CALL ME MILT

BRANDON KELLEY

To my loving wife whose encouragement and support helped me finish this project. To my 6th Grade English teacher, Mrs. Goodspeed, for instilling in me a love of writing and helping me cultivate my passion at a young age. And finally, to Milt, an unknowing and unknown participant in this story.

Dedicated to the loving memory of my mother.

Harnessing the power of adventure and feeling the excitement of the unknown allow us to comprehend things to which the eyes, with their superficial understanding of the world, are blind.

PROLOGUE

"The rum didn't bother nobody," a venerable old man said to no one, a tear streaming down his grizzled face.

He sat on the ground, his shoulders slouched, flames reflecting in his tired eyes. He lamented the burning storage house that held the island's aged rum barrels as clouds of black smoke billowed into the sky, carrying upon it the sweet smell of molasses.

"At least the distillery still stands," he noted, taking solace in his shrine's preservation moments before it, too, caught fire and exploded.

"Well, shit."

On an uncharted island in the Caribbean, a soft drizzle began to fall on an otherwise sunny day in the early years of the 1700s. A slight chill rode in upon the shoulders of a gusting wind, carrying with it the stench of death as the city burned. The cries of the wounded and dying reverberated throughout the secluded cove.

"There's no one here to save you this time, Henry. Right here, right now, it's just you and me. You can either tell me where the treasure you stole from me is hidden, or I can pry it out of your head with my two hands."

Thomas Tew licked the blood from his blade. His shirt was open, revealing a muscular chest and a long, deep scar across his abdomen.

"That won't soon matter much to you," Henry Avery replied, matching footwork with his old foe, engaging him in a masterful pirouette of swordplay.

The two men, weary from fatigue, bloodied and dirtied, were each looking to deliver the decisive blow, giving the victor sole control over the island, and solidifying his respective legacy. Tew struck a defensive posture as Avery lunged at him with his sword high. Tew retreated a step, his back against the opening of a deep cave nestled into the rock at the far end of the beach. Avery's sword came down hard, whistling as it sliced the air. Steel met steel. Avery felt Tew's strength, and as he struggled against his longtime enemy, he noticed a shiny object hanging around Tew's neck, an amulet. Tew began to gain the edge, but Avery drew a second blade from his belt and thrust it upwards into Tew's torso. Thomas Tew smiled, the hilt protruding from his ribcage. Though weakened, he gargled a laugh. Avery's anger exploded. He delivered a punch with all the strength he had left to Tew's jaw sending him reeling backwards into the cave.

"Do it now, Naemi!" he commanded.

The words echoed their way to Tew, stunned and struggling to stand, weakened from his injuries. The cave's darkness engulfed him. The straining rays of sunlight danced on his pallid face. He braced himself against the slick cave wall, wet with condensation. He looked up as Henry Avery dropped to a knee in the sand, his own injuries and the weight of the battle finally overcoming him. Naemi stood nearby, her eyes wide, her body shaking.

Tew struggled to stand, his breaths becoming increasingly shallow. He locked eyes with Naemi as he leaned against the cave wall and slid back to the ground.

Avery stared back into the darkness.

"Naemi, now!" he once again commanded.

Naemi did not immediately respond to his command, terrified of the consequences of the action he demanded.

Avery's eyes locked with Tew's, which flashed a shade of evil that chilled him to his core. A strong wind began to circulate. The sky turned an ominous black.

"This won't be the end of him," she reminded Avery. Tears welled in her eyes.

"Let it be his tomb."

"If he somehow gets free…."

"I don't trust him to die."

"You can't…keep me in here forever," Tew gargled, coughing blood.

"Seal it and let it be his tomb for eternity."

"Every man, woman, and child on this island will also be cursed to live out eternity here, on this island, unable to leave. You know this," she pleaded with Avery. "And those that aren't currently on the island, I know not what will happen to them."

"I can spare a ship's worth of men."

"Henry…."

"Your spells have no effect on you, so what are you worried about?"

She lowered her eyes.

"It's now or never," he told her, turning back to the cave.

She hesitated.

"Naemi, I will not risk him escaping death a third time."

She hesitated further.

"Naemi…," Avery persisted, impatience welled in his voice.

Reluctantly, Neami held her arms outstretched and closed her eyes. She opened her mouth to speak.

"Wait!" he interceded, a wave of realization hitting him. "What is immortality if I can't use it?" Avery stepped closer to Naemi, "Allow me to leave this island whenever I wish." His eyes glowered as the hate rose within him. "But no one else."

"I don't know if I can alter the curse," she admitted. "It is ancient and very difficult, and it could have implications beyond its intent."

"Try."

"I…," she started.

"TRY!" he roared back.

Tew's breathing was becoming ever more laborious in the cool damp of the cave. He tried to crawl back outside, to the warm sand, watching the whole argument with a look of satisfaction. Warm blood oozed down his arm as he clutched with his free hand the blade's hilt still protruding from his chest. He could go no farther. The blood pooled steadily on the ground beneath him. He smirked at the irony in which he found himself.

Naemi closed her eyes and held out her palms towards the cave's gaping mouth. She worked through the amended incantation. Avery grew anxious. Finally, uttered a short spell in a foreign tongue, incoherent gibberish to Avery's ears, she finished. Time had stopped. The cave was sealed. She fell to her knees and held her face in her hands as her tears sprinkled the sugar white sand.

Naemi raised her head and spoke.

"It is done."

"Good. Now tell me about that amulet he was wearin'."

"I have only heard about it, but if the legends are true, it grants its bearer immortality."

"Little use it'll do him now."

Avery picked up a seashell and threw it at the cave. The moment the shell hit the threshold it was propelled violently backwards by an invisible explosion of force.

"Nothing can enter it," Naemi said. "His blood created that tomb and sealed his soul in it for eternity. He cannot leave and no other can enter."

"So that's it then? Good riddance."

"Not entirely. Though unlikely, there is only one way this curse can be broken," she reminded him.

Avery stopped and slowly turned to look at her.

"Tew's blood is the only thing that can open that barrier and free the island," she added.

"And why would I want it opened? His blood is coagulating nicely in the sand inside that cave. I have no more worries about him."

"Immortality can be its own curse, Henry."

"I've built myself a nice little playground here," he said with a hungry smile and outstretched arms. "Immortality in this paradise don't seem all that bad."

Naemi did not speak. She knew Avery better than any man, a fact not lost on him.

"You will come to regret it," she warned.

He sighed, tiring of the conversation.

"Fine. Let's assume I wanted to finish this…though I don't see why that would be necessary," he grumbled, "then how might I end it?"

"His blood transcends his body. You must look to his bloodline to break the seal and separate him from the amulet."

"His bloodline, you say?" he asked, growing curious.

"You know as well as I do."

He thought for a moment.

"He has a daughter," she reminded him. "Henry, inside that cursed cave he cannot regain his strength, but if he is allowed to leave it, he will become too powerful."

Avery glared into the cave, contemplating the threat posed by Tew's remaining power.

"I welcome the challenge. What honor is there in slaughtering a trapped pig?" he said, turning to leave the beach.

"This is only temporary, Naemi. You know it to be true," Tew yelled with all the strength he had left.

Avery turned back around.

Tew winced in pain and, slumping over a small, empty wooden chest left behind by the crew who betrayed him, and breathed the last of the air from his lungs. His body had died.

Naemi and Avery looked on from the daylight into a black void. An ominous laugh echoed from within the suffocating darkness and disappeared into the depths.

Avery inhaled a slow, deep breath to collect himself, a bit unsettled that his vaunted enemy still existed. He sighed and limped back along an old road that cut through the town towards his villa, a beautiful, white Spanish mansion with a rust-colored, terracotta mission-style roof that once served as the cornerstone for a prolific Spanish sugarcane plantation, built before the War of Spanish Succession and used until a local slave revolt sent the plantation owners fleeing back to Europe.

ONE

The small turboprop aircraft touched down on the runway at Manassas Regional Airport in rural northern Virginia. The pilot taxied the plane towards the tarmac just outside of the staging hangar where a few other planes of similar make were being tended to by hopeful flight students, shadowed by their clipboard-carrying instructors, the gatekeepers of the skies.

"Not bad," the co-pilot said through his headset over the hum of the propellers.

"Thanks," the pilot replied. He throttled the engine to idling speed, pulled the mixture knob out, and as the props slowed, he pulled the throttle all the way off and removed his headset.

Ashton Hood stepped onto the tarmac as the sun shone brightly overhead in a clear, blue sky with miles of visibility. Perfect flying conditions. Heat waves rose off the black asphalt distorting the ground at a distance. A breeze blew through the air, bouncing harmlessly off his bomber jacket. He looked to the sky through his aviator sunglasses. He loved the way he felt when he was thousands of feet above the ground. It was an exhilarating feeling. There were no deadlines to worry about or incompetent bosses to deal with. There were no traffic jams, no politics, no worries. He was free, just him and his thoughts.

The instructor, his co-pilot, walked around the tail of the plane, clipboard in hand.

"That was some nice flying today, Ashton. You're really improving," the instructor told him before offering him feedback on areas where he could further tailor his skills.

"Remember, make fine adjustments. You're still a little heavy handed in controlling the plane. Your landing was smooth, and your radio calls were precise. I'm glad you've turned the corner on both of those. Finally, and this is something even us old guys still have to pay attention to, focus on managing your trim. You still haven't quite found the perfect medium, which will decrease your workload and make flying a whole lot easier. It's a skill that can always be refined. Overall, nice job."

"Thanks, Rick," Ashton said, shaking his hand. "Same time next weekend?"

"No can do. I'll be in Lake Tahoe next weekend for our anniversary."

"Congratulations! How long have you been married?"

"Twenty-five years. Hard to believe it's gone by so fast."

"I'm happy for both of you. Give Amy my best."

"I will. How about we shoot for the following weekend? Two weeks."

"Sounds good. Enjoy your vacation and I'll see you in two weeks. You'd better be flying yourself there," Ashton said.

"We'll be flying, but someone else will be taking the controls this time," Rick laughed.

The two men shook hands and Ashton walked to his vehicle, a thoroughly broken-in Ford pickup. Upgrading to something more reliable had always been an option but was now increasingly becoming a necessity. She'd been a good truck through some good times, and it was paid off, and that was hard to overlook. He drove out of the parking lot headed for home, the wind blowing through the windows as he sang along to the radio.

Two

The following day was considerably milder. The first few weeks of spring were in the books, but its grip still held on to the remnants of what had been a brutal winter. The leaves on the trees belatedly began to reappear and flowers were eagerly waiting to peek through their budding cocoons. Inside the Monday morning office, however, the air was stuffy and uncomfortable. A pane of glass was the sole partition separating the two worlds. The bustle inside was growing feverish.

Ashton slouched in his ergonomic chair and stared blankly at the colorful, translucent bubbles bouncing around his computer screen in homage to his extensive duration of inactivity. How much time had he wasted daydreaming in his cubicle? Five minutes? Fifty minutes? It all felt the same to him. Time dragged on in a space where Relativity could be objectively measured. He took a sip of coffee, black, the way it was intended. He reluctantly put his hands on his keyboard and let out a sigh. The bubbles vanished from his screen and the spreadsheet reappeared.

The audible sigh caught the attention of his cubicle-mate, Chad, who spun around in his swivel chair and spoke smugly with a slight lisp, "I don't think the boss is paying you to sleep, Ashton. You finish those audits yet? You know they're due by the end of tomorrow and I'm not staying late to cover for your ineptitude. I know your life is pathetic, but I actually have plans tonight."

Chad Hanson was an ambitious man and eager to replicate his father's business success. He wasn't exceptional looking, though he was fond of reveling in himself whenever he would pass a mirror. He had a round, freckled face, and a soft chin. His sandy blonde hair was short but thick and styled with a man's weight in pomade. He thought immensely of himself and yearned for the aristocratic lifestyle he'd seen in the movies, which imparted upon him a level of pomposity that left little regard for those he viewed as beneath his perceived status. This lifestyle partly manifested itself through his expensive, yet ill-fitting wardrobe that was both lacking in style and ostentatious in taste. He assumed that if he could look the part, then one day he might be cast in it.

Ashton leaned back in his chair and stared at a framed photo of his brother in his Marine dress blues, an American flag behind his right shoulder. His thoughts rekindled his brother's memory as he was often inclined to do, especially when it offered a welcomed distraction from the workplace. Next to it was a larger framed family portrait on the day Ashton was adopted. His mother gave it to him on his eighteenth birthday as he left for college.

It was a drizzly morning thirty-two years ago when a young nun found him swaddled in a blanket and lying in a box on the doorstep of the cathedral to which she belonged. He was wrapped in a white hospital blanket with a single red rose lain across his body. There was no note and no name. She brought him inside and warmed him up. Over the next several days she prayed long and hard before hearing God's call to raise him as her own until she could find a suitable family to adopt him. She gave him the name Ashton and her own surname, Hood.

Sister Anne was young, having just turned twenty-six years old, and took her final vows only a few months prior at the convent attached to the Church of the Little Flower. For years she was unable to find willing parents in her small community to adopt Ashton, which led her to countless sleepless nights questioning God's plan for her.

As Ashton grew older and attended the first years of grade school at Little Flower Catholic School, it was evident he was a quick learner, but he took to solitude rather quickly. Whether on the playground or in the classroom, whenever he found himself in the company of others, he kept to himself, never developing any close relationships with other children.

Then, on a beautiful, unseasonably warm day in late winter, during a brief respite in an otherwise dismally cold and wet week, he was finally adopted at age nine. The young nun cried and embraced him, happy that he now belonged to a good home that would give him the life he deserved. The family had a young son of their own and the two children soon became inseparable.

Sister Anne took Ashton's hand in a gentle, reassuring manner.

"Are you ready?"

He hesitated at first, throwing his arms around her neck. She embraced him as her emotions overcame her. She quickly gathered herself knowing she needed to be strong in this difficult yet joyous time. She stood and gave him an encouraging smile, and together they walked over to his new family. She kissed him on the cheek and reassured him as best she could, straining to hold back her tears while his new mother fought back her own.

Sara Connelly was a pretty woman, an interior architect and volunteer soccer coach. She was married to the kindest man she knew, she would often tell people. Her husband was Doug Connelly, a tall firefighter with a penchant for tattoos and a shameful inability to grow a mustache. Both had a strong Christian faith and had only one child before Sara was left unable to conceive after a hard-fought battle with ovarian cancer.

"This is your new brother, Luke," Sara said to Ashton.

Luke waved at him. Ashton looked down and did not acknowledge the young boy.

"This is your family now," Sister Anne bent down and said to him, looking him in the eyes and cradling his face in her hands. "You listen to your parents and be good, ok?"

She kissed him on the forehead.

"Ok," he answered.

"I love you very much, and I always will," she told him.

"I love you, too, mom."

Sister Anne gave him a warm smile and a long hug, and they said their goodbyes before Ashton and his new family drove away. Ashton chose to keep her surname in remembrance of the woman who rescued and raised him, and his new family fully embraced that decision. A few years later, Sister Anne passed away in a vehicle accident. When Ashton heard the news, he was distraught for months. It was his first encounter with death and losing someone as close to him as she was, was especially hard on him. He visited her grave each year and laid a single red rose next to her marker.

"Do you want to play with my new toy, Ashton?" Luke asked with an affable smile, holding out his new G.I. Joe action figure, Duke.

Ashton took the toy and smiled.

As they grew up together, Luke was the one climbing tall trees, jumping off cliffs, and facing down kids bigger than he was just to prove that he could. It wasn't until he approached his late teens that those adolescent tendencies transformed themselves from a byproduct of pride to one of confidence.

The two boys soon drifted down different paths as their interests and lives diverged. Luke was popular throughout high school. He was two years older than Ashton and had his mom's blonde hair and blue eyes, and his dad's athleticism being a standout baseball and football player. He was naturally talented at both and didn't need nearly the practice time that Ashton did with just baseball. Yet, despite their differences, the dichotomy between Luke and Ashton's personalities served as the adhesive for their relationship. As Luke was more outgoing and charismatic, and Ashton more studious and careful, they quickly formed a tight bond growing up and continuing into high school as Luke adopted the role of protective big brother and Ashton helped him with his studies.

Once Luke graduated, he joined the Marine Corps, following in his father's footsteps of military service, and foregoing his college athletic career. Ashton was proud of Luke's decision and supported Luke wholly in his endeavor, attending his Boot Camp graduation at Parris Island and his graduation from airborne school at Fort Benning, Georgia, where his father, a veteran Army parachutist, ceremoniously pinned his wings on Luke's chest.

A few months later, Luke arrived home for two weeks of leave prior to his impending deployment to Afghanistan. The time seemed to fly by and the four of them were soon standing on the curb outside the airport departure terminal. Luke hugged his mother goodbye and shook his father's hand.

Ashton noticed immediately that there was something different about his brother. He seemed reticent, but behind that reticence, he saw courage, and it was this courage that would soon define Luke.

"Take care of yourself. Swear to me," Ashton said when Luke stood before him.

"Little brother, you know I will. I wish you were coming with me. We'd take down the whole Taliban together!"

He slapped his hand on Ashton's shoulder and the two embraced.

Midway through Luke's deployment, at a forward operating base located deep inside Afghanistan's Korengal Valley, his unit became encircled by a Taliban contingent three times their strength. Air support was called in, but the Apaches designated as the Quick Reaction Force were allocated to another mission. Support would have to wait. As Luke's unit slowly decimated the enemy's numbers and drove the Taliban back into the mountains, a rocket propelled grenade struck the northwestern wall of the small outpost. When the smoke and dust settled, five Marines lay dead or wounded. Luke exposed himself three times to enemy fire to retrieve the three men still clinging to life. The faint sounds of rotors cutting the air bounced through the valley. As Luke was dragging the third wounded Marine to safety, a sniper's bullet found its mark and he fell lifeless just feet from cover.

Luke was posthumously awarded both the Navy Cross and the Purple Heart for his sacrifice and buried in Arlington National Cemetery. His death created a gaping hole in Ashton's life, and he spiraled into depression, losing his ambition, motivation, and confidence. He moved to Virginia shortly thereafter as a way of running from his trauma. He looked up to his brother and the void he left behind was inescapable. Every day became a challenge, each worse than the one preceding it.

Ashton was pulled out of his nostalgia by his cubicle mate's bloviating. Luke was Ashton's hero, but to Chad the military was a fascist indoctrination camp. Chad existed to serve himself. He didn't know the meaning of sacrifice and wouldn't blink an eye for throwing someone else onto a grenade if it meant saving his own skin.

Ashton checked his watch.

4:23pm.

Close enough.

He slowly packed his bag and shut down his workstation with Chad's voice grating on his nerves. When Chad fortuitously stepped away, Ashton seized the opportunity, and with his coat draped over his arm he headed for the exit as covertly as he could.

"ASHTON!" a loud, boisterous voice called from across the office's sea of drab, monochromatic cubicles just as he reached the door.

Ashton turned around reluctantly and saw the worn face of his boss, the firm's middle management in charge of Ashton's team, staring back at him from the threshold of his office. He was an experienced accountant but sorely lacked any modicum of interpersonal or managerial skills. Compounding that problem, Ashton had never been particularly fond of authority figures who were incapable of wielding it, but he rarely raised any opposition in the face of confrontation and often buried his opinions on the matter.

He walked sullenly into his boss's office, feeling the eyes of his coworkers following him. The whispers began in earnest. Ashton looked at the floor ahead of him. His company seemed more like a gossip press than a functioning accounting firm. He stood in front of his boss. A black name plate was affixed to the wall with "Dick Garble" emblazoned in comic sans letters.

"I'm paying you for eight hours of work, not seven hours and thirty-two minutes!" his boss said firmly, his arms crossed on his bulging belly.

"Yes, sir."

The boss continued to dress him down about accountability and work ethic because he knew he could get away with it. Ashton nodded quietly until he was dismissed. Deflated, he slouched and obediently returned to his cubicle. He grew frustrated with himself for not having the gall to tell his boss where to shove it. While his computer restarted, Chad spun around from the online dating site he was perusing on his own screen.

"You really think it's fair to everyone else here that you leave early while we're slaving away? It's not. In fact, I'll probably have to stay late to cover the work you haven't done since lunch. Don't think I haven't noticed."

Ashton ignored him. His computer was taking an unusually long time to restart, so he put his earbuds in while he waited to help drown out the office atmosphere around him.

His brother never had any reservation about speaking his mind when something needed to be said. If an injustice needed to be righted, the little guy defended, Luke had no compunction stepping up. Ashton envied this about him.

He had become acclimated to the routine simplicity of his life, but he yearned to be the dashing captain on a high seas adventure or wealthy secret agent sailing a yacht along the blue waters off the Adriatic Coast of Italy with a beautiful woman on his arm.

Just daydreams.

The workday finally came to an end. While he prepared to shut down for the second time that afternoon, a woman appeared at his cubicle. He fumbled nervously.

"Hey, Lindsey," he said with a crack in his voice.

Lindsey Cochran was pretty-ish, with nice features that he assumed lay underneath all the makeup. She was the receptionist at Roberts, Lee, and Associates, but her true professional passion was her gig as an Avon saleswoman. She never left the house without looking like she was heading to a magazine shoot. Grocery store? Bank? A walk to the mailbox? She was always in heels, her hair done, and wearing the latest fashion.

Ashton found her alluring, if for no other reason than her reputation led him to believe he may have a chance. He had known Lindsey since the day they both began working with the firm six years ago. He liked her, but never garnered the nerve to ask her out. He just watched from afar, awkwardly initiating conversation when she was near his cubicle, and hoped that she would notice him.

There were four women who worked in Ashton's office. Lindsey was the only single one, though she had managed to hook up with most of the other men at the firm, married or otherwise. She knew Ashton fancied her, and she fed on the attention, so much so that she often came to visit Chad just to feed off Ashton's insecurities. It empowered her, and Chad's ego was unable to see that she was playing him like a fiddle to her own satisfaction.

She sat on the edge of Ashton's desk wearing a short, tight-fitting designer skirt and joked with Chad. Ashton wasn't necessarily angry about it, but he couldn't let go of the notion that Chad was a willing pawn in the game she was playing. She laughed at one of Chad's inane jokes before turning her attention to Ashton.

"Any plans this weekend, Ashton?" she asked, leaning over in a low-cut, tight-fitting blouse.

Ashton shifted nervously, fighting the temptation to steal a look.

"No, I don't have anything going on," he said, doing his best to seem nonchalant. "If you don't have anything going on either, would you maybe want to get together?"

As the question came out of his mouth, he felt the blood rush to his head. His body got hot, and his palms started to sweat.

"Oh, bless your heart," she replied. "But there's this new club opening downtown and me and a few girlfriends are going to check it out. My friend Missy knows one of the bouncers. Sorry."

"Ok, cool. No problem. Maybe some other time."

"This guy I met online is going to meet us there, too. He's a professional baseball player and really hot."

"Sounds like fun. I might be in the area. I could meet you there." he suggested.

Chad watched, laughing to himself.

"I don't know, Ashton, I mean, you're a nice guy and all, but I don't think you'd like this place, and besides, we already have, like, an even number of people going so you'd kinda just be tagging along," she countered.

"Yeah, no worries. I don't have a whole lotta time this weekend anyway. I need to finish some projects," he said, trying to save what dignity he had left.

Ashton was of average build, clean cut and unassumingly handsome, not quite the arrogant, bad-boy type that Lindsey lusted over. He never really considered the notion that women might be attracted to him, that was his brother's gift and he often fell into the trap of comparing himself to Luke. A charming, magnetic personality and a pretty face kept Luke in a relationship with one girl or another for most of his teenage life. For his part, Ashton maintained an active lifestyle, regularly involving himself in co-ed sports leagues and personal fitness, and to some degree liked to think he would have made a great officer in the military if he had joined with his brother. He regretted not doing so and on some days was overwhelmed with guilt for his brother's death. If he had only been there with him....

"And I love that skirt on you," Chad remarked, regaining her attention.

"Ugh," Ashton muttered in disgust under his breath.

He looked at his watch.

5:00pm.

He grabbed his bag and coat and squeezed past Chad and Lindsey who didn't bother to make room for him.

"Excuse me," Ashton said, pushing through them.

Ashton parked his truck in the back corner of the parking lot. He opened the door and slid onto the torn leather of the bench seat. The engine started, sputtered, then died.

"Come on," he urged.

He rubbed his hands together to get them warm and turned the key hard again. The engine whined before eventually roaring to life. He cracked the window and sat for a moment.

"Is this really all my life's meant to be?" Ashton mumbled.

THREE

Interstate-495 was gridlocked. The infamous reputation of DC traffic was one thing to hear about, it was something else entirely to experience. Ashton squeezed the steering wheel until his knuckles turned white. A few deep breaths calmed him back down and he loosened his grip, stretching his fingers. He rotated the volume nob so his music would ease him back from the precipice of madness and drown out the incessant blaring of horns. He just wanted to get home and after another long day at work, the quicker he could settle in and unwind, the better.

I could really go for a drink right now.

A traffic accident, two hours, and twenty miles later, he pulled into the parking lot of his condominium complex, a quiet neighborhood just a few miles north of George Washington's Mount Vernon. The community in which he lived was a reasonable accommodation for Ashton, it was quiet and small and near Old Town, a waterfront area along the Potomac River with great restaurants and pubs and small boutique shops. But Old Town was merely a respite from everything he hated about northern Virginia. He wanted desperately to move, but always found himself reluctant when it came to the thought of uprooting himself.

Change created for him unnecessary anxiety and he rationalized the monotony of his situation as the safer, easier option. He was already settled, and any kind of move would be expensive and a hassle to undertake. Eventually, he often promised himself. *Eventually.*

His condo on the top floor, the third floor, was modest, but comfortable. His decorating was mostly modern with some classicism and histrionics sprinkled in for good measure to balance the ambiance. An antiquated copy of the Summa Theologica of Saint Thomas Aquinas rested on the coffee table next to a sculptural piece – a spherical fusion of wood and metal. A framed print of Poussin's *A Dance to the Music of Time* hung above the stone fireplace that warmed the space during the cold winters. He hated cooking and his kitchen reflected that.

Ashton sauntered up the stairs.

"Why hello, there, Ashton," said Mrs. Lewis in her slow, southern twang.

Mrs. Lewis was a gentle woman with a magnetic sense of humor. She was approaching her twilight years but still full of high spirits and a profound appreciation for life. Hailing from Savannah, Georgia, she had lived in her first-floor condo for almost three decades following her retirement, and Ashton was the relatively new kid on the block. Her husband passed away eight years ago and aside from her cat, Dixie, she lived alone. Her three children and five grandchildren routinely visited, providing her good company, and Ashton was eager to lend a hand whenever she needed.

"Good afternoon, Mrs. Lewis. How are you?" he said.

She was kind and one of the smartest people he knew, frequently imparting upon him a wealth of experience. Every Sunday after church, she would invite Ashton into her cozy home for tea and reminisce about her remarkable life. Her stories were rich and could fill a library, and Ashton enjoyed listening to them intently. She was humble, but quite opinionated, and had fun teasing Ashton into debate topics.

Every Thursday night her daughter would drive her to her church for choir practice in preparation for the services on Sunday. She loved to joke, but more than that, she loved to sing, and Ashton would sometimes hear her belting out a Gospel tune.

He'd stop what he was doing and open his door to listen to the notes drift up the stairwell.

"I'm doing quite well, thank you, Ashton. I hope you're about done with whatever it is you're building up there," she teased.

Ashton chuckled, "I'm renovating the guest bathroom, but yes ma'am, just about finished. I'll try to be quieter."

Ashton looked out of the window in the staircase and saw a girl walking her dog across the street. Mrs. Lewis noticed.

"You should really find yourself a girl, Ashton, like that pretty one there who lives across the street."

He blushed.

"Good night, Mrs. Lewis," he said with a smile and a wave.

"Good night, dear."

He locked the door behind him and threw his keys into the bowl on the table by the door. He slunk into the couch and sighed deeply. Strange notes then filled his ears. His first thoughts went to Mrs. Lewis, but this sound was quite different. A steel drum melody lingered for a few seconds before fading away. He quickly dismissed the sound and turned on his vintage record player, Electric Light Orchestra's 1981 album *Time* was under the needle. He took a sip of bourbon and let the music drift over him.

"Ni hao," he said into the phone. "I'd like to place an order for delivery…Orange chicken dinner combo…Yep…Pork fried rice…Cash…Thanks."

He changed his clothes while waiting for his food to arrive. Ten minutes later he was eating the best Chinese food in the area. When he finished, he returned to his bathroom renovation project, applying a new layer of substrate, and installing earthy-hued terracotta floor tiles.

9:59pm.

Satisfied with his progress, he cleaned up and staged the sealant for application during the next round of work. He lay in bed for an hour, restless and awake, staring at the ceiling fan blades as they rotated in slow circles. He threw back the covers and walked into the living room. Powering up his laptop, the blue light from the computer illuminated Ashton's face in the darkness.

He looked up various vacation destinations – the Grand Canyon, skiing in New Hampshire, a Mediterranean cruise. After a few minutes, he had a dozen different webpages opened. He rubbed his eyes, now dry and bloodshot. The options became overwhelming.

Several hours had passed when he finally closed the laptop and went back to bed to try and get a few hours of sleep before starting the rat race all over again.

The alarm was unrelenting. Ashton slammed his hand on the snooze button. Five minutes later, he reluctantly slid out of bed and touched his feet to the soft Saxony carpet. He dragged himself to the bathroom, half-asleep and avoiding his own remodeling mess, and took a long, hot shower.

Dressed, he walked into the kitchen, the sweet aroma of Blackbeard's Delight dark roast coffee filling the condo and poured himself a mug. Soon, the smell of eggs and the sizzling sound of bacon brought him slowly back to life. He took his breakfast to the dining table and opened the laptop.

He took a bite of his crispy bacon, the meat snapping between his teeth, when the sweet metallic sound of steel drums returned. He stopped chewing, but the sound quickly dissipated. He shrugged it off.

What about a tropical vacation? He suddenly thought.

He opened a new search window and typed in "Key West."

The Caribbean had always been on his bucket list of places to visit. An impediment to vacation was Ashton's belief that any absence he took would negatively impact his standing with the firm. Year after year, his saved vacation time lapsed, but his job was stable and paid enough to make him not entirely miserable.

This time, though, he was determined to have something booked before getting his workday started; before he talked himself out of it.

After weighing each of the options carefully, he found himself resigning to yet another local vacation rental property along the Shenandoah River. Suddenly, the sound of steel drums appeared to him again, louder and clearer than before, bringing him back to the images of clear blue water, white sandy beaches, and swaying palm trees. He rubbed his ears, but the melody lingered this time, getting progressively louder before finally disappearing again.

The next few minutes were a blur. His recent memory was foggy, but he found that he had made a reservation for a beach front hotel on Roosevelt Street in Key West, Florida. He squinted at the screen trying to recollect the four-night reservation he had just made.

His flight departed that evening at 7:20pm from Reagan National Airport. Ashton stopped analyzing the last few minutes and rushed back to his bedroom. He grabbed his Italian leather weekend bag, a gift he bought himself upon graduating from Auburn University with his MBA, and before starting his new job in Northern Virginia. He had never used the bag and was excited for its maiden voyage. He bought it in anticipation of seeing the world, but those plans have thus far fallen short of expectations and so the bag sat, buried in his closet, for years. He hurriedly threw clothes, toiletry items, and snorkeling gear inside it and laid out his clothes for the flight. He slammed his laptop shut on his way out the door, twirled his keys, and bounded down the stairs with a smile on his face.

FOUR

The sun sat low in the sky. The morning was gloomy, the air still crisp from the night before. The dew sat atop the grass sparkling like a carpet of diamonds. Ashton was running late, but he paid no attention to the time. Even though he still had an entire workday to suffer through, he was finally taking a vacation and tempering his excitement was going to be difficult.

He stepped onto the sidewalk, digging deep for motivation with every step. The melancholic cawing of crows in the gray, morning quiet sounded like a metronome. He turned the corner around the building to the parking lot.

"Good morning, Ashton!" Kayleigh said, nearly running into him as he turned the corner.

It took only an instant to register, and then he froze, his heart stricken. All the blood in Ashton's body rushed into his head. His words hid in his throat, refusing to leave. The girl he saw through the window the night before was walking her puppy, Kaya, a hyperactive German Shepherd-mix. Every morning around seven o'clock she would leave her building in her pajamas to walk Kaya just as Ashton was leaving for work. He did his best to time his departure every morning so he could see her, which made him feel slightly unscrupulous, but he never thought she noticed him anyway.

A few times since she moved in across the street, they have had opportunities for conversation, but in every instance his mouth parched, and his heart thumped in his chest. Their interactions were brief. Luckily, and much to his relief, her outgoing personality meant she was usually the one to initiate dialogue before Kaya pulled her away to chase a smell.

"Hey, Kayleigh," he responded.

He swallowed hard.

She smiled at him. She was a few years younger than Ashton, with a classical beauty about her, and lightly golden skin. Her eyes were both welcoming and intimidating, and her long, natural blonde hair fell in slight, cascading curls past her slight shoulders.

Four months ago, Kayleigh Mann left a great job in Florida working with the Tampa Bay Buccaneers organization to move to the Washington Metro Area with her fiancé, an environmental lawyer who had accepted a position with the U.S. Fish and Wildlife Service. Although she loved working for the Bucs and made a lot of money doing so, advertising fell well short of her passion, and she didn't see herself working in the field the rest of her career.

Soon after arriving in Alexandria, she accepted a position with a small, private advertising company until something better presented itself. It didn't offer many benefits, but her hours were flexible, which gave her the time to pursue her dream of being an artist. A few weeks later, she returned home early from a conference in Boston and walked in on her fiancé screwing a young, redheaded intern from his office.

Ashton remembered the event clearly and watched it unfold from his living room window, as did the rest of the complex. It was loud and messy, and spilled out onto the lawn. She threw his clothes out of the window as the pretty opportunist scurried naked out the front door, holding her bundled clothes tightly against her body. A few seconds later, her car tore from the parking lot, screeched around the corner, and sped off.

Kayleigh chased her ex-fiancé out the front door. He was shirtless but managed to get his pants mostly on before tripping on a dangling pant leg and falling onto the grass. He jumped to his feet with the audacity to yell at her. Tears rolled down her cheeks, and the more she cried, the louder he yelled. She threw her engagement ring at him and slammed the door in his face, locking him outside. He was undeterred. He carried on for several more minutes before storming off to his car carrying what he could and leaving a trail of items behind him.

"How are you?" she asked Ashton cheerily.

"I'm doing well. You?"

"Well, now that Spring looks to be here, I'm doing great!" she replied. "You seem to be in a good mood this morning."

"I am. I just booked a...," his voice trailed off and he stood still, listening.

It began to drizzle. The sound of raindrops pelting the sidewalk became more apparent amidst the sudden lapse in conversation.

She waited for a few awkward seconds then tried to bring him back into the conversation.

"Booked a what?"

"Do you hear that?" he asked her, ignoring her question.

"Hear what? The rain? Yeah."

"No, the steel drums."

"Steel drums?" She chuckled. "Umm...no."

She looked around trying to hear what Ashton was hearing.

"It's the craziest thing," said Ashton. "It's the fourth time I've heard it."

"Really? That is crazy."

"I'm not sure where it's coming from. It started yesterday. I hear it for a few seconds and then it drifts away, but each time is longer and clearer than the previous."

He saw the confusion wash over her face.

"Sorry, you probably think I'm insane," he said slightly embarrassed.

"Don't be sorry," she said waving her hand at him. "So, are you going to tell me what you booked? You've left me curious."

"A vacation to Key West," he said.

"Oh, I love Key West! I used to go all the time when I lived in Florida," she replied. "When are you leaving?"

"Tonight," he said.

"Oh, wow. Just for the weekend?"

"A little longer. I need some rest and relaxation. You know, come back refreshed."

"I'm so jealous. I wish I could come with you."

His heart skipped a beat. His mind became enthralled with the possibility of taking a vacation with her.

"You'll have a great time," she continued. "I can't wait to hear all about it when you get back."

He swallowed, "Me either."

He stood smiling at her.

"Well, have a wonderful day, Ashton."

"You, too. Try not to get too wet."

He cringed at the words as soon as they left his mouth.

"I'll try not to," she said with a smile.

She gave him a quick wave goodbye as Kaya pulled her through the grass, ready to get home and out of the sprinkling rain.

Convinced that she was way out of his league, he never considered her a realistic prospect. Yet, whenever they would see each other, her smiles were effortless and genuine. She was friendly and kind and during the short conversations they shared together, Ashton managed to develop a genial relationship with her, and an infatuation that soon followed.

He turned and looked at her again over his shoulder, not minding the rain, as he walked to his car. He sat for a moment on the bench seat before turning the key, the car sputtering to life on the first attempt.

Kayleigh held a doggy bag, waiting for Kaya to finish her business. She looked up as Ashton drove past and with her phone pressed between her cheek and right shoulder waved at him with that same glowing smile.

Ashton smiled back then chided himself, "Just ask her out, you pussy!"

He spent the remainder of the commute daydreaming about what it would be like to spend a vacation with Kayleigh. First, they would run through the surf holding hands, then lie in the sand as the waves washed over them. The day would be topped off by an open-air dinner at a fancy restaurant on a cliff overlooking the water below and then back to his room to….

A car horn blared. Ashton swerved his car to avoid the oncoming traffic. His car kicking up a torrent of gravel as he overcorrected and drove back onto the shoulder. Time seemed to stand still. His muscles tensed. He straightened the vehicle and settled himself down with a few deep breaths, then proceeded to shout every swear word he knew. He gripped the wheel tighter to steady his shaking hands. He turned the radio off, refocused his attention back to the road, and drove the rest of the way to work in silence.

Every morning was the same routine. Starting with stop and go traffic on the Beltway, he was typically the first person in the office. The workday was nine to five and, per Dick's office directive, anything else was considered the employee's own time. Nevertheless, Ashton preferred getting to work early and getting as much done as he could without the ubiquitous office distractions and social interruptions that plagued his day.

When he pulled into the parking lot of Roberts, Lee, and Associates, the drizzling rain had stopped, but the sun remained hidden behind a gray sky. Anxiety surged within him, but he tampered the emotion by counting down the hours to his first vacation in six years. He let the music from the radio play. He rolled the window down and put his elbow on the door, letting the crisp, post-rain breeze into the car. He rested his head on the headrest and closed his eyes daydreaming about sailing on the crystal waters of the Caribbean. He smiled contently at the mere thought of escaping, physically and mentally, from the toils of his job.

Just a few more hours.

FIVE

Ashton lumbered begrudgingly across the parking lot as a cold wind cut through his jacket. He pushed open the front doors, which felt heavier than usual, and meandered his way to his desk. He turned on his computer and swiveled in his chair while it booted up, relishing the relative peace. He sat in the quiet of his cubicle for half an hour until the rest of the office personnel started trickling in. The quiet quickly gave way to water cooler chats, adding machines, telephones, and the omnipresent voice of his boss, Mr. Garber, yelling at something or someone.

It was during this time, before his coworkers filed into the office, that Ashton worked most diligently, completing his quarterly reports, and consolidating much of next week's work in the process. He hoped to sneak out of the office a little earlier today to ensure he had enough time to return home and then get to Reagan National Airport. He finished the last of the reports and placed the hard copies in the "out" bin on the corner of his desk.

Amidst the growing sounds of endless typing and buzzing conversation, the familiar yet faint melody of steel drums floated into his temporal lobe. He stood up abruptly, scanning the office, unable to pinpoint the source of the music.

He feigned walking to the breakroom to replenish his coffee, straining his ears trying to hear the sound that was beginning to fade. His frustrations were reaching a boiling point and he began to question his own sanity. He was certain now that a vacation was the only medication that could get him right. As he was pouring his coffee, making use of his trip to the breakroom, the music returned, louder and clearer than he had heard it before. He ran out into the hallway, splashing coffee from his mug, and walked a measured lap around the office. He eventually returned to his cubicle as the music was reaching a crescendo. The music of the steel drums grew louder and louder until it sounded as though the instrument was being played right next to him.

"Where the hell are you coming from?" he yelled.

He could think of no explanations, no logic, nothing that made sense.

Everyone in the office stopped what they were doing and stared at him. The music faded away after its longest session yet, to be replaced by the mocking laughter of his officemates. He returned to his cubicle and slunk in his chair.

Chad rolled in right at 9:30am and slammed his backpack down on his desk.

Ashton's stomach turned.

"Morning, Chad," he greeted.

Despite his personal predilections and opinions towards his colleagues, he did his best to maintain a working-level of professionalism.

Silence was his response.

Ashton shook his head fuming, humiliated by the slight, but didn't say anything further.

As lunchtime approached, Chad leaned over the cubicle wall and started talking to Nick Mandias, an Army Special Operations veteran. Chad often pandered to Nick, seeking his approval and acceptance, which was outwardly characterized by the way he mirrored Nick's country drawl and word choice whenever he spoke to him. On more than one occasion, Chad found himself regaling anyone who would listen of his moot plans for military service, thwarted by some medical ailment or life circumstance, the cause being irrelevant as it often changed depending on the conversation. His parents had started a trust fund for him when he was a baby and when it matured on his eighteenth birthday, he gleefully chose the lavish lifestyle paid for by his parents, went to college merely as a formality, and thus started his journey towards joining the aristocracy in DC. Military service would have to wait, indefinitely.

Nick had just turned forty-two and his wife had made him settle down and get a less demanding and more permanently fixed job. Nick, a tall, ruggedly handsome man with dark, movie star hair, was the office's quality control officer. He liked the work. It was different from what he was used to, but undeniably a nice change of pace. His wife remained faithful and patient while he deployed a dozen or so times to some of the most austere places on the planet. She raised their kids and took care of the household responsibilities all on her own for a good portion of their marriage wondering if, and when, she'd receive the dreaded knock on the door.

Nick had never talked about his deployments or his time in his squadron, at least not to Ashton, but he did find Ashton to be the most relatable guy in the office. Nick liked to keep to himself. He habitually arrived in the office every morning around the same time as Ashton and was always one of the last to leave. His cubicle was empty save for one family photo. He reminded Ashton of Luke in many ways – he was confident and assertive and didn't succumb to office drama or politics. Mr. Garber once took his frustrations out on Nick because he happened to be the nearest employee and Nick, with a surgical politeness that was both commanding and respectful, silenced him on the spot. Dick never spoke to him unnecessarily again.

"Hey brother, you catch the Wizards game last night?" Chad asked knowing Nick was an avid sports fan.

Ashton rolled his eyes.

Nick shook his head and kept working. Chad kept talking.

"I'm thinking about selling my Porsche Boxter and buying an Audi S8."

Nick grunted and kept typing.

"My dad owns an Audi."

Nick threw his pen down and rubbed his face with his hands.

"Fuck me," he sighed then looked up at Chad. "You've been talking about selling that car for months, Chad. Tell you what, *brother*, I'll cover for you here while you take a longer lunch and go buy that bad boy. Audis are great vehicles. You're gonna love it."

Chad stood looking at Nick, not sure what to say, so he cleared his throat and sat back down at his desk. Message received.

Ashton ignored the exchange. He was doing his best not to keep looking at the time, knowing that the day would go faster if he kept his mind occupied. His ensuing thoughts were tangential, jumping from one topic to the next, but eventually he caved, curious of how much time had thus far elapsed.

Two minutes and twenty-three seconds! That's it?

He sighed.

Then, like clockwork, Lindsey showed up for her morning flirt.

Ashton needed a break. He left his desk and walked to the restroom. He cupped his hands under the sink faucet, letting the water pool in his palms. He splashed the cold water on his face and looked up at himself in the mirror for a few seconds before grabbing a paper towel and drying his skin.

The breakroom was around the corner from the restroom. Ashton could think of nothing better to do so he grabbed his lunch out of the fridge. Nothing fancy. He sat at one of the tables and ate alone. Just a few more hours. Cabanas and cocktails were waiting. When he finished and walked out of the breakroom, he saw Chad and some of the other folks in the office, Lindsey among them, heading out to lunch.

While Ashton sat at his desk looking at Key West travel photos on Instagram, Nick came around and pulled up Chad's chair.

"Hey, brother, I know you're heading out for the weekend, so if I were you, I'd try and jet out of here earlier than later."

"Hey man, yeah, I'm hoping to sneak out of here around two o'clock."

"Y'know, between you and me, I think it's a pretty raw deal how Chad and Lindsey treat you. Don't know how you put up with it."

"I don't either."

"You'll never get away from those types. Just have to pay 'em no mind."

Ashton nodded in agreement.

"What time's your flight? You're heading to the Keys, right?"

"How'd you know? I don't remember telling anybody."

"I'm observant."

"Flight's at 7:20pm flying directly into Key West."

"Right on. Key West is not a bad gig," Nick said.

"You've been?" Ashton asked.

Nick laughed, "Brother, I used to fly my Beechcraft G58 down there all the time."

"I didn't know you were a pilot?"

"Oh yeah, picked it up while I was in the service. You do enough deployments and the money rolls in faster than you know what to do with it. When I had some downtime, I took lessons. Bought the plane shortly after getting my license and have been flyin' ever since. You ever want to fly somewhere let me know. If I like the destination, I might just take you up on the request."

"I've been working towards my pilot's license for a few months now," Ashton mentioned.

"No kiddin'? How many hours?"

"Just hit thirty this past weekend. I like being in the air, above all the distractions on the ground."

"I hear ya. What are you flying?"

"A '79 Piper Archer."

"Not a bad aircraft. I learned on a similar bird – a 1980 Cessna 172 Skyhawk. Good luck to ya. It's a fun hobby and a great skill to have…if you can keep her in the air," Nick added.

They both chuckled before Nick added, "Listen, I'm gonna head outta here in a few minutes and grab a drink to honor some old buddies. I see your brother's a Jarhead," he said noticing Luke's picture.

Ashton picked up the frame.

"Yeah. He was a sergeant. Killed in action in Afghanistan and given the Navy Cross."

"Your brother's a hero," Nick told him matter-of-factly.

"He is."

"Where was he stationed?"

"He was a Recon Marine at Camp Lejeune."

"Good buncha guys," said Nick. "Damn good buncha guys. I ran into a couple of 'em when I was operating out of Bragg."

Nick paused.

"If you want to grab a beer before you head out, I'll buy you a round. There's a bar in Herndon called Donovan's. The bartender's an old Group guy. He's good people."

"That sounds great, man. I'll take you up on that."

Nick stood and patted Ashton's shoulder as he stepped past him.

Ashton looked at his watch.

12:44pm.

Nick grabbed his backpack and made his way toward the exit.

"See you there," Ashton said.

"We'll see ya," Nick responded.

Chad, returning from lunch, was entering the building at the same time Nick was leaving it.

"Hey, bro. You taking off?" he asked in the doorway obstructing Nick's exit.

"Yep."

Nick slipped his sunglasses on his face and brushed effortlessly past Chad, letting the door close behind him. He tossed his bag in the backseat of his burnt orange Jeep Wrangler Sahara with oversized tires. The front doors were off, and the skin was rolled back. He shifted the jeep into second and headed for Donovan's.

Ashton's excitement was brewing as cocktails and cabanas danced in his brain. He walked hurriedly and, leaning into his boss's office without stepping a foot inside, rapped on the open door.

"Yes?" Mr. Garber answered dryly, shoveling greasy French fries into his mouth by the handful.

"I finished the first quarter's reports, and the Morrison account is done, just waiting on an email with their concurrence on the documents, but the partners are out today."

There was an uncomfortable pause as Ashton awaited his boss's response. He slowly took a step backwards out of the doorway.

"Good work," his boss said without raising his head.

He belched and Ashton took that as a grotesque sign of dismissal. He returned to his cubicle and quietly shuffled his things into his bag. He peered back at Mr. Garber's office who was pre-occupied with slurping down a large Coke, then walked purposefully toward the doors, keeping his head down, careful not to make eye contact with anyone.

Chad was at Lindsey's desk engaging in shallow conversation. Ashton pushed open the door and stepped into the dreary air as a smile stretched across his face. A raven cawed from atop one of the light posts dotting the parking lot. The car started on the first try for the second time that day. It was going to be a good weekend.

SIX

When Ashton arrived at the bar, Nick had just started on his second draft beer, a near perfect pour in a still frozen glass. He sat alone at the bar watching the Washington Nationals take on the Miami Marlins in a daytime matchup. It was the bottom of the fourth and the Marlins were leading by four runs. The bar was empty save for an old, grizzled man with a wiry beard down to his chest sitting at the opposite end of the bar staring down into the bottom of his mug. He was holding it with both hands, his eyes were closed, and he wasn't moving. He twitched himself awake and Ashton let out a sigh of relief. There was a lingering haze in the air from the cigarette smoke that wafted to the ceiling during the lunch hour. A worn American flag hung over the bar. A light flickered in the back where a scratchy tune rung from the jukebox behind the pool tables, giving the place a grungy, but evocative feel, whose walls held the collective stories of generations past.

The bartender was an older woman who looked to be in her early fifties and wore her experience on her face. Her skin tanned and wrinkled, she had tattoos down both arms. Her long and graying hair was pulled back in a braded ponytail. She was cleaning glassware as Ashton scanned the room, his eyes adjusting to the contrast from the light outside.

"Have a seat," she said in a raspy voice. "I'll be with you in a sec, dear."

"Thanks," Ashton said in return.

"Pull up a chair," Nick said in his familiar drawl waving him over.

Ashton put his jacket around the back of the bar chair and sat down. Nick looked at him and nodded, then turned his gaze back towards the television. Ashton ordered one of whatever Nick was drinking. It arrived in a cold mug and Nick raised his glass to Ashton's. Ashton took a short sip of his beer. Nick drank a quarter of his.

Nick wiped the froth from his mouth.

"I love baseball," he started. "Best sport on earth."

"I can't argue that."

"You play?"

"When I was younger," Ashton said, reminiscing on the smell of leather from his ball glove, the feel of the baseball in his hand, and the sweet crack of the bat as it connected with a fastball. "I miss it," he continued. "What about you? You play growing up?"

"Up until high school, then I focused on football. Football got me into college, but baseball…baseball was always my passion."

"I'll drink to that," Ashton said.

They clanked glasses.

"Speakin' of women," Nick said, changing the subject. "You need to forget about Lindsey. I've seen the way you eye her and she ain't worth your time."

"I know," Ashton admitted.

"I don't get it, man. I mean, you're a smart, good-lookin' dude, you should be beating them off with a stick, and I mean the classy types. You shouldn't be begging for dates from the office whor…receptionist."

Ashton laughed, slightly embarrassed.

They drank in silence as the game went into the middle inning.

"Your brother's a hero, man," Nick said. "I'll say that till I'm blue in the face. But you…you can't live in his shadow or let his memory weigh you down. I don't think he'd want that for you.

In fact, if he was how you say he was, I guaran-damn-tee you he'd tell you that you needed a swift kick in the ass to get you goin'."

"He did tell me that, all the time." Ashton paused, looking into his own mug. "Most people don't realize that he isn't my real brother."

Nick looked over at him.

"I'm adopted. I never knew my real family."

"So? Listen, family's more than blood. Those guys that bled next to me on the battlefield were my brothers, in some ways more so than my biological ones still living back home in Texas."

"I always considered him my real brother," Ashton added.

"You should and nuthin' will ever change that fact," Nick told him.

Ashton nodded.

"To those that went before," Nick said raising his glass.

Ashton lifted his glass and together they cheered the memories of their fallen brothers. Several minutes of silence passed. Nick took another long swig of beer and looked thoughtfully at his drink.

"Y'know, every year I come in here alone on the same day and order four beers," he said. "Just ask Jessie there."

Jessie, the bartender, was wiping down the bar and looked up at him.

"He does," she affirmed. "And like every year, three of those beers are on the house."

She walked over and stood in front of Ashton.

"I hear you also lost your brother?" she asked as she poured him another round and slid it over to him. "This one's on the house, too."

Nick gave her a respectful tip of his dirty, faded ball cap.

Jessie let them be and tended to the older man still half asleep at the end of the bar.

Nick took another swig and sat in silent reflection, looking eerily like the bar's only other occupant, minus the biker clothes and ZZ Top beard. Ashton couldn't begin to fathom what all Nick must've seen and experienced in those foreign and hostile lands. Even if Ashton wanted to ask, it wouldn't be of any use. He knew Nick wouldn't be able to talk about any of the missions he was involved in, though he did make vague mention of at least one other deployment to East Asia.

"I've always come in here by myself, but I've never been alone," he said solemnly, breaking the silence.

Ashton didn't respond. What could he say? Even though he'd lost his brother, he wasn't there when it happened. He didn't watch him fall, bleed, and die. He wasn't the only person among his friends to walk away from a firefight. A confluence of beer and reminiscing about his fallen comrades, combined with someone to talk to suddenly led Nick to open up about his past. Ashton, honored by the confidence he'd been shown, sat and listened.

"My last mission," Nick began, "we were ambushed in a village on the Tajik-Afghan border."

He never raised his eyes.

"It was over quick. It was a surveillance and reconnaissance mission, and thought our objective technically was a success, I lost my team."

"Damn," Ashton uttered.

"RPGs and heavy machine gun fire came in fierce from our left killing Jake, our commander on the ground, and Brian, a sniper by trade. Me and Sean, a young guy, first time with the team but battle hardened, managed to scramble out of the rubble, but he got hit before I dragged him to cover behind a nearby stone wall."

Nick paused and took a swig of beer.

"Sean was a mess. Blood pooling on the ground. Then, just like that," Nick snapped his fingers, "a bullet hit the top of the rock and the fragments peppered his face. I can still hear his screams. When our ammunition was expended, I pulled out my combat knife and prepared myself for a warrior's death, a first-class trip to Valhalla, y'know what I mean? Sean died not too long after. I managed to escape into the mountains and that's when I heard the propeller blades beating the air. Two Apaches approached over the ridgeline and their hellfire missiles lit the sky. Man, did they scorch those motherfuckers."

A smirk appeared on his face as he relished in his enemies' timely deaths.

The emotion faded, however, as he continued, "I," he paused. "I didn't make it out until a few weeks later."

"What happened?" Ashton found himself asking without thinking.

Nick took another swig of beer and thought back on some distant memory but did not speak about it further.

"Eventually, I returned to Fort Bragg and continued to serve before the burden became too much to bear. I decided to retire and moved to Ashburn, Virginia, near my wife's family, and found the least stressful job imaginable."

Ashton looked at him confused, but he wasn't given time to ask his question. They had only been at Donovan's for forty minutes, give or take, when Nick's phone, lying on the countertop next to him, began vibrating. He looked down at the screen.

"Speak of the devil. It's Lipstick 6," he said.

He opened the text from his wife then chugged his fourth and final beer and wiped his mouth. He stood up and grabbed his sport coat from the back of the bar chair and in one fluid motion put his arms through the sleeves and shrugged it onto his shoulders.

"I gotta run," he told Ashton. "Have a great time on your trip and try to relax a little, huh? Loosen up and have a little fun down there and don't do anything I wouldn't do. Better yet, it might do you some good if you did try some things I wouldn't do," he laughed.

Ashton laughed with him and took a drink.

"It was a pleasure," Nick said swatting him on the back.

Nick threw down a handful of bills onto the bar counter, more than enough to cover both of their tabs and a generous tip.

"Thank you, sweetie," Jessie said.

"Anything for you, darlin'," Nick replied with a charming smile.

"Careful Nick, if I wasn't married…," she flirted back, all in good fun.

Ashton turned his attention back towards his beer, or what was left of it.

"Here, hun, let me top you off," Jessie said to him. "He's a good guy, you're lucky to have him as a friend."

Jessie took his mug and filled it with a fresh, cold refill.

Ashton nodded his thanks.

Not long after Nick left, Ashton's own phone began ringing. He took it out of his pocket to see "Boss" emblazoned across the screen.

Do I answer?

If he answered, Dick might make him come back into work for some inexplicable reason and he wouldn't put it past him to do just that. He had snuck out early, after all. But then again, if he didn't answer, Dick would be royally pissed and who knows what actions that might lead to. Either way, it was sure to put a damper on the trip. He decided to answer the phone, hoping to alleviate the anxiety from thinking about it all weekend if he hadn't.

"This is Ashton," he answered.

"Ashton, where the hell are you? It's the middle of the afternoon!" Dick yelled from the other end of the line.

Ashton pulled the phone away from his ear and grimaced as he frantically turned the volume down. He rubbed his ear and put the phone back just as his boss paused to take a breath.

"I'm on my way to the airport. I put a note about it in the email I sent you about the Morrison audit I finished," he told him, hoping his boss would feel foolish for missing the information and let him off the hook.

That was how Ashton envisioned the scenario playing out when he strategically embedded the notification about his imminent vacation at the end of the email regarding the Morrison account. He knew his boss didn't read emails, he merely skimmed the first few lines looking for the most salient points and rarely, if ever, made it to the end.

"I didn't see any note," his boss countered.

"It's there, sir."

"Irregardless," his boss continued. Ashton cringed at the word. "I need you to get back here immediately, we found some discrepancies with one of the merger accounts we just acquired, and it appears several tens of thousands of dollars have gone missing. Consider this your number one priority until it's resolved."

This was unanticipated. Ashton was shocked.

"Which merger account?"

"The Marian Medical account," his boss answered.

"Sir, I'll have to get to it when I get back. I'm on my way to the airport right now. Chad's there, why not have him look into it?

"I don't want Chad looking into it. I want you looking into it. I have my reasons, Ashton, and don't make me ask you twice."

Ashton's heart was pounding in his chest. His nerves were unsettled. He knew he had to get to the airport, and he desperately needed this vacation, but he also needed his job. Ashton took a breath and stood firm, responding with a wavering voice, "I can get it to you first thing when I get back."

There was a long, awkward pause.

"If you don't fix these account discrepancies by Monday close-of-business, you won't have a job on Tuesday!"

His boss discontinued the call.

Ashton sighed. He put the phone on silent and slipped it back into his pocket.

This vacation was too good to be true.

The conflict that raged in his head about his next action was real and it was sucking the life out of him. He didn't want to expend this amount of negative energy mere hours before going on vacation. It was a thought he was determined to push aside until he returned.

Ashton ordered a third beer to calm his nerves. He leaned over it, ignoring the Nationals game that was now in the top of the eighth inning. Ashton looked up at the screen just as the Marlins batter swung sending the ball soaring over the left field wall, extending their lead. Ashton watched with indifference. He threw back the remainder of his beer, gave Jessie a twenty-dollar tip, grabbed his coat, and left the bar.

SEVEN

2:53pm.

Ashton cranked his car and waited as it gasped for life. If he ever won the lottery, a vehicle upgrade was first on his list of extravagant expenditures – a rosso Corsa Ferrari 812 GTS convertible with a crème-colored interior to be exact, and there was no second choice. Ashton grew up with Ferrari posters hanging on his bedroom walls, changing the posters as new models rolled out over the years. He smiled as he thought about the wind blowing through his hair cruising along Route 1 in Big Sur, California, the throaty sound of the exhaust trailing behind him, and the sun glistening off the deep blue waters of the Pacific Ocean.

For now, he had to settle for his old, rusty Ford pickup, which ran more on hope than it did gasoline. It finally sputtered to life. He didn't arrive back at his condo until nearly 4:00pm. He burst through his condo door, nearly tripping over his bag, and immediately began loosening his shirt and tie while making his way back to the master bedroom.

He slipped out of his clothes and hung up his wool blend suit in a relatively empty closet, a staple of any bachelor pad. He stepped into the shower and six minutes later he was toweling dry. He dressed in the clothes he had laid out for himself before leaving for work that morning, gave himself a once-over in the mirror, and, satisfied, grabbed a few other last-minute items he had forgotten, namely a book for the flight and a ball cap. He reluctantly tossed his phone charger in as well but promised himself that his phone would be turned off for the duration of the vacation. He stretched his arms and looked up at the whirling ceiling fan overhead, oscillating just a bit.

That needs to be tightened.

4:19pm.

Plenty of time for a quick dinner. Packed and ready, he warmed up a few slices of leftover pizza and cracked open a cold can of Dr. Pepper. With the directive from his boss still fresh in his mind, he contemplated whether to bring along his laptop, too. He could get some solid work done on the plane, he reasoned, or while sitting next to the pool at the hotel while indulging in a tropical cocktail. But that was counterintuitive to the reason for his vacation.

He decided to leave the laptop on the dining table. No work while in Key West and that was settled. These next few days were for himself. He walked outside and waited on the sidewalk in front of his building for the ride that would ferry him to the airport. He had only been standing on the sidewalk for a few seconds when Kayleigh walked out of her building with Kaya. She waved at him and crossed the street. His heart fluttered.

"Thank you," he prayed under his breath.

"Hi, Ashton!" she said with her perfect smile.

Kayleigh, with her natural beauty and girl-next-door aura, looked as radiant as ever.

"Hey, Kayleigh!"

"Are you on your way to the airport?" she asked.

"I am. My ride is on the way."

"You deserve a vacation. I never see you going out except to go to work, and you've looked pretty stressed these last few weeks. You gotta enjoy life, you know? Make every moment count."

"I know. It's a little surreal. I don't even remember making the reservation," he said with a laugh.

"Sometimes, being impulsive isn't so bad."

"Let's wait and see what happens the next time I decide to run headfirst into a decision."

Kayleigh laughed.

"I hope you have a great time."

"Thanks. So do I," he said with a smile.

A black sedan rounded the turn and drove toward him slowly, reading each individual building number despite Ashton standing on the curb with his luggage.

"That must be your ride. Have fun!"

"I'll see you when I get back?"

He didn't breathe.

"Definitely," she answered as she started away.

He exhaled.

"Are there any restaurants I should try while I'm down there?" he asked trying to keep her around.

"Oh my gosh!" she said excitedly, walking back towards him. "There are so many delicious places to eat, you'll be happy wherever you go, but if you can get to Alonzo's Oyster Bar for happy hour, I promise you'll eat like a king! Their oysters are fantastic!"

"It'll be the first place I try."

As Kayleigh was about to speak, the driver, a young, overweight woman with purple hair rolled down her window and interrupted their conversation.

"Are you Ashton?" she yelled.

"Yeah, one sec."

He picked his bag up off the sidewalk.

"I'm glad I ran into you," he said to Kayleigh.

"I feel like that's been happening quite a bit," she responded with a wink.

He laughed nervously and walked around the vehicle.

"I'll report back on those oysters."

"I can't wait to hear all about your adventures."

She smiled and turned back to Kaya who was sunbathing in the grass.

"Let's go, girl!"

Kaya sprang to her feet, hopping through the grass with excitement, pulling Kayleigh down the sidewalk. She turned and waved back at him, and he responded in kind. He slid into the backseat of the car, his nose immediately turning up at the odor, and settled in for the quick journey to the airport, looking out the window and resuming his daydreaming.

EIGHT

The ride to the airport took about twenty-five minutes. They hit a few traffic jams driving through Old Town, hitting an excessive number of red lights, but otherwise the ride was relatively unencumbered.

5:21pm.

The driver dropped Ashton off in front of the departure terminal and started driving away before he was completely out of the vehicle. He managed to grab his bag from the seat next to him and stagger out of the car before his arm was nearly ripped off by the seatbelt.

He didn't have a bag to check so he walked through the Terminal B departures entrance to the self-service kiosk and checked in before walking down the escalator towards security, which was backed up with a significant line. Ashton waited patiently with businesspersons and politicians, men and women, young and old.

He noticed two people standing a few feet ahead of him, a gentleman who he guessed was somewhere between fifty or fifty-five years old and a young woman in her mid-twenties. The gentleman was tall, slightly overweight, and groomed himself nicely. He had silver hair and a tanned face. His suit was well-tailored, his briefcase was made of conditioned leather, and his comportment was that of someone important. He was laughing along with the young woman, his hand on her lower back. He was clearly flirting with her, and she was letting him. She was shorter than average height for a woman, slim with snow white skin, light freckling on her nose, and strawberry blonde hair that fell onto her bare shoulders. Ashton studied them both, trying to guess their story to pass the time.

He concocted a possible scenario in his head while slowly moving towards the TSA checkpoint. The gentleman, a corrupt congressman, probably from the upper house of the bicameral chamber, and the girl a Capitol Hill staffer working in his office. They were on their way to Italy for the weekend and staying in a villa overlooking Lake Como. Dating would be too scandalous given the wedding ring on his finger and the lack of one on hers. This would be just a tryst while his wife was away on business or at home taking care of the kids while he went on one of his own.

"Sir…," the TSA agent repeated.

The story washed away like sand in a storm, and he handed his boarding pass and ID to the agent. Ashton all but disrobed and walked through the body scanner and out again as his bag was coming off the X-ray conveyer belt.

"Is this your bag, sir?" another agent asked.

Ashton let out a sigh, knowing what was coming.

"It is."

The obese, unkempt agent wearing latex gloves placed it on a metal tabletop and rifled through Ashton's bag looking for who knows what. As Ashton waited patiently, he put on his shoes and belt, and put his keys and wallet back into his pockets.

The rummaging continued.

The agent's breathing was becoming laborious, and he was breaking a sweat.

"Can I help you find something?" Ashton asked.

The agent ignored him.

"Excuse me," Ashton asked again, "can you tell me what you're looking for, so I can tell you where it's located?"

Again, silence, as the agent ran his sausage fingers through Ashton's packed clothing.

"How about you just dump the whole damn bag out?" Ashton said in frustration.

The agent pulled out a cigar cutter from the small, zippered pocket on the inside lining of his bag. He held it up examining it.

"Sorry, sir, you cain't take this on the plane."

"Are you serious?" Ashton remarked.

"Cain't let you take this on the plane. See these here," he pointed to the cutter's two small blades, "these are razors. Cain't take 'em on the plane, lessen you want to check your bag. But you'd have to go back out security and come back through again."

"It's fine," Ashton said, hurrying the encounter along. "Enjoy it!"

"Alright, sir," the man paused for a breath, "have a nice flight." The TSA agent waddled away leaving Ashton's clothes splayed on the metal table.

Ashton tried to repack his bag with a semblance of organization and left the security area. When he arrived at his gate it was quiet and sparsely populated. Ashton sat down in a seat at the end of a row closest to the windows. His flight was next on the manifest, but he still had almost an hour to kill before boarding began. There were a few other retirees at the gate with him, some wearing Naval service hats, others wearing tacky Hawaiian shirts and Birkenstocks.

He walked a short distance over to a restaurant bar to pass the time. The bartender was rushing around serving a dozen other passengers also waiting on their respective flights. Ashton waved him down and ordered an Old Fashioned.

"Tab?" the bartender asked returning with the drink and placing it on a napkin in front of Ashton.

Ashton shook his head and handed him a crisp twenty-dollar bill.

"Keep it," he told the bartender.

"Cheers," the bartender replied and scurried over to another waiting customer.

Ashton held the glass in his hand for some time before taking a sip. On the television mounted above the liquor bottles behind the bar, a Braves game had gone into extra innings. It was the top of the tenth and the Braves held a one-run lead.

C'mon, Atlanta.

A middle-aged woman, weary from travel, sat down next to him. She was pretty, he thought, but her headphones indicated she was not interested in conversation. Ashton turned his attention back to the game. He finished the drink and checked his watch.

Plenty of time still.

He spun around in his chair and looked back at his gate where a couple of flight attendants were now at the counter dealing with a handful of customers looking to upgrade their seats. The door to the gangway was still closed.

He turned back around, hitting the woman next to him with his knee.

"Sorry."

She gave him a look of disgust. She paid for her drink and grabbed her bags in a flurry, hurrying to whichever gate awaited her. He waited for the bartender to look at him and when he did, he raised a finger in the air.

The bartender nodded his understanding and made a second cocktail.

"Here ya go," he said placing it on the napkin.

Ashton gave him another twenty-dollar bill.

"Pleasure," the bartender said and went back to the other end of the bar.

The Mets tied the game on a single to shallow left field. During the next at bat, the runner on first was picked off trying to steal second for the third out of the inning. The bottom of the inning was up next. Ashton threw back the last sip of his drink but before he could place his glass back down on the bar, the familiar melody of the steel drums began to resonate around him. The sound grew gradually louder and clearer as it washed over him. But this time was somehow different, a strange feeling arose within him.

How strong were those drinks?

He shook his head a few quick times.

The bar, the noise, the people in the airport and the terminals were all ripped away, torn from this reality and transformed into tall, swaying palm trees. The crystal-clear Caribbean waters sat like a blanket caressing the powder white sand underneath a pale blue sky. Ashton was transfixed, enchanted by the mirage. He closed his eyes letting the sensation of the wind kiss his face and the smell of salty air fill his lungs. As the feeling of a gentle ocean breeze touched his skin, he smiled, fully engrossed in this vision, the melody dancing in his ears. He stood in a beautiful, secluded cove with emerald water, guarded by lush, green peaks and sheer rock cliffs, and surrounded by thick jungle. Paradise. He opened his eyes and was greeted by the familiar face of the bartender.

"Another?"

Ashton looked around him. The bar was again filled with transient passengers.

"Hey, buddy," the bartender repeated impatiently.

When he got no response from Ashton he walked away.

"I'm going insane," Ashton said under his breath.

"It's hit hard to left-center field! It's going! Going! GONE!! A solo walk-off homer into the centerfield stands! Braves win!" the broadcaster announced excitedly.

Ashton pumped his fist at the victory and, having already paid for his drinks, returned to the departure gate.

"We'd like to welcome any passengers who need special assistance and any families with children under two years old to go ahead and board," one of the flight attendants announced in a chipper voice. This was followed by the usual rush of impatient travelers lining up and waiting for their group designation to be called.

He looked at his ticket, *Boarding Group 5*. When his group number was called, he walked down the gangway where he was cheerfully greeted by the onboard flight attendants, two cute blondes who could've passed as twins. He smiled and returned their greeting. He was seated near the front of the coach cabin, and after placing his bag in the overhead bin, took his seat and opened his book.

NINE

The direct flight from Washington, D.C. to Key West International Airport took a little over two and half hours. The pilots made up quite a bit of time in the air as they rode a strong tailwind at thirty-five thousand feet for the duration of the leg. The plane touched down just after 10:00pm local time. The weather was temperate but humid. The night sky was a deep midnight blue sprinkled with bright stars twinkling in celestial harmony. The moon, glowing white and heavenly just above the horizon, illuminated the glassy surface of the Caribbean Sea.

Ashton walked out into the night and waited for the hotel shuttle to take him to his home for the next few days. The driver dropped Ashton's bags on the curb in front of the lobby doors and jumped back into the shuttle, tearing out of the porte-cochere and back onto Roosevelt Avenue.

The scent of lavender welcomed Ashton as he entered the lobby. It was subtle and pleasing to his nose. He walked across the travertine-tiled lobby to the front desk where a skinny, young man with sharp eyes awaited him with a smile. His uniform was well-tailored with a gold name tag pinned to his chest that read, "Will."

"Good evening, sir. Checking in?"

Ashton set his bag on the floor next to his foot.

"Yes, I have a reservation under…."

"Mr. Hood," Will said finishing Ashton's sentence. "We've been expecting you."

"Great."

"How would you like to pay?" Will asked.

Ashton handed the desk clerk his credit card.

"Thank you, Mr. Hood. Your card will be charged upon checkout. Breakfast will be served every morning from 7:00am until 10:00am, and brunch on Sundays from 8:30am to 12:30pm. Would you like one room key or two?"

"One will be fine."

The clerk handed Ashton his room key.

"Your room number is 4-2-3. Is there anything else I can do for you?"

"Nope, all good. Thanks," Ashton said.

"Very well. Have a great night, Mr. Hood, and enjoy your stay with us."

As Ashton was searching for his room, the phone back at the reception desk rang.

"Yessir, he just checked in…Yessir, I think so…Tomorrow? Yessir, I'll make sure he does."

Ashton stood at the railing outside his room examining the pool deck, eager to lounge by its side as the culture of island life surrounded him. The sky was cloudless and the light from the rising moon splashed the tides. The fishing boats anchored offshore swayed in unison with the rhythmic ebb and flow of the gentle waves.

His room was cold and clammy with a hint of lilac in the air. Switching on the light, he saw that the queen bed was immaculately made, beckoning him to crawl in and relax. He dropped his bag and fell backwards on the covers, feeling his stress wash away as the reality of his vacation started to set in. He smiled and ran through his mind everything he wanted to do the next day, starting with an early morning breakfast to get the day started. The room itself was relatively small, but he paid it no mind because he didn't foresee himself spending a whole lot of time in it. He was on the topmost floor overlooking the interior of the hotel, which itself formed a quadrangle surrounding the expansive swimming pool shaped like an hourglass, traced by equally spaced palm trees and covered lounge spaces shrouded with white linen canopies.

It was approaching midnight, and a couple was making out in the water. The woman was pressed against the edge of the pool and the refracted image of her legs were wrapped around the man. They both still had their bathing suits on, which Ashton found reassuring, and used that as his cue to call it a night.

Morning arrived early, and Ashton slowly opened his eyes sans alarm and checked the time.

6:11am.

He wiped the sleep from his eyes and rolled out of bed feeling the cool stone tile floor beneath his bare feet. He ran the shower as hot as he could stand it, and without a care in the world, stood for ten minutes letting the water wash over his body. He wrapped a towel around his waist, lathered up his face, and shaved his burgeoning five o'clock shadow. He finished his morning hygiene routine, dressed, and walked outside onto the balcony overlooking the pool, smelling the salty scent of the nearby ocean.

The morning air was cool, but Ashton could tell it would soon get blazing hot as the day wore on. The sun was rising above the horizon into a clear baby blue canvas sprayed with wisps of cirrus clouds and hints of dark pink hues. There was a wind blowing in from the southeast. The surf was choppy. He hoped the current weather wasn't an ominous portent of a coming storm.

The pool deck was relatively empty. A few guests were already waiting on breakfast, which wouldn't be available for another ten minutes, with more guests filing down by the minute, so Ashton hurriedly put his claim on a table nearest the pool. The serving staff was rushing in and out of the kitchen preparing the buffet style breakfast. The food spread was extensive and smelled divine, and Ashton realized how hungry he was.

The breakfast area was setup under a large pavilion adjacent to the pool. A tiki bar with a wide selection of liquor and every conceivable brand of rum occupied the far left third of the patio. It was already being fervently tended for the customers eager to get their day started from the bottom of a glass.

The pool itself was inviting. Some of the younger adults were already knee deep in the shallower parts while others prepared their breakfasts from the smorgasbord of eggs, bacon, sausage, fruit, biscuits, and so much more, all spread out in chafing dishes on teal linen tablecloths. Last night's quiet ambiance had disappeared with the sun.

A wet deck sprinkled with lounge chairs was strategically positioned next to the tiki bar. Next to the tiki bar and partially obscuring the breakfast pavilion from view was a grotto with a small, cascading waterfall. It was beautifully built, reminiscent of ancient Grecian architecture.

The sound of the waterfall provided some tranquility, and Ashton grew more excited at the thought of lounging around the pool after he finished eating. With that thought, he walked around the edge of the pool to the patio, grabbed a tray and plate, and stood in line for the buffet breakfast that awaited him.

"Why go back for seconds when you can just put everything on your plate the first go-round? Amiright?" said an overweight man wearing khaki shorts, tennis shoes with crew socks, and a pale-yellow fishing shirt. He directly preceded Ashton in the short line and was heaping food high on his plate, while his wife was busy trying to wrangle two small kids running and screaming around the tables.

"Yeah," Ashton simply replied, grabbing the scrambled eggs serving spoon.

The man continued, unprompted and unsolicited, to regale Ashton with stories of how this breakfast spread compared to others he's had while staying at other hotels. His wife scorned him for not helping with their unruly kids. He broke off the conversation, apologized to Ashton, and hurried to her aid. Relieved, Ashton poured himself a hot cup of coffee that he's been looking forward to since he awoke. The house blend was a little burnt, but it sufficed. He took his time eating his breakfast in relative quiet, relishing in the feeling of having no rigid schedule or plans. When he finished, he leaned back and relaxed with a full stomach, sipping his second cup of joe and engaging in the popular pastime of people watching.

8:05am.

Having eaten his fill and lounging without a care in the world, he finally figured it high time to get moving. He walked around the pool towards the gated exit and on the way, noticed a honeymooning couple on the pool deck sipping mimosas. Not his drink of choice, but it gave Ashton pause for thought. He longed for the feeling of a beautiful woman on his arm again, someone with whom he could share his experiences. His last and only serious relationship broke his heart. They dated for the better part of a year. He was smitten with her, infatuated to the point of blindness as she returned his love by sleeping with an overly competitive paintball afficionado. That part was embarrassing in and of itself, not to mention the overall betrayal he felt. Though he dated since, his relationships were casual and rarely exclusive, and he had yet to feel comfortable enough to open his heart back up to another woman.

Without much more hesitation, he decided to remain at the pool awhile longer in the hopes the gods would bless him with a female companion while on his vacation. The morning was still young, and though it wasn't Vegas, he was sure the same rules applied. He went to the bar. A mojito sounded refreshingly delicious.

The weather was already warming. The bartender, a Hispanic man in his mid-thirties wearing an American flag bandana on his head, was making a Bloody Mary for a heavily augmented middle-aged woman wearing big sunglasses and a wide brimmed hat with a menthol cigarette held loosely between her fingers. A recent divorcee perhaps, but someone with money, who spends her days convincing herself she's thirty years younger than her actual age. When the bartender handed her the dark red concoction, she gave him a twenty-dollar tip with her room number written across the top of the bill. The bartender, obviously used to such overtures, took it without blinking an eye and put the bill in a jar already half-filled.

"What'll it be, my friend?" he asked Ashton.

"Mojito, please."

"Anything else?" the bartender asked as he grabbed a glass and threw ice into it.

"That's it for now. Thanks."

"One mojito, comin' right up. Name's Chris. Shout if you need anything."

Chris grabbed a bottle of Bacardi Rum and immediately went to work with his best Brian Flanagan impression. He knew his way around the bar. Several more customers crowded on either side of Ashton watching the bartender conduct his symphony of liquor bottles, awaiting their turns to order and hoping for a chance to see again the impressive acrobatic display.

"Here ya go," he said, putting a lime garnish on the rim of the glass.

"Can you charge it to my room?"

"Sure thing."

The drink was crisp and refreshing, liberal on the rum and the mint leaves muddled to perfection, just the way he liked it. He took his drink and put his claim on one of the recently vacated, shaded lounge spaces. He lay back, crossed his legs, and put his drink on the table next to him, then interlocked his fingers behind his head. The palm trees surrounding the pool were doing a hell of a job blocking the sun.

Ashton closed his eyes, enjoying the comfort of the cushioned chair mixed with the slight breeze and warm sun, when he was disturbed by the loud laughter of a group of college girls climbing out of the pool on their way to the adjacent lounge space. One of the girls flashed him a friendly smile as she sat down. Ashton smiled back at her.

This was his chance, and he could sense the precious time flying by. Her attention returned to her friends and the ship had all but sailed, but he could still see opportunity's wake as it slipped slowly away. The side curtains were rolled up and tied off on both lounge spaces, providing no privacy between them. He gave her a wave, a couple flicks of his wrists as coolly as he could, but she was no longer paying attention to him.

Ashton felt rusty and a little out of his element. In his younger years, before Luke deployed to Afghanistan, they spent every weekend cruising for chicks with a good degree of success. When their mom, Sara, received the phone call that Luke had been killed in action, Ashton socially shut down, no longer sure where he belonged in the world. He didn't attend parties as routinely as he once had, or any other occasions that lent themselves to large gatherings of people and small talk. As the years passed, he longed for a serious relationship, having since moved past his boyish pursuits. He yearned for a family, but he realized how inextricably linked his confidence was to his brother, a security blanket Ashton clung to since leaving Sister Anne.

Deep in his heart he was convinced that this vacation would cure all that, put him back on the path to happiness and reinvigorate his zeal for life. He hoped, too, it would help him overcome what he felt were too many wasted years wallowing in the black void of depression. His demons were consuming him, and he was watching his prime years from a spectator's bench. Key West, the tropical temperatures, easygoing culture, the crowds and tourism, had provided an exit ramp and a chance to start over. The woman who rescued him as an infant, Sister Anne, admonished him many times during his early formative years, telling him that a wasted life was a sinful one, and he knew it was time to heed those words and take action.

He reached for his drink, drenched in condensation. He casually took a sip while still lying back and jerked forward, erupting into a coughing fit. He wiped the drink off his chin with his towel.

"Are you ok?" the girl asked him.

"Yeah," he coughed again. "I'm fine," he continued, trying to stifle another cough.

"Ok," she said. "Just making sure."

She turned back around and rejoined the ongoing conversation with her friends who were unfazed by the incident.

As subtly as he could, he leaned in.

"I'm Ashton, by the way," he said.

She didn't respond.

Ashton cleared his throat.

"Hi," he repeated, a bit louder this time.

The group of girls halted their conversation and turned in unison. Ashton's eyes darted to all of them, uncomfortable with the attention.

"I'm Ashton."

"Um, hi," the girl said.

The speaker became visibly annoyed and resumed her conversation.

"He called me three times last night! I don't get why guys can't take the hint…."

The girl who had his attention smiled and turned back to her friends.

He tried again.

"I'm Ashton," he said hoping to get just her attention this time.

He started to sweat. He was committed now and either his pride or his dignity was going to get sacrificed. There was no going back. The other girls, sensing that simply ignoring him wasn't going to succeed, urged her to talk to him and so, feeling the peer pressure mount, she played along. She spun around and put her feet up on the reclining chair, bending her long legs and arching her back just slightly. She turned her head to look at Ashton.

There was no going back. What was it like watching the Titanic hit that iceberg, he wondered? Ashton pressed on now that he had successfully interrupted her conversation as the group looked on whispering and giggling amongst themselves. It was a bold move, he knew, but only those who dared to fail greatly ever achieved greatly, but then again, the owner of that nugget of wisdom was shot soon after saying it.

"I'm Ashton," he repeated.

"Michelle," she replied.

"Nice to meet you, Michelle. Have you been here long?" he asked her.

"I'm sorry, what was that?" she asked.

"Have you been here long?" he repeated a little louder.

A little confused, she answered, "Where? At the pool?"

"No, in Key West."

"Oh, um, not really. We flew in yesterday."

"Cool. Same here."

"Oh," she said looking back at her friends for help.

"Hey, if you aren't doing anyth…," he began.

She sat up and sighed with a smile and stopped him.

"Listen, I'm sure you're a nice guy, but I just want to relax with my friends. I'm not looking for anything and you aren't really my type."

He smiled, for it was the only thing he could do.

"No worries," he said.

"Nice job, Casanova. I can't believe her panties aren't flying off!" he imagined Luke teasing.

Can't win 'em all.

Still, he was eager to leave but didn't want to make it look obvious, so he sat back and waited. Finally, he grabbed his drink and drank the rest of it without taking a breath. In one motion he put his empty glass on the ground next to his chair, grabbed his things, and left the pool area.

He entered his room and stood in front of the mirror, staring at his reflection. He wanted a change. He looked at his clothes and decided he needed to buy more fashionable clothing commiserate with the environment. A more fashionable style was at least something he could remedy immediately. It was a starting point. Ashton wanted change and it would begin on Duval Street. If he wanted to feel good, he had to look good, he told himself.

TEN

8:49am.

Eager to put his failed Casanova persona behind him, Ashton grabbed his wallet, gave his hair a once over, and hurried down to the lobby. He approached the front desk where the clerk, a large black man with a clean-shaven head and face, and muscles bulging from his tightly fitted shirt, awaited him. A family stood nearby looking through the varying array of tourist brochures.

"Excuse me, Caesar," Ashton said reading the man's nametag.

"Mr. Hood, good morning. How may I help you?" he responded with a beaming smile and an accent unfamiliar to Ashton.

"I want to do some sightseeing this morning. I was hoping you might have some recommendations."

"Certainly, sir, what is it you're looking to do?" Caesar asked.

"I'm not sure. The main tourist spots, for sure. And a friend referred me to Alonzo's."

"Ah yes, a Key West staple."

"And maybe a little adventure if there's any to be had," Ashton added.

"I can definitely help you there, Mr. Hood," Caesar said pulling a visitor's map from a drawer and spreading it open on the counter. He circled the few tourist highlights the small island had to offer. His hands were enormous and made the map look more like a napkin.

"The island is small enough that you could do all of these in one day and in any order you'd like. But make sure you hit the marker identifying the Southern Most Point in the Continental United States as well as Earnest Hemingway's house. You can't miss those."

He handed the map to Ashton.

"What's the best way to get around?"

"I recommend walking. You're lucky, the weather this weekend is supposed to be unseasonably mild. Otherwise," he continued, "you could rent a bicycle or scooter from us. Most visitors tend to do that when they realize how hot it gets here."

Ashton put the map in his back pocket. The family that was huddled around the brochures finally walked through the automatic sliding doors, leaving the lobby empty save for Ashton and Caesar. Caesar waited for the doors to shut behind them and leaned over the counter.

"Tell you what, if it's adventure you're after, let me put you in contact with an acquaintance of mine," Caesar whispered.

Ashton was bewildered with the unexpected turn of conversation.

"Go on."

"His name is Jermaine. He lives several blocks down the road, near the cemetery."

Ashton leaned in as if to protect their conversation from curious passersby, despite there being none. Caesar scribbled down a phone number on the back of a small piece of paper and handed it to Ashton.

"Call this number and tell him 'the crow flies at midnight.'"

"Seriously?"

"Of course not. But call that number and tell him I sent you."

Caesar stood back upright smoothing his golden silk tie.

"Is there anything else, Mr. Hood?" he asked.

Ashton backed away a few steps. The two men silently nodded their tacit understanding before Ashton turned and walked out of the automatic doors. The doors closed behind Ashton. Caesar picked up the phone and dialed a number.

"Give him some time…No, I don't think he suspects anything…Hard to say…Depends. I've done all I can, per our agreement."

Caesar hung up the phone.

He looked up and saw Ashton standing outside in front of the doors, looking at the map and trying to get his bearings.

Nice guy, Caesar thought.

Caesar lent his assistance to the stranger on the other end of the line because he was paid handsomely for his service. Whatever events were about transpire, it had all been pre-arranged, and as soon as Ashton made the call, the wheels of the unforeseen plan would be set in motion.

Ashton stood for a moment staring down at the scribbled phone number. His took a deep breath, and though his intuition told him that danger wasn't a likelihood, the potential outcomes nonetheless played through his mind. Holding the scrap in his hand, he thumbed the edge of it, uncertain about the decision. He shoved it back into his pocket and decided to walk around for a bit to let his thoughts settle into a clearer picture. He jumped on a passing shuttle and rode it downtown.

The weather was balmy but not as hot as he anticipated. The sky was cloudless. An ocean breeze was blowing strongly through the streets and alleyways. He popped in and out of the souvenir shops and clothing boutiques that lined the narrow streets. Eventually, he reached Duval Street. He hung a left and continued to the bustling waterfront of Mallory Square, replete with restaurants, bars, shopping, and the ubiquitous tourist.

He strolled aimlessly at first, not having a plan or goal in mind, just enjoying the beautiful day, though his thoughts continued to circle back to the phone number in his pocket. Passing quaint conch houses, warmly painted and inviting, he scurried across the road, dodging bicycles and motorcycles, and entered a quaint boutique clothing store to peruse attire more suitable to the locale.

He made the purchase and changed in the dressing room, putting his old clothes in the shopping bag. Leaving them behind, he walked out of the store with his head held a little higher and made his way towards Sunset Pier for an early lunch. Ashton stood on the sidewalk forgetting, if for a moment, Caesar's proposition. He slid his hands habitually into his pockets. Fingering the card, his mind fixed once again on the phone number.

He looked at his watch.

11:10am.

A hotel nearby, shrouded by mossy oaks, seemed a likely place for a telephone. He had read enough spy novels to know better than to use his own phone and implicate himself should anything illegal happen. The lobby was ornately decorated and rated a few stars higher than the one he was currently staying in. He approached the black marble counter trimmed in gold.

"Excuse me, may I use your phone," he asked the concierge, an ageing man, in as proper a tone as he could muster, aiming to give himself more pedigree than what he had, and hoping to have a little fun with the role play in the process. He was fairly certain a bit of an accent crept into his voice as he did so.

"Are you a guest here, sir?" the concierge countered.

"Am I a guest here? Sir, you checked me in two nights ago. I am embarrassed that one so willing to spend so lavishly to lodge in your establishment is so quickly tossed aside!"

"If I could just get your name…," the tuxedoed man started.

"Get my name? Is that the kind of service, or dare I say lack thereof, that's to be expected from this institution? Unbelievable. I'm likely to contact the manager. This is an outrage!"

Confidence and a sense of purpose could sway most arguments and manipulate people just enough. He hoped he had struck the right balance. The concierge eyed him for a few long seconds.

"I am terribly sorry, sir, it was a simple oversight. Our phone is just this way. I apologize for any inconvenience."

"Thank you, kind sir. I shan't forget this and doubtless will lend to your establishment my future patronage."

Ashton angled his body away from the concierge, who stepped away to give him some privacy, and dialed Jermaine's number. It rang three times. He looked over his shoulder at the concierge who was still eyeing him and quickly turned away when a thickly accented voice answered.

"Yeah," grumbled the man on the other end of the line.

"Is this Jermaine?" Ashton asked softly.

There was no immediate response.

"Hello?"

After a pause, Ashton took the phone away from his ear.

"Who 'dis?" the deep voice asked.

Ashton hurriedly put the phone back to his ear.

"Hello?"

"Who 'dis?" the voice asked again.

"Caesar told me to call you," Ashton answered.

A few more seconds of silence passed.

"Where you at?"

"Eaton and Elizabeth."

"A'ight, mon. Stay dere."

The conversation ended. Ashton hung up the phone. His adrenaline was pumping. He could still disappear if he wanted to, there was still time.

While he worked through any internal reservations, he heard a vehicle with a high-displacing engine approaching quickly. The car had yet to reveal itself as the loping sound echoed through the streets. Suddenly, a silver 1969 Camaro SS convertible, with two white racing stripes streaking across the top length of the car, drifted around the intersection north of him.

The tires barked as they caught the pavement and thrust the vehicle forward. The driver raced the vehicle down the street before coming to a screeching halt in front of Ashton, sending a wall of smoke pluming into the air. The car idled choppily as the smoke slowly dissipated, revealing the driver, a figure in dark shades and long dread locks.

"Get in," he said in his low voice. His accent was thicker in person than it had been on the phone. A scowl marred his jaw.

Jermaine eyed Ashton closely as he opened the passenger side door. Before Ashton had settled into his seat and buckled the seat belt, Jermaine smashed the gas pedal and lowered the canvas top. The torque pinned Ashton against the back of his seat. Ashton looked at Jermaine wearily through the corner of his eye. Jermaine put the butt of his cigar into his mouth and clinched the tightly wrapped leaves between his teeth. The end glowed a bright orange as he took a drag. The rich, sweet cigar smoke surrounded his face as he exhaled.

"Where are you taking me?" Ashton asked.

Silence.

Ashton began to regret the decision. Something didn't feel right.

"Let me out here," he demanded.

Silence.

The car was moving too fast to jump out. Ashton turned his gaze back toward the road in front of him. The car continued its accelerating pace, dodging unwary pedestrians and drifting around turns. It didn't really matter much where he wanted to go, he realized. He was committed now and only along for the ride, wherever that ride might take him. The wheels were in motion.

ELEVEN

The Camaro sped south towards the water then followed the road as it turned a sharp ninety degrees westward to Roosevelt Boulevard and a beautiful view of Smathers Beach. The water was a beautiful, glassy, pale green. The white sand was blindingly bright. Having followed through the curve, the car traveled another two hundred yards before coming to a sudden, screeching halt, jerking Ashton forward into the dashboard. He rubbed the back of his neck and grimaced. White smoke and the smell of burnt rubber engulfed the vehicle.

"Here. Get out."

"Thank God," Ashton said under his breath as he opened the door and poured out onto the asphalt. He slammed the door and leaned on the window jam.

"Where am I?"

"Here."

"What does that mean? I have no idea where 'here' is!" Ashton shot back.

Jermaine gave a cool smile in return, showcasing gold-plated teeth. He revved the engine. Ashton jumped away from the car and stood on the sidewalk watching the Camaro's tires spin in the loose sand that had blown across the asphalt road, belching more smoke before catching the pavement and screeching off into the distance. It was soon reduced to a blur, and as mysteriously as the car had arrived, it disappeared.

The beach was nearly vacant. A few sandpipers scurried along the surf, chased by the waves, and looking for any ocean-dwelling treats that washed ashore. A homeless-looking man, sitting in the sand perched against a slanting palm tree with a dramatically bending trunk, was sleeping with his chin resting on his chest, his thick, flowing red hair blowing in the breeze. Just beyond him to the south, a rocky jetty covered in mangroves lunged into the sea. Ashton contemplated the precarious situation in which he had put himself. The beach was deserted. He weighed his options.

He stood underneath a nearby smattering of palm trees, the last bastion of shade before an exposed beach. Taking a moment to collect himself, he used the time to relish the beauty and tranquility of the shore. The sea was about thirty yards in front of him, its waves gently lapping the saturated sand. A white heron startled him as it strolled past, leaving behind it a trail of pronged footprints.

The metallic sound of steel drums began to drown out the ocean and the crying gulls overhead. He walked to the surf, the music once again filling his ears, pulsating, as though it was coming from right behind him. He looked down the beach. Nothing.

"Get out of my head!" he yelled in frustration.

"I'm not in your head, son!" said a gruff voice.

Ashton, startled, turned back around, and stumbled backwards in surprise nearly somersaulting into the water. A large man with a thick, red beard and wavy red hair stood before him, his arms folded, casting a shadow down upon him. He stood over Ashton, tall and stout with a carefree look despite his hardened appearance. The imposing figure was accompanied by another man, comparatively smaller in stature.

"Who…? Where did…? What…?" Ashton rambled.

In a sudden realization he turned towards the man sleeping against the slanting palm tree. Gone. His heart raced. He thought of running while his short and relatively dull life flashed before his eyes. The unkempt stranger saw it coming and threw up both hands to assuage Ashton's trepidations.

"Easy, bub. You can call me Milt," he said in a deep, authoritative tone.

He reached out his bearpaw of a hand and grabbed Ashton's, lifting Ashton to his feet in a single, rapid motion. When he released his grip, Ashton could feel the blood rushing back into his fingers.

"What the hell is going on?" Ashton asked, standing and brushing the sand off him.

"Don't know what you mean. You looked lost out of your mind, so I figured on lending a hand. And if we're speaking truthfully, I half expected you to curl up and cry when you saw me."

"Yeah, well, what do you expect."

"Do I smell bad?" he asked rhetorically to his companion who looked wearily at Ashton, analyzing him.

"You can call me Ashton. Ashton Hood," he said introducing himself.

"It's nice to meet you, Ashton Hood."

"So, do you want money or something?" Ashton asked.

The stench of rum oozed from Milt's pores, but he seemed to Ashton to be entirely too lucid. His hair was disheveled, pushed lazily backwards. His clothes bordered on tattered. His tanned, hairy, barrel chest protruded through a thin, loose-fitting, half-buttoned shirt. His pant legs were rolled up to the knees and his thick-soled feet gave Ashton the impression he hadn't worn shoes in years.

"Money?" Milt repeated with a laugh. "No, I don't need money. Why? Do I look like a vagrant to you?" he said seeming concerned.

"Sort of. I mean, no. I...."

"I'm kiddin'!" Milt clapped back laughing heartily.

Ashton laughed nervously.

"Were you the one playing the music?"

"What music?"

"Nevermind."

Milt put his muscular arm around Ashton's shoulder.

"Well, we've passed with the pleasantries. That makes us acquaintances by my book. How's about we head down to my waterin' hole and get ourselves a couple of drinks or seven?"

Ashton was sure of it. He had just unwillingly made friends with a vagabond.

"I'm gonna pass, but thanks," he said trying to back out of the offer. He averted his eyes from Milt's gaze, feeling the pressure to acquiesce and knowing the situation would only grow more unpredictable, but there was something appealing and disarming about the gesture.

"Tell you what…I'll get the first round. You can get the rest," Milt said with another boisterous laugh.

As his laughter settled, he placed his hand on Ashton's shoulder and guided him forward. Ashton was no longer in a position to refuse the man. The muscles in his shoulder ached as he stumbled alongside Milt. A second man, identical in appearance to the other man accompanying Milt, met them at the curb in a six-seater golf cart.

"Where'd you commandeer this thing?" Milt asked the driver.

"I have my ways," the driver answered.

Milt answered Ashton's unasked question, "Where're my manners. Ashton, this is Marco and the driver here is his brother, Carlos," introducing his two companions.

Ashton nodded.

"You don't talk much, do ya?" Milt asked.

"Only when I have something to say."

Milt and Marco jumped into the golf cart, while Ashton hesitated, standing and staring. As if sensing Ashton's intentions, Milt yelled back over his shoulder, "Don't be making any rash decisions. Get in."

What am I doing? If this is what Caesar had in mind, we're going to have a conversation when I return.

Ignoring his own inhibitions, he sat in the back seat next to Marco. Carlos sped the golf cart north around the curve and onto Waddell Street and headed towards Greene Street. Milt held the side of the roof and put his foot up. He closed his eyes and smiled, letting the breeze blow past him.

TWELVE

A rooster crowed and strutted past Captain Tony's Saloon. Inside was a boisterous, convivial scene, packed with brigands and drunkards, mavericks and miscreants, neither tourist nor local. It was dark inside and it took some time for Ashton's eyes to adjust to the lighting. When they did, he saw bras, dollar bills, an 82nd Airborne Division flag, and license plates from an assortment of states affixed to the ceiling and walls.

"Stay away from the bathrooms, they smell like cat urine," Milt advised.

Milt seemed to fit right in, like a hand into a thoroughly worn-out baseball glove, and in that regard the atmosphere almost made sense. The rum was flowing, the laughter was raucous, and a musty stench of sweat and unnamable odors danced through the dusty air. Milt stood larger-than-life, a giant smile on his face, silhouetted in the larger of the two entrances under a Jewfish mounted above the sign outside the saloon. Ashton's uncertainty and suspicions about Milt soon subsided, and he gave in to the uninhibited debauchery that diffused throughout the open-air bar.

Ashton was quick to notice, however, that the noise and rowdiness of the patrons failed to capture the attention of any of the passersby. Marco and Carlos took a seat on two barstools at the center bar. Sitting at a table in the back with three rough-looking men next to a wall sign that read "Elect Tony Tarracino Mayor" was a slightly overweight tourist with alabaster skin wearing a Margaritaville t-shirt and having the time of his life.

He looked up and gave Milt a wave and a raise of his flagon. Milt raised his own and toasted the man.

Milt walked amongst the rabble, joining in the merriment. Ashton followed in his wake. Milt greeted and shook hands with everyone, clapping them on the back as he passed. It was easy to see the respect and admiration he garnered from those with whom he interacted.

"Have a seat, Ashton," Milt said motioning to a barstool at the end of the bar. The lighting cast a peculiar shadow here making it slightly darker than the rest of the room.

Milt held up two fingers to the aging bartender. The old man nodded and went to work. In the interim, several ragged men approached Milt and spoke in his ear, reminiscent of scenes from the Godfather. A woman came over and sat on his lap for a good while, and for the most part, they all ignored Ashton for the favor of Milt's company. Ashton met the bartender at the bar and drank whatever concoction the bartender placed in front of him. He took a cautious sip.

"I call it a bumbo," the old man said.

Ashton looked up to see the toothless bartender staring back at him.

"A what?"

"A bumbo. Rum. Wa'er. An' a toucha cinnamon."

Ashton took another sip and nodded his satisfaction.

"Not bad."

The old man grinned with pride. Ashton finished the drink in a hurry and called for another. Milt had been so engrossed with his friends that he didn't initially notice Ashton had moved and called for him to return. When the barkeep reappeared with another round of his renowned concoction, Milt called for the same, slamming down several gold coins. The bartender swept them into his thick, knotted hand.

"I thought I was getting the first round?"

Milt laughed again.

"I get the first round, lad. You get the rest," he corrected.

He raised his glass to Ashton and toasted him.

"Ain't a better way to start a day," Milt slammed his glass into Ashton's. "To every day, an adventure!"

Ashton held his mug high in unison with the crowd.

"Another!" Milt said in his deep, commanding voice.

"Comin' ri' up," the old bartender responded.

"Keep 'em comin', old man."

"Aye aye, cap'n."

"I've always had fond memories of this place," Milt said to Ashton. "Hell, this was the first place I brought these two bastards and they've been following me around ever since."

Ashton looked over at the two brothers sitting idly at the bar but did not comment.

"Another for my friend!" Milt yelled while looking down his shoulder to Ashton. "You'd better hurry and finish that one up."

Ashton forced down the last swallow as the alcohol began taking its effect. His face grew warm and prickly. The drinks were getting stronger.

"This is just rum."

"And?"

They continued to drink even as Milt soundly outpaced Ashton. After four rounds, Ashton had just loosened up and joined in on the fun and conversation when the laughter abruptly ceased. He followed everyone's gaze toward a woman standing on the concrete step in front of the lesser doorway. She wore a large sun hat and oversized sunglasses, her hands firmly planted on her hips.

"I've seen that look before," Milt said.

A shopping bag hung from her wrist adorned with several colorful bracelets no doubt purchased from a souvenir shop. The speed at which she was tapping her foot reminded Ashton of something.

What was that rabbit's name?

"Thumper!" he said aloud, laughing and slapping the tabletop proudly.

Her piercing gaze shifted from her husband to Ashton, and he could feel her stare burning through him.

"Sorry, ma'am, that was the booze talking."

The sound of a wooden chair being pushed back on the floor saved him as the man in the Margaritaville t-shirt slowly stood and shuffled towards the woman, his head hanging low and his shoulders stooped. Ashton watched the man saunter to his wife, accepting his fate like a man headed to the gallows.

"Hey honey," the man said tentatively.

His salutation elicited no reaction from her.

"Stand strong, buddy," Milt uttered as he walked past.

The husband meandered his way through the crowd. His wife's gaze was transfixed on him, and she did not seem to notice anyone else in the bar or, and perhaps more apropos to the situation Ashton thought, she didn't care. As the hapless man closed the distance, she grew impatient and marched into the bar to meet him. She grabbed him by the arm, dragging him out and dressing him down on the sidewalk.

"You want to tell me just what you think you're doing? You said you were going to the bathroom. That was an hour ago!" she shouted in a heavy New Jersey accent, wagging her finger feverishly in his face. "And what? I find you in a bar drinking by yourself?"

Yourself?

"You know what they say about scorned women," Milt said to Ashton.

The spirited atmosphere dissipated.

"I was just hanging out with some guys I met. I thought you'd be in there shopping longer," the husband said trying his best to reason with his wife.

She snatched her sunglasses off and turned her head.

"What guys? What the hell's wrong with you?"

The husband turned around and pointed.

"Those guys."

"Time to go," Milt said sliding out of the shadowed end of the bar and tiptoeing out the main entrance opposite the quarreling couple.

Everyone else scurried after him like roaches in the light. Ashton, for his part, was engrossed. Aside from his gentle swaying, he didn't move nor take heed of the exodus. The wife smirked about as sarcastically as any person could and continued her massacre.

"Oh, good, at least you aren't the only low life drowning yourself in booze this early in the day. Two peas in a pod, you two are."

She was now staring directly at Ashton. Ashton looked around, noticed the bar had emptied, and shifted uncomfortably in his seat. He waved nervously at her.

"GET A JOB, YOU BUM!" she yelled at him while her husband looked on with utter shame and embarrassment.

As soon as the happy couple left, Ashton bolted past the game room for the exit. He hung a quick left, then turned south on Telegraph Lane, desperate to escape. The smell in the narrow street was pungent from days old garbage rotting in the tropical heat, but in a small chained off gravel lot opposite the side façade of Durty Harry's Bar, he saw Milt leaning against a white fence chatting with Marco and Carlos. They were waiting casually in the alcove, each smoking a fine Cuban cigar. The fragrant smoke wafted around them.

"Hey! There he is. Glad you made it out alive, bub," Milt said.

"How was I the only person she saw in there?" Ashton said cutting right to the chase.

"Because we left," Milt answered.

His comment was met with subtle laughter from the two Cuban men.

"That doesn't explain why she couldn't see everyone else."

"When you look like us, maybe that was for the best," Milt joked. "But you, you look respectable. Maybe she was just lookin' out for your wellbein'."

"Or maybe she took offense to shitbag corrupting her husband," Carlos added.

Ashton turned to Carlos with a furrowed brow and grit teeth.

"All right, all right. You got me. It was magic!" Milt said with a pantomime, cutting the tension.

Ashton dispensed with the mockery but lingered with the group. Milt eyed him carefully, studying him, and put the cigar back into his mouth.

"Y'know, I don't envy that man," Milt said as he bit down on the cigar. "I've been in his shoes b'fore and I s'pose every man at some point in his life is due to experience such a situation." He pulled his shirt off his left shoulder, revealing a long, deep scar just above his chest. "See that? It's one of many, but that one," he paused to reflect, "I deserved that one. She ran me down and sent a sword through my shoulder. If she could've seen clearly through her tears, she might've hit her mark."

The group laughed.

"You're a sonuvabitch," Ashton said to him.

Milt laughed and took the cigar out of his mouth.

"You're alright, kid."

He threw his arm around Ashton's shoulders.

"I like ya…Ashton, was it? Right," he said not giving Ashton an opportunity to speak. "C'mon then, there's something else I want to show you."

THIRTEEN

Marco and Carlos walked a few paces behind Ashton and Milt as they turned northeast onto Front Street. Milt knew where he was going but was in no hurry to get there. Key West was blossoming. They walked past various species of palms, ferns, and shrubbery, along with the occasional bird-of-paradise flower stretching its orange and yellow finger-like petals toward the sky. Bright purple and pink orchids blossomed up and down the trees, intermingled with the hanging roots of several Ficus.

Milt didn't say a word as they walked. He maintained a frontward gaze, brooding, eyes squinted in the sun. His stubby cigar still clinched between his yellowed teeth. Light wisps of smoke were carried away with the breeze. After a while, he took a long drag from the cigar, exhaling a long train of smoke. The cigar hung wearily between his fingers and then fell onto the sidewalk. He drew in a slow deep breath through his nose and let it out the same way.

"You won't find better oysters!" Milt exclaimed as they strolled up to Alonzo's Oyster Bar. "Go tell that pretty waitress you want a reservation." Milt grinned and nodded towards the hostess, giving Ashton a push.

"Hey, easy," Ashton said to Milt. "Table for four, please."

"Sure. Inside or out?" she asked politely.

"Do you have anything outside by the water?" he asked.

"Everything outside is by the water."

"Then outside is fine."

"Ok," she smiled. "Right this way."

She turned on her heels and led Ashton to his table. As he followed the hostess, he turned around expecting to speak to the rest of his party. Instead, his eyes caught a rather odd fellow more suited for safari than the beach frantically scribbling in a tattered journal.

Ashton was beginning to feel a bit relieved that perhaps this escapade had finally ended, and he could sit back, enjoy his lunch of oysters that Kayleigh spoke so fondly of, and continue his weekend of rest and relaxation.

"Here we are. Your waitress will be with you shortly."

He smiled at her. The table was situated underneath an Alonzo's sign nearest to the "Tarpon Feeding" station. The sailboats moored in the marina rocked on the waves caused by boats passing in the channel. A flock of pelicans floated nearby hoping for a morsel of food scraps.

And so now he sat at Alonzo's alone, admiring the view and the swaths of tourists passing by along the Harbor Walk. He sat back completely relaxed and eager to put the wild morning behind him, finally.

At the table next to him sat a couple who looked to be in their late-30s. The man was reclining leisurely in his chair drinking a rumrunner and enjoying the breeze and a full stomach. He was tall and well dressed in a custom tailored, sky blue, half-linen suit proper for the tropical climate. Underneath his open jacket, he wore a white shirt, the top two buttons unfastened. A pair of brown leather drivers completed his ensemble. His dark hair was combed back with subtle streaks of gray, a distinguished look for his young age. He was engaged in light conversation with the beautiful woman sitting next to him sipping an amaretto sour. Three dozen empty oyster shells and several squeezed lemon wedges rested in the iced tray in front of them.

Ashton was admiring the young woman's beauty when the debonair gentleman leaned over to Ashton, "Menu?" he offered. "We're just finishing up. I recommend the oysters, just like everyone else," he said in a barely discernable southern accent. His regional diction overcome, Ashton assumed, during his many travels galivanting around the globe. Doing what, exactly, Ashton could only speculate.

"Appreciate it," Ashton said taking the menu.

He noticed the man was wearing an Omega Seamaster dive watch with a blue ceramic bezel framing a sun-brushed chrome dial with blue hands. The initials "BK" were monogrammed on the cuff of his shirt protruding just slightly from underneath his jacket sleeve.

They both looked upwards simultaneously as the rhythm of steel dreams danced on the breeze. The man looked back at Ashton and removed his Oakley Holston sunglasses revealing light brown eyes.

"I love the sound of steel drums, don't you?" he asked.

"I did," Ashton answered.

Ashton tried to ignore the music. The stranger's mouth curled slightly up into a smile. He leaned back in his chair and finished off the rest of his cocktail.

"You don't hear those every day," he continued as he pulled out several bills to cover the check. A nice payday for the waitress, Ashton noticed.

The handsome gentleman winked and turned back toward the beautiful sun-kissed woman. She was taking her last sip of the drink she had been nursing and dabbed her mouth with her napkin. Ashton was entranced and didn't realize how long he'd been staring until she glanced up at him and gave a warm wave. Embarrassed, he shifted in his seat and smiled back. The couple stood up together. The gentleman buttoned his suit jacket while the woman slid her arm around his.

"Have a good one," the gentleman said coolly.

"Thanks. You, too."

"Bye," the beautiful woman said with a smile as strands of her brown hair blew across her face. Her colorful summer dress flowed behind her as they walked around the corner and disappeared. Ashton turned his attention back to the menu. As he was opening it and reading through the different oyster options, the waitress appeared.

"Hi, there! I'm Kat. Sorry for making you wait. Can I get you something to drink?"

"Um, yeah. I'd like a rumrunner, please."

"Ok, no problem. I'll have it right out for you," she said with a cheerful smile.

"Hey, ol' buddy!" Milt said as he approached the table with Marco and Carlos in tow.

Milt slapped Ashton on the back just as he was taking a sip of water. Ashton choked on the beverage as it trickled down his esophagus.

"What you need is another cocktail."

"One's already on its way. I don't need another one, you drunken ass."

Milt appreciated Ashton's frankness.

"Well, you got me there," he said bursting into laughter with Marco and Carlos. "You talk to that pretty young lass?"

Ashton sighed, a bit perturbed by the question.

"No, I did not."

"Too bad. Maybe I'll have a go at her, eh?" he said chuckling again and elbowing Ashton in the arm.

This fucking guy.

A silence fell over the table.

Ashton took a few deep breaths.

At that moment, the waitress walked up behind Ashton and placed his drink in front of him. It was refreshing. The perfect complement to a warm day. Ashton pushed the miniature umbrella to the side and took a sip, feeling his cells soak up the cool drink.

"Hey, y'all. Y'all ready to order?" the waitress asked.

She was cute. A born and bred Key West Conch. She wore cut-off jean shorts and a black tank top. Standard business attire for the island, Ashton suspected.

"Indeed, little miss. My friend here will have another one of those pretty drinks," Milt joked. "And three scotches for us. Enough to make my friend here seem interesting."

Milt ordered most of the menu for the entire table.

"It'll be right out," the waitress said.

Milt called after her, "And don't forget the fancy umbrella for my friend here!"

She turned and smiled and gave him a thumbs up.

"That's a lot of food."

"C'mon now, Ashton, oysters are an ocean delicacy and an a-phro-di-si-ac," he annunciated. "I can promise you that from experience."

That comment finally elicited a reaction from the two brothers.

The waitress returned a few minutes later bringing with her a tray full of drinks. Ashton was already asking for another. He pushed his empty glass to the edge of the table.

"How long have you lived in Key West?" Ashton asked her.

Milt looked to his two friends and smirked.

"What is time but a number? A human construct – most of the time. Which reminds me, I have something to show you. Been carrying around this damned thing long enough," he trailed off as he rifled through his pocket. He pulled out a folded, yellowed piece of parchment and gently smoothed it out on the table revealing a series of crude lines and markings.

"What is it?" Ashton asked as he tried to make sense of what he was seeing.

"What's it look like? It's a map."

"I get that it's a map, but a map to what?"

"You'll know when it's time," Milt told him.

"Fine," Ashton said, having resigned himself to Milt's secrets. "There's nothing on this map but lines. It looks like something I used to scribble on the walls with crayons as a kid. There're no terrain features, no grids…."

Milt laughed.

"Do these lines lead to treasure or something?" Ashton asked louder than he intended.

The people at the tables nearest them all turned at the mention of the word. Milt stared them down until they looked away, then sighed knowing Ashton's curiosity would not be satisfied without a satisfactory answer. His task was not yet complete. Milt needed Ashton, though Ashton remained unaware of the role he was about to play, and Milt was determined to keep it that way.

"How'd you come by it?" Ashton asked.

"Now you're asking the right questions. Settle in…."

FOURTEEN

"Can I get you boys anything else to drink while you wait?" the waitress interrupted.

Ashton was hanging on every word of Milt's captivating tale.

"I think you already know the answer to that question, lass," Milt answered with grin.

"You got it. Another round, comin' up," she said.

Milt watched her as she walked away.

"We'll need to be leavin' soon, so I'll end my tale with this, I didn't have much need for money anymore, so I headed back to Ireland and the woman I left behind. But I never made it. A hurricane happened right on my heels. A wave steered me into a reef and marooned me and my crew on a deserted island, though a beautiful one, to be fair. By a miracle it would seem, I made it through the jaws of the bay and its rocky teeth. I hid my ship in an expansive sea cave, salvaging all I could from the wreckage, and then made the island my home. I'm giving this to you because I can sense my days coming to an end."

Milt folded the delicate parchment and handed it to Ashton.

"Coming to an end? And this map then, if it holds any significance, why give it to me?" Ashton asked suspiciously. "Does this have something to do with why I'm here?"

"Just a coincidence," Milt lied. He took a gulp of his beverage. It dripped down the corners of his mouth and into his thick beard.

"Coincidence or not, I still don't understand how I fit into all this. Why aren't you giving the map to one of your friends there?" He turned his eyes towards Marco and Carlos who then both exchanged a glance with one another. "Why did you interrupt my vacation, more or less kidnap me, and lead me all over town?"

"Woah woah woah. I didn't kidnap you. You made the phone call. Two, I don't trust these two bastards," he said thumbing at the two men. "After all," Milt leaned in, "I thought it be adventure ye after," he said, exaggerated his accent for effect. "That's why you came all this way to Key West, is it not?"

"How'd you know about the phone call? And yes, I was hoping for some adventure, but more than that, some relaxation, and so far I've had neither."

"Ashton, my lad, I'm the king of these parts. Didn't you know that?"

"Your drinks," the waitress said as she placed them around the table.

"Thank you, sweetheart," Milt said.

"You're quite welcome."

"You're free to leave whenever you'd like," Milt said to Ashton, realizing the gamble he made with his bluff. Still, he pressed, "I wouldn't blame you if you did. It's a beautiful day. Listen, I've been on this earth a long time, and I've seen and done more things than I care to recall, but there's plenty of adventure in store, so it's your call."

"I just met you, and you damn sure don't know anything about me."

"Don't I?" Milt said stone-faced, his tone deepened. "I know more about you than you think."

After a pause, he winked and sat back in his chair and let out a hearty laugh. The breeze was picking up. It rustled his red hair.

"Then tell me who you are?"

"I just told you. King. Captain. Whatever you like me to be."

The waitress reappeared and Milt opened his arms wide welcoming the trays of food. A feast had arrived.

"I'm starving!"

Despite Ashton's misgivings, his hunger became insatiable as the delectable smells wafted into his nose. Their mouths salivated at the smorgasbord that now lay in front of them.

"Eat your fill, boys. We have a long day ahead of us," Milt said.

For the next half hour, the four of them sat and ate, enjoying themselves, the company, and the variety of seafood dishes before them. Ashton didn't contribute much to conversation but nevertheless reveled in the superb stories and jokes. Milt, his arms crossed about his barrel chest, let out a sigh and smiled. He turned his head and gazed out towards the sea. The boats in the harbor rose in sync with the rippling waves. A beautiful blue and yellow macaw flew in on the breeze and flapped its wings in a wonderful display, landing on Milt's shoulder.

"Time to go," it squawked.

"I hear you, Tuki, thank you. In a minute."

The tropical bird squawked its displeasure.

"Ashton, you've sat here all lunch and barely uttered a peep."

"I've tried," he responded, "but you won't answer my questions, so what else is there to say?"

Milt opened a packet of Lance Captain's Wafers and fed one to Tuki.

"Tell me a story," he said.

"I don't have any."

"Son, no man on this earth goes through life not having stories. Every experience, every decision we make, every opportunity we take or don't take, has something to teach us. And don't get me wrong, not every experience is created equal. I've hunted big game on most continents, traveled to remote places, and encountered some interesting folk who have some even more interesting ways of doin' things. It's the experiences that change us at a fundamental level; the ones that reveal truths about ourselves that make the best tales. If you didn't have any before, I suspect you'll have some soon."

Milt finished his drink. Ashton had been drinking water since halfway through the meal, concerned he wouldn't be able to stand if he continued on the binge he'd been on since Captain Tony's.

"Now it's time," Milt said rising from his chair.

Ashton remained in his seat and fingered the rim of his glass, pensive, thinking.

"I've seen that look countless times. Men don't come to the Caribbean without wishing they were pirates, even if for a day," Milt said with a laugh.

"You're right," Ashton decided, pushing his chair back.

Tuki squawked and flew away as they left the restaurant.

At the northern most point of Key West Bight, floating lazily at the end of the pier beyond the super yachts and luxury sailboats, power catamarans and walkarounds, was a white hardtop cruiser with twin outboard motors. The boat was worn and thoroughly used, clearly no stranger to usage. Forty-five feet in length, it was smaller than most of the vessels in the wharf, but impressive all the same. It had a fly deck in the bow and behind the transom in the stern, a swim deck. The pilothouse was enclosed on three sides, and below-deck housed the living area. Hand painted messily on the hull in royal blue, contrasting brilliantly with the off-white color of the boat, was its name, *Mami Wata*.

"There she is! Always a fine sight to see 'er restin' there on the water. I've had my share of loves in the past but this one will always have my heart."

Milt turned to Ashton with a boyish grin plastered on his face, "I can ride her all day and she don't get tired nor complain a bit!"

Ashton managed a laugh. "It could definitely do for some TLC."

"Aye, that she could," Milt replied. "She's a good boat all the same. Reliable."

Milt ran his hand along the gunwale.

"After you," he said as Ashton climbed aboard.

Marco and Carlos clambered aboard behind him, followed by Milt who untied the rope from the cleat. Carlos went inside the cockpit and started up the engines while Marco, on the fly deck, hoisted the anchor. The engines sputtered to life and spit out a cloud of white smoke. Milt took the helm, and as the boat pulled away from its slip, Tuki flew into the pilothouse and took up his perch on Milt's shoulder. Milt piloted the boat slowly out of the bight. After passing Sunset Key, he angled the boat and thrust the throttle forward, giving it some trim. The boat launched southward skipping over the first few rolling waves before settling on plane and heading out into deep sapphire waters.

FIFTEEN

The *Mami Wata* glided over the tranquil waters of the Caribbean. Milt's hands rested easily on the polished cedar helm. A smile plastered on his face. He lit a fat, sweet smelling cigar and took a deep drag, savoring the sweet taste of the tobacco. The cloud of smoke quickly dissipated riding on the wings of the wind that streaked across the deck.

The sun was still shining intensely and the splashes of water that hit their face whenever the bow of the boat met the crest of a wave was a welcomed refreshment. White gulls circled in the air framed by a pale blue sky. After an hour's ride skimming across the cerulean water, Milt throttled down and brought the boat to an idle near a shoal. The sandy ripples of the seabed were visible from the surface as was a sprawling reef that stretched to a steep drop plummeting into the abyss. Ashton watched as a large stingray glided underneath them.

"Where are we?" he asked.

"Mr. Hood, ain't it obvious? This is Heaven itself!" Milt pronounced as he walked out of the pilothouse and basked in the sun. He took a deep breath of the fresh, salty air. Marco and Carlos had moved below deck and rifled through some of the gear that was stowed away.

"Go to the fly deck and toss the anchor overboard," Milt told Ashton while coiling a large piece of rope around his muscular arms. "There are beasts and fish of all kinds that roam the deep. Some you'd think were out of some myth or storybook. Believe me on that, when you were suckin' at your mama's tit, I was battling real sea monsters."

OK, old man, Ashton thought.

"Toss it over the port side in the sandy bank there, away from the reef."

"Port side?"

Milt let out a sigh and pointed to the left. Ashton tossed the anchor into the water. Marco and Carlos appeared top deck and threw down four netted dive sacks.

"What're we looking for down there?" Ashton asked.

"Dinner," Marco replied. "Here," he added, tossing a pair of swim trunks to Ashton.

The boat rocked slightly as the men moved about.

"Just remember not to breathe when you're down there," Carlos sneered.

"And watch the current or there'll be nothin' between you and the dark deep," Marco warned.

Carlos dove in first and followed the anchoring line to the bottom. Ashton followed him. Milt stepped over the transom and onto the swim deck.

"This was a mistake. It'll never work," Marco acknowledged as he and Milt looked into the water at the two men descending to the bottom.

"The hard part was getting him on the boat," Milt countered. "Once he's on the island, it'll only be a matter of time."

"But if he finds out…."

"He won't find out," Milt assured him. "It took me thirty-three years to find Tew's bloodline, and I didn't get this close to fail. We need to get Tew out of that cave. I need to finish what I started and end this infernal curse so I can finally know peace."

Milt placed his mask on his face and dove into the water toward the reef. The coral and ocean flora were vibrantly colored and teeming with various species of marine life. A Great Hammerhead shark swam gracefully above them, disappearing into the blue before reappearing minutes later. As the two men descended to the reef, a school of Blue Tang swam past, quickly changing direction to-and-fro in unison. At the bottom, Milt reached underneath a large rock, the disturbed sand quickly obscuring his hand, and pulled out the largest conch shell Ashton had ever seen.

Ashton swam around for a few seconds more before having to resurface for air. Carlos shook his head at the novice. When he returned to the reef he found his own conch, but he found his prize guarded by a territorial Moray Eel darting out of its home to greet him. Ashton managed to grab the mollusk, barely avoiding the strike, and threw it in his bag.

"Not bad for your first time," Marco lauded at the surface.

Ashton unloaded his haul of two into the cooler.

"Should we be worried about the Great Hammerhead down there?"

"Nah," Milt said. "Hammerheads are the kittens of the sea. We're fine. It's those two bull sharks you need to be worried about."

"Bull sharks?" Ashton repeated, exasperated.

"You'll be fine. Just keep your wits about ya."

They descended again. Curious marine life had begun to congregate around the abundance of food being stirred up by their scavenging. Milt was the first to take notice as the largest of the two bull sharks was becoming increasingly aggressive. He motioned with his thumb for the group to resurface, keeping their heads on swivels as they ascended. The hammerhead was circling below, but well beneath them.

"We're missing one," Ashton said, treading water on the calm surface. "Where's Carlos?"

He put his mask back on and stuck his head underneath the surface searching for the fourth member of their party. Milt and Marco hung on the ledge of the swim deck while Ashton scanned the reef. Carlos was in a crevice near the shelf.

"He's still down there trying to wrestle a conch from an octopus," Ashton reported.

Milt put his mask on and looked for himself as Marco attempted to swim down to his brother. Milt grabbed his ankle just as he passed beneath him.

"It ain't worth losing both of you," he told him.

"He doesn't see the shark!" Marco said with alarm, noting the larger of the two bull sharks approaching from behind Carlos.

Against his better judgment, Milt let him go and Marco again descended towards Carlos, but before he reached the reef, the second bull shark brushed past Marco's leg and approached Carlos from the side. Carlos was still engaging with the octopus, having brushed off the Great Hammerhead just moments before. The octopus's snaking tentacles clung desperately to a jutting rock. Marco hovered in place, watching the scene unfold and monitoring the hammerhead swimming near him before it, too, swam down toward Carlos in concert with the other two sharks.

Stubborn fool! Marco thought.

The Giant Hammerhead that now took a keen interest in Carlos was swimming in tightening circles. The sharks continued to lurk, while Marco was helpless to watch. Then, in a flash, the large bull shark made its move, lunging at Carlos in a flash and biting his left forearm.

"NOOOOOO!" Marco yelled, his cries muffled under the water. His words mere bubbles floating harmlessly to the surface.

Amidst the red cloud, the octopus used the screening to scurry back underneath its rock. Carlos clutched what remained of his arm as he squirmed in agony, kicking furiously for the surface. A cloud of bright red blood diffused quickly through the water, trailing behind him. The two bull sharks, in a well-coordinated dance of death, encircled Carlos. Marco could only watch in horror. The smaller shark bit Carlos's left shoulder and his arm floated helplessly to the sea floor. The three sharks moved in and preyed on Carlos until all that remained were a few fleshy bones, dinner for the reef-dwelling creatures. Marco returned to the surface hoping Carlos had at least drowned before he became a shark feast. Without a word, he climbed back onto the boat, shaken by the gruesome scene and the loss of his brother. His face was emotionless and passive.

"We gotta do something!" Ashton said trembling with adrenaline.

"We're in their world. Can't blame them for their instincts. Carlos knew the risks," Milt said with a deadpan countenance. "It's time to go."

"Time to go," Tuki squawked again. The bird spread its wings wide before launching into the clear afternoon sky.

Ashton knew Carlos's death was going to be impactful to his two companions and though his death was disturbing, Ashton withdrew his emotions and collected himself for the betterment of the group. If the events of his life had taught him anything, it was the ease in which he was able to internalize his feelings.

"Hoist the anchor, Marco," Milt said once they were aboard.

Marco stood frozen on the swim deck staring into the water. Ashton sympathetically heaved the anchor aboard in Marco's stead, and then hurried about the deck securing the loose items. With the anchor safely stowed and the gear secured, Milt spun the helm hard to starboard and throttled the engine, launching the nose of the boat high into the air. It landed on the crest of a wave sending a heavy spray of water onto the deck. No one uttered a word. Marco stood beside Milt in the pilothouse and spoke with him in inaudible whispers, then went below deck. Milt fixed his gaze on the horizon.

After nearly twenty minutes sitting on a rear cushioned seat, staring at the wake and the pod of dolphins giving chase, Ashton approached Milt. He was half a step inside the pilothouse when Milt spoke, his voice rising over the dull hum of the motors.

"Gonna be some time before we get where we're goin'," Milt said flatly without turning around.

His hair was blown stiffly back by the salty wind. Ashton took the cue and returned to the aft deck, his gaze again fixed on the wake trailing the speeding boat. The sun was inching ever closer towards the horizon. The large, orange orb painted the western sky in streaks of orange, pink, and purple hues. Ahead in the distance, southeast of their position, an ominous storm cloud began to materialize.

Amid the looming gray sheet of rain, a veiny bolt of lightning shot across the sky. The wind suddenly shifted, accompanied by a slight chill. A gust carried with it the clean smell of rain. Ashton looked past the bow into the distance and stepped into the pilothouse for shelter. Tuki flew low across the deck before circling back, and once again landed on Milt's shoulder.

"Are we going through that?" Ashton asked, ignoring the macaw's arrival.

"No choice," was all the response Milt cared to muster.

"Looks foreboding. What's on the other side?"

"Home."

"How long till we get there?"

"Depends."

"On what?"

Milt, growing irritated, rubbed the bridge of his nose.

"You don't say nothin' all day and now you feel like talkin'?"

Ashton didn't respond.

"Hunker down, this ride's about to get rough."

Milt sat back in the helm chair. Ashton walked down the narrow steps below deck to the cabin. The room was surprisingly spacious with all the accoutrements to make it comfortable. Marco was sitting on the small, sectional sofa, holding his face in his hands. When he heard Ashton come down the stairs, he sat upright and slapped his cheeks to collect himself and hide his emotion.

Ashton was silent. An old black and white picture in a cheap wooden frame caught Ashton's attention. It was a silhouette cutout of a woman, a style made popular in the seventeenth century. It struck Ashton as odd to see such a picture in this current day and age, and his attention was soon caught by an old but polished brass sextant.

"You know, I was against bringing you along," Marco said suddenly as he channeled his anger towards Ashton. "Prove me wrong."

Ashton looked at him sideways, ignoring the comment. He understood Marco's current state, probably better than anyone. Marco had to blame somebody and if blaming Ashton helped him reconcile his brother's death, then so be it, Ashton thought to himself.

"How'd you meet Milt," Ashton said, changing the subject to get Marco talking about better days.

Marco's scowl eased from his face, his heavy breathing abated as he slowly calmed himself.

"Havana."

Marco grabbed two crystal rocks glasses and poured a few fingers of whiskey. Taking his seat by a small teak table, he crossed his legs and took account of the approaching storm through the porthole. Still a few miles out, he guessed.

"Carlos and I were mercenaries for Castro then," he began. "Before we ended up in Cuba, we found ourselves wherever guerrillas were needed, bringing with us weapons and money. Africa. South America. Mission after mission we exported our expertise to failing governments until, you might say, we grew consciences while in Cuba. It hits different when it's your own people, family, and friends that are affected. Carlos and I, along with a handful of other mercenaries that had turned against Castro were meeting in my uncle's place. Milt walked in unannounced. Surprised us all. We were well armed and had our guns pointed right at him, but he just laughed. He said he was looking for men and that he'd pay well. So, Carlos volunteered us. The others chastised us for abandoning the cause, but the next day, those guys, those revolutionaries, along with my uncle, were arrested and shot in the street by Castro's police."

"Unbelievable," Ashton muttered in astonishment.

"The government accused Carlos and me, in absentia, of subversion. Held a sham trial and everything. They killed our parents and tortured our younger brother, and the regime's been hunting us ever since."

"I'd venture to bet this life you now find yourself living is a step up from where you were."

Marco stared at him but did not answer. The boat began rocking violently as the storm grew in intensity. The rain, sounding like a thousand hammers beating the deck aboveboard, refused to ease.

"We'd better get back topside, see if Milt needs a hand," Ashton suggested.

"Indeed."

Ashton followed Marco to the top deck. The storm was picking up. Milt navigated the boat expertly through the outer edge of the storm, battling the winds and massive swells. The boat lurched skyward as it crested each wave.

"Here we go, boys!" Milt hollered.

Ashton's balance was moot. The boat listed starboard sending him nearly overboard. He grasped the gunwale and lunged towards the amidships fighting chair. The *Mami Wata* crested another wave. Tilting back downwards, Ashton tumbled forward and down the stairs back into the cabin. He was bruised, but unhurt. He made his way back topside. Water cascaded down the steps making them nearly impossible for his shoes to grip. As Ashton reached the top, his trailing foot slipped and he slid down two steps, knocking his shin, before he caught himself. His leg was bleeding and throbbing with pain as he climbed.

"Hold on!" Milt yelled, not taking his eyes off the raging sea.

Ashton stood up on the deck, the wind and rain tearing at his face. Blood mixed with water. He held his arms in front of him shielding the onslaught of rain from stinging his skin and slowly moved towards the helm where Milt was enthusiastically riding the storm. He looked like Major Kong straddling the atomic bomb like a rodeo bull, Ashton thought for a brief second before being reminded of the jarring brutality the storm was bearing down upon them.

Dread filled him as a towering wave rose to meet the boat, and as the *Mami Wata* climbed the wave's face, its bow pointing near straight up to the heavens, Ashton fell backwards and slammed against the transom, banging his head. His cell phone was flung from his pocket and into the abyss. Instinctively, he threw out his arms to stable himself and caught loose cargo netting affixed to the inboard port side hull. His left hand clinched tight before his mind had time to think about it. His body jerked to a sudden stop and a fiery, sharp pain birthed itself in Ashton's left shoulder. He let out a scream, drowned by the deafening sound of the storm's roar.

His consciousness was waning. The pain had given way to shock. With the little strength he had left, he reached over with his free hand and pulled himself closer to the net. As the *Mami Wata* rode down the slope of another wave, Ashton thought for a moment he saw a speck of burning light in the distance. A large swell rose before the boat and the fleeting light was blocked from view. Ashton slid his left arm through the weaving to better secure himself just as his body went limp and the world faded to black.

SIXTEEN

When Ashton awoke, the boat was gently rocking in a sheltered and secluded cove. Water softly slapped the hull. The weather was still with only the slightest hint of a breeze. The sun was beginning to set, illuminating the cove in a golden glow. Jungle covered mountains climbed skyward on all sides save for a narrow inlet to the north connecting the cove to the open sea. Gulls cawed as they floated aimlessly overhead.

As he slowly regained his consciousness, and images came back into focus, Ashton was able to take stock of his condition. His body was already sun-dried, and his clothes were draped over the side of the boat drying. He propped himself up on his elbows, still a little bewildered at the circumstance in which he now found himself as he tried to piece together the moments before and after hitting the transom. His left arm was slung in a white cloth across his chest, his shoulder set, but throbbing. He attempted to move it, but his shoulder screamed in response to a sudden wash of dull pain.

Ashton picked himself up and sat on the gunwale. Marco, in a melancholy daze, was refitting the *Mami Wata* with supplies purchased from the harbormaster, located just at the end of the dock and the first of many such shanties that comprised the rather decrepit and weathered town.

"It'll subside, in time," a clear voice said from behind him.

"What happened?" Ashton asked, still disoriented.

"You dislocated your shoulder. How you managed to secure yourself during that storm and not get swept overboard is an impressive feat, I'll admit ya that. Not bad for a little guy.

Welcome to Emerald Cove. Try to keep your wits about ya, huh?"

Ashton turned and raised his eyes to see a large man with long, black, curly hair tied in a knotted bun on top of his head. A massive tribal tattoo covered his wide back, and a thick, hemp necklace with a white shark's tooth rested against his bare, muscular chest.

The islander hoisted one of the stowed chests from the *Mami Wata* effortlessly onto his thick shoulder and took it to the beach as Tuki squawked and circled overhead before flying away into the distant jungle. Ashton managed to stand, but his legs faltered, and he collapsed onto the deck. Collecting his balance and strength with several steady breaths, he glanced over the side of the boat as he pushed himself back to his feet. The water was clear as glass. Barnacles crusted the pilons running the length of the rickety dock. A sea turtle and a small school of rainbow parrot fish swam through the sea grass under the hull. He looked at his watch. Stopped. He shook his wrist.

The Sentinel Cliffs towered above him, twin jagged rock faces on opposite sides of the cove guarding the entrance, tapering down to white, curving beaches ushering the inlet into the sea. The stone precipices slowly gave way to an encircling jungle beyond that was so green, so wild, so alive. Atop the eastern cliff, perched precariously on its edge, was a mammoth but crumbling stone structure. Emanating from the top of the ancient, char-stained orifice, burned a blazing fire, licking the sating air.

A quarter-mile stretch of crystalline sand dotted with palm trees, makeshift shelters of tattered sails and sheets replete with a variety of textile fabrics, and a couple rowboats turned over with their keels facing skyward buffered the town from the water. Cargo boxes lay half buried in the sand. The breadth of the beach from the shoreline to the coastline, buttressed by large and small boulders alike, spanned nearly three hundred feet. It was the prettiest stretch of shoreline Ashton had ever seen.

A ramshackle town had been built between the beach and the inland jungle, nestled in the shadow of the looming hills to the south. It was an old city with sandy streets. Most of the buildings, rustic and dilapidated, showed signs of the original beauty. Stone edifices peaked from behind crumbling and pealing pastel-colored stucco. While the earliest buildings of better construction still displayed some of their prominence, once brightly painted only to have succumbed to the years. They now sat with their facades chipped and faded; their long, wooden storm shutters warped and sun-bleached. The town once constituted a bustling and eclectic hideaway. Pink houses with iron-railed balconies abutting yellow ones; baby blue next to soft, salmon red, reminiscent of La Boca's Caminito Street. Time had relegated the town to just another one of the many, nondescript fishermen's villages sprinkled throughout the Caribbean.

Ashton grabbed his clothes, still damp, and covered his nakedness, careful not to further aggravate his shoulder. He left the bandage hanging on the gunwale, worked his shoulder through the aching pain, and walked down the plank onto the creaking dock heading for the beach. His seafaring partners, Marco and Milt, were nowhere to be seen. He counted upwards of sixty men lingering on the beach and a handful of women of the working-class sort, some engaging their clientele right in the open. Merriment filled the air.

A large warehouse stood near the docks and occupied the westernmost part of the beach just beyond the sand, battling the overgrowth and framed by a waterfall that fell into a pool feeding into the harbor. At the eastern part of the beach was a large cave shrouded in vines and hanging vegetation. To the south, on a hill behind the shanty town at the edge of the jungle, stood a beautiful Spanish manor that once stood as caretaker to a prosperous sugarcane plantation.

The soft, white sand was still warm, a hangover from the scorching afternoon and soothing to his bare soles. As Ashton meandered through the pockets of people drinking and debauching on the beach, he went largely ignored though he did notice more than a couple curious glances. Some of the men on the beach sat in groups around small fires, the kindling and tinder cracking under the flames. There was no telling how long they had been drinking, but the rum was flowing abundantly, and the laughter was hearty. A contingent of older men were gambling and playing cards on an old wooden stump now serving as a table, while others were involved in intense bouts of bartering. The remaining men, who had not yet succumbed to complete inebriation, were doing their best to court any available woman in sight.

Near the waterfall, a hammock swung between two palm trees arching outwards over the surf, gently rocking its sleeping occupant shaded by the long palm fronds hanging lazily overhead. He looked to be in his mid-thirties with a healthy but unkempt beard. He wore a pair of tattered khaki shorts and a gray tank top. An empty bottle of rum rested on his chest with his finger stuck in the neck. His foot hung over the side brushing the sand. A wide-brimmed straw hat shielded his face. He lay relaxed and content as though this were the only place he ever wanted to be.

Ashton stood with his toes buried in the sand for a moment to soak in all he saw, astounded at the beauty of the cove, feeling as though he had stepped into a Daniel Defoe book. The events of the day began to wear on him, and he felt he would soon succumb to exhaustion. His stomach growled for food. Two men were sitting on a large piece of driftwood, cooking fish and roasting a small piglet over a fire. A bottle of half-empty rum passed between them. It looked to be a delicious feast and

Ashton approached, led by his nose and drawn by the overpowering aroma. He knelt, sitting back on his feet with his knees in the sand.

"Excuse me," he said, but the words hardly escaped his parched throat.

The men continued to ignore his presence.

"Excuse me?" he repeated, louder and more forcefully.

The older of the two men was short, bald, and more robust than his companion with a wooden peg below his left knee. He remained silent, never lifting his head, concentrating on a small piece of wood he was diligently carving, slowly releasing the mermaid trapped inside it. The other man was tall and thin with moppy hair. His left eyelid was sewn shut on account of his missing eye.

The man with the peg leg looked up at Ashton and asked rather impatiently, "Can I 'elp ya, mate?"

"I'm not exactly sure where I am, but I've had nothing to eat since breakfast and saw that you were cooking some food. It smells delicious."

"Yeah. And?"

"Might I join you?"

The one-eyed man laughed.

"Who the fuck is this guy?" he asked his companion as they mocked the newcomer.

The bald man continued his studious carving as the two of them laughed at Ashton's expense long enough for him to get the point. Ashton let them be and walked farther down the beach towards a small wooden bridge that spanned a shallow stream fed by the waterfall running down the western rock face and culminating in small pools on the eastern side of the beach near the cave. It was the only dry crossing point connecting the beach to the town, the stream having split the coastline from its small, undulating dunes covered in marram grass.

"Probably best you avoid much talkin' to that bunch."

The islander he met on the boat, dwarfing him in stature, joined him on the bridge with the last box from the *Mami Wata* on his shoulder.

"Name's Christian," he said.

Ashton shook his hand, reflexively wincing in response to the man's bone crushing strength.

"Ashton," he replied shaking the pain out of his hand.

"Try to stay outta trouble…Ashton."

"Is this…is this Tortuga?"

Christian replied with a hearty laugh, "No, son. This here's New Nassau."

The islander strutted down the sandy path to its confluence with what seemed to Ashton to be the main thoroughfare bisecting the town, running down the middle of New Nassau from the bridge to the manor and the jungled mountains to the south. The wide lanes were a sand and shell composite, compact and dusty.

Ashton followed closely behind Christian seeing the disrepair of the buildings up close as he passed them. It was clear to him that they were built with the intention of longevity, not as a temporary hideaway. Still, other structures appeared more hastily constructed and now, partially collapsed. Ashton walked past a church with a tall spire standing alone at the convergence of two roads and glanced inside. The staircase leading to the choir loft was in such a state of dilapidation that the second floor was inaccessible. The nave was slovenly. The pews broken and shuffled out of place. The roof had partly caved in over the sanctuary. A giant crucifix hung unscathed high behind a marble altar split down the middle.

He saw an elderly couple sitting on the porch of their shanty house across the street from the church and underneath a large mossy oak. The window shutters were left open to let in the breeze and sunlight. The woman was knitting, while her husband engaged in a rousing game of checkers. The game was hotly contested and the gambling, as judged by the coins stacked on the end of the table, was high stakes.

New Nassau inspired grandeur in Ashton's mind.

"So, give me the macro version. Aside from *New Nassau*, where am I?" he asked Christian.

"Shipwreck Island. It's a haven, fer...less reputable men...men of the sea, one might say. Men who decided not to go in fer the machinations of traditional society."

"Shipwreck Island? Really?" Ashton mocked.

"Yeah. Why?"

"Nothing. It's just...that seems kinda lazy, doesn't it?"

"I don't get your meanin'?"

"Let me guess. A ship wrecked here at some point in the past?"

Christian ignored the quip. Ashton carried on getting acquainted with his new surroundings. Questions could wait. He had no idea where he was, but at this point, it didn't really matter. He was here and would remain so for a while, at least, he reasoned.

Making his way along the roughshod street, the buildings stood closer and closer together. Businesses and ventures began replacing residences. Taverns, brothels, a general store, all well frequented by the town's inhabitants. Gambling, whoring, and drinking abounded, often spilling out of the establishments and into the streets. The town crawled with unforeseen danger and ill repute enough to make take heed of his surroundings.

"This place has seen better days," Ashton said.

"This place has seen a lot of days."

Christian turned onto a smaller transverse path with Ashton still lagging a few strides behind his long gait.

"Get outta the way!" a voice yelled from behind as stamping hooves hauling a loaded cart brushed past Ashton, knocking him to the ground.

Christian sidestepped the horses and swung at the haphazard driver, missing him but splintering the back corner of the cart with the impact of his hand. From the ground, Ashton watched as the cart corrected itself and rolled along the uneven road kicking up a small cloud of dust behind it. Several oaken barrels darkened by their seeping contents were packed in the bed, jostling with every bump and pothole, as it rolled its way out of the town, past a skeleton of a building long forgotten and largely swallowed up by vegetation. Its destination, Ashton surmised, was the Spanish villa at the top of the hill just before the road curved and disappeared into the dense jungle. The honeyed smell from the cart wafted into Ashton's nose.

"No shortage of rum around here," he noted.

Ashton spun around to find himself alone. Not able to immediately locate Christian, he hurried to the intersection, looked left, and saw Christian just as he lowered his head and crossed the threshold of a two-story building filled with singing, hollering, and the occasional staggering patron pouring out into the street. Above the door frame hung a roughly cut wooden sign shaped like a sea turtle that read "Green Turtle Tavern."

SEVENTEEN

The sun had disappeared behind the peaks leaving behind it a diminishing ambient glow across the cove. Ashton followed Christian's footsteps through the doorway and into New Nassau's oldest tavern. There were several to be sure, but the Green Turtle Tavern was a bit more reputable if one could loosely apply the word. The floor-to-ceiling plantation shudders were swung open, inviting in the breeze. Inside, the air was malodorous. Several candle-lit lamps and torches were affixed to the bracing columns. From the center of the ceiling, a large, circular, iron chandelier hung, its tiers of candles lit and ready to vanquish the incoming darkness.

Ashton immediately took notice of Marco sitting at the bar slouched over a near empty glass. It was impossible to know how many times it had been refilled, but judging by Marco's disposition, it had been quite a few. Marco threw his head back, his hair matted and tousled, and emptied the remainder of the glass's contents. He missed the bar top and dropped the glass on the floor. He sunk in his stool and nearly fell over, but Christian, anticipating the impending accident, rushed to grab him. His muscular arm held Marco as he tilted off the edge of the seat and hoisted him back upright. Christian signaled to the bartender that Marco's night of drinking was done and leaned him forward to rest on the bar top. Two men sitting together nearby each threw down several coins and offered their best drunken lines to the bartender who entertained them if only for their continued patronage.

"Thank you, boys," she said, corralling the coins and turning her back.

They left the tavern with their arms around each other's shoulders, propping each other up and stumbling as they went. Marco, his head now resting on his folded arms, began crying hysterically. Ashton could not take his eyes off the bartender. She was strikingly beautiful. She wore a colorful dress tailored to reveal some skin and accentuate the tight curves of her body. Marco now grunted to himself. Ashton shifted his attention from the beauty behind the bar to the drunken beast in front of it.

"Marco?"

Marco looked up, his face sullen, eyes blood shot and red.

"Now that I've had some time to think about it, it's all starting to sink in," he said choking on his words. "My brother was all I had…." The words got trapped behind a trembling lip.

Christian sat at a table nearby, giving Marco his space, and held up a finger while keeping one eye on Marco's comportment. The bartender rounded the bar carrying a flagon full of ale. Ashton caught himself staring as she brought Christian his drink. She looked up and met his gaze, smiling at him as he awkwardly tried to divert his eyes. Christian chuckled his amusement.

Marco leaned over the bar and grabbed the rum and another glass. His balance was off. His stool shot out from under him, but he reactively grabbed Ashton and managed to keep himself from crashing to the floor. He stabled himself on buckling knees and refilled his glass, spilling most of it on the wooden countertop. He looked at Ashton daring him to intervene, then swallowed the drink in a gulp. He hiccupped, and his eyes rolled into the back of his head. The glass rolled on the bar top as he fell backwards in a drunken stupor. Ashton reached for him, but just missed. Christian took his time finishing his drink then stood and casually grabbed Marco by the waist of his shorts and flung him over his shoulder.

"Is he alive?" Ashton asked alarmingly.

"Yeah, he's alive. Just passed out drunk is all," Christian responded nonchalantly.

"Where are you taking him? He looks like he needs attention."

"Medical attention?" Christian scoffed with a bout of laughter. "All he needs his sleep."

Night had fallen when they exited the tavern and walked up the road to the large house on the hill. Marco, draped over Christian's shoulder, bounced limply with each step. When they arrived, the lights were on in only one room. Smoke billowed out of the chimney. Christian put Marco down on the porch, leaning him against one of the columns fronting the house, and strolled back into town as if he had just dropped off the neighbor's mail.

Ashton remained behind, concerned with Marco's current state and convinced that he had some level of alcohol poisoning. He tried to jostle him awake and get some sign of life from him, but Marco just slumped over and fell into the cool grass. He still had a pulse and was breathing. Ashton let out a sigh of relief. A heavy, brass knocker adorned the ornately carved, double front doors of the manor. Ashton knocked three times, the echo of which reverberated inside the empty halls and rooms of the house. He waited. A silhouette moved inside the lit room. Heavy footsteps approached. The door swung open spilling light outside.

"Well, look who it is!" Milt cheered with open arms. "I was beginning to wonder if you'd ever make it off my boat. Come on in. Hope you don't mind us leaving you on the deck of the *Mami Wata* after getting you all fixed up. Nothin' like dryin' in the open air naked as the day you were born."

Milt turned and strode back into the Grand Hall. Ashton shut the door behind him. It closed with a thud and knocked loose some dust clinging to the ceiling. The interior architecture was impressive. The fixtures gilded. The baseboards and crown molding were artfully crafted with no shortage of decorative details. The staircase in front of him was wide with brilliant purple carpet cascading down the steps.

"Marco…," Ashton said pointing over his shoulder.

"He'll be fine. Marco can hold his liquor better than most men twice his size, and after what happened to his brother, as far as I'm concerned, he's earned the right."

Through a pair of large, glass French doors was the Grand Hall, a cavernous room with vaulted ceilings, two chandeliers, and several large Renaissance paintings. A large, polished grand piano sat in the near corner. An exquisitely designed oriental rug lay spread across the whole of the room, on which sat a red three-seat canape near the window, and by the fireplace, two beautifully upholstered Louis XIII armchairs.

A crackling fire at the far end of the Grand Hall provided light from a marble fireplace large enough for a child to stand in comfortably. Four floor-to-ceiling windows, opened to take advantage of the cool night air, were evenly spaced apart and framed by identical grandiose drapery of the finest silk-velvet material from South Asia. Each dark sapphire cloth was embroidered with lines of periwinkle and silver damask woven patterns. The windows presented a panoramic view of New Nassau and, beyond the town, the sparkling green waters of Emerald Cove. The windows, Ashton saw as he stood peering through them, were covered in a fine layer of grime.

No wonder he has them open.

The air in the room smelled of tobacco and rum. A lone barrel, tapped, and with a lit cigar resting on its lid, was tucked away in the corner, probably delivered by the same cart that nearly ran Ashton over, he reckoned. Milt picked up the butt of the cigar and motioned with his hand to one of the Louis XIII armchairs.

"Have a seat."

Ashton sank in the plush, comfortable chair. He looked over his shoulder taking in the rest of what the room had to offer. Marble busts, a pair of encased flintlock pistols, and a suit of Spanish armor really tied the room together, providing it a particular level of luxury and sophistication. One piece that caught Ashton's eye was a lavishly built French clock, clearly handcrafted, and depicting a scene from a provincial Alpine town.

"Here," Milt said, offering Ashton a drink and taking a seat in the companion chair.

"None for me, thanks," said Ashton, holding a hand up.

"Wasn't a question, son."

Milt thrust the glass into Ashton's open palm that still hung in the air. The sweet, aromatic smell of the liquid sloshed in the crystalline glass. He placed the decanter on the three-legged, mother-of-pearl inlaid side table between the two armchairs.

"Carved this myself," Milt noted, rubbing the round tabletop. He took a sip, finishing half his glass.

"You did this? Is that cherry?"

"Indeed."

"Where'd you get the mother-of-pearl?"

"I acquired it."

"Well, however you got it, it's nice."

Ashton watched him drink the remainder of his glass in a single gulp, then, feeling pressured to do so as well, took a reluctant sip of his own. He coughed.

"Strong," he choked.

His eyes watered and his face turned red. Milt smiled. For the next hour, Ashton regaled Milt with the story he owed him. He spoke about Sister Anne, the Connellys, and Luke's ultimate sacrifice in Afghanistan. Milt conceded that he wasn't too familiar with current events, having spent most of his time on Shipwreck Island, Key West, and the waters in between, but was intrigued about Sister Anne.

"You never learned who your real parents were?"

"No. All I have to remember my birth mother by is that red rose."

A full moon had risen over the cove during the course of Ashton's tale. The muted light shone through the windows and illuminated those parts of the Grand Hall the fire didn't reach. Ashton heard a groan outside the windows and remembered Marco was still on the porch. He placed his glass on the mother-of-pearl tabletop and nearly leapt over the back of the chair. He dashed across the room and pulled open the front door. Marco was conscious and sitting up, holding his head in his hands.

Relieved that Marco was once again conscious, Ashton tried to coax him out of his stupor with mundane questions and anecdotes. Marco groaned as a string of saliva drooled from his mouth. He rubbed his head and winced in aching pain. Milt came up from behind with surprisingly featherlike footsteps, startling Ashton, and hoisted Marco gingerly to his feet. He wrapped his arm around Marco's ribs and walked him into the house. Marco's feet dragged the ground as he struggled to keep pace, so Milt picked him up and carried him up the stairs to one of the four bedrooms on the second floor.

EIGHTEEN

Marco lay asleep, snoring loudly on a large four-post bed. The rest of the furniture was shrouded in white linen, covered long ago when the preceding occupants fled the small island for distant worlds with expectations of returning to their finery. A window in the room had been left open, letting in the noise of the jungle that encroached inches closer to the manor with each passing day. Chirping crickets, croaking frogs, singing birds, and other unidentifiable sounds were sure to keep any other person awake, but Marco slept, and snored, a sound that was itself indistinguishable from those of the jungle.

Milt descended the staircase, its banister covered in a fine layer of dust, to find Ashton staring out a window towards the distant inlet. Milt returned to the corner barrel, letting its contents splash into his glass and onto the floor.

Ashton turned.

That explains the smell.

"The best rum in the Caribbean," Milt said without turning around.

He held his glass in front of his face, looking through the crystal glass and appreciating the ambrosial nectar.

"I keep a reserve here on the island separate from the swill the rest of those animals prefer. Like a dog to flesh they'd devour it without truly savoring its magic."

Milt drank, inhaling deeply through his nose as he savored the sweet notes of the drink.

"I've known them for many years," Milt said, pausing for another sip.

Ashton noted the slight change in his tone. A sense of regret in his voice. Milt poured another glass and topped off Ashton's who now had twice as much rum in his glass than before, and twice as much rum than he wanted. He forced a sip.

"So, this island is yours? Is that why you're the one occupying this house?" Ashton asked, beginning to press Milt gently for some answers to his many questions.

"This house belongs to me, but the island, New Nassau, that belongs to no one person. Each man and woman here does as they please. We have a code, Mr. Hood, and though we may not look it, we're every bit as civilized as the outside world. Make of that statement what you will."

Milt reclined on his canape. He took another mouthful of rum, swishing it in his mouth before swallowing. Ashton watched him. His eyes were glazing over. He was not his usual self, at least as far as Ashton knew him, and he seemed clearly distracted. The night's chilly darkness seeped into the Grand Hall. Ashton heard the faint whisper of a draft whistling through the wide halls and corridors, emanating from an unseen room somewhere in the east wing recesses of the sprawling villa. Ashton turned, half expecting to discover an apparition haunting the halls of the old mansion.

"I don't have much need for a house this size anymore," Milt said into his glass.

The flames of the fire, now roaring, reflected in his dark eyes.

"This house has a lot of potential if given the time and materials to fix it up," Ashton added.

Milt didn't respond but sat in silence for several long moments looking into his glass.

"The house. This town. I am their steward," he said jumping to his feet, his chest heaving. Anger carried on his voice, "and look at what they have become!"

Ashton realized that Milt's conversation was directed inward, a conflict within himself. Still, Ashton pressed him.

"Protecting them from what?"

"You may well see soon enough," he said with a snarl.

A passion burned behind his eyes and Ashton shifted in his seat. Milt finally looked up at Ashton.

"And that's why you're here," Milt told him with an unnerving smile.

"I don't know why I'm here and frankly I don't even know where *here* is! I just wanted a weekend vacation. Somewhere away from the burdens and stresses of my own life. I've been rehashing the day's events that led me here and I can't explain why I joined you. All I wanted was a place to relax and…."

"Relax? If you wanted to relax, lad, you wouldn't have gotten on my boat," Milt countered. "You were looking for adventure! I could see that in your eyes when you were standing on the beach like an abandoned dog. You needed to break the monotony of your wasted life. You craved something different, and I gave it to you. You'll be thanking me soon enough."

"I…maybe. But you've barely answered any of my questions. I still don't know who you are and why you brought me here."

Ashton's patience was reaching the end of its rope, and Milt knew he still needed him to play his part in this game. He was careful not to reveal his hand too soon.

"I'm whoever you need me to be. Want me to be Santa Claus? Spring-heeled Jack if you're into that darker sort? How about God, would my deification suffice?" he asked with a bellowing laugh Ashton hadn't heard since Key West. "Whoever I am, I fear I'm now failing you as a host, though even that role must come to an end. The sun has set, and I have some things to see to here. Head down to the beach and eat some of that prized conch we brought back. And try to do some of that relaxin'. As for why you're here, you're on vacation, remember?"

Feeling a bit frustrated at being played for a fool, Ashton saw himself out without another word. Deep shadows were already being cast across the valley as the full moon sat solemnly in the night sky, covering the island in a bluish hue. While Ashton was walking back down the hill along the short but winding dirt road into the town, he was passed by several of the island's rougher looking men heading in the opposite direction and moving with a sense of purpose. Curious, he turned to watch them stroll into the manor and close the door behind them. He headed back to the Green Turtle where Christian, still drinking, and yet, still surprisingly unencumbered by drunkenness, was engaged in a rowdy card game at a round table on the opposite side of the room.

"Bullshit! Let me see your cards, you cheatin' son of a bitch!"

Christian reached over the table and grabbed the man, nearly comparable in stature, by the collar and yanked him close. The man grabbed hold of Christian's wrist and drew himself closer.

"You wanna dance?"

"I don't feel like giving lessons today," Christian said through grit teeth.

Paul Lime, an unsavory character with sensitive pride and a reputation for being easily disposed to violence, locked eyes with Christian and grinned as they both continued sizing up the other. One of the two remaining cardplayers at the table leapt up and ran out of the tavern.

"Easy boys, not in my bar," the beautiful woman behind the bar commanded, clearly not her first experience with this kind of altercation. "I don't feel like cleaning up your mess tonight."

"Just a friendly disagreement 's'all," Lime said. "Ain't that right?" he asked turning his eyes back to Christian.

Christian had a provoking smile on his face, then looked at his bulging arm grasping Paul Lime's collar. "This disagreement seems one-sided from my angle."

The bartender rolled her eyes and then shifted her gaze to the scrawny man frozen in his chair at the table, a puddle growing at his feet. She let out a sigh, like a mother unable to wrangle her unruly children.

"There are other, less reputable establishments on this beach that you can grace with your presence, Paul." Then, turning to Christian, "Christian…," she said, and it was all she needed to say.

Christian loosened his grip and Paul Lime straightened himself, smiling while his eyes shot daggers, and left the bar. The scrawny man was red as a beetroot, the crotch of his pants stained wet. Embarrassed, he apologized repeatedly as he shuffled out the door and continued to do so until he was clear out of ear shot.

The night air circulated through the tavern. The fronds on the palm trees outside the plantation windows swayed, creating a gentle ambiance irrespective of the turbulence inside.

"Sorry about that," the woman said, noticing Ashton still standing near the doorway.

Hungry, he was on his way to the beach, acknowledging that despite all else Milt's idea to cook up some conch held water, but he stopped when he heard the commotion inside the tavern. She smiled and waved him over to the counter. Her silky brunette hair was tied up messily in a windswept updo, revealing her slender, olive-colored neck.

"Have a seat. I'm Jiya," she said.

Her voice was soft and subtly accented with undertones of some exotic dialect. It rang like a song in his ears.

"Jiya." Ashton repeated. "That's a beautiful name."

"Thanks," she responded, it was my great grandmother's. "I haven't seen you around before. Did Milt bring you here?"

Ashton found himself looking at her a little too long. *Blink!* He was unashamedly drawn to her smile and the smokey aura of her soft, almost translucent, green eyes. She was beautiful, and he was smitten.

"Hey. You still in there?" she said playfully.

"Sorry. What was the question?"

She smiled. "You're here because of Milt, right?"

"Yeah. We met in Key West. To be honest, the whole circumstance was a little strange how it all took place."

"What do you mean?"

"I'm not sure."

"Hmm."

"And what does that mean?" he teased.

"What does what mean?"

"'Hmm.'"

He sensed some reservation in her voice when he affirmed that Milt had indeed brought him to Shipwreck Island. He didn't raise it outright to her.

"So, you know Milt?" he asked, happy to have conversation with her.

It was an easy enough question, he thought, to break the ice.

"I do," she answered. "I've known him for some time."

Ashton waited, thinking there was more to her answer, and there was, but she didn't say any more about it. Jiya took note of his nerves and reached below the bar. Her hands moved quickly, expertly filling two glasses with a bronze-colored liquid. She pushed one of the glasses in front of him and threw hers back in a single motion before Ashton had a chance to even reach for his.

Is there anything else to do here besides drink?

"This all you got?" Ashton asked, his stomach turning at the thought of drinking again.

"Rum is the drink of choice on this island, and the worse it tastes the more plentiful it is, but the good stuff typically finds its way up to the manor. Nobody fusses about it. Rum is rum to these poor bastards. In here, you get what you get, which still isn't all that bad, especially once you've had a few."

"I suppose being in the Caribbean, I might as well drink the drink of the islands."

He hurried it down to get it over with. It burned like he was drinking lighter fluid, though he took new appreciation in the variety Milt offered, noting the wide disparity in quality.

"This is awful."

Jiya laughed.

"Where does it come from?"

"Right here on the island. It used to be better, but when the sugarcane fields stopped being harvested, we had to start making our own with what was left."

"How long have you been here?"

"Too long."

"Looking at the condition of the town...."

"New Nassau," she informed.

"Right. New Nassau. Looking at the condition of New Nassau, it seems this place is rather transient."

"Quite the opposite, actually."

"How so?"

She leaned over the bar. The smell of coconut radiated from her.

"It's going to sound a bit crazy," she said.

"Try me," Ashton prodded as he leaned inward.

Their faces were near each other. Ashton could feel the chemistry and his excitement grew.

"Well, let's just say that I came here about three years ago."

"That's not bad. You made it sound like you've been here a lot longer."

"But really, it's been over three hundred years."

Ashton's eyes widened.

"I told you it was crazy."

"A little bit, yeah."

"It's the truth."

"So that makes you, what? Three hundred forty years old? Give or take?" Ashton joked.

"Twenty-four," she corrected him.

"So, what? You've been twenty-four for three hundred years?"

Jiya answered him with a look. Ashton showed his displeasure of being made a fool twice in one night. Jiya noticed.

"I'm sorry. I know it must sound ridiculous, but it's not. I promise."

There was sincerity in her eyes. Still, Ashton maintained his skepticism.

"What's in this rum?"

"If I was in your shoes, I'd feel the same way. Trust me."

"So you've been alive for three hundred forty-four years?"

"There's evil here," she warned.

"What kind of evil?"

Jiya didn't answer. She removed their glasses and wiped down the bar.

"I'm sorry," Ashton said following her down the bar. "It's just…that's not something you hear every day…or ever, for that matter."

"It's ok. I'm sorry," she started, realizing the position in which she put Ashton. "You're the first outsider to arrive here in over three centuries."

She laughed, hearing the absurdity after saying it aloud. "It does sound ridiculous." Ashton laughed with her.

"There are many stories that are meant to be told, that should be told, but never make it to the ears of anyone who will listen," she said.

"Like what?"

"It doesn't matter."

"Sure it does."

She smiled at his persistence. "You're sweet."

Ashton responded with a smile of his own.

"There's much you don't know and it's better that you don't. Another drink?"

"No, thank you. I've had more to drink today than I think I've had all year."

Jiya poured herself a shot of rum.

"So, can you tell me your story? How did you arrive here?" he asked her, taking a seat on a barstool.

She drank her shot, walked around the bar, and sat next to him.

"That's a long story."

"I've got nowhere to be, and I'd love to hear it."

"No, you wouldn't."

"Why would you think that?"

"Because as I said, it's a long story, and not a happy one."

"You just said how no one wants to listen, and here I am, genuinely interested," he rebutted. "But if you don't want to tell me, that's ok, too."

After a thoughtful pause, Jiya gave voice to her story long kept silent.

"My family and I were sailing back home when we were attacked. Several ships pursued us, and when they caught us, they boarded our ships and slaughtered everyone."

"Wow, I'm sorry to hear that," Ashton said.

"When their captain found out who I was, he spared my life."

"Who were you?

She hesitated.

"I was someone of importance once in a land far from here," she continued.

"Like a princess?" he asked with more surprise than he intended.

"Not anymore. It's difficult to be a princess when you have no kingdom."

"What about this place? What about New Nassau and Shipwreck Island?"

"Does this look like a kingdom to you?"

Ashton wasn't sure how to answer.

"Where's your home? Can't you go back?" he said getting back to the topic.

"This is my home."

At that moment, Christian said goodnight to Jiya, kissing her on the cheek. He carried a bag full of coins and a smile on his face.

"Time to go, boys!" Jiya announced to all the others still in the tavern. "I know you don't have any more money so there's no more business for you here tonight."

The remaining old, crusty patrons groaned and slowly stumbled their way out of the tavern and immediately collapsed into the weeds alongside the road. The snoring started immediately. The sounds were synchronized and grew louder with each breath.

"Well, since it looks like my business is finished here, I'll start closing up," Jiya said to Ashton. "It looks like a beautiful night out. Why don't you head down to the beach and I'll meet you down there when I'm done. I can smell the food from here. We can continue our conversation, too, if you'd like."

"Sure, yeah, I'll see you down there," he said with excitement rising in his voice. "Do you need help cleaning up or anything?"

"I'm good, but thank you," she said with a smile and began directing two of the beer wenches under her employ.

Ashton walked out of the tavern with his head high and strolled down to the beach dotted with campfires and buzzing with the sounds of drinking and singing. A large piece of driftwood rested on the shore, its limbs scratching the air, grasping for nothing. Two smashed cargo boxes lay partially buried next to it. Stars were beginning to appear in the indigo sky. A beautiful view under the moon's glow, framed by majestic cliffs that drew sharply down, escorted by several teethy rocks jutting from the water leading to soft, sandy banks angling the inlet out to sea.

NINETEEN

The white sand beneath Ashton's feet was soft and cool. His stomach was full, having eaten his fill of his earlier catch. The sound of the waves gently lapping the shore was magnified in the relative quiet as the groups slowly dispersed. He walked down to the edge of the water until his feet were in the tranquil surf, sinking into the foreshore. Farther east down the beach, a couple of men still lingered, delaying the night. He noticed beyond them the cave he saw earlier in the day, so dark it contrasted with the night, an unnaturally occurring blackness. He glanced back towards the town, the tavern still in eyeshot. Its lights were on, so figuring Jiya was still cleaning up, Ashton decided to take a few minutes and satiate his curiosity.

As he passed the beach's remaining imbibers and made his way toward the cave, he saw that the void was partially obscured with straggling vines and dying vegetation hanging down the rock face in front of the gaping hole. He pushed them aside and peered into the dark. He saw an orange glow flickering off the walls in the deep of the cave, and just as quickly as he saw it, it was extinguished. He felt the breath getting sucked out of him as the suffocating darkness returned. Ashton's heart pounded. He felt an intrinsic pull to enter, but fear gripped him and he backed away from the cave's mouth.

"Don' think I'd be goin' in dere if I was you," a strange voice warned followed by a prolonged cackle.

Ashton spun and saw a spindly old man standing in the sand. He was bald with milky blue eyes owing to his blindness. He had few teeth and a slightly exaggerated curve in his spine.

Startled, Ashton backed away. His heel caught a small plank of wood protruding from the sand, and he fell. When he looked again, the old man was gone.

Ashton, frightened, walked briskly back towards the driftwood resting just a few feet from the surf as the tide started to come in. He sat and stared at the water, a source of calm for him, and gathered his emotions. The moonbeams flickered off the waves in a chorus of light. He sat, waiting for Jiya to arrive. The cool, salt-tinged ocean breeze soothed his nerves as much as his skin.

"There you are," Jiya said as she approached from behind, startling him for a second time.

"Oh, am I glad to see your face," he said.

He stepped over the driftwood and went to meet her. He pointed in the direction of the cave, but his words failed him.

"The uh...uh...uh...," he sputtered.

Jiya followed his finger and saw where he was pointing.

"It's just a cave," she said quickly. "Come, sit."

She grabbed his arm and sat with him on the log. She kept her arm interlocked with his.

"It's really beautiful here," Ashton said. "But...."

Jiya looked at him, waiting for him to continue.

"But that cave, there's something about it. And there was this old man standing near it. A ghost I think."

"It's just a cave. Nothing more. Just a dark, damp hole," she said trying to assuage his concerns. "And if you think this cove is beautiful, you should see the rest of the island."

"I don't know. This is going to be pretty tough to beat if you ask me."

"In the Green Turtle, you asked me where I was from. I mean, before New Nassau," she continued.

He was glad she was feeling comfortable enough with him to speak more on the issue and he didn't want to mess that up or hinder her. He sat silent, looking at her.

"Originally, my family was from the western India, from a coastal city on the Arabian Sea. My memory of it has faded over time," she said while gazing into the distance. She slipped off her sandals and dug her toes into the sand. "But I remember it's distinct beauty."

She continued on about her home, describing its beauty and her upbringing.

"And how did you come to know Milt?" Ashton eventually asked.

She looked at him, locking eyes with his for just a moment, then turned her gaze back towards the sea as tears began to well. She turned back to Ashton and smiled back the tears that never fully materialized.

"That's a bit complicated," she said.

She grew silent, retreating to the memories she had long since buried.

"And you? Where are you from?"

"Virginia."

"And how did Milt find you?"

"I sort of ran into him on a beach in Key West. I was on vacation, but, well, somehow here I am. Not quite what I was expecting…wait, what do you mean, 'find'?" he asked. "Was he looking for me?"

Jiya smiled, realizing her slip.

"He doesn't usually bring people here," she said.

"But he brought me here for a reason? He alluded to that earlier."

"I'm not sure."

"Carlos is dead and Marco's drifting into deep depression. Whatever reason he had I hope it was worth it."

"No one really knows his intentions. He keeps to himself here, mostly."

"But I'm glad he brought you. It's nice to meet someone handsome and normal for a change," she said with a blushing smile.

"Same here. I mean, you're beautiful. I mean, I…," Ashton stuttered.

"It's ok," she said interrupting his babbling and putting her hand on top of his.

Her hand lingered. He froze. She smiled.

"So, are there, um, others like you here? I mean, royalty types?" Ashton asked.

"Oh, no. There are no types or titles here."

"I'll be honest, I still don't know where here is. Or who Milt or anyone else is on this island. These people, the buildings, the aura, there's something strange about it all."

Jiya gave him a look.

"These people," she started, "they're pirates, mostly Milt's crew, but soon others began finding their way here, too. Prostitutes, wayward sailors, freed men, he recruited them all before time stopped and the island became shuttered to the outside world."

"Pirates, you mean?"

"Not so much anymore, but at one time…."

"And Milt?"

"He was their captain."

Ashton sat pondering on the revelation that he then realized explained so much.

"Can you leave like he can?"

"No. Milt is the only one who can, and he comes and goes as he pleases."

"So, you're a prisoner here?"

"In more ways than you think. Which is why it's nice to meet someone new. Despite everything, I've managed to make myself a pretty good life here. I don't want for anything and I'm on a tropical island. How bad could it really be?"

Ashton sympathized with her for the anguish she kept hidden.

"I couldn't imagine being trapped in one place for as long as you have."

"Maybe someday I'll be able to see the world again. Perhaps you can show me."

Ashton's smile was wide.

"Of course! And I'd love to see your home."

His naivete was cute, she thought.

"This really is a beautiful island."

"You have no idea," Jiya said with unrestrained youthfulness.

The excitement on her face, and her childlike wonder, really brought her to life. She often spent her days alone in the inland parts of the island where clear springs, underground caves, waterfalls, and thick jungles defined the landscape.

With the tide rising, they moved off the log a few feet and laid on their backs with their heads in the sand, staring up at the sky. For the next hour, they talked.

"Come on, let's go, I want to show you something." Jiya said injecting a bit of excitement into the night.

She waved for Ashton to follow her as she trotted through the sand, over the footbridge, and up the sandy road leading through the town. The moon was full and illuminated their path. Ashton was right behind her, though becoming increasingly winded as they trotted quietly past the manor on the hill and into the forested foothills.

They entered the jungle and continued along the narrowing path until it was only wide enough for two people to walk abreast, running past tamarinds and kapok trees. Ashton pushed through the pain growing in his side. His legs were getting heavy. The distance between him and Jiya grew as she effortlessly sprinted forward as if running on a cloud.

The dirt path that entered the jungle well-worn and clearly distinct became increasingly overgrown as it wound its way through the trees, meandering past moss-covered stones and over snaking roots and trickling streams from unseen sources. The ambient light that washed over the cove was soon beaten back by the fierce resistance from the canopy above. A few beams managed to sneak their way through the tree cover, giving Ashton a slight glimpse of the environment encircling him. The piercing hum of the jungle filled his ears. Jiya was now several paces ahead as Ashton lumbered along, pushing himself to keep up. His legs ached. His lungs burned.

"Where...are we...going?" he managed to yell through desperate gasps of air.

They had been running for near half a mile on coarse, hardpacked sand when they began a sloping ascent up a large hill, the route twisting and turning around boulders and tall Ceibas. As he trudged onwards, he could no longer see Jiya nor hear her voice, his pulse beating hard in his ears. Nevertheless, he pressed on, willing his legs to turnover as the fear of becoming lost crept into his psyche, and worse, any opportunity he may have with Jiya on this perfect night. He dug deep and found the fortitude to ignore the pain and push onward. The jungle seemed to be growing thicker and the noises emanating forthwith were becoming much more perceptible in the growing silence.

"Jiya?" he yelled through abated breath.

A muffled roaring coupled with a slight salinity that accompanies any freshwater mist commandeered Ashton's senses. While he looked around him, distracted and frantically searching for the young beauty, he had failed to mind what lay before him. He came to a skidding halt, loosening the dirt beneath his feet that carried him to the edge of a thirty-foot cliff. Below him, at the base of a tall waterfall that poured over the side of a smoothened rockface, was a turquoise pool encircled by large boulders and lush vegetation. The pool twinkled in the moonlight that poured in through a wide opening in the forest canopy revealing a clear night sky, a calming site juxtaposed to the foreboding jungle.

The moon and stars shown down their light illuminating the pool and everything around it. Jiya was treading water in the center. Her hair was slicked back and clinging to the nape of her neck. Her slender, feminine frame was barely visible beneath the surface. Her clothes were neatly folded on a flat rock that sat on the edge of the cliff to Ashton's right, guarding a steep slope with protruding roots and natural steps leading down to an earthen embankment on the water's edge.

Ashton's heart entered his throat. Whether it was because of the cliff's height or because a beautiful, naked woman was waiting for him below made no matter. The discomfort was twofold, but one clearly outweighed the other. He stepped out of his clothes and placed them haphazardly in a bundle next to Jiya's. His hands instinctively covered himself as the night air chilled his skin.

"Jump! C'mon, don't be such a baby!" she pressured.

Ashton took a breath and stretched his arms out wide, exposing himself to her in all his glory. As he calculated the distance and trajectory needed to avoid the hidden boulders that surrounded her in the shallows, Ashton kept his eyes on Jiya gracefully treading water with an approving look on her face. He took a few steps back, closed his eyes, and with a few running strides, leapt away from the cliff, eyes clinched shut and hoping he was far enough out to land safely in the dark spot of the pool. His arms flailed wildly as he continued to fall. The sudden cold almost forced his lungs to inhale. He opened his eyes wide and swam frantically to the surface where the welcomed air raced back into his lungs. He brushed his hair back and wiped the water from his eyes. Her body looked as if it had been sculpted by Bernini himself.

"What a rush, huh?" she said swimming over to him, the water shimmering off her skin.

"I can't believe I just did that!"

"Welcome to Caiman Falls, my most favorite place on this island. Up there, behind the falls," she said pointing, "is Vida Spring. It feeds the river under the mountain."

She swam up to him, wrapping her arms around his neck until her body pressed against his. Her slightly pruning hands grabbed his face, and she kissed him gently on his lips. He kissed her back. She smiled at him, biting her lower lip, and then playfully retreated towards the waterfall. Just before Ashton caught up with her, she disappeared behind the roaring wall of water. He followed her in and found himself inside a seemingly endless tunnel. A river cut through its rocky foundations, the faint light from the flowing water reflecting on the walls as it cut its way underground. Jiya climbed on top of a rock ledge and stood naked, water beading off her velvety skin, her slender body toned and well proportioned. Ashton held onto the rock with eyes wide and mouth agape at her glistening form.

"No one ever comes to this place but me," she said hands on her hips. "Well, and the alligators."

"Alligators?"

Ashton pulled his legs from the water and scurried onto the smooth stone surface, polished over countless millennia. His mouth was dry as cotton. It was one thing to be naked on a cliff and then hidden underneath water, but now he couldn't hide from her, for better or worse.

"Yes, but don't worry, there's only two of them that I know of, and they were on the other side of the island a couple of days ago. They wouldn't have gotten here so quickly."

"Still. How can you be sure?"

"Because I know this jungle like the back of my hand."

"Fair enough," Ashton said. "I trust you."

"You should."

Jiya turned to face him. Her eyes darted down and back up again. She blushed.

"Like what you see?" Ashton said with a self-deprecating smile.

"Not bad," she replied.

She took his hand.

"This is the Río Alma."

They walked cautiously on the slippery surface farther back into the wide tunnel.

"This is my sanctuary. My favorite place to come when I need to be alone," Jiya said. Traces of light still reflected off the walls, but visibility was waning as they continued walking. "I remember one afternoon shortly after I arrived, when I ran off into the jungle and found this place." Jiya paused in reflection. "My life had been torn from me. That cliff," she said motioning back to the one they had leapt from, "snuck up on me and I fell over the ledge down into that pool. I swam into this cave and found the river, but have never bothered to explore it further, and I don't know where it leads."

Returning, they walked back through the waterfall, and dove again into the pool. They swam towards the bank, and Jiya led them up the earthen staircase back to the top of the cliff. She threw Ashton his clothes, taking one more subtle but approving glance at him as he stood as God made him. Ashton averted his eyes, respecting her decency, as a man should. He stood behind a young bay rum tree as she got dressed.

When they were both fully clothed again, she walked over to him to let him know she was ready. Her hair hung wet behind her head. They walked back to New Nassau, taking their time and enjoying each other's company. The conversation was great, and he was growing more comfortable with her, and she with him. They laughed and joked as they shared personal stories from their own lives. The time passed quickly and before they both knew it, they were back on the edge of town and walking towards the Green Turtle.

Ashton and Jiya pushed through a throng of drunkards congregating in the road and belting out a song. Jiya unlocked the door and when they entered the tavern, Ashton danced with her.

"This is a terrible song," he joked.

"Shhh," she said as she rested her head on his shoulder. A smiled plastered on her face, she allowed him to lead, much to his delight.

She caught herself experiencing a feeling she had only felt once before. Before her life was ripped away from her. Ashton held her in his arms in a moment of unanticipated intimacy. Seizing the moment, he kissed her.

"Do you have a place to sleep tonight?" she asked him.

The thought never crossed his mind as the realization of his homelessness suddenly hit him. "No, actually. I don't."

"I live above the tavern. If you want, you can stay with me tonight," she offered.

"I'd like that."

Jiya took his hand and led him upstairs, and they soon found themselves embracing each other's trembling bodies, and for the first time since before she could remember, Jiya felt truly wanted.

TWENTY

Ashton awoke well before dawn to a chorus of croaking frogs. He sat on the edge of the bed and stared out of the second-floor window at the old town fast asleep around him, painted in silver light, and paying extra care not to wake Jiya lying peacefully beside him. She was on her back draped from the waist down in a sheer, transparent sheet, which served little purpose in the tropical climate. A look of contentment was on her face, one that had not been there for many years. Her long hair was fanned out on the bed linen. Ashton admired the radiance of her body visible beneath the fine fabric. Her breasts were exposed and her caramel skin aglow. Her long legs intertwined with the sheet that clung to the curves of her hips. He took his time getting dressed and walked downstairs.

The entire second floor of the edifice was once used for deeds of ill repute before it became the Green Turtle Tavern. Originally a brothel, the tavern became Jiya's driving force and she was determined to turn it into a respectful establishment despite its reputation and state of disrepair. It was a beautiful building, constructed opposite the harbor master's shack just off the wide swath of sand that led to the water. It was one of the first buildings built in the cove when it was first settled by Milt and his crew, and it served as the first establishment pirates would encounter upon mooring their ships.

The first buildings they constructed – the brothel and tavern, a change house, harbor master, residences, and warehouse – were built with the finest wood on the eastern side of the island and stones brought down from the western mountains. Milt's villa was constructed with the finest materials and fabrics purchased from Africa and the Near East and adorned with items captured from the Grand Mughal's treasure fleet, attacked near the entrance to the Red Sea in the late seventeenth century. The house's magnificence towered over the town below it in both size and splendor.

In some ways, Jiya saw the tavern as a representation of herself. For years after her arrival, Jiya was forced to endure a residence with Milt in the villa on the hill. Thoroughly desiring her independence and emancipation from Milt and the island, she marched into the tavern one rainy afternoon and put an end to the depravity practiced by the habitually drunken pirates. Milt happened to be in attendance that day and witnessed the authority with which she spoke. When she finished her demands the men in the tavern laughed. She patiently waited with arms folded until they finished and defiantly told the barkeep, an old, foul-smelling man, that the bar was now in her charge. The tavern again erupted into laughter. Milt walked over to her and stood beside her.

"You heard her, get out, and don't bother finishin' your drinks," he barked at the miscreants.

Despite her initial impulse to bristle at Milt's gesture, it served her ends. As a princess, she held firm to the air of grace she exuded as granddaughter to the Grand Moghul, while obfuscating the hypocrisy she was loathe to accept for the moment. The laughing ceased. Milt swelled his chest and stepped toward the men who, in unison, hurriedly fled the tavern.

"It's all your's now, sweetheart," he said and proceeded to help her clean up the place, her place.

"I can take care of this on my own," she said to him.

His dark eyes looked sharply down at her. She could see the years of pain and burdens beginning to weigh on his countenance. He nodded and put the handful of mugs he was holding on the table nearest to him and departed. The tavern was now hers and the one thing in her life she could control.

All that night, she toiled, cleaning and organizing, decorating the tavern to her liking. She transformed the entirety of the second floor into her personal living quarters. It was a far cry from the luxury she was used to, but it gave her privacy, and that was all she could hope for given her circumstances.

Ashton walked down the wooden stairs and through the main tavern hall. The outside air was still and humid. He saw up the hill that smoke still wafted from the chimney. Curious, he strolled up the path to see if Milt might still be awake. The lights in Jiya's loft were still darkened. She was still asleep, and he'd be back before she woke. The sun would be up in a couple of hours, he reminded himself.

The heavy front door to the villa was again unlocked, so he took the liberty of letting himself in. It was eerily quiet save for the metronomic ticking from the French clock in the Grand Hall. Embers in the fireplace glowed. There was a small flame that had yet to die. It licked the air. Dying whiffs of smoke rose into the chimney. Milt was slumped over in one of the throne chairs snoring loudly. His right arm hanging limply just above the carpet where a cup lay on its side. His crystal decanter sat empty beside him.

Ashton picked up the goblet and set it on the small side table next to his chair. A cashmere blanket was wadded up in the corner next to the fireplace. He grabbed it, shook it out, and draped it over Milt. A noise, coming from the room opposite the Grand Hall, startled him. He crept cautiously into the dining hall where a long table sat with a dozen ornately carved chairs with richly colored cushion seats placed around it. Dusty dinnerware covered in cobwebs dotted the table and floor. Tapestries like those in the Grand Hall hung about the tall windows, which were adorned with more oil paintings of various unknown personages and landscapes. A second, smaller fireplace occupied the center of the western wall.

Ashton continued his exploration of the abandoned rooms and halls. Tucked away in the southeast corner of the house were two large doors. He pulled them open. The rusty hinges creaked. He entered another smaller hallway and found that vines and other local flora had broken through the cracked walls and shattered windows. A draft swirled and whistled through the dilapidated corridor.

He tried another door on his right. It was locked and so he continued straight ahead to the next set of doors, identical to the previous pair on the opposite end of the corridor and pushed them open. The room was adorned with several jeweled and hand-crafted artifacts from around the world. Along with bookshelves full of old books, there were various maps of foreign lands and nautical charts. At one end of the room, in front of a large bay window, was a mahogany desk, on which rested several pieces of parchment and a large leather-bound journal stuffed with loose pages filled with scribbles and note takings. A wine red justaucorps with gold trimmings was draped over the back of the tall, plain desk chair. Cobwebs and a thick layer of dust covered most surfaces in the room.

Ashton explored the room, randomly thumbing through books and stacks of paper before stumbling upon the journal. As he opened it, a loose sheet of paper, dated 4 May 1705, fell from its binding. The writing was mostly faded and difficult to read. He looked through the journal, filled with records and ledgers and other seemingly random business-related materials. He turned his attention to the lone piece that fell onto the table. It was a personal note that appeared to be hastily written, but only a few fragmented sentences remained legible.

"...was disemboweled by cannon shot.... ...getting older; my wealth having exceeded my wildest dreams.... ...I fear I may never see you again...."

"What the hell?" he said under his breath as more questions formed in his mind.

He replaced the fallen page and returned the way he came, stopping in the dilapidated corridor to look out one of the windows peering towards the east. A faint hint of light began to spread across the horizon. Realizing he had spent more time in the villa than he intended, he hurried back through the dining hall, glancing into the Grand Hall on his way past the staircase and out the front door. Milt was gone. He hurried back to the tavern and walked up the stairs where Jiya was still sleeping. He wondered if perhaps she was dreaming about him the way he had about her just before he awoke. It didn't matter. He took off his clothes and laid back in the bed beside her draping his arm around her waist. He drifted off to sleep and back into his dreams where she awaited him.

TWENTY-ONE

When he awoke again a few hours later, the sun, already beaming, hung low in the sky with the temperature near scorching. The town was bustling. He squinted in the early morning rays shining through the window and wiped away the sleep. He spun around and sat on the edge of the bed.

"Jiya?" he called.

This time it was she who had risen early. He dressed, tiring of his original clothes, still dry and stiff with salt, and walked downstairs hoping to find his exotic beauty, but she was not in the tavern. The events from the night before circled in his mind. The atmosphere in town was lively and raucous. A makeshift market turned the main road into a bustling congestion of people, tents, and carts. The brothel madame stood outside showcasing her finery and tempting the island's occupants to spend their coins for a moment's pleasure.

Ashton walked through the crowds back to the beach. The long, crooked palm trunks gave the cove a calming vibe. Gulls circled overhead. A smile of contentment stretched across his face. This, an island paradise, was everything he wanted. He did a quick scan for Jiya, but she was nowhere to be seen. He sat down again on the large piece of driftwood half buried in the sand, shaded by a palm, passing the time in the morning sun with not a worry in the world and reflecting on last night.

While lost in peaceful thought, a harsh whisper beckoned him. He looked around but saw no one. It was clearly a voice he was hearing, but there were no discernable words. He looked towards the cave and when he turned back around, an old man suddenly appeared next to him on the driftwood. He stared straight ahead with milky eyes and a toothless smile.

"Don' recommend goin' in dere," he said with a laugh. His words lighter than air. "Dass jus' ol' Pierre's advice."

"You again?"

"Pierre St. Croix's me name."

"Nice to mee-," Ashton stopped suddenly.

Ashton heard the whisper again and fell into a trance-like state. The old man had disappeared. When he heard the whisper a third time, he looked to his right and stood involuntarily. The cave seemed to rush towards him; he felt a severe sense of vertigo, and yet he was drawn to it. He lurched clumsily toward the blackness as the whisper became incessant and grew in intensity.

"ASHTON! STOP!" Jiya yelled from behind as she sprinted down the beach towards him.

All activity on and near the beach came to a screeching halt. Standing into the void, Ashton was transfixed by the same orange glow he had seen dancing on the smoothened stone walls in the deep recesses of the cave. He heard Jiya's plea, which nearly pulled him from his hypnosis, but the allure of the flame and the call of the whisper was overwhelming. Ashton reached out his hands trying to grasp the distant glow as the outside light was quickly swallowed up by the dark. He entered. He walked slowly, shuffling his feet along the sandy ground. The intensity of the firelight grew with each step, but he could not yet see a source for the flame. Jiya slid to a halt at the edge of the cave just as Ashton entered it. He was beyond her reach. Tears filled her eyes. She never understood the evil that lay dormant inside the cave, only that it existed and that it was terrible.

"ASHTON! COME BACK!" she yelled, but her words were unable to penetrate the thick, rotting air. The wheels were in motion.

She strained her eyes as she peered in, fearing the worst for Ashton and the horror that awaited him, anxious for his return. Milt arrived and stood several paces behind Jiya with a scowl, deadly serious and eagerly anticipating the inevitable. His arms were crossed about his chest. His eyes were dead black, like those of a Great White, soulless and menacing as it prepared to devour its prey. Ashton had been dutiful, whether he knew it or not. Destiny, to Milt's great pleasure, had finally reared itself.

"So it begins," he said under his breath as the corner of his mouth turned up in a brief yet restrained smirk.

Ashton made his way through the cave, walking slowly as he felt his way into the darkness, allowing the wall to guide him as his fingers glided along the cold, wet rock. The ground had become more hard-packed, a combination of broken shells and sand, as he descended the slight slope farther underground.

An expansive cavern culminated at the end of the tunnel. The air was thick and damp. A hole in the rock overhead let in a whisper of light enough to illuminate the chamber, revealing a crevice in the rock face before him. As his vision adapted, Ashton walked quickly towards it. His foot stubbed against a stone sending his body reeling onto the hard-packed ground. The trance-like force that gripped him had vanished. He stood, dazed, and looked around the cavern taking in his surroundings for the first time. He identified a cleft in the rock leading his path deeper into the cave. His heart rate quickened, and his body stiffened as fear took hold. He was standing in near darkness without a clue how he got there. He managed to stand himself upright, and dispensing his urge to flee, he continued onward. No longer able to see the beach, he gave way to a growing curiosity and eagerness to discover what lie ahead.

Contorting his body, Ashton side-stepped through the increasingly narrow cleft hewn through the stone wall. By the end he was sliding on his knees until he pulled himself through the other side and stood in another cavern, the air increasingly colder, his breath visible. When he emerged on the other side, he found a smoldering pile of wood and ash. He put his hand over the kindling. Still warm.

A crumbling ledge rose to his left. Ashton climbed up the slope to where several large stones had collapsed, blocking passage to whatever lie out of reach on the other side. Dejected and about to give into his loss of fortune, he saw in his periphery a whitened object contrasting mightily with the darkness surrounding it. He walked closer and saw a familiar shape, albeit one he had never seen before with his own eyes. He gasped and stepped back before collecting himself and regaining his composure.

"C'mon, Ashton," he castigated himself. "Just a skeleton. Get ahold of yourself."

There was still flesh on the bones. The jaw was slack. The eye sockets were empty and black. It was still clothed in vibrantly colored woolen and silk garments and a large feathered, tri-cornered hat. Its right arm wrapped tightly around a wooden chest. Ashton peeked inside to find it was filled with gold coins. A small blade, rusted and spotted with dried blood, protruded from its rib cage. Around its neck, affixed to a thin leather cord, hung an amulet. Ashton removed it and held it in his hand, marveling at its intricate beauty and the strange script drawn around the circumference of the artifact.

Suddenly, out of the shadows in a recess opposite Ashton, something began to stir. Smoke swirled around the corpse in front of him, gradually morphing it into a suggestible human form. The ashen pile roared back to life as the flames clawed the air. Ashton threw his hand in front of his face to shield the heat and took several steps backwards. The heat grew unbearable. Pocketing the amulet, Ashton hurried back through the split in the rock and scurried to the other side, not yet caring to contemplate what he just witnessed.

When he believed himself to be in relative safety, if just for a moment as he ran unashamedly away from the apparition, he risked a look behind him and saw a figure moving quickly towards him. It continued to grow in form. Something had awoken it, Ashton thought. He couldn't make out a body, much less a face, but as it materialized, terror gripped Ashton as the ghostly abomination pursued him back to the entrance to the beach. Ashton ran for his life, summoning his legs to remember his high school track days, but those days were long gone. His legs became tangled, and he crashed to the ground. The amulet spilled out of his pocket. He quickly threw it around his neck, tucking it into his shirt. He scrambled on his hands and knees towards the mouth of the cave when he again heard the hoarse whisper behind him.

Ashton couldn't understand what the voice was saying, nor did he care to. He resumed his sprint towards the beach and dove out of the cave. The sunlight hit him like a freight train, blinding him as he landed at a pair of thick legs, his mouth full of sand. Breathing heavily, he looked up to see Milt staring down at him. Milt grabbed Ashton's arm and pulled him to his feet, brushing off his shoulders and looking him over. Jiya rushed over to Ashton and gave him a hug nearly knocking him back to the ground. A crowd had gathered behind Milt.

"What did you see?" he demanded.

Ashton stared blankly back at him.

"Ashton, I need you to answer me, and be specific. What did you see?"

"I don't know. There was a skeleton and…something else, I don't know…. I really don't know what I saw," Ashton rambled, still trying to grasp what had transpired just a few moments before and whether his eyes had played a masterful trick on him in the dark.

Milt studied him for a few seconds, then gazed over Ashton's shoulder and into the cave. He saw nothing.

"Come with me," Milt said finally.

Milt ushered Ashton away from the cave and back up the beach. Jiya walked on the other side of him, holding his hand, the tears in her eyes now dried, having given way to relief that Ashton was not hurt, allaying the fears she now insisted were sensationalized by rumor.

TWENTY-TWO

The beach had all but cleared out except for a few stragglers who stayed behind greedily counting their newly acquired coins from the day's trading extravaganza, the earlier event already forgotten. The two men who earlier gave Ashton such a cold welcome on the beach upon his arrival were sitting outside of their shabby, makeshift tent, still perched among the tall sea oats and beach elder swaying gently in the wind.

As Ashton passed them, he glanced down and gave them a nod. The man with the missing eye had just successfully got his fire going when he met Ashton's smile with a sneer. The bald man finished cleaning a pair of blackfin tuna and yellowtail snapper and threw them on the flames. The sun was beginning to beat down on the two men, Ashton noticed, turning the bald man's head a bright shade of pink.

"Damn good catch today," Ashton overhead them saying.

"Lucky that current didn't get us. I could see the water star'in to churn, ready to swallow us up."

"I know, but 'ere we are dining on this fanciful feast! Ain't nuthin' can kill us, ey."

Both men laughed and retreated into the shade of their sheeted canopy watching their fish cook.

"*This* is all that's left of the rum?" the bald man yelled exasperated.

He swirled what little remained of the bottle's contents.

"Cool yer horses," his friend commanded as he reached under his blanket and pulled out a new, uncorked bottle.

The smell of the cooking fish entered Ashton's nose and he fantasized for a second about stealing their catch and running off to partake in a banquet of his own. Spiteful vengeance for their earlier transgression. But he, Milt, and Jiya continued past them into New Nassau. Milt's arm was still firmly around Ashton's shoulder as they made their way back into the late morning bustle of the town where most men were hard at work with the usual imbibing, an activity likely to last them well into yet another night.

As the two men on the beach enjoyed their recent catch, a dark, misty shadow appeared before them. They looked up simultaneously as a figure materialized and cast their eyes upon a large, menacing, wraith-like figure, more human than shadow, with a short beard and a scar down the right side of his emaciated face. There was a deadness in his eyes that made the two men shiver. His clothes were dingy and tattered. The figure took off his soiled tri-cornered hat, looked at it with a steely gaze, and tossed it aside. He ran his fingers through his hair and turned his face skyward, letting the sun warm his taught, pale skin.

He looked at the bald man and addressed him in a harsh tone, "William Hobbes."

"A-a-aye?" the bald man stuttered, trembling.

The figure breathed deeply and, in a firm, commanding voice said, "Get me my amulet."

Hobbes stood and lowered his eyes in a contrite manner for fear of disrespecting the man he suddenly recognized.

"Aye aye, cap'm," he obliged.

The figure that stood before them turned and, reverting to his shadowy form, re-entered the cave, unseen by any others, and disappeared back into the darkness to bide his time.

"Shit, mate, it's been three hundred years since we've seen him in the flesh. If I'd had known today was gonna be tha day, I'd have washed or somethin'," the one-eyed man remarked.

"It was a matter of time, Squints," Hobbes said sullenly to his lanky compatriot. "No prison and no kind of voodoo magic was gonna 'old him foreva'."

"We oughta find that amulet," Squints reasoned.

"Right…you know what he's talkin' 'bout?"

"…I have no idea."

The fish that remained on the fire was beginning to burn. They yanked what they could salvage off the logs and sat back under their tent passing the bottle of rum between them. They stared blankly into the distance and did not speak for a good while.

"We'll get to it after dinner," Hobbes finally offered.

"Aye. After dinner. Where's the rum?"

Squints threw the bottle back. The rum spilled down his cheeks.

TWENTY-THREE

Ashton sat next to the bed upstairs in Milt's manor while Marco continued to rest. He held the amulet in his hand and looked upon it for the first time since finding it in the cave, examining the trinket and trying to decipher the meaning behind the markings on its surface.

"What's that?" Marco asked eyeing the blue-tinged piece of cobalt in Ashton's hand.

Ashton quickly pocketed the amulet.

"Nothing. Just a souvenir I traded for in town. How're you feeling?"

"Been better."

Ashton felt terrible for the predicament in which Marco found himself, having suffered the same pain and heartache with the loss of his own brother, Luke.

"I'll leave you alone to rest."

"I'll be up in a few minutes. I've slept long enough."

"Take your time, Marco. There's no need to rush."

Ashton left the room and put the thin, leather cord around his neck slipping the amulet back under his shirt. Music was playing as he made his way downstairs where Milt was expertly playing the piano, his fingers dancing over the ivory keys. The tune sounded familiar. Ashton stood just around the corner of the entrance to the room listening, careful not to disturb or interrupt the maestro at work.

Ashton leaned against the wall for a few minutes more enjoying the music before leaving Milt to play in the solitude he preferred. He took his time walking back to the Green Turtle, a smile on his face anticipating seeing Jiya again for what he hoped would be another eventful night. Halfway down the hill, though, Ashton still could not stave off the lingering questions that continued to rage in his mind. Solitude would have to wait. He turned back around. He knew where to find Jiya and would catch up with her later. For now, he hurried back up the dusty street and threw open the front door. The music slowed for a couple of notes, then resumed. Milt was unmoved and unfazed by the intrusion.

"It's time to start answering some questions," Ashton demanded.

The music stopped. Milt turned his hard gaze to Ashton. He took a gulp of rum and set his glass down on top of the piano as he brushed passed the intrepid newcomer.

"Already?" Ashton asked rhetorically. "The sun's barely up."

"Follow me," Milt said gruffly.

He took a sharp right out of the Grand Hall and continued down a dark hallway on the western wing of the house, leading Ashton to a heavily locked room at the far end of a stretch of broken stone tiles. Inside, he struck a match and lit an oil lamp hanging on the wall illuminating the room in a flickering light. The stained-glass windows on the southern wall were largely devoid of light as they fended off the encroaching jungle. The room was empty save for one large, wooden chest that sat atop a dusty handwoven carpet of various shades of faded colors. Milt turned the key that protruded from the lock and unlocked it, pulling out a stack of papers, writings and a variety of drawings, mostly, the pages of which were yellowed and musty.

"All of this you see – the island, this town, this villa – all of it...," he began, recollecting his memories while he read through the scribbled pages. "It's all the result of a vision a single man had long ago. And now, that vision is at a crossroads."

"What man?"

Milt handed the papers to Ashton who could make no sense of them. Scribblings he couldn't read, maps of places he couldn't identify. He dropped them back in the chest.

"At one time, he went by the name, Henry Avery."

Ashton began to connect the dots with the details Jiya provided the previous night.

"The pirate who disappeared with his treasure," Ashton added.

"Some say that. Others say he retired. But the truth is a little more complicated than that."

Milt launched into a history lesson, describing Avery's piratical tenure and the legend of his disappearance, pacing back and forth across the room and getting pulled deeper into the past.

"I'm familiar," Ashton told him, himself a student of pirate lore.

"Are you?"

Milt slid the chest to one corner of the room and rolled up the carpet, revealing more of the stone floor beneath. He slid his thick finger between two flat stones, triggering a latch that popped up out of the grove. Milt grabbed it and hoisted. A stone staircase spiraled downward. Milt descended slowly. Against the gritty stone wall, he scratched a match head and the phosphorous tip burst into flame. He touched it to a torch hanging on the wall. The smell of burning oil quickly wafted through the tight staircase.

It was a long descent, but as they went lower, the air grew considerably cooler. The stale smell of mildew and the lack of airflow made the air pungent and intolerable to breathe. When they reached the bottom, Milt placed the torch through a small iron ring affixed to the stone wall. The glow from the torch lit the walls on either side of the stairwell revealing streaks of dark red smeared and dried on the stones. Before them, a heavy, bolted door blocked their way. The thick wood covered in gouges and scratches, as if made by both sword and fingernail.

Dark blotches stained the roughened exterior. A gruesome remnant of darker times long since passed. Milt pulled from his pocket a long iron key attached to a leather string. He slid the key into the keyhole and turned it a full revolution. The lock released with a click and Milt put both of his hands on the door, heaving it open with one great push. The door lurched open, creaking as it moved on its rusted hinges. Milt grabbed the torch and the two men entered.

"Where are we?" Ashton asked.

"Inside a room that'll answer your questions," Milt responded, the light flickering on his face and casting long shadows about the underground chamber.

TWENTY-FOUR

Christian, who lived in one of the grittier dwellings on the island, stood in the threshold of his front door, barefoot and shirtless. He inhaled deeply the salty air and casually walked out of town unnoticed. He made his way into the jungle following the western cliff to avoid cutting through the town, passing empty stables along the way until finally he reached the tree line. The trees seemingly parted before him as he continued onward, burdened with an unseen weight that he hoped to relieve at the conclusion of his trek. He had not looked forward to the task he knew he needed to complete, but it was long desired, and it was time.

Christian trudged south, alone in his thoughts, gliding through the brush and overgrowth. The path he was on had all but disappeared, given in to the wild of the island. Having thrown off the shackles of his previous life, he now sought to reconnect with his former self. He waded through a mangrove swamp that led to the inlet of the Río Plata. On the eastern bank, a long, crudely carved canoe was tied loosely to a thick banyan tree. The grass had grown tall over the years, obscuring it to the unobserving eye. Christian untied the rope and drug the boat across the pebbled shore down to the water and pushed off downstream. The current was quick, and he used the one oar sparingly, opting to enjoy the tranquility for some much-needed introspection. The river gently meandered west through the jungle for a couple miles before guiding him to an opening in the trees at the confluence with another river. He steered his canoe left, breaking away from the Río Plata and taking the larger, slower moving Río Lenta southwest. After a few miles, the river widened. Christian guided the small boat towards the narrow, southern shore at a wide bend in the river, and pulled it onto the sandy embankment.

Forest surrounded him on all sides, feeding into the foothills of Mount Deluz, the island's tallest peak located near the western coast. To ancient peoples, the mountain was considered sacred, and a place believed to hold special powers granting a way of communicating with one's ancestors.

Christian strolled through a small, grassy plain to a spring-fed pool. He took his clothes off and laid them neatly at his feet and jumped in. The water was crisp and rejuvenated him. He soaked for several minutes before getting out and lying down to dry in the sun. His hands behind his head, he stared up into the blue sky as white clouds floated overhead. The birds were singing jubilantly in the nearby thickets. The crickets and cicadas were conducting a harmonious symphony.

After his short rest, Christian set off, passing vibrant flowers of all colors and sizes blooming along a well-trodden animal path leading to the base of Mount Deluz up ahead. As he began his climb, the air was touched by the sweet smell of pine, which made the hike pleasant, the scorching heat notwithstanding. Sitting atop of the sacred peak was an ancient altar, long in disuse and ruined by time and the harsh elements of the Caribbean. When Christian first arrived on the island, it was uninhabited, and he relished in its resplendent beauty and the peaceful solitude it provided. It was some years later when he encountered Milt and his shipwrecked crew and before long, pirates from all over the west gravitated to the new pirate haven. But Christian turned his eyes back east and sailed into unknown waters on the other side of the world.

The summit provided a panoramic view of the bucolic surroundings, the lowlands and jungle, and the sea beyond. Christian took a moment to take in the breathtaking views before he continued with his intended purpose. He approached the ruined altar and knelt before it. There was a time when he often climbed to the pinnacle of Mount Deluz, to this altar, to connect with his ancestors. Now, he had come to forsake them.

"It has been a long time since I last called upon you."

He looked around at the ruined structure in front of him and shook his head. He looked back up towards the sky.

"I do not regret my decisions or for my actions against my brother, and I do not ask for your forgiveness. I came here to ask you for mercy and to welcome me upon my death."

He hung his head in penitence. He grabbed a handful of earth – dark, moist soil – silky to the touch and held it in his hand. A thick swirl of black smoke rose from the ancient chimney and rose high into the sky. A wind blew over the outcropping on the peak.

"Tane," it whispered.

Christian ignored it and rubbed the earth between his palms. It grounded him, made him feel closer to nature and eased his mind.

"I no longer answer to that name," Christian muttered as he walked away.

He took his time descending the mountain down to his brethren on the coast. His old self was behind him. Now, he was fully one of them – a pirate and mortal.

TWENTY-FIVE

Ashton sat in a lavish wooden chair, on a cushion made of purple and silver silk, surrounded by barrels and chests and boxes overflowing with treasure, listening intently to the story of Henry Avery that Milt continued to share with him. A vibrant Persian rug was sprawled out in the center of the expansive cellar that sat beneath the manor. It was a large, stone room with many nooks and darkened angles. Water seeped in from cracks in the stone. There was a coldness to the air. The one torch illuminated but a fraction of the space. As Milt spoke, it seemed to Ashton that he was reminiscing on an experience, rather than describing a legend.

"So, what *did* actually happen to him?" Ashton asked incredulously.

"He managed to elude his would-be captors and disappeared back to England. Unfortunately for his crew, they weren't as careful. Spending frivolously and bringing unneeded attention to themselves, they eventually, one-by-one, hung from the end of a rope or drank their fortunes away until they became vagabonds, dying nameless in ditches. It was said that Avery succumbed to the latter, but in fact, my lad, he did not. He sailed to Ireland a few short weeks after arriving in Devonshire, looking for a girl he once loved…and lost. He found her, eventually, but not as he left her. Her grave marker was all that remained."

Milt stared at the ground, his eyes showing signs of pain, Ashton saw.

"Having nothing left, Avery sailed with his immense treasure and a newly recruited crew back to the pirate kingdom he established in Madagascar. He called it, Libertalia. When he arrived, he found it governed into the ground by a bloodthirsty man he once considered a friend. You've met him. That...semblance of a human you ran into back in that cave on the beach. His name is Thomas Tew. His tyrannical rule in Avery's absence destroyed that burgeoning colony. He was ruthless. Bloodthirsty. He attacked ships and vessels with complete disregard, killing and enslaving with impunity all on board. I'd venture to guess whatever part of him you encountered in that cave means to finish what he started."

Milt put his hands behind his back and walked to the center of the room, standing half hidden in shadow. He began slowly as if transported to another time, reflecting on a past long gone.

"When Tew heard of Avery's return," he continued in a soft tone of regret and sorrow, "he aimed to kill his old friend and consolidate his power once and for all, but Avery prevailed, wounding Tew and leaving him for dead. Avery resigned himself to the fact that his pirate kingdom was lost and so he set sail for England, deciding then it was best to retire alone in a land he knew so as to live out the rest of his days in peace." *Peace*. He paused to reflect on the word. "He sailed into the Atlantic, passing the Cape of Good Hope and continuing west as he raced to avoid a hurricane swelling off the coast of Africa. The storm system caught up with Avery in the Caribbean Sea and pushed his ship into the reef on the southern end of this island. It tore a hole in the hull, but he was able to limp it into a hidden cave, keeping it safe.

"When the storm passed, he and his crew abandoned the ship and started their trek inland. The storm had cleared a lot of vegetation on the island and uncovered an old Spanish coquina fortress, Castillo de Luna, with a buttressing town built from stone and wood. Avery chose this location on the eastern side of the island as his new hideaway. Its position, though on high ground, was largely obscured and invisible from the ocean and the nearby waters were treacherous, marred by sunken British and French ships.

"For years this place flourished, but Tew was able to track Avery and eventually found him here. Tew should have died from his wounds long ago, but he has a way of surviving death. I watched him in battle as a cannon ball ripped his belly open," Milt recounted with a reignited fury.

But then his face turned as if he had come to a sudden realization. Fearful of exposing himself too much to Ashton, he comported himself and continued, "After his fight with Avery in Madagascar, I suspect that some of the natives found him and healed him. And despite a few of the tribes having deep knowledge of local medicine, there was a power there that was felt, but not understood."

Milt, as if having a premonition, turned to Ashton, "When you were in the cave, did you notice an amulet around Tew's neck?"

Ashton's face flushed.

"No. I didn't see one," he said, his face flushing. "Why?"

A bead of sweat drew on Ashton's brow. Milt eyed him but played his thoughts close to his chest.

"He wore an amulet when he was sealed in that cave those many years ago. There're rumors of such relics. Rumors I heard while in Africa. They grant a power to its bearer," Milt trailed off as if in deep thought. Milt studied Ashton before finally breaking off his stare.

"When Tew landed on these shores, he and his men snuck up from behind the mountain and set fire to the jungle surrounding the ancient fort. As the blazes rushed towards New Nassau, forcing Avery and his men from their stronghold, Tew and his men engaged them in open battle. Some men were consumed by the flames, others by the sword."

"So why not return and reclaim Castillo de Luna for yourself and rebuild Avery's dream of Libertalia?" Ashton queried.

"I haven't the want. Back then, my crew sought to wipe away any reminder of Tew, and those that fought with him were indentured to rebuild New Nassau. With Tew gone, they no longer felt the need nor desire to rebuild Libertalia and so voted to let the fortress become swallowed once again by the jungle in favor of the lethargic, lustful lives they now live. Tew's treachery was too much to bear and so here it was that they chose to remain free men. Eventually, the memory of Tew faded and life went on."

Milt strode over to a long wooden chest and opened it, looking down at a sheathed sword. Ashton stood behind him. Milt touched the supple leather, then shut the lid.

"How was Tew alive in that cave, if that was indeed him?" Ashton asked, still looking at the box.

"Come. I want to show you something else."

They ascended from the room and walked to the atrium in the rear of the house. They exited through the backdoor that opened to a large yard, surrounded by a makeshift picket fence and a smattering of tree ferns and golden dewdrops. Inside the fenced space rested several makeshift headstones and wooden crosses. Some had names etched in them, while most did not.

"A cemetery?" Ashton asked.

Milt walked to an unmarked grave.

"Her name was Naemi. She helped Avery that day by placing a spell on the cave, sealing Tew's body inside it," he told him, leaving out the details and Ashton's role in the plan.

"Who are in these graves?" Ashton asked.

"All heroes to the cause," Milt answered. "Anne Bonny, you may have heard, was rotting in prison waiting for death before her father bought her freedom, but she never made it to him. She came here to hide out for a while, but she died from pregnancy complications soon after."

"Anne Bonny?" Ashton repeated excitedly.

"Her son is still here in New Nassau."

Ashton couldn't believe what he was hearing. History was being rewritten before his very eyes. Her grave marker was nearest to him, next to another old slab of stone, whose upper right quadrant had long ago broken off. Inscribed across what remained was a barely legible name that read, "Edwa…," and next to it a stone that read, "Ned Low," and finally, "H. Morgan."

"If you're wonderin', Henry Morgan didn't look nothing like the picture of that fella on the rum bottle," said Milt. "I searched and found his grave where Port Royal once stood and reinterred it here. He would find no rest in the sea."

"Who's Ned Low?"

"Ned Low was brutal even to Tew's standards, and he often caused problems here until he raped a prostitute down there in the brothel and got shot in the back walking down the stairs. We disagreed on his tactics, but he was a Brethren all the same."

"A shot in the back sounds like an appropriate death."

"They strung her up from the ceiling bannisters for it, too."

"Damn."

"They all deserve their peace," Milt remarked, not exhibiting any emotion or sympathy for any of them save one. His attention returned to Naemi's resting place.

"She never forgave herself for helping Avery that day, and in the end that regret ate at her until she withered away."

"Why isn't her name written on her gravestone like the others?"

"She didn't think she deserved to be acknowledged for what she had done."

Ashton found himself pitying them.

"We have work to do. I need you to find my quartermaster, Christian."

Back in the Grand Hall, Milt poured two generous glasses of rum. Ashton took his glass reluctantly, but together they drank their fill until Ashton could barely stand. The sound of Milt's laughter as he recounted stories with each of the pirates grew heavier and heavier. The room started spinning out of control and Ashton fell face first onto the oriental rug. Milt continued to laugh as he raised his glass in a mocking salute and Ashton drifted off into unconsciousness.

Three hours passed before Ashton woke up. He groaned and raised his head from the puddle of drool on the rug. He struggled to push himself upright but managed to find his way to the canape. He sat for a few seconds before stumbling to the window. He pushed open the panes and vomited into the rose bushes.

The heat from outside beat against his face. Feeling better, he followed his nose into the dining hall just as Milt walked through a doorless entrance out of a large, tiled kitchen where he had cooked up an enormous lunch. Ashton sat at the end of the dining table and lay his head on his arms.

"Glad to have ya back. You hit the mat pretty hard, bub. Eat up."

"That rum we were drinking…I gotta admit, wasn't half bad."

Milt laughed.

"Half bad? Son, your palette needs some refining, not to mention your tolerance level."

"So it would seem."

As Ashton left the house to find Christian, surprised to learn of his lofty, number two position in New Nassau, Milt noticed Marco, who was now standing on the bottom step of the Grand Staircase, and gave him a sly smile. Marco nodded his approval.

"Well done," Marco said to him.

Milt raised his glass.

"It cannot be stopped now. Stay with him. I will begin my preparations."

TWENTY-SIX

Hobbes and Squints finished their meal on the beach and walked to a separate tavern, farther down the beach from the Green Turtle, with a large sailcloth awning and inside, an open-air courtyard. Music and dancing filled the air. It was smaller in size to the Green Turtle and of lesser repute, but it satisfied the needs of the more unsavory types inhabiting New Nassau. A large woman belted out powerful notes as she swung her wide hips on stage to the delight of the crowd. Pushing aside the temptation to join in on the fun, Hobbes and Squints made their way to a back table to discuss their likely course of action to accomplish the task that been imparted to them.

A lumbering, foul-smelling man slammed into their table, slapping his meaty hand onto the tabletop to capture the attention of the two conniving pirates. His one good leg was heroically supporting his wide girth as his knees started to quiver. In his other hand he held a small cask of rum in which he had yet to find a bottom.

"Heard you was lookin' – *hiccup* – for men," he slurred. "I'm a fight – *hiccup* – I can pirate."

He took another large swig. The drink ran down the corners of his mouth and into his thick, black beard. Hobbes turned his nose up at his stench.

"What's yer name?"

"Horatio – *hiccup* – Thundersnatch."

"Looks like yer havin' a hard nuff time battlin' that drink in your hand, but maybe your wife can fight with us," Squints mocked.

Thundersnatch steadied himself and cocked his right arm. He squeezed his fist and took a swing at Squints. His momentum carried him straight to the ground, catching the side of the table as he went and flipping it onto his back where it would serve the rest of the night as a round, wooden blanket. Hobbes and Squints stepped over his unconscious, snoring body and continued moving inward through the crowd. In the corner of the room, they saw a lone man sitting with his back to the wall reading a book.

"Evenin'," Hobbes said approaching.

"Good evening," the man replied in perfect Queen's English. He looked up at the two men over the top of his reading glasses. "Can I help you, gentlemen?"

"You might indeed."

The two men looked at each other and grinned before pulling up two chairs and sitting down across from the man.

"My name's Hobbes and dis 'ere's Squints."

"Squints? Is that the name your mother gave you?" the man asked.

Squints looked at Hobbes who shrugged his shoulders.

"Uh, no, sir," Squints said.

"Well, never you mind. What can I do for you? And make it quick."

"First of all, we asked you yer name," Hobbes said, trying to assert dominance.

"They call me Shepherd," the man said without blinking or taking his eyes off them.

"Why do they call you that?" Squints asked.

"Don't know."

"Well, uh, Shepherd, see we're here recruitin' some men…," Hobbes began to explain.

"Let me stop you right there," Shepherd said as he put his hand up. He took off his reading glasses and rubbed the bridge of his nose. "I don't give a damn what you're doin here, and I've already tired of your company. I must ask you to now leave me in peace."

"But don't you wanna hear our…," Squints pleaded.

"No. I don't," Shepherd interrupted, ending the conversation.

A vein in Shepherd's forehead bulged. His steely gaze made the two pirates uncomfortable, and feeling defeated and confused, left him alone with his book.

"Maybe we should lower our standards," Squints advised.

"I'm thinkin' yer right."

"What kind of men you lookin' for?" a gruff voice suddenly called from within the crowd.

A husky, shirtless man with dark tattoos all over his body approached, towering over them. Hobbes and Squints stared up at the pirate in awe.

"Men exactly like you," Hobbes told him. "Meet us t'morrow night out by the ruins and we'll explain ev'rythin'."

"Is there payment?"

"More than you can imagine, friend. Say, what's yer name?" Squints asked.

"Lime. Paul Lime."

"Awright then, Limey, 'til tomor…"

Paul grabbed Squints by the throat, his fingers wrapped nearly around the circumference of his neck and lifted him effortlessly off the ground.

"Don't call me Limey…and I ain't your friend."

Squints scratched at the man's hand as his face turned red.

"O…O…Ok," he choked.

Paul let go his grip, sending Squints crumpling onto the floor holding his neck and gasping for air, and left.

"Bring yer friends!" Hobbes yelled after him.

Hobbes helped Squints to his feet.

"Best just call 'im Paul, mate."

"Where to next?" Squints asked in a hoarse voice.

"Let's see what else kinds of eyes and ears we can buy," Hobbes answered as he continued to meander into the crowd.

"And enlist more men!" Squints added.

"Obviously," Hobbes said with a roll of his eyes.

TWENTY-SEVEN

"He seemed to buy the story. It's safe to say he doesn't suspect his relations, but even if he did, I've convinced him well enough that Thomas Tew is the enemy in all this," Milt said confidentially to Marco as the two walked the streets of New Nassau. "And now that he's broken him free, I finally have the chance to free myself of this dreadful prison," he added with disdain.

"Hey, guys," Ashton said, approaching at a trot.

"Ashton," Milt said jovially. "Forgive me for not staying, your timing is rather unfortunate as I must take my leave of you both."

He whisked himself off and disappeared down a narrow, winding side street. Ashton and Marco continued strolling through the town leaving Milt to his own machinations. As dusk approached, a light rain began to fall, muddying up the dirt roads and paths.

"I assume you also knew that Milt and Avery are one in the same?" Ashton asked.

"You pieced that together, huh," Marco asked unsurprised. "But that was a long time ago. He hasn't gone by that name in some time." Marco stood close to Ashton and put his hand on his shoulder to emphasize his next point. "And I recommend not bringing it up to him."

"I'll be honest, he's not what I expected in a legendary pirate king."

"How do you mean?"

"I'm not sure. I guess I expected someone…different."

Marco did not respond.

"It would explain his fascination with Thomas Tew," Ashton began to theorize. "And the cave…."

Marco knew Ashton to be intelligent, and realizing he was heading down a dangerous path of discovery, Marco fervently changed the subject away from Tew.

"Hey, let's share a drink to our fallen brothers," Marco said, feigning bonhomie.

He threw his arm around Ashton's shoulder and ushered him inside the Green Turtle.

"Who's Naemi?"

"I don't know much about her aside from what he's allowed to be known, but my guess is he loved her. Milt holds himself responsible for her death."

"How'd she die?"

"That's not for me to tell."

"How is Milt able to leave the island?"

Marco smiled at his inquisitiveness.

"Less questions, more drinking," he said, holding up two fingers to Jiya.

Ashton smiled brightly at Jiya as she winked at him and placed two glasses on the bar top. The tavern was crowded, which kept her busy. She quickly moved on to the other patrons. A loud shout caught their attention. Christian was engaged in another contentious game of poker and had disgruntled the other players when he folded his hand upon seeing the two men enter the tavern. He knocked the table as he stood, much to the consternation of the other players.

"Marco! You're alive!"

He threw his arms around the man and lifted him off the ground.

"You look a lot better than you did earlier, that's for sure. Sorry about your brother."

"I feel a lot better. And thank you."

"Don't thank me. I should be thanking you for getting me out of this game. I've been hemorrhaging money for the last two hours," he said with a smile.

Christian, sensing some new news was afoot, asked, "What's on your mind?"

"Tew's awake," Marco replied.

Christian's face grew somber.

"When?" he asked gravely.

"Earlier today."

"It was me," Ashton admitted. "I entered the cave and the next thing I knew, there he was, sort of."

Christian studied Ashton for a moment, then approached him slowly.

"I knew this guy was going to be trouble."

"Easy, big fella," said Ashton, retreating a few steps back.

"You have no idea what you've done," Christian snapped.

Ashton backed himself against a wall. The distance between him and Christian continued to shrink with each giant step Christian took towards him.

"You're right," Ashton responded, taking a half step forward, standing tall. "So go ahead and get on with it."

Christian smiled, "Gladly."

His rock of a fist came flying at Ashton's face. Ashton reflexively ducked just as it crashed through the wall. The other patrons in the tavern quickly scurried over and hovered like ravenous vultures anticipating a bloody beatdown. They circled around the two men as Christian licked the blood from his knuckles and grinned.

Christian swung again, but Ashton ducked under his arm and got behind him. Christian quickly realized the vulnerability of his position but not before Ashton landed several kidney shots and crawled up his back to put him in a rear naked choke. Christian laughed at the effort, but soon the hold began to have its effect. Sensing a change in fortune, the crowd shifted from jeering Ashton to cheering him. Beer was flying, money was changing hands, everyone but Ashton and Christian seemed to be enjoying themselves.

Milt showed up just as Christian pried Ashton's arm away from his throat and regained some leverage. He stood in the back laughing at the sight of Christian whirling around with Ashton holding onto his neck for dear life. Christian attempted to punch over his shoulder. Milt was enjoying the spectacle and even wagered some money of his own as he muscled his way to the front of the ring and urged the two of them on.

Ashton and Christian were oblivious to the crowd they were attracting. Christian wanted a quick example to be made of Ashton, while Ashton was just hoping to come out of it with all his teeth. He punched Ashton in the chest, and contacting something hard, he recoiled his hand in pain. Ashton was knocked to the ground, the wind knocked out of him. As Christian grew frustrated, his face changing varying shades of red, he managed to get a handful of Ashton's hair. He grabbed Ashton's shirt, yanked him up, and, in a snap, threw him into the crowd. Ashton landed in the arms of a wiry, blind man.

"Pierre?"

"Don't get whooped!" Pierre St. Croix chortled. "You still have a bigger part to play yet."

Ashton glared at the strange man. The crowd shoved him back into the center of the circle. Ashton maneuvered around the perimeter. Christian lunged and Ashton dodged. Again, Ashton tried for the rear naked choke, but Christian was quick to not show his back a second time. Ashton scurried around the circle again, parried a punch and countered with a right hook that caught Christian on the jaw, surprising them both. Christian wiped the blood from his lip and laughed his amusement. Ashton tried his luck again, but Christian grabbed his fist mid-flight and twisted Ashton's arm, bringing him to his knees. Christian kicked him in the chest sending him flying back into the crowd.

A few rowdy pirates quickly scooped him back onto his feet and shoved him once again back into the ring.

Ashton brushed off the dust in a defiant manner. Christian was beginning to be impressed with the tenacity of his opponent. He feigned a move and Ashton dodged the phantom punch. Christian, encouraging the crowd, allowed Ashton a cheap shot. Ashton took it and punched him in the stomach, then immediately shook the pain out of his hand. Christian, toying with Ashton, shoved him backwards into the crowd, who then shoved Ashton back towards Christian a third time. Milt was bent over laughing. Ashton ran around the outer edge of the circle and ended up pausing just in front of him. Milt patted him on the shoulder and spun him back around just in time for Ashton to duck out of the way of Christian's incoming jab. Christian's fist found Milt's right cheek, and the crowd went silent.

Milt rubbed his jaw, a fire kindled in his eyes. Christian was dumbfounded and stood with mouth agape searching for words. The crowd stood still as statues waiting to see how Milt would respond. In the confusion, Ashton came from behind and grabbed Christian's ankles, pulling them forcefully backwards. Christian crashed to the floor, landing face first with a thud. Ashton pounced on his back and secured the rear naked choke. Milt went back to cheering on Ashton who still had not let go of his hold. Milt grabbed him and peeled him off Christian, hoisting him onto his shoulder and parading him around the bar to great fanfare.

Christian, his pride the only injured party, was slow to get up. The crowd followed Milt and Ashton to the bar where Milt bought the place a round of drinks. Jiya had been watching from the bar, enjoying the fun, though when she saw Ashton's body hurtling through the air, it worried her for just a brief moment.

Christian made his way to the bar and spun Ashton around. Fear welled inside Ashton, anticipating the large islander raining down retribution for embarrassing him. The crowd grew silent once again. Milt looked on attentively. After a few tense seconds, Christian smiled and held out his hand. Ashton took it, and Christian squeezed it firmly, perhaps a little too tightly for Ashton's comfort, but he had earned Christian's respect.

"Well done," Christian told him with a quick tussle of Ashton's hair.

A bead of sweat trickled down Ashton's forehead as he let out a sigh of relief.

"Next round's on me," Christian offered to sustained cheering.

The crowd was drinking faster than Jiya could refill their chalices. Ashton was jumping up and down with the rest of them, singing and hollerin', and enjoying the attention. As the night wound down and the tavern slowly emptied, Ashton found himself at a table with Christian, Jiya, Marco, and Milt, who was two dozen drinks in when he stopped counting.

"Gentleman, I bid you a fond goodnight," Milt said with a flamboyant bow.

He nearly toppled over from the gesture but composed himself and retired to his manor. As the remaining four chatted, Christian chimed in, "So, let's talk about the elephant in the room," he said.

"I don't see no ephalent," Ashton said with accompanying giggling.

Jiya took his mug away from him.

Ashton stood to protest.

"Best not to belabor the point," Marco advised, pulling him back down into his seat.

"Tew's free," Christian began.

"No one saw him leave the cave, but I'd bet he's preparing to fight," Marco cautioned.

Christian's face was expressionless. "We knew this day would come eventually and we can rightly gather what his intention is. We need to make sure we stop it from reaching that point."

"Agreed," Jiya said as she walked back to the table.

"Let's regroup in the hour before dawn by the old stables under the cliff," Christian ordered. "Get some sleep. And you, my friend," he said, turning to Ashton, "need to sober up."

Christian patted Ashton on the cheek as his eyes started to glaze over. The group adjourned their meeting. When Marco and Christian walked outside to go their separate ways, the night was quiet, and the moon was peeking through a break in the heavy cloud cover. Jiya escorted Ashton upstairs and prepared him for bed. Lying beside her, he fell asleep in her arms.

TWENTY-EIGHT

As dawn approached, Marco met Ashton outside the Green Turtle Tavern and together they walked towards the stables, built into a recess in the mountainside and sheltered partly by an overhanging slab of stone. The horses were absent, accustomed to coming and going as they pleased. The group sat on the soft piles of hay inside the grotto-like stalls, watching the rain fall while waiting on their compatriots.

"The rain's a nice respite from this incessant humidity," Ashton noted as he welcomed the cool, accompanying breeze on his skin.

Thunder cracked. Lightning lit the sky. At the apex of the hour, Christian, with his thick, curly hair matted and wet, together with a dozen other men, arrived.

"Early mornin' thunderstorms foretell trouble," Christian noted.

"I've never heard that."

"That's what my people believe."

"Who are they?" Ashton asked.

"I found some friends willing to help. Turns out word about Tew's resurgence is spreading quickly, and most are eager to join in on the fun," Christian responded. "Some, though, with the curse bein' lifted and all, have decided to brave the open waters for more fruitful seas."

"That's suicide," said Marco. "They must know that, curse or no curse, once they get close…they'll be…they'll never make it."

"Those men are cowards and better for us if they're not in our way," Christian reasoned.

"What about the rest of the men in New Nassau?" Ashton asked.

"Most of these men at one time or another accepted this new reality and gave up any chance of returning to pirating. But bein' a pirate is about freedom as much as it's about adventure. I'm sure there are some here who still share that belief, and if they do, we have to find them. But we need to be careful. There are still some who'd rather continue their bloodthirsty habits and lust for plunder. They'll undoubtedly be lookin' to Tew for direction to increase both their riches and their body counts."

"Gou gai bu liao chi shi," replied a stranger in the back.

Ashton looked over the group. This speaker of tongues sported a shaven head except for a long, braided ponytail.

Seeing the blank faces, the stranger proclaimed in broken English, "A dog cannot stop itself from eating shit."

Laughter erupted.

"I will kill any man that follows Tew," the foreigner calmly warned.

"Who's he?" Ashton asked.

"Not sure, really," Christian answered. "We sailed together once. He was my Quartermaster.

"Your Quartermaster? And you don't know who he is?"

"He didn't talk much. I do know his name's Chen, and he hailed from Shanghai, originally, but fled when he was eleven or so, having stowed away on a junk headed for Formosa. He was supposed to be a eunuch or somethin'. He mostly keeps to himself, except when we're ported somewhere. If I had to count," Christian began to laugh, "I'd say he has around eight or so wives by now; tends to get one every place we visit. Helluva sailor, though."

As the rest of the group talked and reacquainted themselves, Ashton continued his conversation with Christian.

"How'd you come to know him."

"I was on a trading voyage passing through the Formosa Strait when our ships got caught in a typhoon. Mine survived, his sunk. My crew of Singaporean merchants found Chen clinging to a wooden plank. An unsavory bunch they were, but they brought him aboard and he was quickly adopted by the crew and christened into our seafaring way of life. It didn't take long before the merchants I employed took to piracy to defend against the Chinese barbarians plaguing the Orient. As their captain, I obliged them.

"We eventually made our way to the Indian Ocean where we spent our time stalking the trade routes. It was more lucrative than the trading business, if you get my meanin', but we were never successful at it. That's where we met Milt. We sailed together for some time before he left for the Caribbean. Chen and I stayed in Arabia with the rest of my crew, lying low for a bit, but we were soon discovered. My crew was captured and hacked into pieces, rest their souls. The bleeding pulps of what used to be their bodies were thrown into the water as fishing chum. Chen and I managed to escape and found our way here, following Milt's course. I still knew the way and we arrived after that curse, so we aren't trapped here like the rest. These men'll do fine doin' whatever we need 'em to do."

"That sucks for your crew!"

"It happens," Christian added nonchalantly. "It's the life we chose."

"Well," Ashton said, looking over the group, "this is a good start, but there's still work to be done."

"Fourteen men," said Milt, startling them. "It's not near enough."

"What do you suggest?" Ashton asked.

"First, we need to figure out who's sympathetic to our side and isolate them from Tew's allies. Then, we hit them before they hit us."

Milt faced Christian and put a hand on his shoulder, the two imposing men, old friends, standing eye to eye.

"We have a lot of work to do, old friend. Take Ashton and Marco and a handful of these men and go to Lost Cay. I need you to talk with the locals there."

"You got it," Christian agreed. He turned to the group, "Any of you speak their language?"

"I do...kind of. I used to trade with them," a tall man answered, raising his hand reluctantly.

"Good, then you're coming with us. The rest of you, start making some friends. Chen, we need to segregate this island as quickly as possible."

Christian handpicked four men, Marco among them, along with an aged man, seasoned with experience, the interpreter, and a young man eager to earn his keep, and led them toward the docks, hugging the cliffs to ensure their movements remained out of the watchful eye of New Nassau as much as possible.

"Ashton," Milt said as the others rushed off, "when you return, Beacon Hill will be lit. Look for the light and follow it straight in. You'll know it when you see it. And once you're on the azimuth, do not veer from it, no matter what. Do you understand what I'm telling you?

"I can navigate well enough. What happens if I veer?"

"Don't."

"Humor me."

Milt sighed and relented.

"There's a terrible maelstrom that's been known to develop around those parts, between here and there."

"That's pretty vague."

"Maintain visual of that light," Milt repeated, pointing his thick finger at Ashton's chest for emphasis.

"I will."

Milt clapped Ashton on the shoulder, "I like you," he told him, then nodded a silent goodbye.

Ashton hurried to catch up with Christian and the others just as they reached the docks. Behind him, Jiya came running up from the town, hoping to intercept the group before they departed.

"Ashton!"

"What are you doing here? How did you find us?" he asked, caught off guard by her presence.

"I'm not going to be left out of this. I don't know what you're doing, but I'm going with you. I woke up and you were already gone, so I went looking for you and saw you leaving the stables. Good thing you guys don't run very fast."

"Let's go! The sun'll be up soon!" Christian yelled to them.

Ashton ushered the men into the *Mami Wata* and untied the rope from around the piling. He took Jiya's hand, and they stepped into the boat as Marco backed it away from the dock. Leaving Crooked Inlet for open water, he spun the helm north towards Lost Cay and pushed the throttle forward, speeding over the flaccid, turquoise waters of the Caribbean Sea.

TWENTY-NINE

Milt paced anxiously in the Grand Hall of his manor. Candles flickered in the pre-dawn darkness. The windows were open, and the wind was starting to pick up, ruffling the curtains. A squall was developing off the northern coast. He stopped and stood in front of one of the windows, wringing his hands behind his back and staring out over the town hoping for Christian and Ashton's success, knowing his advantage rested on it.

He poured himself a drink and watched as the faint silhouette of a vessel sailed its way past the Sentinel Cliffs and through Crooked Inlet towards an uncertain fate. Milt knew what lay in store for them. He knew the risks were high, but he needed to be done with Tew and his mind was bent on achieving that end at whatever cost.

Assured that the events that would shortly unfold were now beyond his control, he retreated to the back of the house, through the secret hatch in the stone floor, and down the stairwell into the musty underground cellar. He lit the entirety of the room. Some dozen torches were burning on strong, square columns bracing the rest of the house above him. Gold, jewels, weapons, foreign fabrics, and fine furniture abounded. Milt sat on the low-back chair with the purple and silver cushion, taking in for one quiet moment all he had conquered.

A black flag lay crumpled on the floor in the far corner. Milt picked it up and clutched it pensively in his hands, staring at the profile of a skull and the crossed bones underneath it, then let it drop back to the floor. A long, rectangular box with studded brass, rested beside the flag. It was locked shut by a large iron lock, rusted and forgotten. He pulled a key from his pocket, the second on his iron keychain, and unlocked the old chest. Inside, a fine leather scabbard rested on a pile of hay. He lifted it carefully from its resting place and, holding the perfectly weighted weapon, wrapped his hand around the gilded hilt and slowly pulled out a cutlass, revealing a burnished steel blade. A smile crept over his face. A power filled him, and with the sword in hand, he walked past the tattered flag and back up the stone staircase, locking the heavy cellar door behind him.

THIRTY

As dawn broke with dark storm clouds looming ever closer, Hobbes and Squints led a small contingent of pirates south into the mountains beyond New Nassau. They made their way along a winding, overgrown animal path to conceal their movements, and as they navigated through the dense jungle, the rain began to fall, penetrating the thick canopy overhead.

It rained for a solid hour, but when it stopped and the sun shone again, the members of the pirate horde, with each step, became increasingly strained under the oppressive humidity, slowing the pace of the convoy to a crawl. The point man, a young, well-to-do Irish teenager with auburn hair and born into an aristocratic family, stopped suddenly. The jungle heat was growing more stifling by the second. The men behind him all took a knee, like a row of dominoes falling in sequence, weary from dehydration. Some even resorted to disrobing themselves to get cool, leaving their exposed bodies vulnerable to the swarms of mosquitos that followed them like prostitutes following a field army.

The blonde kid turned to the line of pirates behind him.

"I think I hear water," he said excitedly.

The men all bound to their feet and rushed forward, crowding the boy and listening intently for the sound. The noise of a waterfall slowly broke through the impenetrable quiet.

"I hear it, too!" another man shouted.

"Aye, same here!" said yet another.

"Nice work, Mac," Hobbes said with a rustle of the boy's hair.

In seconds, the group was rushing to the roar of crashing water. As the men hacked and hollered their way through the brush, the sound gradually became louder until finally a stream of sunlight broke through the dense vegetation. Several men rushed forward to peel back the leaves and tree branches and stood on a precipice overlooking a water hole fed by a tall wall of water. Mac and another young pirate standing next to him, a close friend since childhood, cheered and jumped together from the forty-foot cliff down to the cool water below with reckless abandon, persuading two others to follow their lead before they were halted from behind.

"Wait!" yelled Hobbes to those readying to jump.

"What for?" shouted one of the men in frustration. "It's bloody hot and that water's the best-lookin' thing I've seen all day. No offense to all you lobcocks."

Hobbes approached the edge and looked down.

"We shouldn't have left the path. I've heard stories 'bout this place. S'posed to be cursed."

"Yeah, well what ain't?"

Hobbes watched as the men below splashed carefree in the water.

"Look!" Squints said as he pointed to three large fresh-water alligators sunbathing on a small sandy beach opposite the waterfall.

The gators slid into the water and deftly swam to their unassuming prey. The men struggled to hear the pleas of their party over the thundering sound of Caiman Falls, and they remained blissfully unaware that they were being hunted. The two young pirates splashed and floated on their backs, unable to hear the warnings shouted to them from above. One of the pirates, stout and proud, rushed down the muddy, steep embankment that led from the cliff down to a perch just a few feet above the pool. But by the time he reached the bottom, all that was left for him to do was watch in horror as the first victim was pulled underneath the water.

"Damn shame," Hobbes said apathetically. "That Mac would've made a fine pirate."

The remaining pirate managed to swim through the waterfall and into the river that led under the mountain as the alligators followed closely behind. It wasn't long before the water had turned from a tranquil, cobalt blue to a churning, crimson red as the alligators executed their death rolls, tearing flesh from bone like slow roasted pork.

"Let's go," Hobbes said to the rest of the men still frozen in horror by the gruesome fate of their comrades.

The group walked cautiously around the northern spring that fed the waterfall and river below it. As they continued deeper into the jungle, following the comparably small Río Niño, they eventually came upon a fork. Heading south, they followed the main waterway downriver for five more grueling hours, after which the dehydrated and demoralized group finally reached the outskirts of Castillo de Luna that once served as the center of Captain Avery's pirate kingdom.

Hobbes left two men at the river to retrieve water for the rest of the group. A loud crack of thunder boomed overhead. The sudden downpour flooded the dirt path that led over the hill and into the small valley enclosed on all sides by mountainous walls. The rising water level saturated the ground around the two pirates, making the mud so thick it sucked one of the men's boots right off his foot.

"With all this rain, I don't know why we're still havin' to get river water," one of the men huffed.

"'Cause we was told. Now move and watch your step before you slip and plunge us both down into that ragin' torrent."

Cautiously, the men stood on the riverbank and filled two large bladders each. One of the men screamed, dropping both bladders into the mud, and jumped back with a face as pallid as the sun-bleached stones of Libertalia. Lodged in debris just below the surface was the face of what remained of one of the men devoured by the alligators.

"I ain't drinkin' no water with dead people in it!"

"Technically, he ain't no person no more. Not really sure what you would call that."

They dropped the water bladders and raced back up the hill. At the top, the rest of the pirate cohort worked diligently for the rest of the afternoon and well into the night, clearing away the overgrowth suffocating the ancient citadel.

THIRTY-ONE

As the sun broke the horizon, Marco piloted the *Mami Wata* expertly through the barrier reef that guarded the cove just as the winds began to pick up and the waves started to swell. Facing the open ocean, he held the throttle down as far as it would go, willing the boat to go faster and outrun the impending storm. He set his course for Lost Cay.

With Marco and the interpreter topside, Christian, Jiya, and Ashton went below deck and poured over topographical maps of the cay. The north and east sides of the island were rocky and precarious, the west side was too far from their inland destination. The south side of the island, however, had a long shoreline that buttressed the jungle, making it the most ideal landing location. They relayed this information to Marco and waited with dark clouds and a gray sheet of rain now far behind them.

"Land ho!" Marco shouted as he steered the boat toward the south side of Lost Cay, looking for a safe, inconspicuous place to moor.

The south side of the island was flat but heavily forested. The crystalline white sand beach was unspoiled, dotted with palm trees just before retreating into a wall of coconut trees, seagrapes, and mahoe trees. Several flat, sandy islands dotted the waters just offshore to the southeast.

Christian threw the anchor overboard fifteen yards from shore near a mangrove forest that spilled over the beach and into the shoreline. With the *Mami Wata* out of view of the main beach, the six of them leapt over the side into the chest deep water and waded ashore. Ashton stood on the beach with his hands on his hips, staring at the lush jungle.

"How do we find this tribe Milt spoke about?" he asked as a spear glided through the air and found its mark in the eye socket of their interpreter.

"I don't think we have to worry about that," said Jiya.

A squad of native warriors quickly approached and surrounded Ashton and the others, pointing their spears and arrows at them. They were bare-chested, wearing only loin cloths and head adornments made of tropical bird feathers, and necklaces around their necks, each comprised of a varying number of bones. Their bodies were lean and covered in paint.

"What do we do?" asked Ashton nervously.

"Put your hands in the air. Show them we're unarmed," Christian instructed the group.

One of the warriors broke through the circle and stood in front of Ashton. There was a long, deep scar on his right thigh. His headdress was bigger and more colorful than the others. He didn't wear a bone necklace. He didn't have to.

The warrior studied Ashton for several seconds before turning his attention to the others. He walked over to Jiya and ran his stubby fingers through her fine hair, then motioned to one of his men who seized her by the arm.

"Let go of me!" she yelled as she fought against her fleshy bounds.

Her fist broke free from the grip and caught her captor's jaw, causing the others to move in and thrust their spears to within an inch of the group's collective heads. The warrior restraining Jiya pulled out a crudely fashioned knife and held it against her throat. The other warriors took rope and bound the rest of their hands. The leader turned and walked back along the beach. Ashton, Christian, and the others were hurried into a single file line and made to follow him, while Jiya and three of her captors broke off from the party and entered the jungle by another route.

"Hey! Where are you taking her?" Ashton demanded with a threatening tone to his voice.

The lead warrior walked to him. Ashton dug his feet in the sand and stood firm, refusing to divert his eyes from his menacing stare. Ashton's heart raced as his nerves held steady. After several tense seconds of staring at one another, Ashton's lip curled up in a snarl, his body was tense. The warrior laughed and turned away to continue their march.

"I said let her go," Ashton demanded again through grit teeth, his feet still dug in the sand.

The end of a spear prodded him in the back. He spun, grabbing the spearhead in a flash and yanking it from the grip of the warrior holding it. Ashton snapped it over his knee and swung his fists, bound together at the wrists, in a parabolic arc, hitting the warrior closest to his left underneath the chin and sending him hurtling through the air. The shocked warrior leapt back to his feet and charged at Ashton.

"Hold!" the lead warrior commanded.

The charging warrior's mouth was full of yellow, rotting teeth covered in bright red blood. He stopped inches from Ashton, furious with the command he had been given. He grabbed Ashton's arm and yanked him forward. Ashton stumbled but caught his balance as the party resumed their trek down the beach before heading into the jungle.

I should be at a tiki bar right now.

They continued trudging through the jungle in silence for what seemed like an eternity when they finally entered a clearing. Several earthen huts made of wood and thatched roofs were arranged in a wide circle, serving various uses and functions, and in the center stood a towering wooden longhouse built on massive stilts of carved, rounded tree trunks, each one telling a story. It appeared to be a place of worship, at least at that moment. A high priest stood tall at the top of a long flight of stairs surrounded by several small, stone ovens that sent smoke pillaring upwards. Below, the chieftain wore a full, towering headdress adorned with a variety of exotic flowers and feathers. He sat on an elevated throne carved of stone and jewels in front of the building. His torso was painted sky blue. A bonfire roared between the two exalted figures as the village daughters danced around it, singing in an unfamiliar tongue.

A second priest, thinner and much younger, brought out an image of a sea beast held high over his head, carved in relief on a large cross-section of tree trunk. The priest incanted several verses of what Christian knew to be a prayer to this creature they so fervently worshipped – a prayer just before a sacrifice. The group was ushered to the base of the stairs.

Ashton spotted Jiya as they filed past the chieftain. Tied up and naked, she knelt, humiliated and bloodied, next to the chieftain's throne, tears streaming down her cheeks. Her eyes, searching for help, were filled with terror. Ashton met her eyes and tried to give her a reassuring look despite the circumstance in which they found themselves.

"I don't want to die!" the youngest prisoner who had been so eager to join the party lamented as he cried and pled for mercy.

"William, quiet yourself!" Christian urged from behind.

The chieftain stood and raised his arms, silencing the tribe, making William's blubbering much more pronounced. He spoke in his indigenous language while Ashton and the others could only look on helplessly. After a short speech, he motioned with a wave of his hand to proceed and resumed his seat. Drums began to beat in a slow rhythm as the priest turned to the carved relief and began another series of chants. The tribe bowed low at their waists, their arms stretched forward above their heads and repeated the verses. A warrior separated William from the rope that bound him to the others and led him up the tall stairway. The young man fell to his knees crying, squirming, and begging for his life. Without prompting, a second warrior assisted in subduing William, grabbing him by the other arm and hauling him, together with the other tribesman, to the ornately carved and painted altar that awaited its victim with much eagerness.

When he was brought to the foot of the altar, the priest washed William's torso, arms, and legs with water, then leaned him over the small alter. A third warrior, larger in girth than the others, stepped forward holding an axe. As the young man pleaded for his friends to save him, the blade fell as the chants reached their crescendo, and William's head rolled down the steps, painting them as it went. Cheering erupted as the headless body was carried down to the fire and placed on a spit, turning slowly to roast the flesh.

Fully comprehending the peril that awaited them, Ashton realized he had precious little time and so plotted his move. Most of the warriors were wholly focused on the proceedings at hand, but several others caught Ashton's eye as they ventured inconspicuously back into the jungle. The same two warriors who hauled William to his death yanked Marco by the arm and led him towards the stairs. He carried himself with dignity. As the tribesmen collectively turned their attention to the priest, Ashton kicked the warrior standing nearest to him on the side of the knee. His leg cracked and bent awkwardly inward, and he fell to the ground, writhing in pain. Ashton slammed his foot into the face of the crippled warrior, stole the bone knife from his belt, and cut Christian's bindings. Christian picked up the spear belonging to the fallen warrior, and in a blink, hurled it at the chieftain, finding its mark in the center of his chest and pinning him to the back of his throne chair. In the disarray following the chieftain's assassination, Christian worked to free the others. Ashton hurried over to Jiya who, in shock and still kneeling, was splattered with the chieftain's blood. He picked her up but struggled to carry her to safety.

"Give her to me," Christian said, and took her from Ashton, cradling her against his wide chest.

"Follow me! This way!" Ashton said.

Together, the four remaining members of the group plus Jiya tore off through the jungle, heading in the general direction back to where they thought the boat was anchored, not bothering to look behind them. Christian, with Jiya in hand having passed out from the shock, brought up the rear.

"They're coming," Marco informed them.

"Let's go, boys, keep up or it's your ass. We can't afford to lose no one else," Christian said as he raced past the others despite the load he was bearing.

THWISSSH.

Three arrows landed right in the middle of the trailing man's back. He let out a muffled yell, unable to breathe, and the aged pirate doubled over, dead. Christian glanced back as another arrow flew past his face and lodged in a tree just off his shoulder.

"Faster!" he yelled.

Ashton followed Christian back to the *Mami Wata*, his heart pounding in his ears, his focus tunneled, not paying attention to much else besides Christian's heels and the limp body in his arms. An arrow whizzed past Ashton's head and he dove to the ground. He jumped back to his feet just as Marco ran past. An arrow flew past them and struck Christian in the back of his leg. Ashton turned to see the warriors quickly gaining ground, and as he did, a large stone hit him on the forehead, knocking him back to the ground. Marco, just a few steps ahead, stopped and hurried back to help him up, and as Ashton's vision cleared, he saw Marco lying unresponsive and bleeding next to him.

He felt a thick hand on his shoulder. Christian snatched him to his feet and pushed him forward. He looked back again as they raced towards the sound of breaking waves on the beach. Two of the warriors took their prize and drug Marco, fighting with what little strength he had left, reaching for anything his hands could grab, back into the jungle. The urge to run after Marco was overpowering.

"No sense going after him. He's gone," Christian cautioned, somehow aware of Ashton's thoughts.

A gull's cry alerted them to the beach. Ashton pushed onward. Running a step ahead of Christian, he crashed through the brush, a wall of vegetation marking the natural boundary between the jungle and the sand and ran headlong into a palm tree. He found himself back on the ground. A coconut fell between his legs. Clinching his teeth and grimacing through the pain reignited in his shoulder, he forced himself to his feet. Christian, having flung Jiya over his shoulder, came up behind Ashton and hoisted him onto his other shoulder.

The sun was getting low in the sky. Christian threw Ashton into the water. Ashton swam sidestroke back to the boat, favoring his left shoulder as Christian waded beside him, keeping Jiya's head above the surface. As the pursuing warriors breached the daylight, they launched their weapons towards Ashton and Christian in a final attempt at kill or capture. The two of them split and went around either side of the *Mami Wata*.

Christian climbed aboard first and laid Jiya in the pilothouse next to him. He cranked the engines as Ashton swam up to the starboard side, reached his right arm up, and grabbed hold of the cleat on top of the bulwark.

"You on?" Christian asked.

"Yeah," Ashton yelled back.

He held on as Christian piloted the boat to the safety of deeper waters. As the *Mami Wata* powered through the battering waves, Ashton held on for dear life. When out of reach of the natives' weapons, Christian slowed the boat and reached over the side, grabbed Ashton's arm, and with a swift tug, hoisted him out of the water.

Ashton sat gingerly holding his left shoulder and leaned back against the side of the boat as it skipped over the water, racing back to Shipwreck Island. The beauty of the sunset and the cool sea spray allowed him a brief respite, but it wasn't enough to cloud the violence that had befallen them. Jiya awoke shortly thereafter, and Ashton quickly helped her below deck and wrapped her in a blanket. He gave her some water and as soon as she lay down on the bed, she was asleep. He went back topside. Christian was swallowing a large swig of rum and was working on ripping the arrow out of his leg while keeping one hand on the helm.

"Just a flesh wound," he said casually.

Ashton handed him a bandage.

"He was a good man," Christian said. "First his brother, and now him. How you holdin' up?"

Ashton didn't immediately answer.

"Let me take over. Go get some rest and take care of that leg," he at last ordered Christian.

"How's your shoulder?"

"It's fine. Just sore."

"You gonna be ok?"

"I'll be fine."

Christian patted him on the back and went below deck.

"Keep your path straight and do not veer," Christian reminded him.

Ashton remembered Milt's instruction.

Watch for the light.

THIRTY-TWO

The last color of the day was gone. Night had fallen as the first sprinkling of stars unveiled themselves in a moonless sky. The boat glided across the glassy water leaving behind it a long wake that disturbed the surface. Ashton stood at the wheel, his eyes heavy and dry.

"Hey," said Jiya sympathetically.

There was a gentleness to her voice that helped calm him. She placed a hand on his uninjured shoulder.

"I'm sorry for what happened back there. It was my fault," Ashton said.

"No, it wasn't. We had no idea what to expect."

Ashton shook his head.

"What happened to you, I…."

"Don't blame yourself. I asked to come along."

"Listen, we don't ever have to talk about what happened."

"It's ok. I was just roughed up a bit. Nothing else happened. It would've been much worse if you hadn't taken action. That was extremely brave what you did. You, Christian, and Marco…the ones we lost…I'm alive because of you."

She held his face and kissed him.

"I'm glad you're ok," he said.

She squeezed his hand and smiled.

Ashton turned the wheel slightly, adjusting the boat's bearing, and at that moment, a faint light revealed itself in the distance. He lined up the bow and headed for Emerald Cove. The boat slowly passed through Crooked Inlet and made its way to the anchorage. Ashton pulled the boat up to the dock, and

Christian secured it by tying a rope around a pile. The night was quiet, the beach empty, and the town devoid of its usual debauchery, save for a few lit establishments for lonely pirates desperately seeking company from the ladies of the night, oblivious to the day's misfortunes. Fires could be seen dotting the mountain ridge in the far distance. Ashton jumped out of the boat with purpose.

"Where are you going?" Jiya asked him as he hurried off.

"Milt and I need to have a little talk," Ashton answered.

The door of the manor was locked. Ashton pounded. No answer. He peered inside the closed windows. The lights were on, but the Grand Hall was empty. He knocked again, and again, no answer. Ashton pounded again. Finally, the bolt clicked, and the heavy doors swung open.

"How'd it go?" Milt asked.

"Are you kidding me?" Ashton asked incredulously. "That's it? Marco and two others are dead! And I'd be dead, too, if it wasn't for his sacrifice!"

Ashton took a breath to regain his composure.

"You sent me to that island knowing full well what awaited us. Marco died and became a meal for a tribe of cannibals. Jiya barely escaped with her life!"

Ashton grew increasingly frustrated with the overall opaqueness of Milt's behavior.

"I like your fire, kid. That ember in your soul was the first thing I saw in you," Milt told him. "Now, before you say something you might regret, I want to give you something."

Milt unwrapped a tarnished cloth revealing an expertly crafted sword as beautiful as the day it was forged. Its gilded hilt was made of smooth leather, inlaid with a thin, gold thread and a ruby embedded in the pommel. The blade was long and shimmering. Milt held the weapon in his hands, admiring its craftsmanship, transfixed on its beauty. He brandished the sword in his right hand. A formidable weapon. Ashton shifted his weight nervously. The room seemed to shrink as Milt became more imposing. A fire burned again in his eyes. Milt took a breath through his nose and exhaled slowly. The pressure in the room eased. Milt presented the sword to Ashton. He marveled at the weapon, forgetting his reason for confronting Milt in the first place.

"Why are you giving me this?" Ashton asked.

"Because you embody what it means to be a pirate. It was chance we met in Key West, but it was fate that you came to Shipwreck Island."

"Was it?"

Milt smiled. Ashton was growing tired of Milt's games. He turned for the door. Standing in the threshold, he gave Milt a last glance.

"There's a great story yet to be told," Milt said to him.

"I appreciate the offer, but I can't lead pirates."

"Why not?"

"Because I'm not one."

"Look. There ain't much use for pillagin' and plunderin' any more. Libertalia was supposed to be a haven for freedom and liberty, but it failed. Those men out there will need a leader to escort them into the modern age when our two worlds come crashing together, because they will.

"That tribe I sent you to contact was marauded on that island by Tew when he first came here. They don't fancy pirates and that was the risk of sending you. But like you said, you ain't a pirate so I took a chance that they'd be open to a meet."

"Well, you were wrong, and men were killed."

"More men will lose their lives," Milt added.

"Which is why I'm not going back."

"You don't have a choice if you want any hope of defeating Tew and his army. That's the weight of being a leader. You need to trust me. Return to Lost Cay."

"Tew's not my problem! He's yours," Ashton shouted back, his chest heaving and face red.

Milt stepped in close and narrowed his eyes.

"Is he now?" Milt said.

Ashton eyed him. Milt controlled himself and stepped backwards through the threshold, standing in the glowing light of the Great Hall that spilled through the doorway.

"Courage is what separates great leaders from weak ones – courage to do what must be done," he told Ashton.

"Don't fuckin' talk to me about courage," Ashton snapped back.

"There ya go! More of that kind of language and you'll be well on your way."

"He's right, Ashton. We do need to go back," Jiya said walking up to the porch.

"You remember that they tried to eat you, right?" Ashton reminded her.

"Their chief is dead. There's likely confusion, maybe even a power vacuum. It's worth it to try and take advantage of the mess they're in."

"She makes a lot of sense, Ashton," Milt said, folding his arms triumphantly.

"What do you propose, Jiya?" Ashton asked her.

"Well, for one, I don't suggest turning myself over again to be skewered like a roasting boar."

"That's too bad. That was my plan," Christian added from behind her shoulder.

Jiya snapped her head and shot him a sideways look.

"There's an animal trail that leads to the camp from the rear," she said turning back to Ashton. "I saw a few of the women heading in from that direction carrying baskets of fruit when I was being led to the camp. So, it's unlikely the men use it much, if at all, and I think we can exploit that."

"Get someone else. I'm no pirate," he reaffirmed to Milt and then he departed.

"We'll see," Milt intoned to himself, sheathing the sword as Ashton took his leave.

THIRTY-THREE

Milt strapped the scabbard around his waist and gently slid the magnificent piece of elongated steel back into its hold. He exited the manor through the rear gardens and began his trek into the mountains, assured in the knowledge that the end game was at hand. He entered the thick jungle just as thunder rolled in the distance. Another storm was brewing.

THIRTY-FOUR

"Where'd you get this boat from anyhow?" Squints asked.

"Found it wrecked over by Horseshoe Point. Some fisherman must've sent it into the rocks a few years back. I got her patched up pretty good though."

Hobbes brought the refurbished boat to rest at the edge of the surf at Isla Cruz, a small, but thickly forested and swampy island due east. He wedged the boat in the saturated sand while the gentle waves nudged it at even intervals. Six men jumped out into the ankle-deep water and pulled it further ashore, anchoring it to a palm tree to prevent the tide from taking it away.

"I still don't understand what we're doin' 'ere?" Squints asked uneasily.

"That bilge rat that's been hangin' around lately still's got that amulet."

"How do you know?"

"Cause I seen him with it. He was walkin' to the Green Turtle from up on the hill and he was lookin' at it. Didn't think nobody seen 'im. But I seen 'im. Clear as day I seen 'im from the window of me own house."

"Then we take it from him. Easy," Squints suggested.

"Easy? Nah, time ain't right. Besides, Tew said that ol' witch, Naemi, may have something in one of 'er books, some kinda spell or somethin' that can bring him back to full human form if'n we can't get that amulet back."

"That makes sense."

"Of course it does. Now let's get to work and find that book," Hobbes ordered.

"I don't like this place. That ol' witch had that evil magic. No tellin' what kinda curses she has 'ere 'round her home," Squints bemoaned.

"She's been dead fer a long time. Now grow some balls and git goin'," Hobbes barked in response.

The six men crossed the beach and entered a mosquito-infested swamp. The water was shin deep and a heavy fog hovered over the murky, vaporous surface. They made their way single file, trudging through the mud, with Hobbes in the lead. Squints consistently fell behind, complaining with every step as his peg leg sunk in the mud.

The second man behind point, tall and spindly with dreadlocks that hung in a bundle down to his lower back, spoke up killing, the silence, "You know where ya goin' mate?"

Hobbes turned around and with one punch, knocked him out cold.

"Tie 'im up to that tree and leave 'im for the gators, and don't let another one of ya question me again."

Two of the men bound him tight against a cyprus tree. The heat and humidity were stifling. Another of the men collapsed in the water. The man behind him stood him up and slapped him hard across the face to wake him up. They continued the slow, tedious trek through the swamp, the quickest route to their destination at the center of the small, waterlogged island.

Time was relative in this place, and after what felt like days, they finally came across the first piece of dry land they had seen since leaving the beach. A stilted house stood soundly atop the compacted ground, nestled amongst a smattering of thick, strongly rooted trees. It was strangled by vines and enveloped by thick, hanging moss.

"I think we found it, boys," Squints yelled from the back.

No one dared utter a sound. They all felt apprehensive thinking the place to be haunted.

"If I was going to build a house fer a creepy ol' witch, it'd probly look sump'n like dis."

"Stop yer chatterin' and start searchin'!" Hobbes commanded. "You," he said pointing, "keep a look out."

The remaining four men, including Hobbes and Squints, clamored up a rotted, wooden ladder, weathered gray and covered with lichen, while the fifth man remained on the ground and provided security.

THIRTY-FIVE

Ashton, Christian, and Jiya sat in Christian's kitchen discussing their next move. There was a knock at the door. Christian moved silently, holding a silver candelabra. He flung the door open and brought the piece of metal down on the visitor, pulling up just before he made contact with his smooth head.

"Dammit, Chen, I nearly killed you."

Chen pushed his way into the modest house. Christian shut the door quickly behind him. He spoke with Christian at length, too softly for Ashton and Jiya to overhear. After some time, Christian entered the kitchen and stood before them.

"Several of Tew's henchman took a salvaged boat to Naemi's home on Isla Cruz, apparently looking for a book of spells or something, I didn't quite catch everything he was sayin' to me."

"How does he know this?" Ashton asked.

"I asked Chen to follow Hobbes and that one-eyed fella with the peg leg. They've been leading a group of pirates to Castillo de Luna. He overheard them discussing their plan, and when they took off, which, according to him was just a couple hours ago, he came to report."

Ashton stood and addressed Chen.

"What's in that book?"

Chen, able to understand the question, answered in his native tongue.

"He's not certain, nor am I to be honest, but it likely has somethin' to do with giving Tew his human form," Christian said.

"We have to stop them," Ashton said earnestly.

"Then let's get to it."

"We need to keep this quiet. Just the four of us," Ashton said looking at Jiya, Chen, and Christian.

They went back to the docks and idled out of the cove. When they arrived at the beach at Isla Cruz, they kept their distance around a bend and out of sight of the other vessel.

As Ashton, Jiya, and Christian waded through the swamp, several pieces of torn, frayed rope floated by them.

"Be careful. They could be anywhere," Jiya warned.

"And by 'they' you mean them," Christian said pointing to five men crashing through the swamp's outer edge and onto the white sand.

"Son of a bitch!"

Ashton retraced his steps until he recovered the short distance and arrived back on the beach.

"Chen!" he yelled in a loud whisper.

Chen, having already seen Hobbes and the other scallywags, fired up the *Mami Wata* as Jiya climbed aboard and Christian and Ashton pushed her back from the shore. A lightning bolt struck the water directly between the two boats.

"Get in front of them and cut off their escape! If they didn't notice us before, I guarantee they know we're here now," said Ashton.

"Then what?" Jiya asked.

"Then…we…uh," Ashton stammered.

"We'll force them to the east. They'll know what awaits 'em there, and they'll be trapped," Christian interjected.

Whitecaps appeared, and the sea began to swell. Dark, imposing, storm clouds rose tall into the sky. The wind was gusting hard, and the gulls had vanished to the safety of their island nests. A sheet of rain began pelting the two boats. The vessels raced south, arching toward the clouds with their bows shooting into the air as they crested the waves.

"We're going to capsize!" Jiya pleaded.

"Keep going!" Ashton commanded.

Christian pressed the boat onwards, blinded by the dark sheet of rain until a crack of lightning lit the sky around them.

"Zai nali!" Chen yelled pointing out the other boat just off their starboard side.

Christian angled the *Mami Wata* hard to starboard. Lightning flashed again. The boats were close enough that Ashton could see the fear in the faces of their enemies as the *Mami Wata* intercepted the other craft on its port side. A wave crashed into the small fishing vessel. As it started to list, its crew leapt into the raging sea. Within seconds, the boat had capsized, floating hull up and bobbing on the surface.

"We can't leave them to drown," implored Jiya, grabbing Christian's bicep and urging him to turn around.

"If we stay, we'll go down with 'em," he countered.

Jiya looked to Ashton with compassion in her eyes.

"Dammit," Ashton reluctantly conceded. "Spin her around, Christian. Pick up who you can, but don't jeopardize the boat any more than you have to, then we head for the safety of the cove. This storm's only going to intensify."

Christian obeyed.

Hobbes and Chen swam to the *Mami Wata* looking like a pair of wet dogs. A third man yelled from a short distance away as he flailed and floundered, barely staying afloat. He was roughly built, with a thick beard and long, thick brown hair.

"Throw him a line," Ashton shouted, pointing to the struggling man.

Chen grabbed a large coil of rope and tossed the end of the line to him. The man grabbed it just as he went under the surface.

"Pull him in!"

Once onboard, he coughed up water then proceeded to vomit. Chen bound their hands and feet and locked them below deck. Exhausted, they did not resist.

"I don't see any others!" Christian yelled.

The storm grew stronger.

"They're gone. Get us out of here!" Ashton said.

Christian spun the boat around, facing it into the wind, as a wave lifted the boat and dropped them hard into the trough. He laid on the throttle. The engines sputtered.

"Engines are flooded."

"Keep trying!" Ashton yelled as he ran to the stern.

Another wave carried the boat high into the air and dropped her back down again. The *Mami Wata* was dead in the water and drifting parallel to the waves.

"Another hit and she'll capsize!" Christian yelled over his shoulder to no one. "Leaving us all to the mercy of the sea," he finished under his breath as he gripped the helm tighter.

Ashton struggled against the gale, clinging to the side of the boat with all his strength to avoid being washed overboard as he made his way aft.

"Take the helm," Christian ordered Chen, and went to help Ashton.

Christian grabbed a crowbar on the way out of the pilothouse and powered through the wind. Reaching the transom, he swung at the portside motor, hitting it broadside. It sputtered back to life as a wave bore down upon them. He then struck the starboard motor and waited two excruciatingly long seconds before it, too, jerked to life and the *Mami Wata* was back in business.

"Good girl," Christian said.

He and Ashton turned and trudged back to the pilothouse. Christian gave Chen a thumbs up who then eased on the throttle. He turned the boat into the oncoming wave. The bow rose skyward, sending Ashton hurtling backwards. Christian grabbed Ashton as he tumbled past and pulled him into the pilothouse. Jiya was seated on the floor, holding on for dear life. Chen relinquished the helm.

"Hold on," Christian told the others as he slammed the throttle down.

They sped off as Christian steered them back towards the guiding light of the island. When the waters calmed down a bit, Ashton went below deck to check the status of his prisoners. They were alive but bloodied and bruised from being tossed about. Hobbes was feverishly shouting obscenities, but Ashton ignored his obstinance and returned topside, satisfied with their condition.

The *Mami Wata* limped into Emerald Cove, irreparably damaged, and floated towards the docks. Several men were awaiting them with ropes and hooks to secure her before she destroyed the entire mooring. She drifted precariously close to the cliffs. Christian struggled to maneuver away from a rock, the top of which protruded just above the surface, and it ripped a hole in her hull. The boat, already structurally weakened by the storm, began to splinter and nearly broke in half. Ashton and the crew were thrown into the water by the force of the impact.

The prisoners below deck did their best to stay afloat as they fought the rush of water and exited the gaping hole. Ashton started swimming to shore. He kicked a hard object, turned, and saw Hobbes's unconscious body bobble and slowly sink below the surface. Ashton wrapped his arm around his large, flabby chest and towed him to safety.

"Don't make me regret this."

Hobbes's lifeless body was starting to drag Ashton, already exhausted, under water.

Squints couldn't escape the breach and sank with the boat to the bottom of the cove. One man ran into the water to retrieve the remaining prisoner, still bound and floating on the surface, while another dove in from the dock and took Hobbes from Ashton. The two prisoners were drug onto the soft sand of the beach, their skin pale, their lips blue. The rain had slowed to a drizzle.

"This one's dead," one of the shoreman said of the rough-looking man.

"Take Hobbes and keep him tied up in that tent there until morning," Ashton instructed once on the beach. "Keep two guards on him."

Jiya jumped on Ashton, throwing her arms around his neck and hugging him hard. The crew stood watching the last remnants of the *Mami Wata* sink down to the sandy bottom of the harbor, joining the graveyard of ships already there.

"It's too bad about those men," Ashton mumbled.

"It's too bad Hobbes didn't share their fate," Christian retorted.

They sat on the driftwood staring at the water, the twinkling stars reflected in the calm waters following the storm.

"I was beginning to like that boat," Ashton said.

Jiya smiled and rested her head on his shoulder.

THIRTY-SIX

Morning had broken, and a cooling breeze blew through palm fronds, turning them into natural wind chimes while New Nassau continued to sleep. Ashton awoke to the sound of raindrops pelting the windowpane. He rose from the bed, careful not to wake Jiya sleeping silently beside him. He walked downstairs around the back of the bar and through a waterlogged wooden door and sat in an old rocker on the back deck. Six large, empty rum barrels clustered together neatly were filling with rainwater. Ashton let the rhythmic sound of the falling rain engulf him while he drifted into deep thought.

He was soon brought back to reality when two slender arms appeared out of nowhere and wrapped themselves embracingly around his neck. He tilted his head back to see Jiya staring down at him.

"Good morning, hero," she said, her voice sweet. "I'm glad that storm didn't completely wear you out last night."

Ashton blushed.

She handed him a hot cup of coffee, black.

"I could say the same for you."

She grabbed his hand and gave it a squeeze.

"Want some company?"

"I'd love some."

Ashton grabbed the arm of the chair next to him and pulled it close. She sat in it, crossing her legs on the seat and, holding her cup with both hands, blew on her coffee. They sat together silently for a long time enjoying each other's company and the soothing rain. The sun had not yet crested the mountains surrounding New Nassau, but its presence was made known by the painting of the distant sky in broad strokes of brilliant pink before surrendering to a pale blue and streaky white clouds.

Despite Jiya's comforting presence, Ashton still felt burdened. The loss of life weighed heavily on his mind, and no salty breeze could blow it away. His thoughts soon shifted to his brother and the courage Luke showed in the face of his enemy, but Ashton wasn't his brother, a fact not lost on him. He struggled to measure himself to Luke. Yet, somehow, he had been thrust into leadership of this group, feeling the guiding hand of his brother watching down on him from Heaven.

"It's peaceful here in the mornings," Ashton observed. "The beauty of it all impervious to the chaos and evil that envelops us."

Jiya looked at him without saying a word, knowing there was still more on his mind.

"And it's amazing when you stop and think about it," he continued. "When you stop and think about the beauty and the power of nature and that places like this…this paradise…that they actually exist in this world, you know what I mean?" He knew she did, but he appreciated her just listening. "Consider the vastness of the ocean, or the diversity and awesomeness of the jungle, and who are we? Humans come and go like the tide. We're getting ready to slaughter each other over an island and no matter the outcome, the world will continue spinning, the birds chirping, the fish swimming. Life goes on indifferent to our petty squabbles."

"There's more to it than that, Ashton," Jiya offered.

Ashton turned and met her eyes.

"Sometimes there must be struggle and sacrifice to achieve the greater good for those that come after us, to leave for them what we want but may not be able to obtain for ourselves, and in most cases that greater good is freedom. Freedom to live our lives as we please, freedom to pursue our own dreams, freedom from the evils of men seeking to rule over others. You know better than anybody that freedom must be paid for in blood. These men understand that, too, and will readily accept the dangers beset by such an undertaking. This is bigger than any one of us, Ashton."

Her words resonated with him. He didn't respond but rested back in his chair and thought them over. Jiya put her hand on his arm, and he put his hand on top of hers.

"You're a different man now compared to the innocent and naïve one I met a few days ago," she teased. "How's your shoulder, by the way?"

Ashton had forgotten about the pain, but it suddenly surged back into his mind, and he grimaced.

"It's fine, though it was considerably better when you didn't remind me about it," he teased back.

"Whether you like it or not, these men look up to you now."

"I haven't done anything. They barely know me. Those other guys are seasoned warriors with way more experience."

"You brought them together. You stood when others didn't, and I'm here because you did. You're the lynchpin that's holding them together. Lead them. Let them help you."

"I didn't ask for any of this. I just wanted to enjoy a relaxing vacation away from all the stresses in my own life, and yet here I am, in this *stressful* situation. If it wasn't for that damn steel drum music." His eyes and tone softened. "But I'll have to admit that coming here wasn't all bad. I did meet you."

Jiya smile broadly at him. Ashton stroked her hair, pulled her to him, and kissed her.

"I don't want anything to happen to you," he said to her.

She laughed.

"I appreciate your concern, but I can take care of myself. I've survived worse and whatever awaits us, we're in it together."

"I know."

The rain continued its steady drizzle, and the sun continued to paint its canvas with early morning hues. The rhythmic silence was soothing and pure and brought with it a calm over the island. When the rain eased, they made their way back to the beach.

"Let's see if that shitbag is ready to talk," Jiya said as they crossed the small footbridge onto the beach.

They saw, almost immediately, the empty set of blankets tossed haphazardly to the side of the tent in which Hobbes was placed. The two men assigned to guard him lay unresponsive. Their dark, coagulated blood soaked into the white sand. One of the guards had a knife protruding from his upper chest, while the other had his throat slit from ear to ear.

"HOBBES!" Ashton yelled at the top of his lungs.

His face was red. His teeth clinched.

"That son of a bitch."

Jiya tended to the corpses while Ashton ran back into town to grab the others. Ashton found Chen and Christian sleeping in a bunk bed in the corner of Christian's shanty home and shook them both vigorously awake nearly knocking Christian out of the top bed.

"What are you carryin' on about, mate?" Christian demanded through dry and sleep-infused eyes.

"Hobbes. He's gone."

Christian leapt out of bed and the three men ran to the top of the precarious steeple of the nearby church and scanned the town. It was the tallest building in New Nassau and provided a panoramic view. There was no sign of him.

"See anything?" Christian asked.

"You mean besides a roof in obvious need of repair?" Ashton joked staring at a leaking hole. "But other than that, nothing. He could've left at any time during the night. Who knows how much of a head start he has."

"Hobbes was unconscious," said Jiya, dumbfounded and without looking up as the men approached her on the beach.

"Was he?" Christian asked incredulously.

"He sure felt like it when I was dragging his sorry ass back to shore. I should've left him to drown out there," said Ashton.

"Probably," said Christian.

"But here we are. Now what?" Jiya asked.

"We should find Milt," said Christian.

"No. We need to get back to Lost Cay somehow."

Chen pointed beyond the cove to the beach bordering the eastern cliff and forming the northern edge of Crooked Inlet.

"Well I'll be a sumbitch," Christian said.

Resting on its side, surprisingly unscathed, was the fishing boat Hobbes had salvaged that had capsized in the storm.

"What about Hobbes?" Jiya asked.

"What about him? He's gone and chasing after him won't do any good at this point. Besides, whatever they were searching for at Naemi's old place, they either didn't find it, or it's lost to the sea because he didn't have it on him," Ashton said to the group.

"It still don't feel right letting him run back to Tew," Christian said.

"I know, but that's the hand we've been dealt, and it's time to go all in on that cannibal tribe," Ashton responded.

"Ashton's right," agreed Jiya. "Let's go. I'll fill you in on my idea on the way."

Ashton and the three others looked at each other as Jiya swam for the aground fishing vessel.

"You heard her," Ashton iterated.

They spent little time on the beach cleaning the boat of debris. When they had the boat back in the water, they each stepped aboard. The motor still worked, much to Ashton's surprise. The boat creaked with each movement, but it floated.

"You sure about this?" Ashton asked Jiya.

"Look, this island is more mine that anyone else's and I won't let my home be destroyed by some demon pirate."

"No, I mean the boat."

"Just come on."

Chen took the helm, while Christian and Ashton prepared a pair of makeshift oars, just in case.

"Let's hope this trip ends better than the last," said Christian.

Jiya nodded in hopeful agreement as the boat gingerly made its way back out to open sea.

THIRTY-SEVEN

Hobbes, his hands still bound, ran as fast as his battered, overweight body would take him. In the relative safety of the jungle, he fell to the ground and scooted against a massive oak tree. His breaths were long and deep, his throat scratched from dehydration, his skin bleeding and raw.

He took a few moments to gather himself. The sweat on his skin long ago given way to salt. He closed his eyes as the pain flooded over every part of his body. He struggled to remove the rope knotted tightly around his wrists. As he did so, the rope cut further into his skin. Warm blood trickled down his palms and onto the moist soil.

"AAAGGHHHHHH!" he yelled flailing about in frustration.

His arms were stuck behind his back, braced against his girth. Squirming to free himself, he dislocated his shoulder as he swung his arms over his head. Now in front of him, his right arm dangling longer than his left, he continued scurrying up the mountain. Blood, mud, and sweat comingling on his clothes and skin.

Several hours passed before he finally reached Castillo de Luna. The pirates were busy clearing back the jungle that had overgrown the old bastion. Hobbes stumbled into a cavernous building exhausted. In the corner of a windowless room, the blackness of Tew's shadow stood out against the darkened backdrop. Unable to see, Hobbes stumbled inside and fell to his knees.

"Well...," the wraith hissed.

"All the men are dead, cap'n."

Tew did not respond. His silence compelled Hobbes to continue.

"I have what you're lookin' fer."

"Give it to me."

Tew held out his claw-like hand, an amalgamation of flesh and bone.

Hobbes lowered his eyes.

"Well, I don't exactly have it, per se. It's in 'ere," he said pointing to his head.

Tew sighed and glided across the floor. Hobbes remained silent.

"Speak! You cur."

I hope this works, Hobbes prayed.

He began regurgitating from memory the short incantation from Naemi's book. When he finished, he looked up into Tew's red, beedy eyes, now aflame. Hobbes cowered in fear as Tew disappeared back into the shadows. With Tew's back turned, Hobbes leapt to his feet and ran out of the house, back into the welcoming sunlight and as far from his own fear as his sore and tired feet would carry him.

THIRTY-EIGHT

Milt stood at the edge of the jungle looking on the ancient stronghold, once an indomitable Spanish fortress, now a haven for those who have disrespected the code. The surrounding jungle had been hewn down and laid bare. His gaze quickly locked onto Hobbes scurrying into the city from Milt's left. Milt ducked back into the cover of the jungle. When it was clear, he moved steadfastly to an abandoned and crumbling rampart. Climbing the wall, he crawled over the top and jumped the short distance to the ground. He crept behind one of the buildings and stood flush against its rear façade. Sliding across the wall, Milt peered around the corner just in time to see Hobbes stumble into a large stone building across the street.

Milt darted into a nearby alcove just as a group of pirates sauntered by, heading north along the main path. They were laughing and stumbling along, sharing between them a bottle of rum, swigging mouthfuls at a time as the excess spilled down their cheeks. Once they passed and were a ways up the road, Milt moved discretely out of his hiding place.

"'Ey! Who a'you?" yelled a squeaky voice from behind him.

Milt turned and saw a spindly old man standing in the street.

"You stop right there!" he commanded.

Milt smiled and squared himself to the man. His eyes grew fierce. He stood tall and wide, strands of red hair blowing across his face.

The old pirate drew his rusty sword and started walking toward Milt with an air of authority that amused him. Milt stepped back into the recess between the buildings, baiting the old-timer to follow him. He slowly unsheathed his sword and held it with both hands at the ready. As the crooked old man closed in, Milt turned and swung his blade in a flash, dropping it like a hammer onto the pirate's outstretched arm. The blow knocked the pirate to the ground, cutting through his thin flesh like it was paper. Milt, his eyes black and fierce, stood over the dismembered man.

Bleeding, the old pirate hobbled on three limbs to grab his sword from the arm he lost, the hand still grasping the hilt. He pried the fingers away and climbed back up to his feet. Milt laughed at the spectacle. The old pirate rushed at him again letting out a pathetic yell. Milt parried his attack with ease and with his free hand grabbed the pirate by the throat lifting him from the ground. The old pirate dropped his sword and reached for Milt's hand cinched tightly around his neck. The pirate struggled to breathe, kicking his feet and clawing at Milt's fingers. His eyes bulged from his head.

"Let me help you along," Milt said, his face close enough to the old pirate's that he could smell his putrid breath.

Milt raised his sword and stuck it through the pirate's belly all the way to its hilt until the blade was sticking clear out of his back. Blood trickled off the polished steel. The man's life left his eyes almost immediately and Milt cast him aside into a crumpled heap. He turned and headed towards the stone structure Hobbes just recently entered. As he hurried across the street, another pirate cohort, a hodgepodge of men, turned at the intersection and were now face to face with Milt. Seeing their dead comrade's arm lying in the street, they quickly drew their swords and, without hesitation, charged. Milt met the first attacker, a short, stocky man who was surprisingly agile, with an onslaught of strength, clashing with the stocky man's sword with such a blow that it flew from the pirate's grip. Milt slashed at him, and the attacker's head followed his sword, spinning bodiless through the air. The body stood for a few seconds longer before collapsing to the ground.

Milt countered the thrusts from two more pirates with ease, parried a counterstrike, which struck down one of them, but the third pirate, a tall, muscular man whose scarred face had seen its share of violence, managed to slash a gash into Milt's thigh, bringing him to his knee. Milt winced and grabbed his leg. Sensing the kill, three more pirates rushed in, their eyes wide with bloodlust. Milt stood himself back up, spun away from a flanking pirate's attack and skewered him through the back. He pushed the victim off his blade with his foot and spun again slicing through a second pirate's stomach, spilling his insides as he fell to the ground.

A fourth pirate, obese and sweating profusely, stood out of breath a few yards away, staring down at his fallen companions and reevaluating his decisions. He looked back at Milt with dread in his eyes. The two men stared each other down, though the obese man was frozen with fear. Amidst all the commotion, another several dozen pirates had rallied to the noise, clearly not the stragglers Milt just battled with relative ease. Milt grinned, relishing the fight that was coming and the challenge from worthy opponents.

As the reinforcements lined up behind the lone, fat pirate, Milt let out a deafening roar. He raised his sword and charged. The obese man's eyes grew as wide as his belly as Milt lowered his shoulder and sent him flying back into the horde. Milt charged on. He slashed wildly, his sword high and glistening, bringing it down repeatedly upon them with a hammering force. The pirates, large and broad-shouldered, stood their ground as they were driven down, one by one.

THIRTY-NINE

"There," said Jiya, pointing as Chen turned the boat to port, allowing a wide berth as they sailed around the island.

Chen rounded the leeward side and tucked the boat into the gray light of a narrow canal hidden from sight by a forest of red mangrove trees. It zigzagged as it cut its way inland through the swamp. An overhanging canopy of tree limbs and interwoven palm fronds hung over the water providing more than enough concealment and just enough room for the small boat to glide under.

"The tide's on its way out," Ashton noticed.

"Everyone ready?" Jiya asked

"Do we have a choice?"

"Not a chance."

"You sure about this?" Ashton asked her.

"Nope."

Jiya leapt off the boat's bow and into the water swimming beneath the surface to avoid any possible detection. The others jumped in behind her. A large green sea turtle, looking for seagrass, swam by Jiya, and ever the opportunist, she grabbed its shell just behind the neck as it unwittingly transported her closer to shore leaving the other three in her wake. They waded through the shallows and, coming out of the surf, kept a low silhouette until they reached the underbrush at the edge of the crystalline sand.

"So far so good," said Ashton, peering through the foliage.

The growth on this end of the beach was relatively thin compared to the rest. Sago palms and driftwood dotted the shoreline. An arrow from their previous encounter was still lodged in the blistering hot sand farther down the beach.

"Let's go," Jiya whispered.

Chen filed in behind her and the other two behind him as they entered the tree line and hiked their way inland. When they arrived on the outskirts of the village, the place was deserted. Smoke billowed up from a pile of embers and charred logs in the center.

"It looks abandoned," Christian noted.

"Not entirely. Look," he said, motioning to a dog curled up in the dirt outside one of the huts.

She was trembling and filthy, tethered to a wooden stake in the ground by a rope barely long enough to allow her to stand. Ashton stepped out of concealment and walked brazenly into the village toward the dog.

"There's no one here," he said after a quick scan.

"Where could they have gone?" Jiya asked as she and the others walked into the clearing.

"This island is only so big," Christian added.

As they beheld the ruin of the village, they were amazed. The longhouse lay in a heap of pillars and planks charred black from the flames that, though languid, persisted. The other huts and structures were ransacked or destroyed.

Ashton cut the rope from the dog's neck. The dog jumped up, whimpered in excitement at her newfound freedom, and wagged her tail enthusiastically as she showered Ashton with gratitude and affection. He bent down to pet her head. Her tongue hung from her wide, smiling mouth. Jiya peeked inside one of the huts. The rear door had been hacked open. Blood had pooled on the floor next to the slain native and his wife. Jiya retreated solemnly back to the group.

"They're dead."

"What?"

"I think they were murdered," she said.

"Check the others," Ashton told them.

The dog loyally followed Ashton as he searched. When they finished, they reassembled in the center.

"All but four of the huts are now tombs," said Christian.

"Why are four of them empty?"

As if to answer his question, four warriors appeared out of the brush and surrounded them, arrows drawn on taut bows. The leader of the small group of survivors stepped forward and approached them.

"We should kill you where you stand," he threatened.

He had a stoic quality about him. A proud man still reeling with grief for his massacred family and tribesmen, yet his countenance remained firm and indifferent. Ashton recognized him as the lead warrior from their previous confrontation.

"We didn't do this. We came here to ask for your help," Ashton said somewhat hesitatingly with his arms in the air.

The dog whimpered and cowered behind him.

"Why should we help you. My family is slaughtered. My tribe is decimated. Your kind – pirates from your island – did this."

Rage consumed him. His chest heaved. He raised his hand, signaling his men to release their barrage of arrows upon them.

"Wait!" Ashton said holding his hands out in front of him. "I know who did this to your family, to your tribe. We're fighting them, too. We were hoping you could help us. We can give you the vengeance you seek."

"I don't think four's gonna cut it," Christian mumbled to Jiya.

The warrior lowered his hand. The others subsequently lowered their bows. He studied Ashton, trying to discern his true motives. Ashton kept his focus on the warrior, neither man breaking eye contact. Satisfied, he accepted Ashton's offer.

"We will help you. Help us care for our dead, then take us to your ship."

Ashton exhaled.

Funeral pyres were built for the slain tribespeople, and the few warriors who remained toiled for an hour ceremoniously preparing their bodies for the afterlife. When they were finished, one of the warriors touched fire to the kindling, starting a blaze that quickly came to life under their chieftain. As the flames grew, the warriors fashioned torches and began lighting the other pyres in the tradition of their people. They remained for a few hours longer until nothing was left but smoldering embers and ash.

Ashton called for the dog as the new alliance made its way back to the boat. The dog ceased her sniffing of a purple flower protruding from a nearby patch of grass and pranced happily over to Ashton's side.

"What will you call her?" asked Jiya.

"I'm not sure yet," he answered.

Agwe took one last look at the rubble and charred remains of his village before entering the forest.

When they reached the water, the dog stayed on the beach, too timid to enter the surf yet crying not to be left behind. Ashton turned and sweetly cajoled her to follow. She tested the water, wagging her tail and barking for help. Ashton walked back to her and picked her up, carrying her into the water. The dirt immediately washed off her fur, darkening the water around her. He held her close to him with one arm and bathed her with the other as her legs dangled beneath the surface. A golden-brown coat was slowly revealed. She had a black muzzle and white feet. The sun's light shone off her big brown eyes and Ashton spared no time deciding on her name.

"Amber," he called her.

He waded to the side of the boat and lifted her up to Christian who caringly lifted her over the side.

"It's ok, sweet girl. I've got you," Christian whispered to her.

He leaned back over the side and extended his hand to Ashton. Once everyone was aboard, Chen eased the boat backwards in the shallowing water and out of the mangrove canal.

"My people are no more, but their memory will carry us to victory," the chief warrior lamented.

"What's your name?" Ashton asked.

"Agwe," he responded. "It is my ancestral name. It means, 'Spirit of the Sea'."

"It's a beautiful name," Jiya said.

"I'm Ashton," he said, then proceeded to introduce the rest of the crew.

It was late afternoon when they finally returned to Shipwreck Island. They tied the boat off and clamored out one by one. Amber scampered to the beach and sniffed everything she could as she began exploring her new home.

"I don't think I've ever heard this place this quiet before," Jiya said.

"I'd pay money to keep it this way for just a night," Christian added. "I can't remember the last time I slept through an entire night without some ruckus waking me up."

Window shutters were latched tight and doors were locked as they walked cautiously through the streets of New Nassau. Amber hurried to Ashton's side, her tail dancing in the air behind her as she trotted along. As they passed the Green Turtle Tavern, a small boy rounded the corner, running past them in the opposite direction.

"Hey, kid," Christian said grabbing his arm.

The boy's legs flew into the air and twisted as he came crashing to the ground.

"Woah! Sorry about that. You gotta slow down, lad, or else you'll fly out of your own shoes."

The boy stood up and brushed the dust off his pants.

"Where is everyone?" Jiya asked him.

She knelt and wiped dirt from his cheek.

"They…they've gone. They left a few hours ago for the jungle."

The boy's eyes started to water.

"Hey, it's ok, don't be afraid. Where are you going?" she asked.

"I hate the jungle, so I'm gonna sail away!"

He jerked his arm away and Jiya quickly grabbed it again and straightened him up, looking at him with great care in her eyes.

"Listen, uh…"

"Davey," the kid told her.

"Davey, where are your parents?"

"My mother died when I was born, and my father is in the jungle with the others."

"I think your father is probably pretty worried right now that you've run away."

Davey wiped his eyes. A streak of tears having already cut a path through the dust on his face.

"He told me to stay here and hide."

"C'mon, stay with us and you'll be safe, ok? The jungle won't hurt you," she assured him.

Davey thought it over for a second and looked back over his shoulder at the water before he acquiesced. Jiya pushed his long dirty blonde hair off his face and put her arm around his boney shoulder as she led him into the tavern for a hot meal.

"I could eat, too," Christian announced.

Inside the tavern, Jiya fixed them up a hearty meal. When she brought out the food, Amber waited patiently under the table for a morsel. Ashton gave her a large turkey leg and she walked off with it and lay down by the bar indulging herself in her treat.

"Eat up," Jiya said to the group. "You can get your own ale."

They laughed and relaxed, each enjoying the company of their new friends. As night drew on, they continued their merriment and drank and told stories, listening to Ashton tell many tales of his coworkers back home, which were met with roaring bouts of laughter.

"We can sit here all night and into the next morning carrying on like we are, but we need to start thinking about what happens next. Tew is out there. His camp is growing restless," Jiya said when the joviality settled down.

Ashton finished his last swig of ale and wiped the froth from his mouth.

"She's right. We need to come up with a plan. Milt is out there, too, somewhere in the jungle, and for all his merit and mirth and myriad traits, good or bad, he can't take them all on alone."

"What do you suggest, Ashton," asked Agwe.

The warrior, his torso clad in sky blue paint, stood over Ashton, glaring at him, awaiting his direction.

Ashton pushed his chair back from the table and walked away from the group, rubbing his chin. Amber watched him intently. He paused near the door looking out onto the street.

"I have an idea. Jiya, I'll need your help."

"Great," she said. "What do you have in mind? Something that'll work, I hope."

Amber, realizing Ashton wasn't leaving the tavern, turned her attention back to the bone that had been thoroughly stripped of meat.

"I, too, have a strategy," Christian said drunkenly. "Let's summon our dead compatriots from the shallow earth and the deepest seas and fight Tew and his bastard army with a zombie army of our own!"

"Or how about we tunnel under the city, pile explosives underneath it, and blow it up in one fell motion from the comfort of our beds," said another.

"…or the bar!"

Cheers erupted as mugs were thrust into the air.

"Great ideas! And I can give a call to my billionaire friend who likes to wear costumes at night and fight crime!" Ashton added.

The group sat silent, not understanding the reference.

Realizing it was fruitless to explain, Ashton moved on and spoke to the group.

"I think it's time I showed you something."

FORTY

Hobbes hurried up to the commotion that had stirred on the streets of Libertalia. Upon arriving at the scene and seeing Milt bruised and beaten, kneeling before a pile of broken bodies, he puffed out his chest and strutted with a swagger in his step. He laughed at Milt's predicament, savoring a victory in which he had no part. Milt raised his eyes with a look of disdain.

Coward.

A small contingent of the surviving pirates stood him up and marched him through the streets, kicking up dust as they shuffled along, cheering and openly calling for a public execution. They dragged him, barely able to walk and weary from exhaustion and blood loss, at a pace too unforgiving for his tired body.

When they passed a large, manicured stone building next to a dilapidated wooden apothecary guarding the entrance to a wide town square, two large, barrel-chested pirates gripped Milt's arms and hoisted him onto a crudely constructed platform. The sharpened edge of a sword's blade was pressed against his neck. A trickle of blood ran down his chest. His face was battered and bloodied, his red hair hung dark and matted over his eyes. When he saw Hobbes, he raised his head and smiled. He spit blood at Hobbes's feet as the fat pirate approached him.

Hobbes stood in front of Milt and grabbed his jaw, studying his face. Milt locked eyes with him and summoned the strength to stand, towering over Hobbes with a menacing stare. Hobbes let go of his face and after a few short seconds of adrenaline-fueled fear, hatred and rage overcame him. He clinched his fists until his knuckles were white, then stepped forward and delivered a striking blow to Milt's cheek.

Hobbes winced and shook his hand, working the pain from his fingers. Milt's icy eyes glinted through loosely hanging strands of hair as he let out a blood curdling laugh that boomed all around them. Surprised, the pirates looked around at one another searching for direction on how to handle the auspicious situation. A cold wind blew into the square. An imposing figure stepped from the building and into the sunlight, a deep scar across his torso.

"Hello, Henry."

Milt stood steadfast, still gripped at the arms, his legs shaking under the weight of his own body.

"Tom. What's it been? 300 years?"

Tew moved closer.

"I've waited and suffered a long time for this moment."

Milt gestured a sniff.

"I can smell the rot on you."

Tew reached out his hand and grabbed Milt by the throat.

"It's my time now, like it should've been so many years ago. You took that from me. Allow me to return the favor."

Milt clinched his jaw and strained his neck against Tew's tightening grip. Tew's eyes were flaming fiercely, his intensity mounting with each breath Milt took as they numbered nearer to his last. As Tew felt the life exiting Milt's body, Milt summoned his remaining strength and ripped himself away from the arms of his captors and stood in defiance within an inch of Tew's ethereal face. Tew's hand snapped back to grip Milt's throat.

"Give my regards to the witch," Tew uttered with the sinister smile of one who is anticipating victory.

Milt's face turned red, his veins pulsed, the muscles in his neck bulged.

"Call me…Milt!"

He gripped Tew's wrist and pried his old nemesis's hand away. Tew's fingers feverishly clawed at Milt's neck. The stalemate continued until Milt slowly separated himself. He let out a roar and brought his fist down upon Tew's collar bone. Tew collapsed to his knees under the brunt force.

"Perhaps this time I'll take your head off your body and ensure you never return."

Three pirates rushed Milt and attempted to restrain him. He let out another earth-trembling yell and grabbed the nearest pirate's sword from its scabbard and hit its owner on the head with the hilt. The pirate stood dazed, and Milt plunged the blade through his heart. Another pirate reached for his own sword. Before his hand touched the hilt, Milt swung his blade and sliced open the pirate's chest. A scrawny, jaunt man attempted the same and as he thrust his sword, Milt parried easily and slashed him deep across his abdomen, spilling his bowels. Tew took advantage of the confusion and slunk back into the shadows.

After Tew vanished almost as quickly as he had appeared, Milt stood alone and turned to face down the rest of his would-be captors who stood in awe at the speed and power Milt exhibited. Some of them took off for the jungle while the majority stood, shaking, with swords drawn and pointed at Milt as they slowly moved to encircle him. Milt's left hand was pressed against a wound suffered on the side of his abdomen.

Milt backed up defensively, anticipating the encirclement. He lifted his left hand to his mouth and licked the blood from his fingers. He roared at the group of pirates like a demon-possessed chimera. He felt himself returning to his old ways, a feeling he long searched for and took comfort in. Almost on cue, thunder rolled in the distance and a darkness rapidly approached with wrath riding upon its shoulders.

FORTY-ONE

Amber lay napping at Ashton's feet, finding solace and comfort in the company of her new master. A candle burned low in a pool of wax in the center of the round table as it flickered in the dark, casting shadows across their faces in the late hours of the night. One of the pirates lit a cigar, the tip burned a bright glowing orange as wisps of smoke surrounded his face and slowly rose to the ceiling. He laid the matchbook on the table. Ashton reached under his shirt and pulled the amulet from around his neck, placing it next to the candle.

"I've heard of that thing. Tew's been lookin' fer it!" erupted one of them in disbelief.

"And you've 'ad dat dis whole time, 'ave you?" another angrily chided as he threw his chair back and stood over the table glowering at Ashton.

"If Tew's been looking for it, why didn't you tell us you had it?" Jiya asked as she leaned forward in her chair.

Ashton remained silent, staring down at the amulet, as did Agwe, who stood a few steps behind those sitting around the table.

"Ashton," Christian prodded.

"That amulet supposedly holds magical properties," Jiya said. "It's the source of Tew's strength."

"How do you know that?" Ashton asked suspiciously.

"It doesn't matter. If it's helping Tew stay alive, we have to destroy it," she said.

"I know," Ashton acknowledged. "I tried destroying it the night I found it, after you were asleep. I went outside and tried smashing it with rocks, throwing it against the tavern wall. Nothing worked. So, I decided the next best thing was to keep it close to me."

"What does the inscription say?" Christian asked.

"I have no idea," Ashton admitted. "Look, I've never been much of anything in my life and now, here I am, in possession of this powerful relic and fighting to reclaim Libertalia, a place that for me didn't exist until just a few days ago, and still doesn't for the rest of the world."

Ashton stood abruptly and walked to one of the open plantation windows. Amber perked up in curiosity then lay her head back down on her paw and went back to sleep. The moon was rising in the clear sky, illuminating the mountain peaks below it. Jiya walked over to him and put her arm on his shoulder.

"It's beautiful, isn't it," she said, trying to calm him down.

"The second most beautiful thing I've ever seen," he answered.

He looked at her and put his forehead against hers.

"I never asked for this. I never wanted this. But after coming here, after meeting you, this is where I want to be."

Jiya smiled.

"Eventually, though, you know I'll have to go back," he told her.

"I know."

A soft thunder rolled in the near distance. He wrapped his arm around her waist and held her close.

"No matter what happens, I'll never forget our nights together, especially that first night at the waterfall," he told her.

Jiya blushed, "and afterwards."

Ashton smiled.

"Wait, that's it! The waterfall!" he suddenly realized.

"What do you mean?"

"At the waterfall. The river that ran through the mountain."

"The Río Alma?"

He took a moment to ponder his epiphany.

"I think I know where it leads," he said, excitement rising in his voice.

"Where?"

"C'mon," he grabbed her hand and returned to the table.

"Now that you guys are done having a moment, can we get back to figuring out our next move?" Agwe insisted without emotion.

"Listen. There's an underground river, not far from here. Some of you may know of it. The trail that leads from the south end of New Nassau into the jungle takes you to a waterfall near the top of that mountain," Ashton said pointing to the peak silhouetted in the window frame.

"Aye, Caiman Falls. We all know it," spoke one of the men.

"That river, the Río Alma, runs to the other end of the island. It'll bring us a little closer to Castillo de Luna, and, more importantly, it'll bring us there undetected from a direction they won't expect," Ashton explained.

"How do you know this?" Jiya asked him.

"You'll just have to trust me."

"So, the blind leading the blind, then. What else have we got to lose at this point," said Christian.

"My man!" Ashton said, enthusiastically slamming his hand on the table. "Grab your gear – weapons, water, whatever you need, but travel light."

The men threw back what drink remained in their cups and leapt from their chairs, scrambling out of the tavern. Ashton turned to Jiya and put his hand on her arm, feeling her soft skin.

"You should stay here, but I know you won't."

"Bullshit I'm staying here. I'm coming along."

"I figured. Promise me you'll keep yourself safe, no matter what happens when we reach Libertalia."

She winked at him and pulled a flintlock pistol from behind the bar. Tucking it into her waistband, she walked upstairs.

"You coming?" she said without turning around.

"I'll be up soon. Milt offered me a sword earlier. I think I'll go get it. Might come in handy."

Ashton now stood alone in the center of the tavern with Amber sitting patiently by his side.

"Don't go gettin' in her way!" a strange but familiar voice said.

Ashton looked behind him. Agwe was seated in a darkened corner busy sharpening his knife and arrowheads. Another roll of thunder rumbled in the distance as the rain started to fall on the island. Amber whimpered and stood between Ashton's legs. Ashton turned back around and saw the blind old man with his toothless grin.

"Where do you keep coming from?"

Pierre St. Croix pointed to his eyes, "You keep an eye on her," he said then scampered off.

Ashton looked down at his glass, his hand was trembling. He let out a sigh and swallowed the last bit in a heaping gulp. He set it empty on the table and grabbed the matchbook sitting next to burning cigar butt.

Outside, a cool wind blew through the streets as a rain fell softly, but steadily. Dark storm clouds encircled the island, obscuring the moon. The wind was picking up. Ashton's muscles were aching as he made his way up to Milt's villa with Amber trotting faithfully beside him. He pushed open the door letting in a draft that whistled through the corridors. He shut the door behind him and walked into the Grand Hall dripping wet, pondering the impending events, hoping his plan wasn't as foolhardy as it sounded in his mind. A lone torch burned, it's light flickering off the walls.

"Now where's that sword?" he mumbled as he began looking around the room.

A noise from out front startled his senses. The hair on the back of his neck stood erect. Goosebumps pocked his arms. He heard the noise again, a rustling, feet moving. He ran to the window but saw nothing but shadows, edges blurring together.

In an instant, two figures leapt out from their concealment in the bushes. Two stones came flying through the windows, shattering glass about the floor. Two men climbed through in a rush. Ashton was caught flat-footed. Precious seconds were squandered. He turned to run, but just as he did, one of the intruders hooked his fingers in the collar of Ashton's shirt and yanked him backwards. The second man lowered his shoulder and drove Ashton into the piano and knocking the breath out of him. He crawled to the staircase. Amber bit down on the man's arm. He threw her off, her teeth tearing his flesh. Ashton propped himself up on his elbow as both men jumped on top of him. Amber leapt back up, unfazed, and chomped down on the right leg of the man nearest to her. He let out a scream and let go of Ashton.

"Hey!"

The men turned to see Christian standing in the doorway. Lightning cracked behind him illuminating his silhouette. One of the assailants grabbed the leather cord hanging around Ashton's neck and yanked the amulet away as he dashed out of the shattered window. Ashton struggled to his knees, shaken but otherwise unhurt.

"You're dead!" Christian yelled as the assailant scampered back into the jungle.

While their attention was fixed on the escaping man, the other managed to flee through the front door. Christian returned to Ashton at the foot of the staircase and helped him into the Grand Hall.

"Good girl," Ashton huffed as his breath slowly returned. He gave Amber a rub behind the ears.

"They really got you good," Christian said. "You alright?"

"Yeah," Ashton sputtered, wiping blood from his nostrils.
"What happened?"
"I don't know," he said. "It happened so fast."
"Did you recognize them?"
"No."
"We'll find 'em, whoever they are, and we'll finish this so you can get back to your vacation."

Ashton leaned forward, slouching over and looking at the ground. He took a breath and turned his head to look at Christian.

"It's too late for that," he said. "Tew will have that amulet by daybreak."

He stood himself up, "Get ready and meet me back here like we planned."

"You're in no condition…."

"Don't say that to me. This has to get done." Ashton shrugged off the pain and limped towards the door. "And don't tell the others what happened."

"Aye, not a word."

"Stay here, girl," Ashton said softly to Amber with a pat on her head.

Ashton left Christian and disappeared into the shadows of the villa. Amber watched him leave then walked over to the carpet in front of the fireplace and curled up for a nap. His footsteps echoed through the halls. In the back of the house a parrot cawed. Ashton walked down to the cellar, carefully descended its slick, stone steps. The air was damp and stale.

Remembering the matchbook in his pocket, he lit the torch in front of the door. The flame grew, licking the air and dancing on the walls, glistening off the moisture that covered the stones. Ahead of Ashton stood the heavy wooden door. He was still taken aback at the scratches and blood that defiled it. Ashton tugged on the iron ring, rusted and bolted into the wood, and heaved the door open. He stood for a moment staring into the dark room. The musty smell was strong, and he grimaced with

each inhalation of the foul stench. The room was cloaked in shadow. The sword he saw earlier, resting in the chest, was no longer there.
Dammit.

FORTY-TWO

The two men who had ambushed Ashton reached Castillo de Luna without stopping, per their orders upon leaving. Hobbes awaited them at the portico of a large building buttressed against a sheer limestone cliff at the far western end of the ancient fortress-city. They fell at his feet panting, exhausted and thirsty. Hobbes peered down at them with his hands tucked in his pockets.

"Well?" he asked. "Did you get it?"

One of the men looked up and spoke in between breaths.

"It…took us…all night…but…we found him…."

"And…," Hobbes urged them on.

The other man held up the amulet without a word.

"He practically gave it to us," the other said with a grin, having caught his breath. "One of the others came behind us, the big one, but we got away with no problems."

"No problems?" Hobbes said. "He saw ya!" He turned to look at the second man, "and he busted you up pretty good. He knows who you are, and he knows you came 'ere! I told ya not to be seen and to be quick about it! Idiots."

The two men looked at each other incredulously.

"Aye, you did tell us that, but we're the only other ones on the island. He would've come figured out we came here of his own accord."

"You at least killed the newcomer?"

"Not quite," one of them said with hesitation.

Hobbes let out a yell of frustration, unsheathed his sword with his right hand and stabbed the man who made the comment through the chest. With his left hand he pulled out his flintlock pistol and shot the other.

"Clean this up," he ordered two bystanders.

The two obsequious men scurried over and hoisted the lifeless bodies onto their shoulders and carried them off. Hobbes looked down at the amulet, studying it as it lay in his hand. His eyes were transfixed on the beautiful color and the markings that adorned it. Looking for Tew, he stepped into a room blacker than the night. He looked around, widening his eyes and urging them to adjust. A pair of glowing red beads rushed forward out of the darkness.

"Give it to me," Tew hissed.

Hobbes placed the amulet in his hand.

Tew began speaking under his breath, unintelligible to Hobbes's ears. Then the ground rumbled and dust fell from the ceiling. Hobbes ran for the door. The darkness spread, exerting immense force against the walls, sending cracks running through the foundation. Hobbes ran into the street and spun back around in time to witness the spectacle. The rumbling intensified. A light emanated from within the room, temporarily blinding those standing outside as they threw up their arms to shield their eyes from the radiant bursts of energy. Air was sucked into the house before all suddenly went quiet and a final burst blew those standing outside off their feet.

No longer fearful of death, a tall man, muscular and scarred, stood in the threshold. He was impeccably dressed. He was a handsome man with a well-structured face. A scar cut from his forehead to the top of his left eye, splitting his eyebrow in two. Another scar, much deeper, ran down his right cheek and across his neck.

"Captain," Hobbes said with profound respect, falling to one knee and graveling. Sweat poured from his head. Fear mixed with excitement, fear of his old master and excitement for the return of days long passed.

"All's been prepared. The island is yers fer the takin', my king," Hobbes stuttered.

Tew ignored him and walked across the street into a large storage house. It was a tall, two-storied wooden structure that offered views above the trees down to the eastern beaches. The men on the street were mesmerized by what had just transpired, not believing their eyes. Fear spread through the new stronghold like a plague. They all looked to Hobbes for direction for none dared approach Tew and risk his latent power. Hobbes ran in front of Tew's path and timidly pulled the large doors open. Tew walked up the stairs, followed obediently by Hobbes, and stood over a table, a bottle of rum and a stone laying on the topmost corners of an unrolled map. Studying intensely the contours of the island, he spoke to Hobbes without raising his head.

"The first time I landed here, chasing that lucky, inept bastard, Avery, I was arrogant and impatient," he said. "I won't make that mistake a second time."

Hobbes didn't respond.

"Where is he?" Tew demanded.

"I d-don't know, cap'm," Hobbes answered. "He murdered some of my men just out there in the street, then he vanished."

"You mean he escaped?" Tew corrected him.

Hobbes hesitated. Tew snarled and slammed his fist on the solid oaken table. The bottle of rum bounced and swayed precariously before settling still.

"He's still here. Find him!" Tew ordered.

Hobbes backpedaled then turned, leaping down the stairs. A large hand flew into his path and snagged him just as he exited the storage house.

"What's happenin' in dere?" the hulking man demanded.

Hobbes was confronted by a small group of swarthy pirates.

"Let go of me if you know what's good fer ya," he said.

The man released his grip on Hobbes. He was an imposing figure, but simple in mind, traits Hobbes valued in those he sought for his crew, strong but incapable of challenging his authority. Confident in his ability to sway them as he was so apt to do in the past, he folded his arms and let them speak their minds.

"Some of us ain't so sure bringing him back to life was such a good idea," one of the pirates said.

Amidst the grumbling from the crowd, Paul Lime muscled his way to the front, pushing men out of the way like ragdolls. Hobbes's eyes widened. His arms dropped to his side.

"I don't much care for you or Tew. I want the little one. I want to crush his bones into dust. You give me that or I'm coming for you instead," Lime demanded pointing his thick finger in Hobbes's face.

Lime stood close enough for Hobbes to feel his warm breath.

"Fine," he acquiesced, a slight tremble in his body.

Lime huffed condescendingly, with a mocking smirk on his crooked face. He shook his head and strutted off.

"This a fool's errand now," another said in heavily accented English after Lime departed. "I fight for a cause I can get behind. But dis? We goin' to our graves brudders."

"What's done is done," Hobbes said. "We'll be takin' back this island in no time and reclaiming its glory. If you ain't with us, feel free to leave. But there ain't nowhere for you to go, and when we do win and kill all them mutineers, we'll be comin' fer you, too."

"You? What power do you have to stop us, you fat pig," another said defiantly, standing in front of the group.

Hobbes pulled a second flintlock pistol from his belt and fired. The pirate fell dead, smoke rising from the hole in his chest. Hobbes reloaded both firearms and aimed them indiscriminately at the cohort.

"Anyone else have words they'd like to say?"

No pirate spoke a sound.

"That's what I thought."

He ordered two random pirates to clear the corpse from the road.

"I don' like dis one bit," one said as Hobbes walked quickly away from the scene. "I can feel it."

"Feel what?" his buddy asked him.

"Tew," he said. He turned somberly to the other. "I'm tellin' ya, soon his vengeance is gonna manifest itself in a terrible panoply of death an' destruction."

"Wha' does panoply mean?"

"Maybe if ya 'ad an ed-u-ca-tion, you'd know what panoply means," he answered with a roll of his eyes

"I'm serious!"

"It means shit's about to get real bad 'round 'ere real quick like."

"No shit. I didn't need no schoolin' word to tell me that."

"Oh, shut up."

They dug a shallow ditch near the outer wall and dropped the bleeding body into it.

"When I give the signal, we're gon' jump through the collapsed part of the wall there."

"Aye."

They shoveled the last bit of dirt on top of the grave. When the coast was clear, he motioned to his buddy.

"C'mon!"

The two of them scurried over the wall, across the open ground that had been cleared of jungle, and into the trees. When they found the jungle road, they headed north. Paul Lime, on the other hand, walked past the two guards at the main gated entrance.

Speaking to his counterpart the younger guard asked, "Aren't we s'posed to stop 'em from leavin'?"

"I don't think so, mate. Just make sure no one comes in is all," the senior guard answered.

"Right."

Still curious, the younger asked, "Where you supposin' he's headin'?"

"Feel free to ask him."

The younger guard stood silent and watched as Lime headed south towards the old docks near the rocks at Horseshoe Point.

FORTY-THREE

When the two deserters arrived in New Nassau, the town was quiet. An eerie calm washed through the streets. Creaking wooden signs hung from their wrought iron chains, swaying in the wind. A cheer arose from inside a shanty nestled in the shadow of the looming villa on the hill above it. A single light flickered, and the two men made their way towards the sound.

"So, we have a plan then. It's settled, yeah?" asked Ashton.

"Aye, we have a plan!" arose an emphatic affirmation.

"San ren yi tiaoxin, huang tu biancheng jing," chimed Chen.

"Yeah, whatever he said," Christian uttered.

The two deserting pirates burst through the loosely secured door, busting the wooden latch. Eager to escape any outside prying eyes, the force of the two men running shoulder first through the door splintered it from its hinges. The group grabbed their swords and in the blink of an eye had them pointed at the throats of the two pirates sprawled on the floor.

"Who are you?" Ashton demanded as Amber sniffed the unwelcomed guests.

"We just came from Libertalia," one of the men answered.

"Yeah, we don't want no part of that evil. And we ain't the only ones leavin' neither," the other added.

"What do you mean leaving? How many?"

"No tellin'."

"So, you saw you had a losing hand and decided to jump ship and join the winning side?" Ashton asked incredulously.

"I wouldn't exactly put it like that."

"They're spies," Agwe warned.

"No! We ain't no spies. It ain't like that. We want to fight, just against Tew."

Ashton glowered at them.

"Milt's there now."

"How do you know this?"

"We saw him. He put up a helluva fight and managed to escape, but then…," they broke off.

"Then?"

"They put up a search and cornered him. He had his own pile of bodies, but no one man can't take on fifty."

"Lower your swords," Ashton commanded. "Agwe, lower your bow."

"We gotta go now!" Christian bellowed, infuriated.

He marched over to the pirate who shared the ill news and grabbed him by the throat, lifting him effortlessly off the ground, and pinned him against the wall.

"I should skewer you and leave you hanging here on this wall," he threatened.

"Christian," Ashton said. "Put him down. I want to hear what else he has to say."

The pirate dropped to the floor, rubbing his neck and coughing.

"Well? Speak or perhaps I will let my friend turn you both into wall ornaments."

"There's a separate path that leads from Gibbet Pass to the western side of Libertalia."

"That path runs into one of the main gates," Jiya countered.

"Aye, and you'll be seen coming from that way. But as you know, the only way to get overland to the other side of the island is to pass right by it. It can't be done."

Ashton took a step toward the two men who instinctively cowered.

"You're coming with us. Lead us astray or into an ambush, and I'll personally guarantee your deaths."

"Yes, of course," they answered in unison, hands folded, pleading for their lives.

"Ephialtes would be proud," Ashton said to them with sarcasm as thick as their cowardice.

Turning back to the group, he said, "We need to hurry this plan along, given the change in circumstances. We set off for Caiman Falls in five minutes."

"Davey, stay here with Amber," Jiya instructed the young boy.

Davey walked next to the dog and knelt by her side, petting her back.

Ashton knelt and took Amber's face in his hands. "You stay here, girl, and keep guard. We'll be right back."

Amber wagged her tail and licked his hands. She watched as Ashton walked outside and closed the door behind him with a tap on the door to let her know he was still there. The group stood out front ready to move. The two deserters were kept in the center of the file as Ashton led them south past Milt's villa and into the jungle.

Davey came sprinting up to Jiya.

"What are you doing here? I told you to stay back. It's too dangerous!"

"I want to help find my mom and dad," he replied defiantly.

"Fine. Come on and stay with me, and keep quiet," she instructed.

Ashton moved them forward at a blistering pace. The line began to stretch, but they made it to the Falls, tired but motivated. Agwe, fleet footed as any of them stayed on Ashton's heels the whole way, remaining a step behind for no reason other than his unfamiliarity with the terrain.

Ashton came to the precipice of the cliff, the same one which he and Jiya jumped off several nights before. He pulled out the tattered map Milt had given him back at Alonzo's and studied the scribbles on the back of the parchment. Jiya looked over his shoulder. The echo of the waterfall surrounded them.

"Do you know what these lines are?" Ashton asked her.

"Not a clue," she replied.

"Milt gave me this map on the day we met. I had no idea what it was or why he gave it to me, but now, it makes sense."

"How do you mean," Jiya asked.

"It's a map of the waterways that run under the island. The mouth of the river flows into that cave right there," he explained pointing at the base of the waterfall, a blot at the bottom of the paper. "This line here," he ran his finger up the thickest scribble emanating from the ink blot, "I'm betting is Río Alma."

"Then what are we waiting for?" she asked as she ran down the hill to the pool's edge.

Thankful not to be jumping, Ashton followed her down.

FORTY-FOUR

Most of the pirate cohort that had cornered Milt lay lifeless and crumpled atop one another in a gruesome pile of death. The blood of his enemies was splattered on his chest and clothes. Tew was his target now. He marched towards the storage house, none daring to challenge him as they watched him pass.

Thomas Tew, pacing in the empty room with the amulet hanging securely around his neck, waited, calculating his next move against his old adversary. He stopped mid-step. Staring at the wall, a smile smirked across his face.

"It's been a long time, my friend," Tew said without turning around.

"A long time, indeed," Milt replied standing tall at the opposite end of the room.

Sunlight poured in over Milt's shoulders from the louvered window above him. Tew stepped into the light as the two pirate titans faced each other once more. Milt held his old sword, glistening and sharp, down by his side, the muscles in his arm were tense. His grip was strong, and his venous muscles bulged. Tew stood coolly in the middle of the storage house, his arms behind his back.

"Still hideously ugly I see," Milt remarked.

Tew laughed. He grabbed his sword off the table.

"Allow me to offer you the fate you more than deserve," Tew said as he raised his sword.

"Allow me to finish what I started," Milt answered.

The two men clashed. Their swords sparked on contact as steel pressed against steel.

FORTY-FIVE

Ashton and his men stood on the shore of the turquoise pool at Caiman Falls.

"I don't know what to expect once inside," Ashton admitted to the group. "But it's our only shot. Stay close and keep an eye out for those gators."

Ashton led the group around the pool and behind Caiman Falls with the darkness beckoning them. Ashton unfolded the map and looked at it.

"I need some light."

Christian held aloft a torch he had fashioned back in New Nassau. He lit the oil-soaked cloth with one of the matches from Ashton's matchbook. It blazed to life lighting all around them. The light shimmered off golden and silvery veins in the stone that sprawled along the walls and stretched far back into the mountain. Ashton, focused on the task that lay before him, studying the map's lines in the glow of the fire. Christian stood behind him.

"Tip of the spear, eh mate?"

Ashton smiled and gave Christian a pat on the shoulder.

"Follow me," Ashton said beginning the trek into the depths of the island.

They filed behind him, walking cautiously into the unknown. Chen brought up the rear with Jiya and Davey just in front of him. They walked slowly and tightly together as the light from Christian's torch lit their path. The river rolled quickly beside them, guiding them along their route. They came across the first tunnel junction where the river forked. Ashton took a minute to look at the scribbled map and pointed confidently to the right, maintaining their direction of travel.

FORTY-SIX

The journey was tenuous, but Ashton and his group managed to quicken the pace by a half-step as he led them through the twists and turns of the cave's tunnels, across narrow ledges and slippery rocks. Ashton could only guess how long they had been trekking underground. He stopped suddenly.

"What do you think?" Ashton asked.

"We're going to have to crawl under," Christian told him.

Ashton thought for a second. He pulled out a small knife and wiped some of the flaming oil onto the blade and tossed it under a ledge in the rock, the opening barely two feet high. The flaming knife lit up the other side, revealing a small tunnel.

"If we can get through to the other side, we should be able to continue our course," Ashton said.

"I'm in," Christian said.

"Jiya," Ashton called back. "Bring Davey up here."

"Davey," Ashton said when he arrived. "I don't know how much space is on the other side, so I need you to crawl through this hole and let me know what's there. Can you do that for me?"

"That's easy," he said.

He dove through the hole before Ashton could respond and scurried on his belly to the other side.

"It's another tunnel," he yelled back. "It's small, I think you'll have to crouch. And there's a river, but it's smaller than the one on the other side and moving really fast."

"Thank you, Davey. Now come on back so we can see you. We don't want you getting too far ahead of us."

Davey scampered under the rock and back to Jiya's side.

"Nice job, Davey," she said with a high five.

"Which way does the main river lead?" Christian asked.

Ashton looked at the map.

"According to this, it bends off to the west and joins this branch here. See?" Ashton said pointing to the map. "Milt was thorough, there's no debating that, but the Rio Alma heads off in the wrong direction, so it doesn't matter."

Ashton put the map away and low crawled his way through the small opening to the other side. Christian stayed behind with the torch and ushered the others through. After Chen slid his skinny frame under the ledge, Christian handed the torch to him and lowered himself flat on the stone floor, squeezing his large frame through the hole.

"Little help here," he said as he wiggled his muscular torso.

Agwe and the stronger of the two deserters each grabbed an arm and pulled. The deserter's grip slipped, and he fell backwards knocking Jiya and Davey into the rushing river along with the torch, extinguishing the flame. The small burning knife was now their only source of light. Christian popped out on the other side, his back scratched and bleeding, and feverishly joined in on the rescue attempt of Jiya and Davey. Jiya managed to wedge her hand in a small crag and was quickly hoisted out of the water as the river carried Davey quickly away.

"Yell, kid!" Ashton shouted into the darkness.

Muffled cries echoed through the small tunnel. Ashton hurried haphazardly ahead with the small flame, running along the smooth rock surface, racing the river as he chased Davey's cries through the bends and turns. The rest of the group had no light amongst themselves. The faint glow from the light Ashton carried was their only guide. Davey's cries, to Ashton's horror, were diminishing until they suddenly stopped and could be heard no more. Ashton ran a few more steps before slowing to a stop and listened intently for any sounds of Davey. The group closed in behind him, bumping into Ashton as they stumbled forward.

"Easy," he admonished.

"Sorry, Ashton," Christian said. "We can't see shit."

"I can't hear him anymore," Ashton bemoaned.

Jiya approached and put her hand on his shoulder.

"You did all you could."

Ashton lowered his head.

"It was me that knocked him into the river, and for that I am…," the deserter began.

"Quiet," Ashton interrupted.

He tilted his ear down the river. "Do you hear that?"

"Hear what?" Christian asked.

"That sound. It's an echo," Ashton said and began following the river again. "C'mon, Davey may be in whatever space it's coming from!"

The group walked as quickly as they could over the slick surface. The river's rate of flow was increasing, splashing the rocks, making them more slippery than before. A faint roar arose up ahead as a white glow began to materialize. They hurried onward. The light was getting brighter and brighter. Now they could finally see in front of them. They came upon a ledge, and beyond it, an expansive cavern. Shallow pools peppered the cavern floor beneath them. The river they had been following fed lazily out through a large opening in the rock face of the cavern leading out into Halfmoon Bay. Half the cavern housed a great reservoir. Looming tall in front of them, half-submerged and silhouetted against the brightness of the outside, was a large, wooden ship, its masts splintered and hull damaged. Its sails lay in tatters across the deck and nearby rocks.

"*Fancy*," Jiya said to herself in utter disbelief. "This must be Pirate's Landing. We've made it to the opposite end of the island!"

The group stared at the wrecked schooner with awe and reverence.

"Hey guys! Look what I found!" a high-pitched voice hollered from below.

"Davey!" Ashton cried. He and the rest of the group slid down the rock surface and rushed to greet the child. "Are you ok?"

"I'm fine, but I'm little wet. Look at these awesome ships!"

"Ships?"

"Yeah, there's another one floating behind that one!"

Ashton hugged the kid and made his way to the careened vessel.

"Christian, come with me," he then said.

The two of them climbed through a gaping hole in the thick wooden hull and into the belly of the ship. Light glistened off its brilliant cargo.

"That's a lot of treasure," Christian noted.

Knowing what else lay secure under the mansion, Ashton only added, "Indeed."

"Probably best to keep this between us for now," Christian advised. "I don't trust those two scumbags; deserters don't have much character. And we still have a fight waiting for us. Don't need any more distractions. Once we've won, we'll split this money amongst everyone and rebuild Libertalia."

"What's in the ship?" Davey asked when they returned.

"We'll need to come back and finish looking. Right now, we need to keep moving."

They walked around the treasure-laden vessel and beheld the second ship resting next to the *Fancy* but in a perfect state of repair.

"Must be Tew's ship," Ashton surmised.

Ashton led the group past the vessels and out of the massive cavern towards the tiny beach on the east side of the entrance. The sun warmed their faces as the bay lapped the diminutive shore. They began their climb upwards. The cliffside trail meandered sideways above a swirling tide. They hugged the rocky face as the waves crashed against the sharp rocks below them.

"Don't look down. Just keep moving."

They inched their way along the ledge, climbing towards the grassy plain above them.

"There you are, you mutinous knave," a booming voice yelled just as Ashton reached the top.

A behemoth of a man raced towards him.

"Lime," Christian uttered in disgust as he leapt up just behind Ashton and drew his weapon.

"No," Ashton commanded. "He wants me. This fight's mine."

"You can't beat him," Christian warned.

"I'm not backing down from this clown."

Christian handed him his sword. Ashton readied himself. Lime lunged. Ashton parried his sword, but Lime was too fast, too strong, and both men went careening off the cliff and into the waters below, barely missing the rocks. The others, still climbing, watched in dismay.

The group made their way to the top as fast as they could and peered back over the edge. Christian couldn't help but regret letting Ashton face Paul Lime alone. He looked on helplessly as Ashton crawled onto the sandy beach, spitting up saltwater and fatigued from fighting the raging surf. Lime, enraged and murderous, raced out of the surf after him. Ashton stumbled forward and maneuvered back into Pirate's Landing and into the shadows.

Lime lurched forward, stepping cautiously. He grinned menacingly anticipating his kill as he entered Pirate's Landing. A game of predator and prey. His sword was lost to the sea when he fell. Both men were unarmed. Paul Lime preferred it that way. It was more natural to kill with one's hands.

Ashton slunk back into a small alcove. His heel knocked a resting pile of bones. The skeleton collapsed in a heap. Ashton winced at the noise. He slunk back farther, holding his breath. His heart rate pounded in his ears. A shadow appeared, creeping along the uneven surface, followed by its owner. He had a look on his face that savored the hunt. Lime peered into the alcove and gave a sinister laugh, his eyes bulging.

"This was almost too easy. Perhaps I should give you a chance to escape, let you run, make this a little more interesting," he said with a lick of his lips.

Ashton said nothing.

Lime cracked his knuckles. Ashton took up a defensive posture, his hands raised before him. Lime stepped slowly towards him, but Ashton rushed forward and delivered a blow to Lime's chin. His hand felt as if he had punched a rock. Lime wiggled his jaw and laughed. He loomed over Ashton like a goliath, his fists raised high. They came down hard looking to crush Ashton's skull. Ashton rolled forward under his legs. Lime spun around in disgust. He exited the alcove in a hurry and scanned the cavern for any sign of Ashton.

"Here kitty kitty."

Ashton remained hidden. As Lime approached his hiding spot, Ashton stepped out from behind *Fancy* holding a sword. He walked towards Lime and slashed at him. Missed. Lime playfully dodged Ashton's attacks with surprising agility. Ashton came over top with the sword, but Lime reached up and grabbed the blade. He laughed again. Ashton tugged on the sword and finally, unexpectedly, yanked it from Lime's grip. Lime's hand was bleeding profusely. Ashton attacked again and stabbed him in the side. Lime's lackadaisical attitude turned to seething anger. He rushed at Ashton. Ashton retreated defensively. Lime hit him across the head with a back hand punch and sent him flying.

"You and me have unfinished business," a throaty voice resonated from behind Lime.

Lime turned. Christian was standing at the cavern entrance.

"So we do."

Lime turned his attention to Christian. The two men ran at each other and clashed hard. Ashton, still on the ground shook the dizziness from his head. His vision was blurry, and his head pounded. He grabbed a nearby stone and ran to rejoin the fight. Christian kicked the inside of Lime's knee and delivered a crushing punch, knocking Lime to the ground. He spun around him and locked his arms around Lime's neck. Lime stood, displaying impressive power, with Christian holding on tightly behind him. Christian brought his elbow down repeatedly on Lime's collarbone sending him back down to his knee. Lime managed to gap Christian's forearm away from his throat.

Seeing an opening, Ashton threw the stone as hard as he could, hitting Lime square in the face, stunning him just enough to weaken his grip on Christian's arm. Christian tightened his lock around Lime's neck. Lime struggled to breathe. He kicked profusely, then went limp. Christian snapped his neck to ensure his demise.

"You saved my life," Ashton told him, thankful.

Wearied from battle, the two men embraced.

"I hated that guy," Christian responded.

They left Pirate's Landing and climbed back up the cliff face. Jiya was the first to greet them, jumping on Ashton and plastering his face with kisses.

"That all happened so fast, I'm still stunned," she said.

"Nothing to worry about. Christian and I had it all in hand."

"That's right. You should've seen him! A real giant slayer," Christian added.

"We're glad you're alive, Ashton," Agwe said. "But we'd better get moving. Night is approaching."

They hurried east along Gibbet Pass, following the perimeter of the island as the path paralleled the cliff's edge that steadily rose in height eastward from Horseshoe Point. Two gibbets still hung over the cliff where the improved portion of the path began, the bones of their occupants still encased in their iron cages, while a third gibbet lay broken in the waters below.

FORTY-SEVEN

When the group approached the edge of the forest, night was falling quickly. They moved silently through the trees and up a small hill until they reached the clearing where Tew's pirates had hewn down the trees. Sections of Castillo de Luna's fortifications had crumbled long ago, while other parts stood swallowed and forgotten by ivy and other vegetation. Ashton, Christian, Chen, Agwe, and the two deserters moved to the top of the small hill to the southeast. Lying flat on their stomachs, careful not to reveal themselves, they stared down into the short stretch of open land.

"No, you stay here," Jiya said grabbing Davey as he tried to join them.

"But I want to help my father!" he cried.

"We will, but we have to make sure it's safe first."

Davey obeyed but did so with a hint of indignation.

"There," Ashton said, pointing down to the city.

A large gap in the wall seemed to beckon them. Haphazard stonework attempted to fill it, but several stones had fallen and now lay at the base. It was their best chance at getting inside. The wall appeared unguarded but for a single sentry that routinely appeared as he patrolled around the outer cordon.

Seems too easy, Ashton thought, carefully considering his options. But he saw no one else.

"Something doesn't feel right," he whispered to Christian.

When the sentry disappeared, Chen leapt up.

"Let me take them," he said and snuck his way through the tall grass, keeping his profile low.

"No!" Ashton said in a loud whisper, trying to stop him.

Just as Chen reached the wall, Ashton saw movement, but before he could react, a second guardsman greeted Chen with the unmistakable feel of cold steel. His sword stuck him through the neck. Chen coughed a spittle of blood and quietly slumped forward, dead. The others looked on, horrified. Ashton maneuvered to his flank with Christian and the two deserters. Agwe stayed put, his bow drawn and ready. The guardsman who had slain Chen had just returned from relieving himself behind a nearby bush before delivering the deadly strike.

How did we not see him?

The guardsman stood unflinchingly still, listening, and watching the woods where Ashton and the others remained concealed. Satisfied there was no more imminent threats, the guardsman grabbed Chen's long ponytail and dragged his body to the gate, placing his severed head on a pike as a warning to anyone else who may be lurking in the jungle with similar intentions.

Agwe let loose an arrow that flew fast and sure towards its intended target. It penetrated the eye socket of the guardsman. The impact sent him backwards to the wooden gate, nailing him upright near the pike that held Chen's head.

"This is going to fail before it even begins," one of the deserters warned anxiously.

Christian backhanded him.

"Don't be a coward, or I'll cut your head off and stick it next to his," he threatened.

"Who's going to tell his wives?" he mocked defiantly.

Christian punched him square in the face, knocking the man unconscious.

"I never liked that guy."

The group swept down the hill toward the wall as silently as they could. Christian arrived at the gate first and drove his sword into the gut of the roving sentry who had just rounded the corner.

He caught the sentry's limp body and slowly lowered him to the ground, not making a sound.

They climbed over the fallen stones, through the gap, and down the other side into the city and waited, crouched, for a small band of pirates to pass before they sprinted across the street. Bounding from building to building, sticking to the shadows, they hunkered in a patch of thick brush. The sky was cloudless and calm. The palm trees still.

"The main fortress is on the eastern edge overlooking the bluffs. I hear the beaches that way are breathtaking, too. I wish we were here under different circumstances," Jiya said.

"Hobbes," Christian noticed, spotting the overweight pirate strutting out of a cracking sky-blue stucco building. He had blood splattered across his opened linen shirt and a face covered in dirt.

"Is that his first name?" Agwe asked.

"You know, I don't know," Christian answered.

"Quiet!" Jiya said hushing them.

Another pirate walked casually up to Hobbes. The two men talked for some time.

"This'll be the last time we'll be seein' 'is face 'round 'ere," Hobbes said as they departed together and entered the alehouse a few buildings away.

"We have to find Milt," Ashton said.

He made his way across the road and headed for the blue building Hobbes recently vacated. They followed him, one after the other, into the building. The interior was strangely cold. They split up and moved purposefully from room to room. All empty. The door to the last room was locked. Christian lowered his shoulder and busted the lock open. In front of them were dangling pieces of rope suspended above a pool of blood and a table full of rusted, primitive surgical tools.

"He had to have been here," Christian said squatting down and touching the blood with his finger. "Still warm."

Ashton tore out of the room and quickly spotted tracks outside the back door. Two parallel lines, like feet being drug, led off towards the town square to the foot of the church, its spire rising tall into the night sky. In front of its doors, a raucous crowd had gathered. Gallows had been hastily erected. Milt stood captive, his hands bound behind his back, his bare chest and face awash in blood, his countenance patient. Tew stood next to him, imposing and powerful. He was attractive in his youthfulness despite his many battle scars.

Milt raised his eyes as Ashton and his party approached. The crowd silenced as they looked upon the brazen intruders. Milt, feeling reinvigorating, stood himself up and let out a terrible roar, snapping the rope binding his wrists. Reaching across his body, he took Tew's sword from its sheath. Tew, startled by the interruption, hesitated a few seconds too long. He reached for his sword just as Milt raised it above his head and brought it down with deadly force. Tew dove out of the way and rolled off the platform landing hard on the dirt road. Milt jumped down to meet his foe. A young man, unsure what to do, relinquished his own sword and threw it to Tew who snatched it out of the air, somersaulted forward, and lunged at Milt. Milt, with all the quickness of a young warrior, parried and shoved Tew back against a fountain in the center of the square. Milt laughed confidently and strolled over to his enemy. His eyes appearing a deadly shade of black. Tew gave his blade a twirl as he beckoned Milt tauntingly.

Tew's pirate horde drew their swords and the two sides squared off beneath the old church in the center of Libertalia, neither side willing to make the first move while their leaders bore down on one another. Before anyone on Tew's side could flinch, Agwe unleashed a barrage of arrows that killed six men before the first victim hit the ground. Tew's men charged in unison.

"Here we go," Ashton said, standing at the ready in front of his small group.

Ashton led the charge to meet the onslaught. Agwe crawled up a trellis affixed to the exterior wall of the nearest building and perched himself on the edge of the roof picking off Tew's men with his arrows until his quiver of twenty had been depleted. He let go his last shot, a deadly precise blow through the neck of a pirate drawing up behind Jiya, and then leapt to the ground. He drew two long-bladed daggers from his belt and cut down two more of the enemy in quick succession as Ashton and the others came together and regrouped just as an enemy faction approached on their flank, moving to encircle them.

"This went sideways fast," Christian said.

Ashton looked for Jiya as they faced overwhelming numbers and went to her side. A rousing yell came from the west as a muscular fellow in glasses led a large force running through the streets towards the church.

"Now that's more like it!" Christian said excitedly. He had been anxiously awaiting Shephard's arrival following his agreement to lead the men Christian had marshalled.

"Shephard," Hobbes fumed.

He ran at the man, scorned by Shephard's refutation. Shephard brushed him aside easily with a flick of his sword and led the new arrivals into the fray. Hobbes, blood pouring out of his chest, fell over a wooden rail into a pigsty. The swine's hungry grunts were the last sounds he heard before his face fell into filth and his world faded to black.

FORTY-EIGHT

Steam rose from the ground as the heat from the bloating corpses met the blue hour's early dew. Blood and destruction littered the square. The church was ablaze. A bluish-gray light, broken by the raging fire that made it feel like morning had already arrived, enveloped the island. A mist shrouded Libertalia as morning approached. Following a lull in fighting and attempts to regroup, the remaining pirates continued clashing in brutal hand-to-hand combat. Milt, growing fatigued, assumed a more defensive posture in his fight. Tew sensed a weakening in his ancient opponent. He thrust at Milt knocking away his sword and then thrust again, hitting his mark, plunging his blade into Milt's gut. Milt backpeddled before falling onto his back. His blood mixing with the dust in a muddied puddle beneath him. He managed to prop himself up, but Tew placed his foot on Milt's chest and slowly pushed him back to the ground, anticipating his victory. He walked behind Milt and spat on him. Milt didn't move. Amidst the chaos, Ashton locked eyes with Tew. Tew smiled, grabbed Milt's hair, and leaned him up. Ashton pulled his blade from his opponent's ribcage, his hands trembling with exhaustion, and hurried towards Milt. Tew put his blade under Milt's chin.

"NOOOO!" Ashton yelled.

In the heat of battle, Jiya saw Ashton out of the corner of her eye as he pushed through the riffraff. Tew kept his eyes fixed on Ashton as he sawed off Milt's head. Tew held the severed head aloft for Ashton to witness before tossing it aside. Ashton lunged at the pirate captain. Tew brushed him off with ease. Ashton's momentum carried him to the ground next to Milt's headless torso. His anger intensified. He grabbed Milt's sword, feeling its weight and craftsmanship in his hands. With renewed vigor and now wielding two swords, he lunged again at Tew with repeated blows before finally overwhelming Tew's defenses, surprised by Ashton's tenacity. Ashton's sword pierced Tew just above his hip. Tew, in a fit of fury, swiftly overcame Ashton, whose own fear overcame him as he stared helplessly into the dreaded captain's rage-filled eyes.

Tew's was too overpowering. The cresting sun shone in Ashton's eyes. Tew slashed at him, slicing a gash into Ashton's arm in a strike as quick as lightning. Ashton's hand went limp. He dropped the sword. He was off balance. Tew followed with a punishing kick sending him sprawling onto the ground. Ashton, exhausted, propped himself up as his opponent towered above him. He still gripped Milt's cutlass and prepared to thrust it upward, but Tew's boot landed on his shoulder, pinning his arm to the ground and sending a wave of pain coursing down to his fingers. Tew stood over him, his shadow cast long as the sun broke over the trees in the sky behind him, silhouetting his face. Ashton lay his head back onto the dusty road accepting his fate so reminiscent of the one Milt had suffered.

This is it.

Ashton closed his eyes. Tew raised his sword for the death blow. Ashton waited, but the blow never came. Obscured by the deafening noise of battle, he had missed the sound. He opened his eyes and watched as Tew stumbled backwards. The pirate captain dropped his sword and clutched his chest. He looked up and saw Jiya standing before him, tall and defiant, her flintlock pistol raised high. Smoke rose swirling from the barrel. The bullet had shattered the amulet hanging around Tew's neck, causing nothing more than a flesh wound. He stood for a moment awestruck, not believing his misfortune, and slowly came to terms with his new mortality. Tew looked helplessly upon his assassin. Ashton shoved Milt's sword into Tew's chest. The vaunted pirate let out a cry and stumbled forward, pulling the sword from his wound. Anger burned inside him.

"This isn't over," he said through his blood-stained teeth.

"It is for you," Jiya replied, lowering her smoking weapon.

No longer protected by the amulet, Tew fled, hobbling away like a wounded deer, disappearing into the morning fog while the battle continued unabated. No one, at that moment, was able or bothered to give chase. Jiya dropped her weapon and ran to Ashton, who was writhing in pain. Milt's decapitated body lay beside him, his head nowhere to be seen. She knelt at Ashton's side and covered the gash on his arm with a piece of cloth.

"Are you ok?"

"I think so," Ashton said through halting breath.

He attempted to sit up. A sharp pain radiated from a broken rib he received from Tew's kick. His shoulder ached.

"Maybe not," he said lying back down.

"Come on, put your arm around my shoulder," Jiya instructed.

Ashton ignored the fighting and did what he was told. Jiya helped him to his feet and took him inside the nearest house, laid him down on a straw mattress in a small, unadorned bedroom, and tended to his wound. Outside, the fighting was beginning to ease as the pirates took notice of Tew's absence. One by one, Tew's supporters dropped their swords and absconded after their leader, while those who were cut-off from their escape raised their arms in surrender. Christian motioned for several men to bound and hang a handful of the more unsavory prisoners from their own gallows.

"Tew's not getting away this time," Christian said to Agwe as the remnants of Tew's faction scattered past them.

"You have any idea where he is headed?" Agwe asked.

"He can't go far."

"Shall we join the chase?"

Christian gestured to Agwe.
"After you."

FORTY-NINE

Thomas Tew reached Horseshoe Point well ahead of his pursuers, having wrangled one of the loose horses grazing at the southern gate. The salty smell of the sea rejuvenated his lungs. For a moment, as he descended into Pirate's Landing, his blood streaking behind him along the cliff face, he was reminded of a simpler time when the sea was his domain. Where he was king. No rules, just freedom. Those days were long past now, and the bleak realization that he would soon fade from this world was setting in, but he was determined to go on his own terms.

Upon reaching the sandy bottom, he walked inside the littoral cave, the first time doing so since arriving over three hundred years ago. Looking upon *Fancy* and *Amity*, Tew was caught in a moment of reflection – Avery's deception, the treasure he stole. Anger welled inside of him at the mere thought of the betrayal he suffered. He felt no remorse for any of his actions, and he relished his old friend's demise at his own hand.

Tew limped to the *Fancy* just as the distant sound of voices were carried to him by the wind. His heart yearned for the treasure-laden vessel that lie wrecked next to his, but there was no time. He climbed aboard the *Amity*, still preserved, and floating in a small reservoir at the mouth of the cavern. He cursed the circumstances in which he now found himself.

All for nothing, he thought.

A half-dozen of his men, those that managed to escape, scurried aboard after him.

"Raise the sails!" the captain ordered as it sailed slowly out of Pirate's Landing and into Halfmoon Bay.

Christian and Agwe skidded to a halt at the cliff's edge near Horseshoe Point and watched Tew and his crew sail the *Amity* south into open waters.

"We're too late," said Agwe.

They could do nothing more than look on as Tew sailed away from Shipwreck Island. Galloping hooves came running at them from behind at a high rate of speed. The horse, a young colt Ashton named Gus, steadied itself in front of the group. Ashton, seated behind Jiya, slid off, bandaged and lame.

"Looks like he got away," Ashton said.

"We're just glad you are alive," Agwe said. "Not many who have taken on Tew have lived to tell the tale."

The group stood huddled together at the cliff's edge watching helplessly as Tew escaped their justice. The sea breeze whistled past them.

"Look!" Jiya pointed.

Ripples appeared in the cerulean waters just off the *Amity's* port side. Overhead, seagulls congregated and circled. The ripples swelled and the water began to churn as a maelstrom slowly took shape, growing and feeding, sucking the ship into its vortex. A large mouth full of rows of teeth appeared in the whirlpool. Massive tentacles exploded from the depths, grasping for its prey. They watched as Tew's ship turned hard to starboard trying to avoid the hungry sea monster hidden beneath the waves.

"I've heard tales of a demon monster haunting the deep near this cursed island, but I never thought it to be true," Christian exclaimed.

"There may be justice yet," Ashton said.

"It is indeed her," Agwe interjected with shock and amazement. "My people have been worshipping her for thousands of years, though I have never beheld her with my own eyes."

Tew's crew was frantically jumping overboard to no avail. Tew maintained the helm. Facing his doom, he let out a defiant cry as the beast's massive tentacles wrapped themselves around the hull, snapping the ship in half, splintering the hardened wood like kindling. Finally, the sea calmed and all signs of Tew, his crew, and the *Amity* disappeared below the waves. The beast's appetite satiated, it retreated to the depths never to be seen again. Captain Thomas Tew now rested at the bottom of Davy Jones's locker.

"Well, that's that. Good job, gang," Ashton said, understating the affair. "Now who needs a drink?"

The victors erupted in boisterous ovation.

FIFTY

Ashton rejoined those tending to their fallen comrades on the field of battle to retrieve Milt's body. Davey walked happily next to Shephard. Jiya returned to the Green Turtle Tavern. Christian retreated to Mount Deluz to pay his respects to those who came before him, and for keeping him safe and strong during the battle, as was his custom despite turning his back on who he was to embrace who he is, a pirate. Agwe assisted the families in burying their dead before refitting his gear and preparing to depart for Lost Cay. He had no more reason to stay now that Tew was dead, and though the women of New Nassau carried themselves with pride and dignity, hiding all emotion as they set about the task of saying their final goodbyes, he could sense their grief, and it moved him in a way he had never felt before.

"Where's Milt's body?" Ashton asked as he walked amongst the many graves being dug.

"One of the men must've buried him already," a middling blacksmith, who had joined the fight early, guessed.

"He deserved a proper burial behind his manor with the other pirate lords," Ashton said.

"Sorry, sir. Do you want us to dig them all back up and look for 'im?"

"No."

A somber atmosphere hovered over New Nassau as Ashton rode back into town. Amber ran as fast as her four legs could carry her, with her ears pinned back and tongue flapping out of her smiling mouth. She jumped on Ashton just as he dismounted and rolled onto her back for some well-deserved belly rubs.

In the cove's harbor, three frigates, sunken in the cove as part of the curse's effect, had risen from their watery graves and rested now in the former glory on the shimmering surface. The pirates took to refitting them, while the harbor master enjoyed his renewed business.

Ashton found himself drawn back to Milt's villa. He walked underneath the long portico, running his hands against the cedar railing, taking the time to appreciate the splendor of the architecture, a blend of Baroque and Spanish Colonial stylings. He entered the home and stood in the center of the Grand Hall. The wood in the fireplace had burned down to a gray pile of ash.

He felt the silk velvet, floor-to-ceiling drapes tucked into their tiebacks. He strolled into the dining room. Fine dust particles danced in the beams of sunlight penetrating the tall windows. He continued down the main corridor, lit by the rays of sunshine pouring in through the broken windows and rotting roof to the rear of the villa. In the expansive garden behind the house, he stood over the graves of the renowned pirate captains. He walked over to the lone nameless cross, took out his knife, and began carving into the horizontal plank. Pleased with his work, he brushed off the woodchips and blew the dust from the relief. He sheathed his knife, satisfied that Naemi could now, finally, get the recognition she deserved.

He dug a shallow hole next to hers, long enough for a cutlass, and placed Milt's sword inside it. He scrounged two pieces of wood from the manor to serve as a grave marker. Carving Milt's name into its surface, Ashton stuck the makeshift cross in the ground behind the sword's hilt, and there it stood next to Naemi, Ned Low, Anne Bonny, Henry Morgan, and Edward England.

On the opposite side of the island, a solitary figure stood at the water's edge, staring into the cavernous shelter of Pirate's

Landing, his eyes glowing with pride, free from his chains and unrestrained by time.

"Hello again, *Fancy*."

FIFTY-ONE

New Nassau was alive again as night fell and victory was celebrated. The streets were filled with the usual scenes of debauchery. Drinking abounded, while at the Green Turtle Tavern, the rum and ale were flowing like the waters at Caiman Falls. Song erupted inside the building accompanied by dancing and merriment that lasted well into the night.

The following morning, the rising sun shone bright and warm through the opened doors of the tavern. The party continued as Ashton quietly walked outside and strolled towards the beach with his hands in his pockets. He relished the warmth of the sun and the salty breeze. The cawing of the gulls flying overhead were a welcomed respite to the screams and sounds of battle. He buried his toes into the soft sand. The clear, emerald water gently lapped onto the shore, the sun sliding across the surface of the sea. Ashton gazed out over the cove towards the sloping cliffs and the inlet beyond. He glanced at the cave. It didn't look as black as it once did, but the memories nevertheless flooded back into his consciousness.

He walked over and stood at the mouth of the cave admiring the beautiful red flowers that had begun to bloom along the vines that overhung the opening. He smelled their fragrant scent then gently pushed them aside and stepped behind them into the familiar darkness. The curse lifted, and Tew vanquished, the cave was nothing more than welcomed shade from the scorching heat.

Ashton then made his way up the gangplank of one of the ships in the harbor and stood upon its deck. Entering the captain's quarters at the stern of the ship, he found it relatively empty save for an exquisitely made armoire containing fine clothing made of richly colored, and intricately woven Muslin cotton. He then went top deck and felt the warm wood of the helm in his hands. Taking a moment to savor the silence, he found himself considering whether to remain on the island and spend the rest of his life in paradise.

"Hey, you," said a sweet and familiar voice.

Ashton leaned over the taffrail to see Jiya standing on the dock. He took a moment to appreciate her beauty. Her dark hair was pulled back in a ponytail and her piercing green eyes mirrored the sea.

Do I really want to leave this?

"I'll be right down," he said, leaping onto the dock's rickety wooden planks. A board splintered under his foot.

"That was reckless," she laughed.

"It would've taken too long to get to you otherwise," he said, hiding the embarrassment.

"Smooth," she grinned.

He gently caressed the soft skin of her cheek. Despite fighting all the previous night, she looked more beautiful to him today than ever before. He pulled her close and kissed her with all the sensuality he could muster.

"I wondered where you ran off to after you snuck out of the tavern. Anxious to leave, huh?" she teased.

Ashton smiled. He took her hand and held it in his own, and the two of them began walking back to shore.

"You know, if you stay, they'll love you forever...I'll love you forever," Jiya added.

Ashton kissed her.

When they returned to the tavern, the atmosphere was even more lively than when he stepped away from it, as if the night had never ended. Jiya rounded the bar and hurried back with two ales in her hands and took a seat next to Ashton. His heart was as full as his chalice. He laughed and entertained his companions. Christian approached, also carrying two mugs of ale, both for himself.

"You're gonna need some colors of your own now," he said, taking a seat on the other side of Ashton.

Christian, with a full mug in his hand, threw his muscular arm around Ashton's shoulders, spilling beer down Ashton's bandaged arm and into his lap.

"I haven't given much thought to that," Ashton said. "Any ideas?"

"Well, there has to be a skull, of course," Jiya insisted.

"Of course. That goes without saying."

"Ashton," Agwe said stoically. "I must return to my people."

"Now's not the time to be somber, Agwe. Your people are warriors, and they deserved to be honored as such. When you get back to Lost Cay and begin to rebuild, let me know if there's anything you need from me."

"Thank you, my friend," said Agwe.

"Aye!" Christian said, raising his mug high in the air.

"Brothers!" Agwe hailed in return.

"Brothers!"

"...and sisters!"

"Aye! And sisters!"

The three men cheered together and all of them turned their mugs to the ceiling.

"Boom!" yelled Ashton triumphantly, slamming his mug down before the others.

Neither man responded, for no response was needed. They only nodded toward Jiya who was leaning back in her chair, her goblet already empty.

"Boom," she said.

Ashton laughed, having been beaten.

"To the victor," he said with a ceremonious bow.

"Not to cut the party short, but I think it's about time we head back to Pirate's Landing," Christian advised with a subtle look.

"Agwe, join us for one more mission?" Ashton asked.

"I think I have time for one more."

The four of them left the Green Turtle for the stables. A handful of horses had willingly returned following Tew's defeat, the evil veil over New Nassau having been lifted. Ashton and Jiya mounted a white horse, and Jiya wrapped her arms around Ashton's waist as he led the other two riders into the jungle towards the southern end of the island. Ashton was more beat up than the rest of them and had no compunction with taking it slow. The three horses each hauled behind them a small cart. The four riders rode through Libertalia where the remnants of Tew's old crew that had not been made examples of on the gallows were all busily restoring the old pirate kingdom to its former glory. With a few friendly gestures, the four riders galloped past Castillo de Luna and through the rear gate. A cloud of dust rose behind them as they continued onward to Horseshoe Point.

The horses reared up at the cliffs where the old road intersected Gibbet Pass. Ashton settled his horse and paused for a moment admiring the view. Taking care not to squander the beauty of the Caribbean Sea and the horizon beyond, the group sat horseback beside each other, watching and appreciating in silence.

Ashton gave a slight tug on the reins and his horse slowly backpedaled away from the ledge. The roar of the waves crashing on the rocks below was music to his weary ears. The gibbets overhanging the ledge swung listlessly in the breeze.

"Christian," Ashton called.

Christian rode up on his dark brown horse.

"The world has changed dramatically in the last 300 years. These people on this island aren't going to recognize it when they see it. As you move to transition to modernity, give them peace to live out their lives without fear. Woodes Rogers, George I…they're long dead."

"You can count on us," Christian assured him.

Ashton nodded.

"C'mon," he said to his horse with a click of his mouth.

The mare reared and pivoted, then slowly trotted along the cliffside road towards Pirate's Landing. The wind was picking up, whipping now across the lowlands near the cliff's edge. When they reached the descent to Pirate's Landing, they filed down the cliffside to the rocky bottom below, skirting the rock wall as the tide receded. Sunlight poured in, lighting their way into the cavern.

"Where's the *Fancy*?" Christian said with exasperation.

Ashton walked deeper into the vast cavern. In a small grotto shrouded in shadow, a glint caught his eye. It was different from the striations of the gold and silvery veins that coursed through the belly of the island, but it was golden indeed. He looked behind the trickling wall of water, and in the dark of the recess saw a mound of gold bullion, jade statues and ornaments, jewels from all over the world, silk and woven fabrics, oil paintings, and other innumerable treasures of immeasurable value.

The group worked meticulously throughout the day hauling the treasure up the cliff face as quickly as they could, ensuring the most valuable and precious pieces were taken first – the art, furniture, fabrics. But as the tide returned, the water slowly flooded the many fissures and sunken points, submerging what golden coins and trinkets remained strewn on the ground, which slowed their progress. Making matters more difficult, the rocky basin below the cliff's ascending path became wet and precarious as waves crashed into it. All was not fraught with such dismal prospects, however, as the sun set slowly behind them in the pale orange sky, the entrance of the cavern framed the burning orb perfectly, flooding it with rays of light that reflected into beautiful colors and painting the slick stone walls, ceiling, and grounds with a cavalcade of shimmering brilliance.

Jiya's eyes welled with tears.

"It really puts things into perspective, doesn't it? The beauty of nature, as if yesterday's violence never occurred at all," Ashton said.

"Time has a way of repairing the world," Christian added.

With the last bit of treasure hauled from the *Fancy's* longstanding resting place, the group began the long ride back to New Nassau.

FIFTY-TWO

The following morning also did not relent to the celebratory festivities that carried over from the previous night. A few hours of rest and the townspeople awoke reinvigorated and excited to embark upon their new lives free from the island's centuries-long curse.

Ashton awoke in Jiya's arms, the smell of coconut on her skin, their bodies contorted around the furry lump at the foot of the bed where Amber lay curled in a ball sleeping without any concept of space. Ashton rolled out of bed and put on his clothes. Amber did not bother to get up, but merely raised her eyes at the sound of his movement then quickly drifted back to sleep.

The dawn's cool morning breeze greeted him as he walked down to the cove and sat on an empty wooden crate under the shade of a low-arching palm tree. It was quiet. His mind needed the rest. The surf lapped lazily onto the beach while the gulls floated carefree overhead. He glanced to his right. Still in the hammock, in the same position as when Ashton arrived on the island, the bum in the tank top slept, his finger still plugging an empty rum bottle.

Where has that guy been?

He glanced to his left.

"Geez Almighty," Ashton said falling off the crate. "How do you keep popping up like that?"

Pierre smiled back at him with his toothless grin.

"I am everywhere, and I am nowhere," the old mystic answered with a cackle.

"You do seem to always show up at opportune times. So, what is it this time?"

"Sometimes dere be nothin' to hear. Sometimes, nothin' is the best somethin'."

"It's hard to argue with that."

The drunken bum in the tank top swung the rum bottle from his finger as he sauntered over. His balance shifted. He stumbled sideways and fell into the soft sand. He lifted his head, half his face covered in white sand and his sunglasses cocked on his face.

"Nice to see you still alive," Ashton joked.

"Of course I am, el cap-i-tano," he said snapping to attention and offering a mocking salute.

The man swayed.

"One condition," he said.

"Condition for what?"

"Take me back home on that old timey pirate ship of yours?"

"Where's home?"

"Florida!"

With a hesitant nod of affirmation, Ashton agreed.

"Be here 8 a.m. tomorrow morning."

The man pointed at Ashton with the finger still stuck in the rum bottle. He stumbled to the docks and jumped in the water, swimming for a nearby schooner. He climbed up a rope ladder to the deck and made himself comfortable in the cargo hold.

"I've been meaning to thank…," Ashton started, but Pierre had vanished.

Ashton moved to the newly vacated hammock and swung his legs inside, nestling himself in the netting. He interlocked his fingers behind his head, closed his eyes, and resigned himself to contentment while the breeze blew past, rustling the coconut palms that shaded him from above.

A little while later, Agwe and what remained of his warriors crossed the footbridge and began loading a sloop with four large chests full of booty, his share of the treasure. Ashton swung out of the hammock and joined his friend on the dock just as Agwe descended the gangplank for the last chest.

"What are you going to do with your share?" Ashton asked.

"I'm going to rebuild my village and reestablish trade," Agwe replied matter-of-factly. "And maybe add a little modernity." He nodded towards the beach, "Some of my men have elected to stay here."

Ashton turned and saw three of his men, each embracing a New Nassau woman. Ashton laughed.

"Can't say I blame them."

"Neither can I," Agwe said with the slightest smile.

The rest of the crew boarded and he was ready to set sail for Lost Cay. No word needed to be said.

"All set, Chief," one of the warriors called.

"Get us under way."

He shook Ashton's hand.

"The title suits you," Ashton told him. "Take care of yourself, my friend. And maybe don't eat any more people."

"They were never to my taste anyway," Agwe smiled back.

Top side, Agwe leaned on the gunwale of the quarterdeck and gave a wave. The sloop pulled away from the dock and turned into Crooked Inlet. Ashton stood on the docks a while longer. A sea turtle swam underneath him, gliding among the fluorescent coral growing on the rocks that littered the seabed. He went back to relax in the hammock, taking heed of Pierre's sage advice of just doing nothing at all.

"Are you going to stay out here all day?" Jiya asked, taking a seat in the sand beside him, her long legs stretched out in front of her.

"Nah, just wanted to enjoy the scenery," he said petting Amber who was happily greeting him.

"I'm glad the rain decided to stay away. It's turning into a nice day," she said.

"And hot," Ashton added wiping a bead of sweat from his brow.

"Let's go for a swim!"

"Now?"

"Yes, now," she said, taking his hand and pulling him from the hammock.

She ran down the dock and leapt into the warm, crystal-clear water. Ashton ran after her, pulling his shirt off as he went. He jumped, curling himself into a ball and splashing her in the face with his entry. Amber watched them from shore, never taking her watchful eye off her master. Ashton happened to glance at his watch.

"Hey, my watch is working again!"

Twenty minutes had passed in a blink. Amber barked as Ashton and Jiya walked out of the water back onto the sandy shore, sun drying and talking about their futures.

"The first thing I'm going to do when I get back is quit my job," Ashton began.

"Yeah?"

"Yeah. The treasure aside, this past week has taught me that life is more than just living day to day. And what good is it if by the end of your time here on earth you've realized the entire span has been an unhappy, regrettable experience? I mean, this is it. This one life is all we have."

"After my parents died, I thought my life was over," said Jiya lowering her head. "I had no other family left. But I grew to love this beautiful island and the nature around me."

"I never really figured out why Milt brought me here," he said turning to look at Jiya, "but I'm glad he did."

Jiya kissed him.

"Want to head back?" he asked her.

Jiya jumped to her feet. Amber sprinted excitedly up the beach and turned, impatiently waiting.

"Go ahead!" Ashton told her, but Amber wagged her tail, waiting obediently.

"I'll take her in," Jiya said and ran after her.

Ashton remained behind for a few brief moments to collect his shoes and put his shirt back on. In those moments, a familiar sound resonated in his ear. The faint sound of steel drums played on the wind.

New Nassau had returned to its usual, transactional self. The brothel was full of customers and gamblers, the Green Turtle Tavern had plenty of business, drunkards were passed out in the street, and the old sugarcane plantation just up the hill near the manor was functioning again. New sugarcane crops were sewn, and farmers began working. Christian orchestrated the planting of the new harvest and the efforts to beautify the grounds. New life had filled the sails of the old pirate kingdom.

The dirt streets were lively. The Green Turtle still had its holdovers from the night before, now either sleeping on the floor or playing cards in a cloud of tobacco smoke. The bell tolled from the old church's bell tower, still functioning on the barely standing structure. Ashton made a mental note to have the restoration begin immediately. Ashton stepped through the tavern's threshold.

Jiya poured two glasses of 350-year-old red wine.

"I almost feel bad for drinking this. Pouring this much money into a wine glass and wasting it on me is almost criminal," Ashton said.

The two of them sat alone at a table near one of the open plantation windows. The sunlight poured in, warming their bodies as the customary island breeze blew through rustling the bushes and cycads just outside. They sipped the wine slowly, enjoying one another's company, as the drunkards in the bar stumbled their way out into the daylight. A pair of red-necked parrots swooped low through the window and perched themselves on a crossbeam inside the tavern, singing cheerily.

"Those birds are really beautiful," Jiya commented.

"They are," said Ashton.

He retreated into his thoughts, doubting his decision to leave in the morning. Jiya, turning her attention from the two birds saw the conflict brimming on Ashton's face.

"What's wrong?" she inquired.

"I'm not sure I want to go back. I want to stay here with you."

"You have to go back, Ashton, but I'll be waiting for you when you return."

"And I promise I'll be back as soon as I'm able."

"I'll be here."

She touched his hand and smiled.

"There you two lovebirds are," Christian said standing at the window.

He was shirtless, exposing his bronzed, tattooed chest. Covered in soil and drenched in sweat, he entered and grabbed a chair, shaking the table as he dropped his arms on top of it.

"You're a mess," Jiya teased him.

"Yeah, that's the truth, but we made some good progress on getting the sugarcane plantation up and running again. The rum'll be in the barrels soon enough and I'm hoping we can restart our trading as soon as the next harvest's done. We've made some good stuff," he said with a wink.

"You ever find out what happened to *Fancy*?" Ashton asked.

"Who cares, mate. Look, speakin' of Milt, his villa needs a remodel. I want you to take a look. And, you might also like to know, I talked with Maribel, the seamstress down the road there. She's prepared to make you your official colors, Captain."

FIFTY-THREE

"First things first," Ashton said standing in Grand Hall of the villa. "We need to repair the foundation and structure, paying attention to the east wing hallway leading to the rear of the house. Don't think it was ever intended to be the arboretum it is now."

"You got it."

"The next thing is to keep the furniture, paint, art, stained-glass windows, and other intricacies as close to original as possible. I want this villa to remain a tribute," Ashton told him.

Christian nodded.

"The last thing…," Ashton began. "Follow me."

He led Christian and Jiya through a nondescript, wooden door in the rear of the house and down a stone staircase in the middle of the room to another heavy, wooden door. He lit the torches inside the expansive cellar to reveal another worldly treasure horde.

"This probably had something to do with the blood on the door," Ashton surmised.

Christian and Jiya explored the room. Old maps and letters, books and scrolls, paintings, jeweled furniture, statues…years' worth of plunder.

"These items and documents in this room answer a lot of questions about the island and shed a lot of light on the lost histories of some of these pirates," Ashton said. "As a kid, I remember reading stories about Charles Vane and Blackbeard, Calico Jack and Black Sam Bellamy. Here are navigation routes used by William Kidd and here's the cypher for La Buse's cryptic text," he said holding up a soiled book of parchments. Christian took the book from him and thumbed through it.

"This stuff needs to be in a museum. I'm sure they'll be reaching out to you before long," Ashton said turning to Christian. "The island is yours now and these people are going to need a governor."

Christian was at first reluctant. He looked at Jiya.

"Don't look at me," she said throwing her hands up in the air, "I don't want to be anywhere near that role."

"Christian, you'll be a great governor to usher New Nassau into the real world," Ashton reassured him.

"If that's how it's to be, I think I'll start by renaming Shipwreck Island. It'll be called from here on 'Libertalia.'"

Ashton shook his hand to signal the transfer of power.

"Have you got a flag design in mind yet?" Christian asked as the three of them walked back of the stairs, leaving the door open behind them.

"Yeah, I think I do."

Christian led him down the hill to a small, faded yellow building along a side road, nestled between the natural colors of various-sized residences.

"Maribel will happily stitch your colors for you," he said introducing him to the old woman.

She wore a heavy, flowing dress, and her silver hair was pulled back in a tight bun.

"Hello, dear," the old seamstress greeted.

"Hello, ma'am."

"Take a seat, young man, and let's get started."

"I look forward to seeing it when it's done," Christian said and exited the old wooden house.

Ashton and Jiya sat down in a pair of wicker chairs, and he began outlining to Maribel the design for his black flag.

FIFTY-FOUR

Dusk was approaching. Though dark clouds were moving in from the east, the rain had managed to steer clear of the island. Ashton and Jiya were eating a wonderful dinner he had prepared over a fire on the beach, and they drank the last two pours of wine from their tin chalices. Set among wooden crates, the meal altogether didn't quite meet Ashton's standard of what he would consider "romantic," but the company and the ambience exceeded their expectations. They sat holding each other and watching the sky change from pink to orange to indigo as the sun set behind the western peaks. They sat together in silence, neither willing to say a word, just enjoying the other's company and the calming, picturesque sunset. The salty air was an aromatic compliment to Jiya's intoxicating scent.

"What do you say we finish the evening among friends? Then we can finish the night between ourselves," she suggested with a wink.

Ashton didn't have to respond. A childlike grin spread across his face.

"Can't we just skip the 'among friends' part and go straight to the 'between us' part?"

They held hands and strolled back to the tavern. It felt homier now than before. Ashton could feel a deeper sense of appreciation for its interior aesthetic and the special place it would hold in his heart knowing it would be his last night inside it.

When they walked in, Christian boisterously announced Ashton's arrival and sat him at a table of honor in the center of the tavern surrounded by the vast majority of New Nassau's citizens. It was standing room only and those not in attendance made good use of the adjacent brothel all to themselves.

"Milt once told me that the underlying tenant of Libertalia was democracy and liberty in their truest forms, and it was under those precepts that Libertalia was established," Ashton began.

He went on to tell the crowd of his plans to depart and appoint Christian as his successor. Christian took the charge with excitement and zeal. Ashton faded into the crowd and sat with Jiya at a table near the far window as the crowd's fanfare shifted to Christian. Christian quieted the crowd and quickly laid out his vision for the island to unanimous consent from those in attendance.

"And finally, I hereby proclaim this island to be renamed in memory of its visionary, Milt."

"Three cheers for Milt!" a voice commanded from the crowd.

When the ovations died down, Christian continued, "From henceforth, Libertalia shall be its name and Milton its capital city."

Cheers went up again.

"Finally, again," Christian shouted over the crowd. "Finally again!" he repeated. The crowd quieted. "We will begin sewing sugarcane in earnest, distilling the best rum in the Caribbean, and engaging in trade with the new world. We will rebuild Milton to its former glory!"

The crowd's excitement at the chance for riches again filled the air. Wild cheers and applause erupted, catalyzing another round of heavy drinking. Christian lifted his mug of ale.

"To Libertalia!"

He threw his head back, spilling the contents of the cup down his face and onto his clothes. He wiped his mouth, refilled his mug, and joined Ashton and Jiya at a table near the window. The three of them smashed their mugs together in celebration and song and chugged their brew until needing to stop for a breath.

An impromptu ragtag band composed of three men playing a concertina, mandolin, and fiddle started playing a catchy tune as a large woman, on loan from the seedy tavern down the road, belted out her polished notes. Ashton, slightly feeling the effects of the ale, grabbed Jiya out of her chair and danced with her for hours to the rhythm of the music.

Jiya came out of a twirl and didn't let go of Ashton's hand. Her hair flowed down her back, and her cheeks colored with the slightest hint of red. She bit her lower lip and gave him a sensual look. She jerked his arm, leading him up the stairs to her room. Ashton slammed the door behind him. The music seeped through the walls. Her passion was electrifying. They continued to kiss, pausing only to rip a garment of clothing off each other's bodies. Jiya laid down on her bed, her naked body glowing and perfect, and welcomed him into her arms, making love until her body quivered.

Thirty seconds later, they were both laughing lightheartedly.

"There's just something about the way you look tonight, I guess," Ashton explained.

"Well, I do have an amazing body," she quipped.

Ashton kissed her again, their passions rising once more.

"Ready for round two?"

Jiya rolled him onto his back and took charge, straddling his hips. Ashton's hands glided up her stomach feeling every inch of her skin. Higher they rose appreciating the smooth contours of her body. She threw her head back in ecstasy and they made love well into the night.

"Three times...wow," she said, exhausted and staring at the ceiling.

"You. Are. Welcome," Ashton said, putting his hands proudly behind his head and extracting a laugh from her.

He opened the windows to let the stars and moonlight shine through, flooding the room in a silvery shade.

"Come back with me, Jiya," Ashton said after a period of silence.

Jiya opened her eyes and turned her head to look at him.

"We have loads of money now and can do whatever we want."

"You know I would love to," she answered. "But I need to help rebuild this place. This has been my home for so long, I wouldn't feel right leaving it now. When you come back, you'll know where to find me."

He smiled, doing his best to hide his disappointment, but the more he thought about it, happiness delayed was better than a lifetime of perceived sadness without her by his side. He rolled onto his back, Jiya laid her head on his chest, and they fell asleep to the euphonic rhythm of the cove – the rolling waves, the rustling palm fronds, the gentle humming of the field crickets, all combining to perform their island symphony.

FIFTY-FIVE

Ashton rose just before sunrise, while New Nassau was still asleep, its occupants having finally exhausted themselves. The roads were deserted save for a few dogs and chickens moving about in the pre-dawn morning. He made breakfast and coffee in the tavern kitchen and brought them upstairs to Jiya. She ate quickly, and together they strolled down to the beach, hand in hand, and put their toes in the cool sand. The sun slowly lit the sky, arousing the many colors of the cove. Christian came down from the schooner having secured the cargo and readied the sails for departure.

"You're up early," Ashton said to him.

"I've been up all night," he said. "Couldn't sleep much so figured on preparing the ship for launch. Speakin' of which, it's bad luck to set sail on a boat with no name."

Ashton thought for a moment.

"The *Angel*," he answered.

"*Angel*. A fitting name."

Ashton turned to Jiya. They stood on the docks, the gaps in the planks wide enough to see a school of parrotfish and a lone white-tip reef shark swimming below them.

"Are you sure you won't come with me?" Ashton asked a final time.

"I want to, more than anything," she lowered her head, fighting back tears. "But I can't."

She felt sick to her stomach with her decision. She looked back up at him. A lone tear rolled down her cheek.

"I understand," Ashton answered. He could call to mind no other words.

She lowered her head again. He put his fingers on her chin and lifted her face.

"Smile," he told her.

She did.

"You're so radiant when you smile."

He brushed her hair behind her ear.

"I'll always remember you this way, young and beautiful, and full of spirit," he promised her.

She kissed him long and slow. He embraced her hard and lovingly, neither one wanting to let go of the other.

"Go on," she told him. "When do you think you'll be back?"

"One of these days, maybe," he answered.

"Don't forget me."

"How could I?"

Her smile was bright.

"I love you," he told her.

Her eyes welled with tears as her smile grew, "I love you, too."

He backed away and walked up the gangplank.

"Come on, girl!" he called from the deck. Amber bounded aboard excitedly behind him. The crew stood by four large wooden chests of treasure awaiting him and his orders.

"Quartermaster!" Ashton called.

"Cap'n," replied Christian as he walked up the stairs from the main deck to the quarter deck.

"Raise the colors."

"Aye! Raise the colors!" Christian repeated to the crew.

Two crewmen unfurled a large black cloth and hoisted it to the top of the starboard mainmast to reveal Ashton's colors as captain of the *Angel*. There, it waved triumphantly in the morning breeze. A white, front-facing skull, with two bones crossed behind it, an opened jaw, and a blossomed red rose in place of the right eye.

"Now she's ready to sail," Ashton said as he craned his neck and beheld his colors for the first time flapping proudly in the wind.

Here's to the next chapter.

Tuki squawked and swooped low, perching himself next to the helm. The *Angel* weighed anchor and drifted slowly away from the dock. Christian, manning the helm, steered her toward Crooked Inlet. The vessel rocked as it sailed past the Sentinel Cliffs. Ashton stood on the taffrail, holding onto the backstay for balance, and watched the numbers dwindle from the dock. All but one. Jiya stood alone. No waving, no tears, just a smile and her shining emerald eyes, like the beauty of the waters on which he now sailed for home.

"Hurry back," Jiya said under her breath as she watched until his ship turned into Crooked Inlet and disappeared from her view.

Tears streamed down her cheeks. She stayed just a few moments longer, then quickly wiped her eyes. Her poise regained, she headed back to the Green Turtle Tavern.

As the *Angel* sailed atop the Caribbean's blue waters, Ashton caught a glimpse of another larger ship, a gray vessel sprinting north in the distance. It looked to be a brigantine with massive sails unfurled and filled with wind.

"Get us more speed, Christian," Ashton said, wanting a closer look.

"Trim the sails!" Christian ordered as his grip tightened on the helm.

The crew tightened the reefing lines and released the main halyard. The fore-and-aft sails unfurled and caught wind. Ashton peered through the telescope. As the image before him came into focus, Ashton saw that the large brigantine looked remarkably like the *Fancy*. On board, a man with a fiery red beard and long, red hair blowing in the wind stood bare-chested at the helm, a smile of contentment plastered on his face. Suddenly, the *Angel's* main sheet inexplicably loosened, and the vessel slowed significantly.

"Secure that mainsheet!" Christian ordered.

The crew frantically hurried to ensure the *Angel* did not lose the chase, but alas, the *Fancy* picked up unnatural speed and disappeared almost as quickly as it appeared.

"Was that a mirage?" Ashton asked Christian as the mainsheet was resecured and the sails once again filled with wind, powering the ship forward.

"No, my friend. I do not believe it was."

"It was the strangest thing. For a moment, I thought I saw Milt."

"Well, that's the thing about legends ain't it. They never truly die."

Ashton scanned for any sign of the *Fancy* but saw only turquoise water.

"Well, wherever he is, I'm glad he has his peace," Ashton said. "Now, bring me that horizon."

FIFTY-SIX

As the *Angel* approached the southernmost tip of Florida, Christian ordered the furling of the aft sail, slowing their speed and coasting around the southern shores of Key West.

"We need to find a place to drop anchor," Ashton said, standing on the quarter deck next to Christian.

Christian glided the ship among several randomly moored vessels. Those sunbathing on the shore and drinking on boat decks all turned to look at the ancient craft as it sailed past them. Ashton and Christian smiled at each other and then waved ceremoniously to the throng of onlookers to their own amusement.

"I'll see y'all boys on the beach!" the bum in the tank top hollered, rushing up from the cargo hold and diving into the green waters.

"Think he'll make it to shore?"

Ashton watched him before noting, "Hard to say. Is he swimming or drowning?"

"That's a badass pirate ship, bruh!" they heard the bum yell as he waded through waist deep water towards Smathers Beach. "It's got treasure and a parrot and...is that Tom Brady? Oh man! Hey, Tom, you're the Goat!"

"This whole time I just thought he was drunk. Turns out he's an idiot," Christian proclaimed.

Ashton and Christian continued watching the beachgoers.

"You'd think they've never seen a seventeenth century pirate ship before," Ashton observed.

"That, or perhaps the open gun ports are makin' 'em unnerved," Christian joked.

"Good point. Best to keep them open then."

Christian laughed.

"You're gonna wanna commandeer that seaplane if you're lookin' to get this treasure out of here," Christian said pointing off the port bow towards a plane resting in the shallow water about sixty meters from shore.

"Always the pirate," Ashton said to him. "Stay with the ship. I need to collect my things before we go our separate ways. I'll be back at dawn."

"I think the men will be amenable to staying. But," Christian warned, "we ought to be settin' sail as soon as possible so as to avoid too much unwanted attention."

With that, Ashton stood on the gunwale.

Holding the rigging, he turned back to Christian, "…and take care of my dog, will ya?"

Ashton dove overboard. Amber walked to the edge of the ship and watched him swim to shore. As he reached the road next to Smathers Beach, a silver Camaro with white racing stripes skidded to a screeching halt. In one fluid motion, Ashton opened the door and slid into the vehicle just as the tires spun, spewing thick white smoke that bellowed into the air.

"Good to see you again, Jermaine," he said to the driver.

Jermaine chewed on his cigar a as he sped the muscle car east down Roosevelt Boulevard. Ashton looked out of the window just as a man, muscular with red hair, stepped into view. He winked. The Camaro sped past. The image was just a blur. Ashton spun around, but the man was gone, like a phantom in the wind.

"He'll be back, girl," Christian said to Amber with a gentle petting between her floppy ears. "Take a swim, boys," he then said to the crew.

The crew hollered and cheered as they threw off their excess clothing and jumped overboard into a pleasant respite from the heat. Christian remained onboard and, going below deck, helped himself to a bottle of one of Milt's vintage rums, a souvenir he'd taken from the villa. He swayed in a hammock as the light streamed in from an open gun port. Amber curled up on a pile of silk cloth bundled nearby against barrels and storage chests, awaiting Ashton's return.

The '69 Camaro came to a slow stop in front of Ashton's hotel. Ashton stepped out of the car and past several guests preparing to check-in.

"Welcome back, Mr. Hood," the attendant behind the counter said with a nod.

"Thank you, Caesar," Ashton replied, returning the gesture.

Ashton labored up the stairs, finally feeling the weight of exhaustion. He opened the door to his room. The cold temperature chilled his body. He took off his shoes and felt the cold stone floor on the soles of his feet. His suitcase lay open on the extra twin bed just as he left it. He placed his clothes and sundries in the suitcase, then changed quickly into his bathing suit and headed downstairs to the pool for a little relaxation.

The hotel pool was crowded. He floated contently, staring up at the pale blue, cloudless sky with shades on and a smile on his face as the reality of the past several days finally came to bear. He let out a quiet laugh, his happiness palpable as his thoughts turned to Jiya and the coconut scent of her body, surviving the onslaught of the battle for Libertalia, and coming home with more treasure than he could spend in a lifetime.

Not a bad vacation.

A burst of laughter erupted nearby from one of the cabanas. He saw Michelle and her friends giggling but paid them no mind. Becoming parched, Ashton climbed out of the pool to the shade of a nearby cabana and signaled for the deck waiter.

"Rumrunner, please."

"You got it, sir."

"Hi," Michelle said walking over to his cabana.

She was wearing a black bikini that left little to the imagination and sat on a cushioned lounge chair next to him, crossing her legs. Her short-cropped hair framed her face, which was painted with subtle amounts of makeup. She was beautiful, Ashton admitted to himself.

"Michelle, right?" he said.

"That's right. Um, remind me of yours again?"

"Ashton."

"Oh, right! Ashton."

A pause ensued. Michelle smiled to hide the awkwardness. Ashton found it pleasant. The waiter arrived shortly thereafter with his cocktail.

"Thank you," he said taking the drink. "For you."

He handed the waiter a Spanish Piece of Eight, a silver coin of high purity stamped 1694. He had found a small bag full of them in the house where Milt was first tortured and found no harm in keeping them safe in his pocket.

"Thank you, sir!" the waiter said elatedly as he examined the rare coin.

He didn't bother to ask him about it, but rather, he quickly pocketed it and went on his way delivering the remaining cocktails on his tray. It was evident to Ashton that Michelle expected him to jump at the chance of engaging her in conversation. The glint in her eye continued to sparkle after watching Ashton hand the deck waiter the silver coin.

"Wow, so you're, like, rich?" she asked.

"Oh, that? No, that was just a souvenir I picked up at the Publix down the road."

She laughed again, not knowing what else to do. Ashton smiled and leaned his head back taking a slow sip of his cold drink. When it was clear to Michelle that Ashton had no more interest in her, she scoffed, and retreated awkwardly back to her friends. Ashton ignored her and settled into the lounge chair, the hot afternoon sun drying his skin, and sat in thoughtful repose. He watched the various patrons around the pool – the kids playing in the water, the elder gentleman applying sunscreen to his wife, Michelle leaving the pool area with her friends in tow – while he enjoyed his second Rumrunner.

It's good to be back.

He had just closed his eyes when a tall, lanky man wearing a cream-colored linen suit, bifocals, and Wolseley pith helmet stood over him, blocking his sun. Ashton shielded his eyes to see a self-assured man with a crooked face. The stranger smiled, revealing oversized teeth. His face crinkled just enough to make the mole on his sharp nose jump. Ashton moved to stand up as the man sat down, placing his briefcase beside him.

Ashton sighed and sat back down.

"And who might you be?" Ashton asked.

"The name's Dwight Hammergold, but everyone calls me Dig," he answered in a smug, nasally tone with a slight Cockney accent.

"Ashton Hood," Ashton responded, completing the introduction.

"I know who you are, Mr. Hood. I've been watching you," Dig said in a deep whisper.

"That's creepy and weird. Now how can I help you, Mr. Hammergold?"

"I know you've been in contact with one they call Milt."

"Milt who?"

"Just Milt, as far as I can ascertain."

"I'm sorry, I don't know who you're talking about."

"I was there at Alonzo's. I watched you eat with him. I'm even staying in this hotel with you," he added, growing frustrated with Ashton's denials.

"Ok, now I feel like I need a shower."

"Don't be coy with me, Mr. Hood. I saw him hand you a piece of parchment at that restaurant. It was a map, wasn't it?"

Ashton reclined back, ignoring him. Dig leaned in and annunciated his words to make sure his next point was well heard.

"I'm also willing to bet there was treasure."

Dig smirked and straightened up when Ashton didn't respond.

"Did you know the treasure in Libertalia was only a fraction of his fortune?" Dig continued.

Ashton opened his eyes, surprised at the level of knowledge Dig held pertaining to Milt and Libertalia.

"That got your attention, did it?" he said with widened eyes.

Ashton said nothing.

"I need to know where that island is, Mr. Hood. I believe it to be called Shipwreck Island."

"Every island in the Caribbean is where it has always been," Ashton answered. "I'd give you a map, but I don't have one."

"Of course not. But did you find his treasure?"

"Look, Dig, I'm sure you have much better things to do with your time. I've already told you I have no idea what you're talking about. I wish I did, but I can't help you."

Incensed, Dig opened his briefcase and pulled out a large, bulging leather bound journal. Loose papers, sketches, maps, and surveillance photos were nearly falling out of it. He unwrapped the leather string holding it closed. When it burst open, several photos fell onto the concrete pool deck, each one taken clandestinely of Ashton since his arrival in Key West. Ashton picked them up and thumbed through them, throwing them onto the white plastic table between the two of them.

"What the hell is this?" Ashton demanded.

He held up two photos, one of him checking into the hotel, and the other of him, Milt, Marco, and Carlos all walking into Captain Tony's. Ashton's faced turned red with anger.

"Now that I definitely have your attention," Dig said with a cheeky smile, "you'll find I have a lot more than pictures in here," he said rapping on the journal's cover.

Ashton let out a sigh and snatched the journal from Dig's weak grip.

"Wait, no, I...," Dig said, grasping for his journal before quickly recomposing himself. "Ok, right then, go ahead and have a look. I am allowing you to look at my journal. I was going to let you examine it anyway."

Ashton thumbed through the thickly bound pages.

"How did you get all this?" Ashton asked.

Dig sat up straight, his hands on his knees.

"I have been watching Milt for a long time. Studying him. Learning everything there is to know about him," he said. "He's an odd one, that chap. There's something…peculiar about him."

"Well, I can't refute that," Ashton said with a laugh that was not returned.

Dig was stone-faced.

"Not one for humor, are ya, Dig?"

"I am one for treasure, and I aim to find him and it," he said with his chin held high.

"And I'm sure you will, Mr. Hammergold," replied Ashton, closing the dense journal and handing it back. "I wish you the best of luck in your quest."

Dig snatched the book back from Ashton's outstretched hand and tucked it back into his briefcase.

"Is there anything else?" Ashton asked.

Dig began to sweat, growing anxious as he sensed his chances of gleaning any useful information slipping from his fingers. His countenance changed. He slumped forward foregoing his usual forced manner and pleaded, "I will give you ten percent of whatever I find. Please, Mr. Hood!"

Ashton laughed.

"Twenty-five percent!" Dig countered himself.

"Mr. Hammergold, groveling is unbecoming, and I've already told you that I have no idea of this treasure you speak of. I'm here on vacation to relax. Nothing more."

"Fine. Fifty percent of the treasure!" Dig begged once more.

"Good day, Mr. Hammergold."

Dig nodded in disappointment and stood, attempting to regain his air of polished pride. Ashton watched him vacate the pool area. When it was clear Dig had gone, Ashton grabbed his things.

"Time to go," he said to himself as he raced back to his room.

FIFTY-SEVEN

Ashton took a quick, long-awaited shower, dressed, and walked with his luggage to the lobby. The local news was on the television discussing a new bill proposed by the city council. There was no mention of the *Angel*.

"Hello, Mr. Hood. Will you be checking out, sir?" Caesar asked.

"Yes," he answered quickly. He handed Caesar his credit card. "A little earlier than expected."

"Very well, sir, you're all finished. I hope you enjoyed your stay."

Ashton smiled, "I did. It's a charming place."

"Indeed, sir."

"Have a good one," Ashton said as he turned with his luggage.

"And to you...Captain," he heard in reply.

Ashton didn't turn around as he left through the lobby doors. A smile crept on his face.

Captain, he thought as he prepared to enter his cab. He turned and hurriedly returned to the check-in counter. The couple in front of him had just stepped out of the way, having received their room keys. Ashton approached.

"I need help getting back to Virginia," he said in hushed tones.

Caesar smiled, "Of course, sir."

Ashton was a pirate captain after all and that apparently meant something in certain circles, even if only to the clerk at the reception counter, but a clerk who obviously had curiously deep connections.

"Can you get to the Bahamas?" Caesar asked in a hushed tone.

"I saw a seaplane off Smathers Beach. I think I can commandeer it."

"You're settling into your new role nicely. I'll make a phone call," Caesar said.

As he dialed, he added instructions for Ashton, "There'll be a small makeshift runway west of Nassau. It's right on the water."

Following a brief call, Caesar hung up the phone, scribbled some numbers on a scratch sheet of paper, and handed it to Ashton.

"Are these the coordinates?"

"Yes," Caesar confirmed.

Ashton grabbed his bags.

"A plane will be waiting for you there, Mr. Hood. A white Gulfstream g280 with blue accents. Tail number H0526K."

"I owe you. Thanks," Ashton said digging into his pocket for a few Pieces of Eight.

Ashton walked quickly through the automatic doors to the idling cab. He placed his bag in the trunk and slid into the backseat.

"Smathers Beach," he said to the driver.

Without a word, the driver started down Roosevelt Boulevard, driving much too conservatively to Ashton's dismay, but it provided a pleasant change from his rides in the Camaro and a moment of leisure to enjoy his last moments in Key West. When the cab approached Smathers Beach, Ashton looked out of the window, the wind cooling his face, and saw the *Angel* still anchored where he left her. A small trawler was rocking gently in the swell. A thin, shirtless young man, with a freckled face, long sandy-brown dreadlocks, and a spindly goatee was loading her up with a cooler and several fishing poles.

"Stop here," Ashton said suddenly to the driver.

Ashton tipped him generously and exited the vehicle, hurrying across the street and through the white sand to where the young fisherman was preparing his boat.

"Excuse me," Ashton called out.

The young fisherman turned around just as Ashton approached.

"If I gave you fifty bucks, would you take me to that ship over there," he asked pointing towards the schooner.

The young man followed Ashton's finger to the pirate ship, its black flag flapping full in the wind.

"Holy cow, man," he exclaimed. "Is that a pirate ship…are those real cannons?"

"It is, and I need to get to it," Ashton said again holding out a fifty-dollar bill.

"Sure thing, man. Hop in," he said as he snatched the bill from Ashton's hand.

He pulled the drawstring on the small outboard motor, and it sputtered to life. He put it in reverse, churning the rippled sand, and then turned the yoke hard, racing the small boat towards the ship.

"Easiest fifty bucks I ever made," he said with a grin.

Ashton smiled back at him but didn't respond. As the boat neared the *Angel*, Ashton could hear the faint barking of a dog growing louder and louder. The fisherman killed the motor and the boat coasted up to the *Angel*'s hull.

"I've only seen these in movies," he said with an abundance of amazement and wonder. "Hey man, is Jack Spar…."

"No," Ashton said curtly. "He's not up there."

A look of disappointment washed over the dingy fisherman's face. Ashton climbed up the rope ladder. Christian gave him a hand and yanked him onto the deck as the small trawler skipped over the placid water.

"That's my way out of here," Ashton said to Christian nodding toward the seaplane.

The crew lowered a dinghy into the water and loaded it with the wooden chests and Ashton's flag, folded and presented to him with respect. Ashton and Christian clambered down into the small, wooden boat. Ashton grabbed Amber, tethered to a rope lowered by one of the crew. The dog stood uneasily in the center of the boat while Christian rowed them towards the seaplane with great speed. When they reached it, Ashton stepped out of the boat onto the float and peered inside. Vacant. He tested the door. Unlocked. He opened the door and studied the cockpit.

I can fly this.

Christian lifted Amber and handed her to Ashton followed by the four treasure laden chests. Ashton almost dropped the last into the water as the weight tested his strength. He slid them into the small cargo hold behind the pilot's seat.

"Amber," Ashton said, patting the co-pilot's seat. Amber obliged and took her seat.

"Feels good to plunder, doesn't it," Christian said standing expertly in the boat with his hands on his hips.

"As long as I don't get caught."

Ashton held out his hand. Christian took it in his, engulfing it. The two friends shook hands without a word. Ashton crawled into the cockpit with Amber patiently awaiting takeoff.

"By the way," Ashton said, "if a spindly man with an accent ever shows up on Libertalia, humor him."

"I'm sure I'll know what you're talking about when I see him."

"You'll definitely know."

Christian sat and prepared to row back to the *Angel*.

"Wait," Ashton said with a quick realization.

He opened one of the chests and took a small handful of golden coins, placed them in a small leather pouch, and handed it to Christian.

"When he stops chasing me, throw him this."

"Who?" Christian asked, taking the pouch in his hand.

Ashton nodded towards the beach as the plane's owner, who was sunbathing with his girlfriend thirty years his junior, jumped to his feet, waving his arms, and sprinting towards the motorboat that brought him ashore.

Christian laughed and gave a final wave.

"Take care of him, Amber," he said and closed the door.

Ashton put the headsets on over both his and Amber's ears.

"Ready, girl?" he asked and started the engine.

Christian rowed the dinghy back to the *Angel* as Ashton rushed through the pre-flight checklist and procedures with the owner closing in fast.

"Fuck it. Close enough."

As the boat approached, the propeller's spun to life, and the boat lurched forward, skipping across the water's surface. The owner closed the distance to within meters of his plane before Ashton was finally able to pull away and lift the plane into the air. Christian gave out a great laugh and then launched the pouch towards the man. It hit the console and burst open, spilling the bullion inside the boat. Back aboard the *Angel,* Christian bellowed orders to the crew and the sails were hoisted, catching wind as Christian returned course to Libertalia.

Safely in the air, Ashton adjusted his flight path to the coordinates Caesar gave him and settled in for the trip, gazing at the horizon and turquoise waters below him, the blues, greens, and whites reminding him of an alcohol ink painting. His pirate flag lay draped over the chests behind him.

The remainder of the flight continued uneventfully. He soon approached his destination in the Bahamas according to Ceasar's coordinates, circled the plane, and readied his approach. His heart was racing as the plane descended. It bounced off the surface of the water a few times before coming to a stop near a rotting pier extending from the deserted shore. Ashton exhaled and stepped out of the plane. Amber stood behind him as an old Bahamian man approached wearing black loafers, white linen pants, a white linen shirt, and a Panama hat. Ashton walked down the pier to meet him and extended his hand. The old man took it but didn't say a word.

"Caesar sent me here," Ashton told the man.

"He's a good boy," the old man said shuffling back to shore. "Come, there's a plane waiting."

Ashton offloaded the chests one by one and carried each one to the end of the pier where an old, rusty Ford pickup awaited him. Once loaded, they drove a short distance to a nearby, roughshod runway. Parked at one end near a rusty tin hangar was the white Gulfstream g280 with blue accents that Caesar described. Ashton read the tail number – H0526K. The truck stopped next to the stairs leading into the fuselage. Ashton loaded his chests into the plane. It was spacious, with four leather recliners and soft carpeting, a bed in the rear compartment, and a bar. Simple, yet luxurious.

A beautiful Bahamian flight attendant asked if Ashton wanted a drink. He didn't. The pilot and copilot stepped aboard, each wearing jeans, ball caps, and dark sunglasses. Amber curled under Ashton's legs. The plane sped down the runway and Ashton closed his eyes, settling in for the long flight home.

FIFTY-EIGHT

Ashton awoke a few hours later when the plane touched down. He stepped out into the waning sunlight surrounded by a pine tree forest.

"Where are we?" he asked the copilot.

"Ferguson Airport. Pensacola, Florida."

"Pensacola? No kidding."

The copilot disembarked the plane and stood with Ashton in the grass next to the runway.

"We were told you'd be needing a van," he said and pointed towards the hangar. "There's a U-Haul parked in the hangar. I'll send in a call and have them bring it over for you."

"Thanks, my man," he said. "I kinda feel like a drug dealer."

The copilot looked at him sideways and ignored the comment. He crawled back into the cockpit and radioed to the hangar to send the van over to the plane. When it arrived, the driver, a sixteen-year-old working a summer job at the airport, leapt out and helped Ashton load the chests, though he was barely able to lift them. The whole process seemed unexpectedly smooth, from start to finish. Ashton hopped in the van and as soon as he left the runway, the plane took off and disappeared above the clouds.

Ashton drove to his parents' house on the west side of Pensacola and parked in the driveway. Amber sat happily in the front seat, panting in the heat, and watching everything around her.

"Ashton? Is that you?" a shrill, shaky voice with a thick New York accent asked from behind him.

Ashton closed his eyes and sighed.

"Hi, Mrs. Heffelweis," he answered.

"Oh. My. God! It's been, what? Foreva!" she screeched.

She waddled down the sidewalk, her hair still in curlers, leaning on her walker. The neon green tennis balls on the front legs were dirty and frayed. Her oversized, floral-patterned nightgown flowed behind her.

"Y'know, it's three o'clock in the afternoon, Mrs. Heffelweis."

"What's that, dear?"

"Nothing."

"Your parents went to Biloxi for the week. I keep telling them gambling is the devil's work, but do they listen to me?" she waited an excruciatingly long time for an answer to a question that Ashton assumed to be rhetorical.

"Um. No, ma'am?" he answered uncomfortably.

"Thank you!" she squealed.

He bristled at the pitch of her response.

"Are you moving back home, dear?" Mrs. Heffelweis then gasped.

"No ma'am. Just stopped in for a visit."

"Oh, that's a shame. You'd really like my granddaughter. I think you two would really hit it off. I'm always telling her she needs to settle down and I want grandbabies before I die."

A nervous laughter snuck out of his throat.

"It was great to see you again, Mrs. Heffelweis. Give my best to your granddaughter."

He turned and stepped back in the van eager to get back on the road.

"You're leaving so soon?"

"Yes, ma'am, unfortunately," he said through the window while backing out of the driveway.

The old lady leaned on her rocker with one arm, while waving vigorously with the other. Her coke bottle, horned-rim glasses nearly sliding off her nose. Ashton gave her a kind smile, she was always nice to him as a kid, spoiling him with cold lemonade every afternoon as he practiced soccer in the street.

He circled the neighborhood and, upon returning to his parents' house, saw that Mrs. Heffelweis had gone back inside her own home a few houses down the street. He leapt out of the van, leaving it running, and placed a sizable pouch full of gold bullion between the glass storm door and front door, more than enough to satisfy his parents' debts, relocate if they wished, and carry them comfortably through retirement.

Before he left the city, he drove through old downtown Pensacola on his way to the interstate and bought a local piece of art, a turquoise etching of a shallow seabed, from Blue Morning Art Gallery on Palafox Street. He gladly paid a generous price to support the local artisans, a hobby whenever he visited small town America, and then he continued to the interstate for the long trek to Virginia.

FIFTY-NINE

Ashton awoke late the next morning warm in his own bed, having driven most of the night. Amber lay sprawled out and snoring on top of the comforter, already making herself at home. His suitcase was still in the living room, unopened next to his treasure chests. He took his time getting up, careful not to disturb his fur princess, and enjoyed a long, hot shower. He shaved his dark stubble and got dressed, but not bothering with a suit, choosing instead something a bit more business casual. He fed Amber and filled a water bowl, took her for a long walk, and gave her free reign of his condo. She jumped on the couch and curled up on a pillow, settling in until Ashton returned home.

His truck started on the second attempt. He took an out-of-the-way route, making a stop before heading to work. When he walked through the front doors of his office building two hours later, it felt to him as if weeks had gone by since he last stepped foot into that gray labyrinth of cubicles. He passed by his colleagues and coworkers unnoticed. He didn't care. He approached Chad and Lindsey, standing at the water cooler and flirting as was their routine.

"Ashton?" Chad said stepping in Ashton's path. "Where were you yesterday? Dick's gonna have your ass."

Ashton stopped but didn't say anything.

"Woah, nice tan. It's about time you learned what the sun is," Chad teased.

"Oh, Chad. Stop!" Lindsey snickered putting her hand on his forearm.

"How long do you think I've been gone?" Ashton asked, suddenly aware that he had lost track of the days since first arriving on Shipwreck Island.

"It's Tuesday," Chad said, laughing loud enough for the entire office to hear. "You missed a whole day of work!"

Tuesday?

Ashton's face revealed nothing. He stepped close to Chad, making him uncomfortable and bit nervous.

"Take care of yourself, Chad," Ashton said with a smile.

Chad scoffed, though he was inwardly relieved. He moved aside as Ashton patted him on the shoulder. Ashton walked back to his cubicle and packed the few personal items that remained on his desk into his bag. Nick sat silently in front of his computer having watched the entire interaction unfold.

"Hood!" a hoarse voice bellowed.

Ashton's boss came storming out of his office.

"Where were you yesterday? Where's the Morrison account I demanded?" he chided.

"I don't think I'll be getting to that today," Ashton replied calmly.

The boss stuttered and stammered, and as the office's eyes were all watching to see how he would respond, the boss did the only thing he knew to save what little face he had.

"You're fired!" he yelled.

Spittle flew from his mouth. His chubby face turned a pinkish hue. He folded his arms atop his bulging belly. Ashton laughed and Lindsey, standing nearby, began to see him in a new light. Ashton walked past her ignoring her advances, and stepped out of the drab, cold office and into the welcoming sun. He threw his bag into the passenger seat of his brand-new rosso Corsa Ferrari 812 GTS convertible with a crème-colored interior. The top was off, and Ashton slid into the soft leather of the driver's seat, putting on his sunglasses.

"Nice ride," Nick said approaching the car. "You win the lottery?"

"You could say that."

"Quite an exit back there."

"I was kinda hoping I would be in and out unnoticed like every other day."

"They noticed you today. Looks like you got a bit roughed up," Nick motioned to Ashton's bandaged arm.

"It's nothing. Just a flesh wound."

"Listen, if you ever want to grab a drink again, give me a call," Nick offered.

"You got it."

"Take care of yourself, Ashton."

"You, too, man."

Ashton shifted the vehicle into gear. The guttural sound from the exhaust carried him out of the parking lot and down the street back towards home. Amber jumped off the couch, impatient to go outside. Ashton walked her down the stairs to the lawn outside his condo complex. She jerked his leash as she trotted through the grass exploring her new surroundings.

"Hey, Ashton," a familiar voice called from across the street. "Did you get a dog?"

"Hey!" he said. His heart skipped a beat. "I did. A few days ago."

"She's a sweetheart!" Kayleigh crossed the street with Kaya. "So cute!"

She knelt to pet her. The two dogs playfully sizing up the other.

"What's her name?"

"Amber."

"Amber? Aw, what a great name – great song, too."

"It is. My favorite, actually. That song, her temperament, and the color of her coat made the name an appropriate choice."

"I love it when dogs have people names. What happened to your arm?"

"Just a scratch. No big deal."

"Well, I'm glad you're ok."

"Me, too."

Amber quickly grew tired of Kaya's playfulness and shifted her attention to the many smells around her.

"Come on, Kaya," she said, pulling on the dog's leash.

Kayleigh whistled at her several times before she reluctantly obeyed and left Amber to sniff in peace.

"See you later, Ashton," she said with a quick wave before being pulled away by Kaya.

Amber watched intently as they left, whimpered, then looked up at Ashton. Her eyes were filled with a love only a faithful dog could provide.

"You, too, huh?" Ashton said to her, scratching behind her ear.

Ashton kept looking at Kayleigh who was busy wrangling Kaya.

"Kayleigh!" he called to her.

She turned around as Ashton ran up to her with Amber in tow.

"Yeah?" she asked.

"Would you like to go out sometime?" he asked.

"I was wondering when you were going to ask me," she said with a beaming smile. "Do you have anywhere in particular in mind?"

"I've never been to Fiji," he said, not entirely facetious.

"Fiji?" Kayleigh laughed.

"Too soon?"

"A little bit. But I'll hold you to that eventually."

"Ever been to Vegas? I have a couple friends who would join us in a heartbeat. We can get a suite at the Wynn Encore, catch a show."

"How about we start with dinner. Pick me up tomorrow at seven o'clock sharp?" she said with a flirtatious smile. There was a sexiness to her charming demeanor that captivated and disarmed Ashton. "I can't wait to hear about your trip."

Ashton smiled.

"My trip, right. You got it. I'll see you tomorrow night at seven," he said barely able to contain his excitement.

"I hope to be impressed. Are you going to take me through a secret kitchen entrance and get us the best table in the restaurant?"

Ashton's jaw dropped to the ground.

"You like Goodfellas?"

"Best movie ever!"

Ashton smiled boyishly.

"And by the way, thanks for the Alonzo's recommendation. But I'll have to tell you, they were good, but they weren't the best oysters I've ever eaten," he continued.

"Oh yeah?"

"I know a better place."

"I'd love to try them sometime," she said with a wave and a smile as Kaya's impatience reached its apex and she jerked her down the sidewalk. "I'll see you tomorrow!" she yelled back to him.

His heart raced. Ashton found himself watching Kayleigh leave. Watching her with a confidence that, for the first time, was real. He found what he had been longing for, more than anything else. His memories flashed to Sister Anne. She would approve, he thought. He looked up to Heaven and said a silent prayer of thanksgiving. His eyes watered up with joy. It was more than a feeling. It was a certainty that his soulmate just said yes to their first date, and he was equally certain his mom had a hand in it.

He strolled around the block with Amber. The sun felt a little warmer on his face, the air was clearer, the songs from the birds singing in the trees resonated with him.

"C'mon, girl," he beckoned Amber.

SIXTY

Kayleigh and Ashton dated for a year before Ashton relocated from D.C. to Florida's Treasure Coast. He opened a dive shop and bar in Stuart along the St. Lucie River, taking prospective treasure hunters and divers around Sailfish Point on chartered diving excursions to the Bahamas and treasure hunting expeditions to the lost Spanish treasure fleet that sunk off the Florida coast in 1715, giving the area its name.

The doorbell rang on his Mediterranean-style, waterfront home overlooking the Atlantic Ocean. Ashton opened the door and saw his beautiful, new wife smiling back at him. Behind her, a moving truck.

"Go on," Ashton said to Amber who nudged her way outside and began playing with Kaya.

"It's about time you showed up," Ashton teased Kayleigh.

Kayleigh stepped into the marble-floored foyer. Sunlight poured in through the windows. A clear view of the ocean could be seen through the open floorplan. The glass doors were opened. A breeze blew in. The sound of the ocean filled the house.

"I wish you would've let me help you drive down here," he said.

"I love the adventure," she responded. "Besides, it gave me a chance to visit old friends along the way."

"I hope you had a lot of time to catch up."

"We did, but why would I stay in North Carolina and Georgia when I could be here with you?"

"They're coming down, aren't they?" he asked resignedly.

"They'll be here next month!"

She cradled his face in her hands and gave him an emphatic kiss as the sea breeze blew past them, the faint taste of salt on their lips.

"Thanks, babe!" she said excitedly.

Ashton whistled for Amber to return but she was content, lying like a sphinx in the grass squinting in the sunlight, so he let her stay awhile longer. Kaya bolted through the front door and Ashton left it open so Amber could return in her own sweet time. Kayleigh unpacked her suitcases in the upstairs master bedroom while Ashton unpacked the moving truck.

"No, don't move, I got it," he said to Amber as she watched from the soft grass, her nose twitching in the air as she studied the smells on the wind.

Kayleigh spent the week decorating and organizing their new home, while Ashton made daily excursions on his charter boat. He named it the *Angel* and his pirate flag flew above the stern.

"Kayleigh?" Ashton called, returning home one afternoon.

"In here," she answered from her art studio, a small room on the side of the mansion facing east with a clear view of the water and the early morning sunrises.

"Care to join me for a walk?" he asked.

"Sure. C'mon, Amber…Kaya…wanna go outside?" she beckoned the dogs.

They walked up the road, holding hands, to the end of Sewall's Point.

"A man came into the dive shop today," Ashton began. "He looked like a wealthy man, up in age, retired, I think."

"What did he want?" she asked him.

"He wanted to charter a boat. For himself. For a month. So, we got to talking and turns out he's an avid diver who's interested in the Spanish treasure. He reminded me of a man I once knew."

"An old friend?"

"Not quite," he said.

"So are you going to take him up on his offer."

"He offered a generous amount."

"I know we've worked through a long-distant relationship before, but I would really prefer not to go through that again, even for a month," she told him.

Ashton raised her hand to his lips and kissed it.

"Don't worry. Nick already volunteered."

"I like him. You two work well together. I'm glad you were able to convince him to come down and work with you."

"It wasn't hard. He hated that job almost as much as I did, and I needed someone I can trust," he said. "So, when I called him, he jumped at the opportunity and actually quit while we were on the phone."

"Are you sure he's ok being on a boat with this stranger for a month?"

"Nick can handle himself. Besides, a year's salary for a month of work is an offer not to be refused."

"This man's offering a year's pay just for a month's worth of work?" Kayleigh asked, shocked.

"He is. It was an odd request, but I accepted it. He was willing to pay for himself and all the potential clients who would have booked a trip during the same time, plus quite a bit more for my trouble."

"I don't blame you for not turning him away."

"I wouldn't be much good at running a business if I did," he joked.

"I don't think your little princess here could've stood you being away for so long either."

Ashton looked at Amber fondly.

"It was a blessing that I found her."

When they returned to their house, a hunter green Rolls Royce Phantom VI was parked in the driveway. Ashton held out his arm, signaling Kayleigh to stop. Kayleigh knelt to hold

Amber and Kaya while Ashton approached to investigate. He peered inside the back window. Empty, save for a taught bundle of rope, an ice pick, and a few loose pieces of climbing gear.

Odd pieces of equipment to be found in a luxury vehicle, and in Florida, no less.

Ashton approached his home cautiously. The front door was open. He pulled a Colt 1911 from his waistband, a gift to him from his stepfather many years ago that he carried religiously. He gripped it firmly at the low-ready.

"Ashton! Good to see you again," a cringy voice called from the living room.

Ashton already had his weapon raised. The man had made himself comfortable enough, slouching on the couch with his legs crossed and arm stretched along the top. A long, scraggly beard grew patchwork on his face. His other hand fiddled with a shiny, round object.

"What the hell are you doing here, Dig?" Ashton demanded.

"Mr. Hood, is that anyway to talk to a guest?"

"Guests are usually invited," Ashton countered.

"That's true," Dig began with an unfounded arrogance about him. "But you'll forgive that oversight once you hear what I have to say."

Ashton stood stone-faced, still pointing the weapon, breathing calmly.

"I have no desire to hear what you have to say,"

Ashton stepped toward the intruder, his arms tense, the barrel of the pistol trained on its target. Dig's pomposity wavered. He leapt to his feet and instinctively put the couch between he and Ashton.

"Listen! I found something," he said in a shaky voice as he flipped Ashton the object he was fingering.

Ashton reached out his non-trigger hand and caught the small object in mid-flight. He studied the tarnished gold coin and smiled. He looked up at Dig who was smiling smugly back at him. Ashton flipped the coin back to him. Dig fumbled the coin and dropped it on the floor.

"I don't know why you showed me that, nor do I care," said Ashton. "Now I suggest, in the strongest possible terms, that you leave my house."

"Do you know what this…can you lower that thing, please?" Ashton ignored him. "Do you know what this is?" Dig continued, holding up the coin, still shocked by Ashton's disregard. "I found the treasure! Avery's treasure! Some of it anyway. I know there's more out there and I know you know where it is. You do have a map, don't you?" His voice began to steadily rise as his frustrations came to bear. "You found his map on that island. I know it, now give it to me! It's the last piece of the puzzle and I need it if I'm going to find his treasure! Do you hear me?" he pleaded with sick desperation and a twinge of anger.

"Get out of my house," Ashton commanded slowly.

Ashton holstered the weapon and grabbed Dig's shirt, yanking the spindly man to the front door and tossing him onto the lawn.

"If you ever come to my home or harass my family again, it won't be some lost treasure you're looking for, it'll be your balls."

Ashton watched as Dig peeled out of the driveway, then he waved to Kayleigh letting her know it was safe to return.

"That turned out to be a little more than I expected," said Ashton as she walked up the path to the front door.

"Should I bother asking who that was?"

"Probably best you don't. He isn't worth the breath it would take to explain."

"The world's filled with too many of those types."

"How long has it been since we've gone on a long vacation?" Ashton asked his bride.

She stood elegantly in the day's last light, and he was reminded again, as he was every day, of her stunning beauty. He smiled warmly at her. The sun peered over the horizon for a moment longer before disappearing in a wave of color that painted the evening sky.

"We're due," she answered.

Three years later...

The green coastlands west of Shannon, Ireland, north of the splendid Cliffs of Moher, stretched down to the rocky shoreline of the Atlantic Ocean. Ashton and Kayleigh's newest home was a cozy abode - a modest two-story stone cottage with a hardwood interior that blended modern conveniences with rustic charm. Smoke billowed from the ivy-covered chimney.

A full, natural spruce Christmas tree, decorated with novel ornaments collected since the start of their relationship, was erected in the living room between the fireplace and a set of French doors leading to a veranda on the rear façade. The doors were framed by dark sapphire curtains, embroidered with lines of periwinkle and silver damask patterns.

"Did you ever tell me where you found these curtains?"

"At an estate sale."

Some secrets were better left secrets.

It was Christmas Eve. As night fell, stars began to speckle the clear, indigo sky. Ashton walked outside and around the house. The wind was crisp and blustery. The grass beneath his feet was soft and lush. He pulled his wool cap down over his ears and chopped several logs to continue fueling the crackling fire burning low in the hearth. The wind settled abruptly, and it became eerily quiet. Ashton, noticing the change, scanned the peaceful, slightly undulating coastal landscape surrounding the home.

Nothing.

He gathered the small logs into a canvas tote and reentered the house through the kitchen. In the living room, he placed the bundle next to the stone fireplace and fed several logs to the fledgling fire.

Ashton shuffled his playlist. "Total Eclipse of the Heart" by Bonnie Tyler was first up, background music that played quietly as they settled in for the evening. The notes danced softly above the crackling fire that had sprung back to life. The smell of cinnamon-apple from a burning candle filled the air.

"I love that song. Reminds me of my youth," Ashton said.

"Every song reminds you of your youth," Kayleigh jested.

"Well, I can't argue that. I remember singing this song with an old buddy of mine at a karaoke bar," he said, smiling at the memory.

"Well, I'm glad I wasn't there for that."

"Would you like some coffee, hun?" he asked.

"No, thank you, but how about some hot chocolate?"

"Coming right up."

Kayleigh sat crossed legged on the couch in front of the fire. Kaya lay curled up on the woven carpet on the floor before her. Kayleigh finished praying her Rosary, then opened her book, Charles Dickens's *Great Expectations*, to her bookmarked page and continued reading.

"Since you're going into the kitchen, put on some Christmas music. Let's get into the spirit."

Ashton brewed up two steaming cups of cocoa. Juxtaposed to the more pastoral architecture of the cottage, the kitchen's modern appliances and aesthetics provided a homey comfort. The crooning voice of Andy Williams's Christmas album helped to set the mood.

Amidst the sizzling fire and sultry voice of Andy Williams, Ashton thought he heard the faint sound of steel drums, a sound he had not heard in several years. Amber, lying sunken in the dark leather couch, raised her head. Her ears perked up and she listened intently, then, unconcerned, she resumed her slumber. Kayleigh took no notice.

The steely music called to mind once more Milt, Jiya, and the others, and his adventure on Libertalia. Ashton petted Amber's head and gave her a kiss on her graying whiskers. He fed another log onto the fire and, standing by the fireside, looked lovingly at his wife, four months pregnant and bundled up in a fleece blanket, buried in her book. He sipped his cocoa and took a moment to appreciate the perfection of his new life.

He walked outside to the veranda and gazed upon the ocean in the near distance. The moonlight glittered off its still surface. A soft snow began to fall, and the faint sound of the steel drums faded, for a final time, into the crisp, silent night.

Crooked Inlet
Beacon Hill
Sentinel Cliffs
Emerald Cove
Tew's Cave
New Nassau
Old Sugarcane Plantation
Mitt's Manor
Caiman Falls
Río Nilo
Río Plata
Río Lenta
Río Alma
Fortress City of Libertalia
Castillo de Luna
Mt. Deluz
Río d'Orléans
Gibbet Pass
Pirate's Landing
Halfmoon Bay
Horseshoe Point